THANK YOU FOR THE DAYS

DAN BROTZEL

BLOODHOUND
BOOKS

First published in 2024 by Bloodhound Books.

www.bloodhoundbooks.com

Print ISBN: 978-1-917449-14-4

For Alex Woolf

'Where can we live but days?'

— *Philip Larkin*

PART ONE: ALL OUR YESTERDAYS

November – December 2021

CHAPTER 1

Funerals are funny things, aren't they? Luke shivered in a thin, ill-chosen jacket as, one after another, all his so-called mates from school – all the eccentrics, sadists and *Dune* obsessives he'd tried so hard to shake off this past decade or more – stood up to make a speech in honour of the absent party. All their annoying tics and traits were on show – the one who still thought he was God's gift to women (despite the two divorces), the one who thought he was interesting and charismatic enough to pull off a bow tie, the bossy one who thought he spoke for everyone else, the one who talked like Andy McNab because he still did weekend jaunts with the Territorial Army, the one who entertained deluded fantasies of being a devil-may-care satanic hell biker – no mean feat on a Suzuki RV125 VanVan (top speed 60mph).

There were so many reasons to despise them all. And doubtless, they had their uncharitable views of him too. To them, he was the pretentious one who fancied himself as a writer, perhaps. Or: the deadbeat one who had never really left home. Or maybe just the one without a proper job, relationship or prospects. (His comrades, of course, were men with wives and even babies, and sterling careers as IT consultants, insurance brokers, landscape gardeners and estate agents.) And yet – in this strange drunken moment, this surreal occasion of high emotion – he felt a terrible, desperate love for them all, and his cursed hometown. As each speech ended in the obligatory toast and the downing-in-one of another plastic beaker of raw burning Smirnoff (a drink he was sure all of them hated, but none dared say), Luke found himself blinking back tears. And he wasn't the only one.

Gavin was dead. Gavin, Gav, their schoolmate, the rugger-bugger animal with the sadistic taste in drinking games, was dead. No matter that Luke wasn't really sure he'd ever had a real conversation with Gav – or not one that wasn't dominated by references to rucks or bongs or blackouts. No matter that none of them had probably liked him that much. Or he them. Or each other. Gav was dead, and he was the first of them to go, and he was way too young. And so were they.

At the service – in which an uncle of the deceased, leading the tributes, had implausibly referred to Gav's electric-guitar scratchings as 'on a par with early Zeppelin' – no one made mention of the likely cause of death. (This struck Luke as understandable, as it was rumoured that Gav had poisoned himself by licking a cowpat that he believed was host to an especially hallucinogenic variant of magic mushroom.) The subsequent booze-up in the old local had led, with terrifying inevitability, to the traditional post-pub gathering in the little playground in the woods behind the pitch and putt by St Armand's Comprehensive, the old alma mater. The naggy one had produced the plastic beakers, the alkie one had produced the vodka, and – after several rounds of singing and hugging and chugging and chest-poking – speeches and toasts had followed. In these, the need for factfulness or originality – neither very much in demand, even at the start of the session – had rapidly given way to an overriding imperative to demonstrate violent emotion. It would be unkind to describe this drunken, faux-nostalgic circle as a ritual of performative grief, and probably not wholly untrue either. But if it maybe wasn't all about

Gav, the feelings weren't themselves all false, they were just maybe about something else.

Luke noticed with detached curiosity that he himself was now holding the Helmet of Truth (don't ask) and was already a good way into his own speech. He stilled his wandering mind as best he could, and tried to focus in on the words his own mouth was pumping out.

'Gav was... a *fecking mensch*,' he heard himself say, using two words he wasn't sure he'd ever used before. 'He always had your fecking back.' Several other people had said this already, so it felt like a safe opening gambit. (He liked the word *feck*, he decided.) 'I remember one time, Gav said to me: "Luke, mate, you only get one ball to put in the scrum of life".' (Good Lord, this was dreadful, though everyone else was nodding along in furious agreement.) 'That's right! He said: "You've got to make every fecking moment count".' Luke stared at his audience, a sage among savages. 'So I say to all of us, here and now: Let's squeeze every drop out of life, lads. We owe it to Gav. *Let's make every single day count.*'

He just had time to pass the Golf Flag of Destiny (don't ask) to the next speaker before staggering over to the sandpit, vomiting violently down his own front and passing out in the silty rainwater of a disused paddling pool.

CHAPTER 2

A few days after Gav's funeral in Luke's town of birth – a sleepy commuter hub an hour to the south of London – there had been a surprising knock on the door of his current residence, the bottom-floor flat of a large terraced villa in Palmers Green, north London. (The first line of Luke's official address was *Rear Basement Flat, 17a Avenue Park Road*, which Holly at work pronounced 'so sad' and yet, at the same time, 'all too appropriate'.) Callers were unusual because to access the flat you had to descend a steep flight of stone steps well below street level, then make your way along an unpromising, overgrown path to a door so far to the side of the building it was almost in the back. You had to really know what you were doing to make the trip, like the tirelessly cheerful postie Monika, or Alan and the kids, who lived upstairs.

This, though, was not a regular visitor but a tall, burly bloke, roughly Luke's age, who wore a boiler suit and whose face was strangely familiar.

'Luke, mate. It's Jamie.'

'Jamie?'

'Gav's brother. I'm sure he spoke about me.'

'Oh right! Yes – often!' Luke lied. He had barely spoken to

Gavin himself in what had proved to be the last decade of his life, and even before that he could not recall his old schoolmate mentioning his family ever. Luke became aware of a writhing brown entity behind Jamie's legs. He was about to enquire, but Jamie was not finished.

'That was bloody beautiful, mate. What you said.'

'What I said?'

'You know, about making every day count. To honour his memory. I heard all about it.'

'Oh right. Well, yes. I think we all said it, didn't we?'

'It was you, mate.'

'Well,' said Luke. There was an awkward pause. 'He was.' He paused again. 'A *fecking mensch*.'

Jamie nodded approvingly. 'The lads have made T-shirts.' He unzipped the top half of his boiler suit – which bore the emblem, Luke saw now, of a much-despised utility company – to reveal a black rock-style T-shirt. "Giving it every day for Gav – Boys On Tour" was the legend.

Luke didn't know what to say. He had never inspired a T-shirt before. This was right up there with his other wordsmithing achievements, which included reaching the semi-finals of the Asda Christmas cracker gag-writing challenge (2019 edition), getting half a joke on a long-forgotten Radio 4 sketch show called *You're Not Far Off*, and – from the day job – writing a series of blog posts that enabled Uxbridge Van Hire to rank briefly on the first page of Google for that hotly contested search phrase, "Van Hire – Uxbridge".

'He wanted you to have him,' Gav's brother was saying now. He pulled the lead he'd been holding in his other hand and the brown hairy liquid thing came into full view. It was an absurd entity, all nose and ears and tail, a strange steampunk sniffing machine with deep pleading hazel eyes, and now it was climbing up Luke's legs and trying to sniff his groinage.

'Have what?' said Luke. He still held out the forlorn hope that

Gav had bequeathed him something more on-brand. A signed rugby ball perhaps. Half a bag of weed. A death metal CD. Even just a pack of Hula Hoops would have done fine.

'Me? *No*! Why?'

'It was one of the last things he said to me,' said Jamie. His voice had become low, intense. 'In the hospital. He said: "Give Ziggy to the one who deserves him most. You'll know them when you see them". As soon as I heard about your speech, I just knew.'

'Oh,' said Luke. 'Couldn't I just have a T-shirt?'

CHAPTER 3

Luke did not want a dog, did not know how to have a dog, but also had no idea how to turn a dog down that had been offered to him as the dying wish of an ancient schoolmate who had allegedly referred to him with exquisite ambiguity as 'the one true friend I never had'. This was news to Luke, and he did wonder if Jamie had misheard the name Gav had whispered, or if there was in fact another Luke that Gav had been properly friendly with in recent years. But before he could get too far with these speculations, Ziggy had been taken up by Milo, an innocent eleven-year-old, and even Grace, an all-too-knowing sixteen, who had been alerted by the little dog's plaintive yelps and had come running down from upstairs. Soon they were cooing over the thing, caressing and tickling its puppy fur (which was surprisingly soft, it had to be said), and had run off down the garden in search of balls and sticks to throw. Ziggy had responded with even more delighted yelps and leaps, and Jamie had smiled approvingly as he strode away up the garden path. Mission accomplished.

'You're not keeping that thing, surely?' asked Dom, in disgust.

'Aw please, Uncle Dom,' said Milo.

'I'm not your uncle,' snapped Dom. 'We've been through this.'

'Yah, yass, we need this,' said Grace, whose Insta likes had begun spiking the moment she started posting selfies *avec chien*. 'Slay.'

Luke had been firmly in the anti-dog camp until he heard Dom come out as virulently anti-dog. Now – and this was the nature of their friendship in a nutshell – the thought that Ziggy might annoy Dom suddenly warmed him to the new arrival.

'Ah, let's just keep him for a while,' he said.

'Hey, Luke. What's all this then?' said Alan, his tedious lanky frame and annoying ginger hair filling up the doorway.

'Oh hi, Alan,' said Luke dismissively. 'Just a dog. Not sure what the landlord will say.' He looked at the kids.

'Oh please, *please* say Luke can keep it, Dad,' wailed Milo. 'We can help look after him.'

Alan looked at Luke, who was now studying the doormat with great intensity. Alan looked back at Milo, his young son, still so eager and uncynical, and at Grace. 'Ew, don't be so wet,' she said, disgusted at her brother's self-abasement. 'DBI!' (Luke had only just found out that DBI stood for 'don't beg it'.)

'You don't want the dog, then?' said Alan with a smile.

Grace shrugged. 'Could be okay.' Ziggy's tail, a tethered vortex of tensile joy, began to vibrate even harder.

'Okay then,' said Alan. 'So long as my tenants keep the place clean, and my kids promise to stop bugging me to get them a dog ever again.'

CHAPTER 4

So it was that Ziggy moved into the rear basement, 17A, and the number of male sharers in the self-contained flat that had once been the bottom floor of Alan's house rose to three. Luke thought that Dom would put up more of a fight about the new arrangement, and indeed he always claimed to 'hate the foul beast with every fibre of my being'. But he noticed Dom would often take Ziggy with him on his slow walks round the park or to the corner shop, where he would bribe one of the young male assistants to stand outside and keep hold of Ziggy while he went in and chose his drinks and pastries. (The assistants didn't mind because Ziggy was a magnet for passing females.) And just occasionally, when Dom thought he was alone with the dog, Luke could sometimes hear him muttering sweet nothings and leaning in for wet puppy kisses.

Luke took to walking Ziggy before work during the week, and it was on one of these excursions through the local park that he had come across a little community library thing, not much more than a fading wooden cupboard with a glass door, mounted on a post attached to a rickety iron fence. Inside the cupboard, an eclectic selection of books was crammed across two uneven shelves.

Over the days, Luke noticed the titles come and go. Some things went sooner than others, of course. Recipe books flew from the shelves, along with thrillers and true-crime sagas. Sports biographies – lionesses, cricketing legends, fighters – did pretty well too. Things with an obvious shelf life – old textbooks, car manuals, comedy annuals – tended to languish forever. And then there was *How To Lose Weight Orgasmically*, which never apparently left but seemed to move around a lot on the shelves, as if it was always trying out new positions. (Luke liked to imagine it was taken out under cover of night and returned at dawn by the same borrower, now impossibly thin.)

Luke had found a few good things in there himself, and always had a look for new arrivals whenever he went past. That's when he came across an old copy of *Chase's Calendar of Events*. He took out the big floppy reference tome, flicked through it and, thinking it might be useful for work, brought it home.

Luke's *work* (if we can call it such) involved writing copy to get companies to rank higher on Google. This activity might be dressed up by his bosses in rather more grand terms when talking to clients – 'we develop powerful content strategies to elevate your brand and deliver meaningful growth'. But essentially Luke and his colleagues boshed out copy – articles, blog posts, ebooks – that included key phrases that clients wanted to rank higher for in search engine results. Phrases like "payday loans" or "steam cleaning north London" or "kosher taxidemist near me".

These were often not obviously compelling topics around which one might easily pen wittily insightful light featurettes, still less articles 'in the style and tone of *Vogue* or *The New Yorker*' as one client (owner of a local liposuction clinic) always demanded. Indeed, one of the key challenges was trying to come up with a reason as to why one might write such pieces of content at all, other than as a pretext to shoehorn in oddly specific links to local businesses and those wildly unglamorous keywords: "24-hour locksmith", "no fee accident claims", "anal fissure clinic – Kentish Town".

But constraints are creative, as they say, and a key part of Luke's job was coming up with ideas and angles that could add a spurious plausibility to the pieces he banged out. Luke had long known there were such things as fake holidays and awareness days, and had quickly seen their potential to help his work. Blue Monday was the perfect excuse to talk about looking for a new job (recruitment agency client), World Backup Day was a great moment to discourse on the importance of computer support (IT consultancy client), and National Payroll Week was a gift for copy to promote that new accountancy firm client.

But flicking through this vast book, Luke discovered now that there were actually thousands of these days, weeks and months. Many of them were very serious, like World Cancer Day or Zero Waste Week. Some were popular fixtures, like Red Nose Day or Take Your Dog To Work Day. Others were nakedly trumped-up PR opportunities, like Nutella Day or Anti-Frizz Month (brought to you by Alberto VO5). Lots were nerdy. And some were just plain silly, like Meow Like A Pirate Day or Zombie Awareness Month.

There were far more of these special Days than actual days of the year, Luke realised. Some calendar days had thirty or more things to observe or celebrate, which could make for some awkward contrasts: National Obesity Day fell in British Pie Week, for example. The silly and the serious were all crammed in together in a most unjoined-up way too: Luke noted that Holocaust Memorial Day (January 27) was sandwiched uneasily between National Peanut Butter Day and National Kazoo Day, which kind of said it all really.

CHAPTER 5

It was actually Milo who first came up with the idea for the silly day challenge as he flicked through *Chase's* 750 pages of pseudo-holidays and Facebook observances.

'Make. Every. Day. Count,' he said.

'What's that?' said Luke, only half-listening. He was munching on a piece of toast and trying hard to ignore Ziggy, who was staring at him with obsessive, scandalised foodlust.

'That thing it says on your T-shirt,' Milo persisted. 'You know, the black one you always sleep in.'

'Oh. This thing.'

Milo read out the slogan: '*Giving it every day for Gav.*'

'Oh, yeah. It's just a gimmick thing.'

'Well: this is how to do it!' Milo tried to hold up the vast book in one small hand to explain what he meant, but it toppled out of his grip and plummeted to the floor, causing Luke to dive head-first over an armchair to stop Ziggy nibbling at its edges.

'Do what?' he asked, feeling the blood in his face still.

'You could do something every day to mark one of these... Days.'

'What an excellent idea!' said Dom, who'd come in on the tail-end of this chat. He picked up the book and began flicking through it. 'You should observe one of these silly holidays every day for a year,' he continued. 'Do it for charity, get in the local rag. Impress a desperate, easily impressed woman. Get a first date, flop badly, try again. Rinse and repeat.'

'That's a ridiculous idea.'

'Well, you're always saying your life has no purpose.'

'Am I?'

'Oh come on, you know you are, you know it doesn't.' Luke often worried that his job was going nowhere, that he spent too much time watching crap telly with Dom, and that it was a long time since he'd had a 'normal' girlfriend. (Though he had, of course, met The One.) But still.

'I don't think I ever said I thought my existence was without meaning,' he protested feebly. 'Don't forget – I had a story shortlisted in the Wivenhoe Flash Fiction Festival a couple of months ago.'

'Oh darling,' said Dom, exhaling his vape with a melodramatic flourish. 'Didn't you know? Everyone who entered got shortlisted.'

Luke made a small noise of something or other. Milo and Dom waited for him to add some words, but none came.

'And anyway, I didn't say your existence was meaningless!' said Dom. 'I merely pointed out it had no obvious purpose, value or function.' Milo snorted with laughter. He knew an epic burn when he heard one. Ziggy wagged his tail with extra vim.

'Wow, thanks for that clarification, Dom,' said Luke. 'For a moment there I was feeling quite devastated.'

CHAPTER 6

It turned out that the answer to Luke's *crise existentielle* – a *crise* so *existentielle* he didn't even know he was in the throes of it – was to accept Milo and Dom's Silly Day Challenge. Dom took up the kitchen whiteboard, and wiped away all the emergency numbers with a flick of his wrist. Then he had a bit of a coughing fit, so he handed board and marker to Milo to jot down the ground rules. The first edition of these rules – a list which would later be held up as a beacon of clarity and simplicity by contrast with future iterations – read as follows:

1. Luke to observe a Silly Day every day of the year 2022.
2. All such observances to be agreed by Dom in advance.
3. Proof to be supplied as necessary.
4. No doubling up on pasta.

There followed the first of many heated exchanges on how to observe a day. Was it enough on National Apricot Day simply to eat an apricot, for example? Was it okay just to do nothing on National Do Nothing Day? Would researching otters online be an adequate way to observe National Otter Day?

Dom had taken a seat at the end of the kitchen table. It was higher than the benches on which Milo and Luke faced each other. This gave Dom a quite undeserved air of authority in the discussion, one he was keen to milk as far as humanly possible.

'Let me see,' he vaped ruminatively, 'you can't just do things that you might do in the course of a day anyway. Like eat apricots.'

'But I hate apricots,' said Luke. 'They make me puke violently. I think I'm probably allergic to them.'

'Oh! In that case, eating an apricot for National Apricot Day would be perfectly acceptable. In fact, I think you should eat six or seven.'

Dom was flicking through the book. His eyes flashed with malice. 'Oh yes, I think there's a lot of fun to be had here.'

Luke did not like the sound of that. He had known Dom since they met on a boozy post-grad media studies course, and – with a shared love of pool, beer and televised sport, and an apparent inability to form proper friendships or relationships – they had been flatmates on and off ever since. As far as Luke could see, Dom's idea of fun was to humiliate Luke. Then, when he pushed it too far, Dom – who was a good ten years older than him – told him to stop being a snowflake. It was all just bantz, wasn't it? Luke was no innocent party in this either, of course. He gave as good as he got, he knew how it worked. But Dom walked with a stick, and was given to coughing fits. Luke had asked him once what that was about, but Dom just snapped something inaudible that brooked no further inquiry. He ignored his condition, whatever it was, and he expected you to as well. Still. As infuriatingly sarky and sadistic as Dom could be, it wasn't easy to let loose your drive for revenge on a man that hobbled.

It occurred to Luke now that his so-called friendship with Dom in the present was not so very different to his so-called friendship in the past with Gav. Which is to say, not much of a friendship at all. If he had a problem or was feeling low, Dom would be the last person he'd go to. Dom would scent blood and store up your frail confidences and vulnerable confessions to use against you for optimal humiliation at a later date. No, Luke would probably end up talking to Milo or Grace upstairs, or to Holly at work or something. If he was honest, he shared quite a lot with Ziggy on their walks. Of course, there was always Yasmine (The One), and from time to time he poured out his heart to her in long emails. But he didn't want to seem needy, and because of the language thing he wasn't sure quite how much she understood. Also, most of his issues were about her in one way or another, so she wasn't always the best person to turn to. (Plus his emails kept bouncing back.)

'What's this thing about no doubling up on pasta?' asked Luke.

'Well,' said Dom. 'I can't help noticing there's a lot of food-related Days. These look like a bit of a cop-out to me. We can't have you ticking the box for National Ravioli Day *and* National Tortellini Day, now can we?'

'Ri-ight,' said Luke slowly. 'And how come you get to approve the challenges?'

'To keep you honest, of course. Also, you'll need to keep a blog, so people can see what you're up to.'

'I see.'

'So we're agreed then?'

'Well, hang on. I see what's in it for you, Dom. You get a year's worth of opportunities to humiliate me. But what's in it for me?'

'Whatever do you mean? Surely the glamour of the quest? The memory of Gav? The satisfaction of a brave mission accomplished?' Luke looked unmoved. 'Did I mention the desperately easy-to-impress ladies?'

'It looks like it might be fun for a week or two,' Luke said. 'But after that it could get quite tedious.'

'I see,' said Dom curtly. 'Playing hardball, is it? Very well. Come with me. You better see this too, Milo.' He ushered Luke into the TV room, with a curious Milo and Ziggy following close behind. With another of his grand flourishes, Dom swept back a fading dustsheet.

'You're not serious.'

'I fecking am. Full use. Of The Chair.'

'For how long?'

'The whole of the following year. Unrestricted, exclusive access.'

Luke eyed up The Chair. It reclined, it had pockets, its charms were so hotly fought over that no one had sat in it for months. He stroked its ample velour arms, primped its profound cushions, one of which Ziggy was already trying to mate with.

His eyes lit up. 'For The Chair?'

'For The Chair.'

'You're on.'

'Blimey,' said Dom, eyes doing that glinting thing again. 'I never thought it'd be this easy.'

PART TWO: MAKING EVERY DAY COUNT

JANUARY — DECEMBER 2022

JANUARY

CHAPTER 7

'Merry New Year! Rise and shine! New year – New you! Let's ring in those changes, people!'

Luke had risen at 5.30am on the first day of the new year. He hadn't really meant to be up so early, but he and Dom had overdone the Baileys the evening before, and all through the night he kept waking up with a headache and dry mouth. (Also, music and laughter kept drifting down from Alan's floors, where they sounded like they were having much more fun than his night in with Dom and Jools Holland.) On his way back from the night's third trip to the loo, Luke suddenly recalled his and Dom's year-long armchair challenge, and he decided to kick things off with a bang. Or a police horn.

January 1 was Ring A Bell Day, according to *Chase's Calendar of Events.* Dom had dared him to walk up and down the road and welcome in the new year with a rousing dawn peal. He didn't have an actual bell, but he did have Milo's old Raleigh Chopper. A little red gizmo strapped to its handlebar came with fire engine, police siren, revving motorbike and even howling wolf mode, not to mention half a dozen different light settings.

So Luke wheeled himself out early doors, his long legs

awkwardly bestriding the little bike, and began to toot its various horns. Mrs Hart, the old lady in the residential home opposite who stared out of the window all day, was already up, and waved back politely. A milkman whistled. The road Luke lived in was a short one, a sort of cul-de-sac behind Palmers Green train station, and with the fresh-faced enthusiasm of a new era's dawn, he had visions of knocking off the first day's challenge with ease. Somehow he thought everyone would get it.

But then a dog started running down a driveway towards him. An irate balding man with a tangle of chest hair spilling out from a greasy-looking vest threw back his curtain and hurled a string of obscenities. Someone threw an actual shoe. More dogs began barking. A lady in a flannel nightie came charging out of her front door and threatened him with a hairbrush. It was as if the whole street had come out against him. He wheeled the Chopper back rather faster than he set out, his optimism almost as deflated as Milo's punctured back wheel.

'What the feck were you thinking?' said Dom on his return. He was leaning on his bedroom door frame, looking rather grey and spluttery, even for him. His usual impeccable hair was a tired-looking mess. This was a person who had not intended to see in any part of the first morning of the new year.

'Come on, you remember!' said Luke. 'It's the first day of the challenge! We've got to *make every day count*!'

'How on earth did it come to this?' said Dom with a shudder, as if he didn't know, and slammed the door in Luke's face.

Luke retreated to the kitchen of the flat that he and Dom shared, made a coffee and looked at the time. It was 7.15am, so he went to liberate Ziggy from his crate. The chocolate cockapoo cub nosed his way out ready for the day, stretched front legs and trunk in an effortless downward dog, then hauled himself up onto a sofa. Luke braced himself as Ziggy, tail now wagging furiously, began to administer the frantic licks to his owner's face that were an essential element of his morning routine. He leant in gingerly, careful not to get his glasses slurped over, and patiently stroked Ziggy's tummy while his cheeks were slathered and his ears expertly nibbled. 'Remind me why you're here again?' he whispered. But Ziggy's ears were covered with great furry flaps, and it was possible the message hadn't sunk in. Few messages to Ziggy did really.

The daily challenges had begun. As he sat sipping his drink and looking down Alan's garden, Luke reflected on this strangely auspicious day, and wondered what the year ahead held in store for him.

CHAPTER 8

Because Dom was apparently 'very hot on accountability', Luke and Milo had set up a blog to track his progress across 2022 – called simply Make Every Day Count – and began with a couple of posts explaining the challenge and the charity angle. But which charity? Luke didn't expect to make much money, but he thought it would be nice to nominate one just in case. He thought of doing something in honour of Gav, but the latter's Darwin-Award manner of passing didn't lend itself to any obvious good cause.

He thought about breast cancer, which had taken his mum, or stroke, which had affected both her parents, but it was very hard to choose. He tried googling deserving causes and found himself confronted by a vast swirling maelstrom of need: so many charities, each trying to do its bit and get its voice heard in the clamorous awareness marketplace. Every health condition underfunded and misunderstood. Every social injustice scandalously ignored. Every environmental issue an emergency, and time running out fast.

Luke wasn't cynical about any of these; quite the opposite. He found himself caught up in every website he read, and filled with fervour to do his bit and bring about some positive change... But then he read another, and another, and soon felt oppressed. All he had wanted to do was enjoy the feelgood buzz that comes with a bit of worthy fundraising. But there were just so many causes out there – all of them deserving, all of them under-supported – that he felt obliged to try and rank them in some way, which was quite impossible. How did you choose between heart disease and cancer? Come to that, what was the 'best' (most deserving) cancer? After an hour or two of this, he ended up feeling guilty and exhausted.

'Come on, stupid dog,' he said to Ziggy. 'Let's walk.' Ziggy was already lying across the gap at the bottom of the front door and needed no second invitation, though he did as always go through the pantomime of refusing to accept having a harness put over his head. As usual, Luke had to spend ten minutes luring him out from behind the sofa and under the kitchen table before the puppy would finally consent to a process which – as he ought to well know by now, since it happened at least three times a day – took a matter of a few seconds, was completely painless, and was the necessary and inevitable prelude to his two favourite pastimes in the world: chasing balls and sniffing other dog's arses. As so often, Luke ended up giving him a big chunk of chicken to short-cut this tedious palaver. 'You really have to wonder who's training who,' drawled Dom.

As a dog walker who frequented the same two or three parks every day, Luke had got to know a great many fellow owners, though never by name. One of the first things he discovered about this strange ball-throwing, treat-laden breed was that to ask any of them for their human name instantly marked you out as a total pervert. In the park, you were never Luke or Zoe or Bob; you were 'Ziggy's dad' or 'Benzo's mum' or 'the lady with the biscuity Cavachon'. (Incidentally, every time he met a Cavachon, Luke was wild with envy. He wished he could swap his cockapoo for one, or least perform some sort of magical breed transplant. Cavachons were like cockapoos on Mogadon – docile, short-range and compliant rather than hyperactive, deceitful, disobedient roamers. Well, his was anyway.)

Dog owners can spot a newbie a mile off, Luke discovered, and were always very free with their advice. This seemed very helpful at first, but Luke quickly discovered that one dogsplainer's opinion, however passionately held and authoritatively dispensed, was usually contradicted by the next one's. Raw food, crates, socialisation, recall, getting the dog 'done'... everybody had a different view on the key issues. Queen among dog walkers was a woman in Oak Vale Park called Kay, who held forth, eternal cigarette in hand, for a couple of hours every morning from the vantage point of her mobility scooter. People seemed to hang on her every word, even though – as far as Luke could see – her dogs were the worst behaved in the whole park.

'Hands up who still keeps their dog in a crate,' she demanded one morning to her followers. A handful of hands went up, Luke's foolishly among them.

'Ah, but that's not a crate, my friends. That's a bloody *prison*. What sort of message are you sending to your dog with that?'

Behind her, Luke saw that Ziggy was being assaulted by her two dogs, one a vast shaggy Alsatian cross and the other a nasty, yappy little Jack Russell whose aggressive behaviour presented a textbook case of Small Dog Syndrome.

'Whose one is that?' Kay demanded, pointing at Ziggy. Meekly, Luke said it was his. She pointed her smouldering fag at Ziggy. 'You know what that is, don't you?'

'Er, no.' Kay was mid-performance; no other answer was possible.

'Your one's still got his balls. That's what that is.'

Later Kay cornered Luke in the wooded area at the top of the park by the allotments.

'Does your one still bite?' she asked, as the Alsatian glowered at him warningly.

'Er, he just nibbles a little,' Luke said nervously. 'Soft mouth.' (He was proud of this terminology, which he'd only learnt yesterday, even if it wasn't really true in Ziggy's case.)

Kay drove her scooter up close, until he could share in the smoke from her fag. 'You know what to do if he bites you, don't you?'

Luke said he did not.

She leant in, until he could feel the heat from her ciggie. 'You *bite the forker back*.'

'Goodness,' said Luke. 'With all these tips, I'll have to have you on speed dial.'

Kay nodded, as if this was a development she'd been expecting. 'Give us your phone and I'll punch my number in.'

'Bloody hell! Back in a sec! Come here, Ziggy!' shouted Luke, looking off in the distance with what he hoped was the expression of a man who had just seen a toddler about to fall off a railway bridge. Man and dog ran away as fast as they could, and had been dodging Kay in the park ever since.

Now he ran into the mum of Teddy, a boisterous Labradoodle puppy who was only a couple of months older than Ziggy, and as usual they stopped for a chat. Teddy and Ziggy would wrestle and race each other for hours, given half a chance, leaving the humans to discuss all sorts. Truly, it was amazing the things dog owners told each other. Widow(er)s reminisced about their late partners, agonised parents talked of tense stand-offs with teenage children, hearty-looking boomers confided the most personal health issues. A couple of weeks back, Luke had met a man from Finchley who was out walking his daughter's dog. The man talked about all the dogs he'd had to have put down over the years. 'Funny how they always look you right in the eye before they slip away,' he said. A strange expression came over him. 'And it's always me they look at. Never the wife.'

Teddy's mum, to give another example, had revealed that she was on long-term compassionate leave to care for her husband, who had long Covid. She was worried her son was on the autistic spectrum. Her seventeen-year-old daughter wasn't speaking to her because Mum wouldn't let her boyfriend stay in her bedroom

27

overnight. All this and more she was happy to tell Luke, just never her human name. It wasn't done.

Luke, over-caffeinated as ever, told her plenty back in turn. He told her about Yasmine (The One), and tried not to notice the sad head-tilt thing she did as he explained where they were at. (Funny how many people did the head tilt when he talked about The One.) He told her about his ridiculous job and how it was getting him nowhere. How his bosses were a dysfunctional father-and-daughter team who inflicted the messed-up psychodrama of their relationship on the rest of the office on a daily basis. How he probably couldn't even stick it if it wasn't for a few good mates like Holly. He told her about Dom, and how he was now involved in an absurd Silly Day Challenge that threatened to take over his life and leave him at the mercy of his sadistic flatmate for the whole of 2022. And how he couldn't even find a charity to raise money for without feeling guilty about neglecting all the others.

'Simple,' she said. 'Do it for one that's completely neglected. Do it for the Trigeminal Neuralgia Association.'

'Never heard of it,' said Luke.

'Exactly.'

'Are you sure that's not a made-up one? Maybe a scam?'

'If only.'

Teddy's mum was affected by trigeminal neuralgia herself. It turned out to be a form of facial pain caused by blood vessels resting on the branches of a nerve in the face, she told him; the pain can be so acute and long-lasting that it can leave you unable to work or even leave home. Many people have been driven to contemplate suicide because of it, and yet no one has ever heard of it.

'It took me twelve years to get a diagnosis,' Teddy's mum said. 'Today is a relatively good day. But on bad days I just sit in my room, rocking with the pain and the side effects of all the painkillers and antidepressants.' She'd had several teeth removed by an unscrupulous dentist, just on the off-chance that it might help with the pain, which she said felt like shards of glass being pushed into your face. It hadn't helped.

'But today's a good day,' she said again, and Luke noticed for the first time how her eyes smiled but her mouth struggled to join in. 'It's worse in the evenings, or when I'm stressed or tired.' As well as being a hidden and almost unknown condition, she told him it didn't count as a disability, so even though you could be completely incapacitated by it, you wouldn't get any government support. 'People are losing their houses over it, and no one's even talking about it.'

'Wow,' said Luke. 'I had no idea.'

'No one does.'

'Well, that's my sponsorship question sorted.'

'Thank you!' said Teddy's mum. 'I think it's a brilliant thing you're doing. And so does Teddy.' Teddy did appear to be smiling up at Luke. Luke might once have been taken in by this, but he recognised it as the same smile Ziggy flashed just prior to launching himself at the kitchen table in a bid to steal some toast. Luke threw each dog a treat. There followed a long, thoughtful companionable silence, punctured only by a few good-natured yowls as Teddy pinned Ziggy to the ground.

'Thanks for sharing all that,' said Luke at last. 'But it does make me wonder: how much more do we need to reveal about each other before we're allowed to know each other's human names?'

Teddy's mum laughed and extended a hand. 'I'm Michelle.'

CHAPTER 9

With the blog up and running, and the donation page in place, Luke soon fell into the rhythm of daily challenges. On Hypnotism Day (January 4) – first day back at work – he borrowed a Paul McKenna book and tried to hypnotise Holly: 'You WILL meet a decent bloke!' Holly was famous in the office for a long string of unsuitable dates and dodgy boyfriends. There was the one who always FaceTimed his mum when they were out on a date. The ones (plural) who just wanted to talk about their ex. The one with the unsightly toe fungus. The one who collected bus tickets. The one who didn't agree with the idea of women bosses or politicians. The one who phoned while in mid-poo...

One could go on. Holly had a well-polished monologue about all this, which she'd trot out in the pub every so often, always ending with a couple of choice new additions. But Luke sensed that – despite the comedy of the situation – there was a sadness beneath it all, and she really did want to meet someone; certainly, she was always ready – and ridiculously optimistic – to go on another blind date or try a new dating app. You could do a lot worse than Holly, and it was incredible that none of these losers could see how lucky they were when she showed up to meet them.

Over Christmas, Holly had met up with a guy who she thought might break the pattern at last.

'He was really nice,' she said. 'We went for a lovely walk on Hampstead Heath, and he was really sweet and thoughtful. Bought me little presents. Asked me questions and actually listened to what I said in reply.'

'Uh-oh. I feel a catch coming.'

'It was only by chance that I discovered he had three social media accounts in completely different names.'

'And there it is. You were dating the Tinder Swindler.'

'Was I? It's hard to know. Maybe I got the nice authentic persona, and some other poor women got the nasty, toxic ones.'

'That does sound promising. I do like the idea of parcelling out the nasty bits of myself and giving them a different profile.'

'Yeah. Then maybe just block them and become like this really perfect person.'

'Except I suppose you'd never be able to cancel your shadow selves completely. They'd probably just languish in some digital netherworld somewhere, ready to come back and haunt you at the worst possible moment. Sort of *Dorian Gray* for Gen Z.'

'Well, quite,' said Holly. 'But let us turn to business. New words, please.'

'Ooh yes. Let's see what we have.' One of the things that made Luke and Holly's work bearable was a side project of theirs, the devising of a comprehensive *Dictionary of Office Life*. The purpose of this book – which would no doubt take decades to complete but would be seen by posterity as the definitive work on the subject – was to capture those little phenomena of office life which everyone knows about but no one has as yet found a word for. For example:

Chair-speration

Noun. The damp patch of sweat that collects between shoulder blades and coccyx after you've been sitting in the same chair for too long. Also, the shiny patch on a synthetic leather chair caused by same.

Or this one, all-too-familiar to them both:

Dreadline
Noun. The cut-off point for handing in a piece of work which you know isn't any good.

Or this – one of the pair's favourites, inspired by a habit of their boss, Greg:

Hypsnotic Trance
Noun phrase. The almost catatonic state that comes over people when they forget they are picking their nose in full view of the rest of the office.

'So what have you got for our Big Dic today, H?'
'Well, I was so knackered and depressed yesterday I almost didn't make it in today,' she replied. 'Just couldn't face it. But I did come up with a couple of pertinent terms:'

Illowance
Noun. The unspoken four or five days per year that you allow yourself to take off sick when you're merely hopelessly hungover.

Admin Day
Noun. A day where you put aside all your usual work to devote yourself to all those funny little jobs that never get done at home e.g. paying bills, phoning your mate in Australia, photocopying the footie team fixtures etc.

'Oh yes,' said Luke. 'That's me today. And, er, most Mondays actually. Tuesdays too, sometimes.'

'Ooh,' said Holly suddenly, pointing at a smart-looking imitation Moleskine notebook Luke had been given for Christmas. 'Is that new?' This reminded Luke to mention that he believed Holly suffered from a serious condition that he at last had a name for:

Pencil Envy
Noun. The inexplicable frisson that comes over certain people in the stationery aisle, coupled with an insatiable need to buy yet more unnecessary notebooks, highlighters and gel pens.

'Guilty as charged,' she agreed.

The new terms were all duly accepted into the *Dictionary*, and Luke promised to revert soonest to cascade some toilet-adjacent lexical items to the New Words Committee (members: Holly and Luke).

'If you could, please,' said Holly with mock officiousness. 'In the meantime, I will attend to my Hint Tray.'

Hint Tray
Noun. The plastic shelving on the corner of your desk, used only by your manager, that is crammed with cuttings, press releases and various other notes relating to speculative projects that you both secretly know you will never get round to.

'Yeah right.'

Chapter 10

More days passed, as they will. Dom and Luke got into a rhythm of agreeing Days to observe the night before, with Dom taking pics for the blog and sniggering a lot, and Luke repeatedly repenting his flatmate's choices on the morrow.

On Whipped Cream Day (January 5), he was tricked into doing something unspeakable involving Ziggy, semi-nudity and a tube of the squirty stuff. On Show & Tell At Work Day (January 8), he commandeered a slot at the fortnightly knowledge-sharing session (usually a tedious succession of fanciful Flop Chart Presentations) to deliver a talk about his Silly Day Challenge.

Flop Chart Presentation
Noun. Any presentation using pretty graphs and fancy animations to mask an absence of real ideas or useful information.

It seemed to go down quite well, and the lack of questions afterwards reassured Luke that he'd hit that sweet spot of dogged indifference he'd been aiming for.

'Sounds like fun,' said Greg. 'Well done, Luke. Not quite sure why you couldn't have chosen a real charity, but still.' Luke tried to explain, but Greg was already hurrying everyone along to the final item on the morning's agenda, a presentation from Muriel.

'Er, what's this one on again, Muriel?' asked Greg. He glanced nervously at his watch. For Greg, knowledge-sharing was something you said you did to sell potential recruits on your wonderful 'culture'; it always alarmed and vexed him when people expected it to actually happen for real. After all, this was valuable billable time they were all wasting: time and Google wait for no one, as he liked to say, and while his team were all huddled together in cosy woke mindswaps, the competition was snapping at their heels.

'It is definitely on-topic, Muriel, isn't it?'

Muriel, a mum of four sweaty, boisterous boys under twelve, was in the habit of giving talks that veered off into domestic issues which, while no doubt of value in themselves, were not considered by the management team (Greg and Phaedra, father and daughter) as central to the mission of the company, which they had recently reformulated as follows:

Wordy Gigs:
We write the words that make the whole world click.

'Oh yes,' Muriel said with a smile, still fiddling with her memory stick. 'Highly relevant to everyone, I'd say. Or at least it should be.' And here she glared at a number of people around the table, most of whom happened to be male.

'Right then!' said Greg, calling everyone to a sort of attention. 'So now let me hand you over to... Muriel!'

The first slide showed a picture of a load of dirty knives and plates wedged precariously into a plastic rack. Muriel, whose PowerPoint animation style was infuriatingly retro, pressed her clicker again, and the title of her talk whizzed in at an alarming spinny cadence not seen since the 1990s. (A deckologist would have had a field day, they really would.)

Deckologist

Noun. An expert in deckology, a minor branch of psychology which claims to be able to derive insights about a person's character by analysing their PowerPoint animation style.

The title flashed a few different colours, shifted left, right, up and down, before settling into place at last:

Dishwasher loading: Best practice and handy hacks

A collective groan went up around the table, but Muriel was unmoved.

'It's for your own good,' she said. 'Same as I told my boys.' Now she flicked to her first slide, a caricature image of a wooden spoon, its cartoon arms folded crossly. 'Now I'm sorry to have to repeat this, guys, but please try to remember: *You do not put these fellas inside the machine. Ever.*'

When Luke told Dom about all this, the latter was so tickled at the idea of grown-ups having to do show-and-tells that he decided Luke could do one every month for one of his Days. In the meantime, he had Luke encourage everyone to declutter their workstations for Clean Up Your Desk Day (January 10).

For the desk challenge, Luke had the bright idea of enlisting the support of Muriel, who brought an uncompromising zeal to the activity. (One of Luke's favourite Muriel subject lines was "CARNAGE IN THE KETTLE AREA!!!" which she sent out two or three times a week, usually accompanied by a line of angry-face emojis and a pic of a kitchen surface 'desecrated', as she put it, by a couple of used teabags and a light sprinkling of cake crumbs.)

Muriel got the design team to knock up a flyer bearing a hi-res full-colour, bulldozer-and-pigeon-strafed image of Bordo Poniente in Mexico which, covering 940 acres and receiving more than 12,000 tons of waste every day, was widely considered the world's very largest open-air landfill dump (at least until its closure in

2011). "DOES YOUR DESK LOOK THIS?" ran Muriel's first headline. Below this, a second banner – "TIME TO TURN IT INTO THIS" – was accompanied by an image of Salar de Uyuni, the legendary salt flats of Bolivia which were widely held to be the smoothest, flattest – and therefore most uncluttered – place on Earth. And of course, like any good marketer, Muriel had not overlooked a crisp call to action (CTA). "JANUARY 10: TIME TO GET CLEANING YA FOOKING MUTHAS".

'Isn't that CTA a bit on the nose, Muriel?' Luke wondered.

'You have to smash these kids over the head or nothing gets done,' she said with a sigh, leaving Luke to wonder whether she was still talking about her co-workers or her children, or whether in her mind there was really much difference.

'And that's not all.' She sighed again, tugging at a forlorn Marigold.

'Oh? What's up?'

'We're into the third day of a massive Rinse Aid crisis, and still not a peep out of Greg or Phaedra. Still too busy bickering.'

Greg and Phaedra's disputes followed a well-worn rhythm, from sniping to shouts to sulky silences that could last for days but were eventually and inevitably followed by toe-curling make-up sessions between Daddy and his little girl that – for those forced to witness them – were easily the most disagreeable phase of the whole cycle. The fact that Phaedra – a graceful Keira Knightley lookalike with bold green eyes and flaming red hair – towered a good foot over her dad, who in size and figure was more of a Danny DeVito, only added to their weird aura of dysfunction.

It was a funny old dynamic: Phaedra had had the idea for the business, and brought to it all her contacts and sales skills. But Greg wrote the cheques to fund his precious girl's baby project, and he could be staggeringly mean and petty at times. Plus, bankrolling his daughter's project made him feel entitled to poke his nose into everything that went on at Wordy Gigs. Phaedra's eye-rolling resentment of all this was like that of a grown-up child who can't afford to leave the parental home. (She was in fact living with her folks again temporarily, having just broken up with her fiancé of many years.)

'Do you have any Paras, Muriel?' said Luke, changing the subject. 'Not feeling too clever today.' As well as managing all the sales, marketing and dishwasher-related aspects of the business, Muriel was also Wordy Gigs' unofficial Office Dealer.

Office Dealer
Noun. The motherly type who's always got a drawer full of paracetamol, Anadin, Lemsip and Alka-Seltzer. Vital to keep this character on side.

'Course I do. Follow me.' She ushered him to a row of filing cabinets and opened a drawer to reveal an Aladdin's cave of pharmaceuticals and first-aid paraphernalia. Ironically, Muriel's own desk was covered in teetering towers of papers, books and files, which cascaded down the back and under her desk. When anyone tried to point out that the desk-cleaning exercise ought maybe to apply to her too, she would shoo them away, saying, 'The key is to focus on the low-hanging fruit'.

Greg came in next morning bearing a disorderly sheaf of her flyers, all torn and trodden on, which he said had spilled all down the stairs and out into the street.

'Who signed off on these? They must have cost a bomb!' he demanded. 'And why are there so many? I found Michael the Cone sitting on a couple more boxes outside.' It seemed Muriel had slightly over-ordered – somewhere in the region of two thousand for a team of seventeen, half of whom worked remotely – but she said she was storing them up for next year's Day.

'They've made a hell of a mess,' said Greg. 'Did you know about this, Phaedra?'

The expression on the face of Phaedra, who had been smiling absently at her phone screen, instantly blackened. 'Oh my God!

That is so unfair! I cannot believe that you would say that! Why is everything *my fault*?'

Greg sputtered, 'I only meant...' But he didn't get a chance to finish his sentence, because his daughter had stalked out of the other office door, the one leading to the toilets, and slammed it behind her.

'That went well,' said Greg. He flinched a little with each crash of a cubicle door being violently slammed. The office walls shook a little. He looked a little lost.

'Muriel,' he said hopelessly. 'Would you mind going into the loos and seeing if...?'

But Muriel had already gathered up a box of tissues and was heading in the direction of the ladies. Along with kitchen monitor and office mother, another of Muriel's unofficial roles was that of mediator between Phaedra and Greg. It was a job only she could do, and it was probably why Greg let her hijack sales meetings with presentations about unclaimed lunch boxes (her regular Tupperware Amnesty days were much admired, albeit ironically) and kitchen theft (she once put up a Wanted poster when her beloved KEEP CALM AND SWEEP THE FLOOR mug went missing).

'I'll talk to her,' she said, sighing.

CHAPTER 11

Following the desk-cleaning, Luke was tasked with doing a tour of the neighbourhood with a shopping trolley containing all Alan's African violets, ivies, ferns, aloe veras and bromeliads. This was, of course, to mark Take Your Houseplant For A Walk Day (January 12). He was just waving back to the old lady in the window, who was nodding her encouragement, when he was stopped by the police on suspicion of vagrancy, theft (daylight shrubbery, perhaps) and criminal damage.

Only the pleading eyes and tremulous sniffing of fellow trolley-passenger Ziggy was able to prevent the incident from being escalated. It transpired one of the officers was the granddad of a boisterous goldendoodle called Lola. Luke was let off with a stiff talking-to on condition that he first coo over about three hundred doggie pics. Then he got another stiff talking-to from Alan, who was unhappy because Luke had decided to water all the plants before returning them, little knowing that over-watering is the number one cause of houseplant fatality. And then he gave *himself* a stiff talking-to, because he realised too late that Dom had confused Take Your Houseplant For A Walk Day – which actually falls in July – with Houseplant Appreciation Day, and that if Luke had been more vigilant he could have avoided this whole charade in the first place.

At such moments, haunted as he was by the expression of manic glee on Dom's face every time he picked up the big *Chase's* book to plan more humiliating observances, Luke began to wonder whether the Days thing was getting out of hand, and whether use of a mere chair – even a chair as comfortable and coveted as *The* Chair – was adequate compensation for everything he would have to go through to win it. And so, one Sunday evening in mid-January, he called Dom and Milo to a meeting to review ground rules. It was time to renegotiate.

Arguing that Dom's suggestions showed signs of becoming increasingly demanding and humiliating, Luke secured an agreement that he could veto one of Dom's challenges per month, and also get a better hearing for his own ideas. In compensation, Dom negotiated the right to play one Joker every month – a challenge that had to be accepted whatever it involved. Luke agreed to this subject to certain pre-conditional caveats which, knowing Dom, he insisted include: No Law-Breaking, No Public Singing, and – remembering the notorious evening when Luke had had to ingest a teabag and a slug after losing another bet with Bill – No Eating Things Which Aren't Actually Food.

Milo did his best to capture all these new and revised clauses, the small print of which had now spread from the original kitchen whiteboard onto a flipchart purloined from Luke's office, to a kids' chalkboard Milo had had to bring down from his own bedroom. (A few days later, Luke added No Cosplay after a difficult Tube commute on January 19, aka National Gimp Day.)

CHAPTER 12

January 14 was Take A Missionary To Lunch Day. Luke didn't really know any missionaries, so he knocked on the door of a few nearby churches until one answered. This turned out to be a spiritualist church, and soon Luke was sharing a table at a kebab place with Janine, Chief Psychic Demonstrator at the Temple of Inner Fire. She was a tall, very straight-backed lady in her late sixties, Luke judged, with neatly cropped auburn hair and the most extraordinary piercing blue eyes.

Janine made no claims to be a missionary, she said, but was always up for a spot of *shish*. When Luke explained about his challenge, she nodded and said, 'Oh yes, I see. Time is our humility.'

'I'm sorry?'

'You want to conquer time. But for now we are trapped in time like a fly in amber.'

'Ri-ight.'

'Only spirit lives outside time.'

There was a long silence that slowly felt to Luke as if it was straying beyond what was socially acceptable. The conversation teetered on a precipice. He nodded, just in time.

'You think by living the days up close you can escape their mortal dominion,' said Janine. 'Tell me, are you the sort of person who often takes on extravagant quests?'

'I... don't think so,' he said doubtfully. For some reason, he found himself picturing Yasmine (The One).

'By the way: do you want any more of these falafel?'

They chatted of this and that, and then Janine suddenly stopped and grabbed his arm.

'Do you by any chance know someone by the name of... Ivy?'

'I don't think so.'

'I see them in your future.'

'Oh. Are they dead?'

'Let's hope not!' She giggled, reaching for another helping of tzatziki.

A little later, Luke asked for the bill, and Janine thanked him for the food. As they were leaving, he said, 'It's been very nice to meet you, Janine. But do you mind my asking: Why did you agree to come to lunch with a complete stranger?'

'Well, the hummus here is *amazing*.' She chuckled. 'Also,' she said, 'I thought you were in spiritual distress.'

'Ah. But now...?'

Janine opened her bag. 'Here's my card,' she said. 'You just call me any time.' She smiled again. Her eyes looked right through him, into his cramped and floppy soul. 'Remember, Luke, *days are all we have*. Days are to be embraced and inhabited, not conquered and ticked off. Sufficient unto the day thereof. There is a whole day in a single moment, and a whole life in a single day.'

Luke thought about her words. 'Does that mean,' he ventured, 'that there is a whole life in a single moment?'

Janine thought for a moment. 'Yes,' she said.

CHAPTER 13

On January 20, Get To Know Your Customer Day, Luke phoned up Reggie from Hornsey BoxLife, the north London storage specialist who was Wordy Gigs' longest-standing client. Greg said that the oldest clients never got enough attention, so this was a great chance to kill two birds with one stone.

There were, of course, two reasons why people didn't get in touch with Reggie from Hornsey BoxLife more often. One was that he needed little attention because he was for some reason endlessly impressed by the team's ability to spin content gold from his line of work. Luke's own masterworks in this area included "10 Great Storage Scenes From The Movies", "The 17 Most Unusual Items To Have Ever Been Left In Storage" and "Are You Allowed To Live In A Storage Unit? And Other Storage Myths Busted". Most winningly, Reggie from Hornsey BoxLife never seemed to notice that these extraordinary works of faction could have been easily cobbled together by anyone with access to Google.

The other reason that people tended not to speak to Reggie from Hornsey BoxLife too often was that he was very emotional, had no self-edit button and was very hard to get off the phone. Oh, and there was a third – he was always trying to sell you storage.

Holly and Luke frequently fantasised about cutting him up and leaving him to dissolve in acid in one of his units. Storage was like a traditional gym membership: the business model relied on you forgetting what you were paying for and/or not having the energy to move all your stuff out again. If Reggie from Hornsey BoxLife could be persuaded at gunpoint to open a storage account himself – you'd think he'd probably get a nice discount – then he could go on paying for his own corpse's incarceration for months before it was discovered. Indeed, if the acid did its job he might never be found.

'Out of context, this might all sound rather ghoulish,' said Holly.

'Yes, but really it's a victimless crime.'

'Well, not for Reggie from Hornsey BoxLife.'

'I think you're forgetting how endless the calls are.'

Still, Luke dialled the number and Reggie answered at once. Actually, it was quite a nice chat. Reggie talked about his children, three and five, and how he never got any sleep anymore. There were lots of anecdotes of the 'kids say the funniest things' variety: the time Reggie's daughter referred to a church as 'an astronanut's castle', the time his son asked a beekeeper if there was such a thing as 'dragonfly honey', and – in an unexpected twist – the time his son got angry with Reggie trying to make him do his teeth in a hurry and told his dad: 'Your heart stinks'.

Reggie stopped talking after that; Luke could just hear great hulking sobs. He imagined a whole storage unit, full to bursting with Reggie's tears. He was so distraught that Luke could barely make out his final offer to Luke of twenty-five per cent off a premium unit for the first six months.

Over the course of the following day – which happened to be National Hugging Day – Luke tried in vain to meet Dom's challenge of hugging one hundred people in twenty-four hours. In the event, he'd managed about ten by home time – the kids upstairs, Dom (sort of), Holly (twice; nice smell), Michael the

Cone (best described as differently odiferous), Muriel – and Clive from the Pay Per Click department. (He'd seen Alan standing behind the kids, hesitating to offer a manly embrace, but Luke just couldn't face it.) Luke gave Clive an extra-hard squeeze because his job – which involved writing the words for the paid ads that come up alongside the normal results on a search page – was generally considered to be even more boring than everyone else's. Half the office queued up to embrace Clive, in fact, who became quite overcome.

As a rule, Luke was quite a huggy sort of person, in a spontaneous way. But going up to people out of the blue and asking them to embrace him was quite different. He toyed with the idea of asking the security guard in Tesco, but was deterred by a stern warning look. It was Friday night, so there was nothing for it but to retire to The Devonshire Maid with the gang, have a few beers and loosen the old inhibitions. Clive got the landlord to announce that Luke was doing a sponsored hugathon for 'the cancer' ('they'll never believe that other thing you said'), and by the end of the evening, he had done several laps of the pub, dispensing hugs and collecting coins in a pint pot. The whole thing was really rather moving.

Holly went round with him, shaking the pot and drawing the more inhibited huggers out of their shell. 'Come on – it's all for a good cause!'

'You got a good one there, mate,' said someone. 'Quite the partner in crime.'

'Holly? Nah, we're just mates. I'm far too normal for her,' said Luke. 'She only likes weird blokes.'

'And I'm much too available,' said Holly. 'He only likes inaccessible women – preferably in a different time zone.'

CHAPTER 14

On Just Do It Day (January 24), Luke sat down and penned Yasmine another of his long emails. He explained the challenge, reiterated his faith in her, reminded her that as far as he was concerned, she was – in every sense – The One. He even sent it.

As if in answer to his prayers, next day promised to be extra special. Or not. Luke got in from work to find his flatmate waiting for him:

'Luke! You've had a message from The One!' cried Dom.

Luke's heart skipped several beats. 'Yasmine! Really? But she never calls!' He felt panic, elation and a nasty nauseous burning sensation all at once.

'I know!' said Dom. 'And she didn't today either! It's National Opposites Day, silly!'

'Oh.'

'Unless, of course, the bit I just said about her *never* calling is the opposite. Meaning, in fact, she did call.'

'Wow! Amazing! *Really?*'

'Yes!'

'*Really?* What did she say?'

'I mean No, silly – the opposite! She never calls. You know that.'

The last day of the month was Bubble Wrap Appreciation Day. Luke liberated a roll of the stuff from the Wordy Gigs stationery cupboard, took it home, and with Milo got down to some vigorous popping, stomping and squeezing. ('You used to love doing that when you were little,' Alan told Luke with a quiet smile. Luke scowled.)

But Luke was aware of a general feeling of anticlimax, a feeling that bubble wrap wasn't quite as... *poppy* as it used to be. 'Whither, oh whither, the bubbles of yesteryear?' wondered Luke aloud. He took to Google, and discovered that, sure enough, a new pop-less version of the product had been introduced in 2015. Luke wasn't the only one to regret this development. In a 2019 tweet, someone called Elon Musk declared pop-less bubble wrap 'a sign of the apocalypse'.

Looking back on the month, Luke couldn't help feeling he had in many ways had the better of Dom. True, there had been some embarrassing moments – the chafing burns from the gimp suit would fade in time, but the mental scars perhaps never. But there had been lots of fun moments too – the group hugging, doing silly things with Milo, the strange encounter with Janine the spiritualist that he couldn't stop thinking about.

True, National Opposites Day had been a disappointment – a classic Dom trap he'd walked into with both eyes closed. (Note to self: find ingenious, slow-burn way to get own back on Dom. Again.) But he was in an upbeat mood, more energetic and positive than he'd felt for a long, long time. For one thing, he'd completed the first month of this very silly Silly Day Challenge. A long way to go, but still; quite something. And another thing, rather more significant, not to say fecking momentous, was the first comment (not by a bot) that had appeared on the Make Every Day Count blog:

Go Go Luke! I love what u do
The author: someone called Yazz028. The One!

FEBRUARY

Chapter 15

Luke had first met Yasmine, aka The One, aka 'The One Who Never Calls' (Dom), on platform 7 of the Gare de Lyon, in Paris. He was on his way to visit friends he'd met when working as a teaching assistant in a *lyceé* near Avignon, and – in the naive belief that Paris was a compact walkable place where everywhere was within a lazy stroll of everywhere else – he had contrived to miss his connection by about forty-five seconds.

Sweating and cursing on the *quai* as the train edged away from him at a sarcastic snail's pace, he had attracted the sympathetic gaze of a tearful Yasmine, who had just been seeing off her beloved mother. They got talking and somehow ended up in a café.

Yasmine was half French and half Tunisian. She had never met an English person who could speak a bit of French before, and even Luke could see she was charmed by his accent. He, in turn, was charmed by her whole person, by her soft voice, her smile, her wonderful white teeth, by her modest allure, her graceful way of sitting on a bar-stool, by her chic breathable nail polish (of a shade called 'Bittersweet', she informed him with a shy, exquisite smile). By her whole *being*, basically. After just five minutes of delirious connection, he wanted to say to her: 'Oh just move in, will you?'

And it was perhaps only thoughts of his dank mottled futon and the rinds of mould around his shower tray that held him back.

Luke contrived to miss two more trains, but all too soon the hour of his unavoidable departure came round. The pair exchanged numbers and email addresses, but Yasmine told him her number was only to be used in emergencies; she was best reached on email. And so it was that Luke embarked on the great epistolary romance of his life.

Over a series of messages, Luke and Yasmine poured out their hearts to each other, wrote loftily and demurely of their feelings, exchanged confidences and confessions, shared hopes, fears and dreams, and endlessly plotted for the day they would finally be together. True, the correspondence was a bit one-sided. Luke wrote in English and Yasmine replied in French, but the word count on his side probably did, over time, come to outnumber hers (by a few magnitudes). But hey – what was the point of 'dating' a content pro if you didn't like getting sent loads of content, right?

Over time, though, Yasmine's replies became ever more muted and non-committal; she seemed happy to validate his feelings but less and less keen to volunteer her own. And then, really rather abruptly, her replies began to dry up almost completely. Luke's novelistic declarations would be met with terse one-liners, or no answer at all. When, out of a sense of rising panic, he switched to phoning, he found that his calls would invariably go to an automated voicemail, and eventually to a 'number not available' message. Something was happening to his love, he was sure. She was in some kind of trouble or need. But he did not know how to reach her to help.

Yasmine had never seemed to have much of a digital footprint and so, despite his repeated efforts, he was never able to track her down online. It was also an unfortunate fact, best kept from heartless scoffers like Dom and professional sympathisers like Holly, that he was not absolutely sure of her last name (she seemed to have two or three different ones, which she used interchangeably). Increasingly, he began to wonder if she had vanished forever. Or perhaps she had just given up; long-distance relationships aren't easy at the best of times, and theirs had very little foundation in face-to-face reality. In his darkest hours, he took to wondering if Yasmine had ever actually existed. But no: whatever had happened to The One, his One, their connection had been real and profound; he was sure of it. He often speculated that an overbearing father figure had discovered their correspondence and intervened to put a stop to things. It was a relationship that was deemed inappropriate; and Luke could only agree. Only Yasmine's love could have saved him from his own unsuitability, he felt, in this as in most things.

Luke continued to write to Yasmine, switching now from email to proper writing paper and an ink pen. With these new, rather more literary props in hand, his missives became increasingly plangent, confessional, agonised. As he completed each one, he sealed it in a blue airmail envelope, and filed it in an old shoebox under his bed. Without a postal address, there was no risk of him ever sending them.

He wasn't perhaps one hundred per cent honest about the situation with other people, however. Whenever he expressed sympathy after hearing Holly's latest crap date story, she'd always say something like, 'It's okay for you; you've got Yasmine'. He'd just give a tight little smile in response which she usually interpreted as 'coy' or 'smug'. (Incidentally, Holly had just binned a bloke she met online who agreed with every single thing she said; she got so frustrated she started to say more and more outlandish things just to provoke him into disagreeing; after about half an hour of this he finally caved, confessing that when it came to compulsory mass euthanasia for the over-seventies, he was sorry to say that he did 'take rather a dim view'.)

All of which was to say that Yasmine's encouraging comment on his blog was more than a tad welcome. On January 24 (Just Do It Day) after weeks and weeks of dithering on his part and silence on hers, Luke had finally sent her an email explaining about the Make Every Day Count blog. And here was his reward. He had been brave, and Fortune had favoured him. Thanks, Fortune, thought Luke; we haven't always seen eye to eye – and I may have directed the odd desperate sarcasm your way in the past, for which I apologise – but it's good to have you on board. At last.

CHAPTER 16

Luke was in such a good mood that he took on Dom's Joker Challenge for the month without a murmur. Dom went early with an idea for Robinson Crusoe Day (February 1). As they didn't really live near any desert islands as such, the flatmate from hell decreed that the obvious next-best thing was for Luke to spend the night on a traffic island.

Flush still with Yasmine's encouragement, Luke built himself a small encampment of cardboard and canvas under a tree on the grassy green circle outside Oak Vale Park. He took with him several blankets, a sleeping bag and a pop-up festival tent. Holly sweetly supplied a comfort pack including Kendal mint cake and a flask of hot chocolate. Alan supplied a pair of thermal long johns from his fishing bag. Ziggy came with him too, and they snuggled up together for extra body warmth.

Not long after he'd settled in, a burly bloke who must have lived in one of the houses opposite the roundabout strode over to challenge Luke on what he was doing. Before Luke could reply, the man went into an (obviously well-rehearsed) rant about how charity sleep-outs were just a fake exercise in poverty porn cosplay for guilty middle-class liberals. Luke lamely tried to explain what he was actually doing, but ended up feeling he was only making the other man's point for him. Later, the man's wife came out, apologised on behalf of her husband and gave Luke a bag of two-pence pieces and random foreign small change 'for your funny cause'. Although it was a relatively mild evening for the time of year, that time of year was still February. The traffic from the nearby North Circular was incredibly loud, so much louder than one ever noticed in the day, and it never relented. From the park nearby, he heard terrible blood-curling sounds of animals screeching and wailing. Luke lasted till 1.30am, about the time he took a blurry red-eyed snap of a curious fox cub poking its head into the tent. Ziggy tried to sniff the cub's behind, and Luke decided it was time to scoot before the parents turned up. Dom was unusually lenient next morning, and accepted Luke's efforts as adequate. Next day he went off on one of his frequent (and never explained) absences.

On February 3, Luke popped up to see Milo and Grace with a tub of salted caramel to enjoy Eat Ice Cream for Breakfast Day. (Grace said she'd have preferred Oreo or mint choc chip, but she would make an effort.) And the day after that, he presented Monika the postie with a bottle of wine.

'What's this for?'

'It's National Thank A Mail Carrier Day!' Luke explained.

Monika, who was Swedish, had never heard of such a thing. She and Luke just stood there, not making eye contact, not sure what should happen next. Grace and Milo watched from Alan's doorway, enjoying all the awkwardness.

'We, er, *appreciate* you!' Luke said at last.

'This is... unexpected,' said Monika. She looked like someone who had just won a prize in a competition they hadn't entered, and was wondering what the catch was. But still, wine is wine, and eventually she stashed the bottle in her bag and went on her way.

Luke noticed as Ziggy ran after her that the puppy's bum was rather matted, which at least gave him a vaguely acceptable pretext for observing Shower With A Friend Day (February 5).

CHAPTER 17

In the office the following week, Luke alerted Holly to the fact the world had now entered Dump Your Significant Jerk Week (second week of February).

'Pretty much every week is Dump Your Significant Jerk Week for me,' she said with a sigh. She had another date that weekend coming up – with a man who said he wrote 'legal spam emails' for a living.

'It sounds dreadful,' she said.

'Well, you never know,' said Luke. 'And it's not often that we get to feel superior to any other kind of writer. Should be worth it for that alone.'

'This is true.' In the meantime they chose to mark Satisfied Staying Single Day (February 11) with a walk around Clerkenwell, Barbican and Holborn. They came across Coram Fields, a playground and park set in the colonnaded grounds of an old foundling hospital.

'I remember this place,' said Luke. 'I used to come here when I was little, I think.' As well as a café, swings and Astroturf pitches, the pair spotted a farm corner. Some of the animals roamed freely round the whole space, like the sheep and the goats.

'This would actually be a cool place to take someone on a date,' said Holly. 'See if they get it.'

'I was just thinking I should take Yasmine here,' agreed Luke.

Luke pointed to a sign that said adults were only allowed to enter if accompanied by a child. 'We'll have to come back here with Milo,' he said.

Holly's phone started to ring. Luke saw a look of consternation on her face. It always alarmed him, because her natural expression was so open and curious. There was something very poignant when her features clouded over like that.

'Oh God, it's him again.'

'Who?'

'Scrabble Man.'

'Come on, hand it over.' Holly paused. Luke beckoned with his palm. 'It's time. You know it is.' Still she hesitated. 'Come on,' he said. 'I've got a new voice and everything.' This clinched the deal.

'Hello, who's this?' Luke demanded into the handset. He sounded like a children's presenter imitating one of the sheep in the playground. Holly had to stifle her giggles.

On the other end of the line, a flat-toned, slightly confused voice introduced itself as Bobby.

'Well, I'm Alan,' Luke interrupted bleatingly. 'I'm Holly's boyfriend. And I'll thank you not to keep calling this number.' Bobby – best known for spending half an hour on his first date with Holly listing all permissible two-letter words in Scrabble containing an X, J or Z, not paying for a drink and referring to her throughout as Heather – was quite nonplussed by this turn of events, and quickly hung up.

Luke handed the phone back to Holly, who was still laughing. 'Don't thank me; it's what I do,' he said.

'I'll thank you not to keep calling this number!!' she mimicked. 'Who were you channelling, Mrs Miggins?'

Luke looked hurt for a moment. 'Well, it did the trick.'

'I know,' said Holly, squeezing his arm for a second. 'Thank you.' She paused. 'Funny how you chose the name Alan,' she said. 'Do I bring out the father figure in you?'

'Stop that,' baa-ed Luke in his best ovine voice.

Chapter 18

There was more name-choosing to come. Dom, who had arrived back from wherever he'd gone as suddenly as he'd left, convened Luke, Milo and Ziggy for a new Ground Rules meeting. He expressed concern that in his absence some of the challenges had become too easy. On February 9, for example – Read In The Bath Day – he discovered that Luke had merely... read in the bath! (Luke, who as a student had been fond of spending whole days like this, was pleased to discover that he retained the gift of *aquadexterity*, which the spoof Oxtail English Dictionary had once defined as 'the ability to turn bath taps on and off with one's feet'. The accompanying pic on the blog was inadvertently over-revealing, as Luke had only realised the morning after. Prior to being hastily cropped out as soon as he spotted it, the image of half a flaccid cock had inspired one cryptic comment: 'Thank you so much for your contribution to the debate. You really advance my understanding of issues. Please check my crypto page!!')

The charge sheet continued. On February 10 (Teddy Day), Dom accused Luke of merely... sleeping with Tipsy, one of Milo's teddies! (Milo was keen to point out that he no longer slept with cuddly animals; he just had a few hanging around his room for old time's sake, and was in fact keen to get shot of them.) And the day after that, to mark National Latte Day, Luke had merely gone out and… ordered a latte! What kind of challenge was that?

'I'm naturally a cappuccino man,' said Luke. 'So, you know, it was quite a struggle. I got Holly and half the office one too.'

'I'm afraid you're just dialling it in now,' drawled Dom. 'Need I remind you what's at stake here?' They both cast a wistful glance at The Chair, on which Ziggy was snoring deeply. In all honesty, the chair thing was losing its sheen for Luke, and seemed to have been completely taken over by the dog now anyway. Dom sighed. 'Also, Luke… Need I remind you: How is you drinking a coffee going to impress anyone who might be observing your activities?'

Luke sat up. Dom had obviously spotted the comment from Yasmine, which was annoying, but he had a point. 'Okay, okay. What do you have in mind?'

Dom vaped thoughtfully as he produced a sheaf of papers. 'Tomorrow is Get A Different Name Day (February 14),' he announced. 'I've looked into it, and it's actually very easy to do.'

'What is?'

'Changing your name by deed poll. You just fill in a few things, and then just alert the various authorities of your surname. It shouldn't be hard for you, it's not like you own a car or a home, or have any shares or insurance or anything,' he scoffed. 'It'll mostly just be your credit cards. Look – I've even paid the deed poll fee for you. Here's the form.'

'And I can change it back?'

'Course you can. Just as easy.'

Luke sighed. 'Okay, but what name will I take? If it's going to be Cockwomble or Trouser-Breath, I'm not doing it.'

'Of course not.'

'Or Warm. I will not be Luke Warm.'

'No, no. We'll choose it at random from this bowl. All the suggestions are eminently sensible – they are in fact the Top 25 most common surnames in the UK, according to a recent survey. Milo – the bowl, if you please.'

Luke knew this survey well, funnily enough, as he'd recently written a piece called "Should you take your partner's name?" for a wedding-shop client. Its appearance in this context reassured him somewhat.

He pulled out a note, unfolded it, and groaned.

'Oh no.'

Dom took a look, and gave a satisfied grunt. 'As I say, eminently sensible. Milo, dispose of the bowl's contents, if you will.' Milo took the bowl, unzipped Tipsy's tummy (for Tipsy had once doubled as a pyjama case), and tipped all the notes into its stomach.

'I was thinking more in a bin?' Dom said with a sigh.

'It's fine,' said Milo. 'Tipsy eats anything.' He squashed the little toy dog to his chest with odd intensity for a lad who claimed he was about to throw all his old cuddly toys out.

'Just sign here, if you will.' Luke picked up Dom's biro, did the necessary, then threw the pen down, deep in thought.

'Can I just get a pic for the blog?' said Dom, smiling. 'Hold up the papers please, that's it.'

CHAPTER 19

Luke was spoilt for choice on Do A Grouch A Favour Day (February 16). Alan and Dom were both card-carrying grouches, obviously, but their very grouchiness made Luke reluctant to offer to do anything for either of them.

At last, he girded his unwilling loins and knocked on Alan's door just after breakfast. 'Thanks for the loan of the long johns the other day,' he said. 'They were a big help.'

'No worries at all.' Alan seemed surprised to see Luke still lingering on the doorstep, so he added, almost furtively, 'Fancy a cuppa?'

'Okay.'

They sat in awkward silence at the kitchen table for a while. Ziggy, who Alan looked after on some days because he worked largely from home, was lazing drowsily in an armchair in the big open-plan living space visible through a gently curving arch. Next to the chair, a coffee table bore a photo he knew too well. Luke scowled.

They chatted of football and work, but the chat had a difficult stop-start quality they couldn't seem to get beyond. At last Alan said, 'It's really good what you're doing, Luke. The

Make Every Day Count thing. I love all the posts you've been writing.'

Luke shifted uneasily where he sat. 'Okay. Thanks.'

'Can't believe you're seeing it through.'

Luke looked up, suddenly defensive. 'You don't think I can stick to anything?'

Alan put up his hands in a placatory gesture. 'No, no! I mean: I wouldn't have believed anyone could do it. I know I couldn't do it.'

Luke took a sudden interest in his tea, apparently appeased.

'Proud of you, Luke. Really am.'

At these words, Luke stood up. 'I just can't do this,' he snapped, and stormed out.

He hadn't done that grouch much of a favour, he reflected afterwards. Dom was prepared to accept the odd 'noble failure' as he called it, so long as there was a funny post to accompany it, or better still a comically compromising picture. But Luke hadn't gathered much in the way of material for today so far, so he knocked on Dom's door and offered to make him a cup of tea. Dom eyed Luke suspiciously, as if preparing for the unleashing of some sort of trap.

'Come on!' said Luke. 'Can't someone do a grouch an honest favour?'

'Ah!' said Dom. 'Yes please. Two sugars for me. And then I've got some dry cleaning that needs picking up. There's a few other bits and pieces. I'll have the list for you by the time you've brought the shirts back.' Luke took a pic of the enormous list of tasks Dom came up with – which included hoovering his car, polishing three pairs of shoes, and buying him a load of health-food supplements – and wrote a sarcastic post about his flatmate's relentless demands, and how he'd had to take a day's annual leave to get them all done.

It was curious, he reflected as he knelt by the kerbside and tried to scrape the ingrained mud out of the hubcaps of Dom's Audi, that none of the tasks he'd been set would bring him inside Dom's actual room, a mysterious locale which he had only ever seen from without. What he could see looked normal enough, but Luke's curiosity was naturally piqued by the fact that Dom kept a lock on his door which he always used when he went out or away. Dom and Luke had known each other for years, and Dom was always storming into his room to complain about the dog or throw some letters at him. Really, given how many years they'd co-habited, it was incredible how little he knew about Dom. What did he do for a living? What were his actual health issues? Was he seeing anyone? Where did he go when he went away? Dom had started off in journalism, like Luke, but early on had lucked into a job writing for a newsletter offering share tips. He seemed to have benefited from some of this advice himself, because soon he had 'gone freelance' (whatever that meant), and eventually given up writing or any kind of regular work altogether.

Now, as he liked to say, Dom just 'played the markets'. But he never said much about what he invested in, or whether he was up or down. You'd think a day trader's prospects could be quite easily inferred from their mood, be as volatile as the markets themselves. But if you were to try and guess Dom's success rate from his state of mind, you could only conclude he was on the world's biggest ever losing streak. Unless he was one of those clever anti-investor types who bet the wrong way the whole time, making thousands of little losses, and then cash in when there's a rare black swan event? (Or something like that, Luke didn't really understand.)

The blog was picking up a bit of interest now, at any rate. Some of it was not necessarily from humans. There were a number of messages that seemed remarkably similar. They said things like: 'Thank you so much for advance my understanding of issues!! I share here an article of my own you have inspired...' Luke foolishly clicked on a few of these, only to discover that they invariably led to pages flogging crypto, or payday loans, or porn. But a little bit of money had trickled in for the Trigeminal Neuralgia Association, and best of all he had opened up a new channel of communication with Yasmine. One reason he was happy to give in to Dom's absurd demands was that she seemed so pleased with what he was doing. Witness her second comment:

Oui Luke! Keep going. I feel you are doing this for both us. Nous deux.

Both us. Wow. It had quite the ring to it. *Nous deux.* That was French, so sounded even better.

CHAPTER 20

On Supermarket Employee Day (February 22), Luke and Holly popped out at lunchtime. They had decided to go round the whole of their local Tesco and offer every member of staff a Krispy Kreme doughnut. It was a nice challenge because, well, who doesn't like being offered a doughnut? In the event, they bought Tesco own ones, because they were so much cheaper. The staff didn't seem that fussed, perhaps because they had access to them anyway.

A couple of days later, they were back at the store and were received with even less warmth. It was International I Hate Coriander Day (February 24) and Dom had suggested a small demo was in order. He and Holly made some placards and improvised a couple of T-shirts, each bearing a picture of a bunch of leaves with a red stop sign stamped over it. They were moved on from the veg section by a security guard (today looking even less huggable than usual), and took their station outside, next to Michael the Cone. Michael customised a rhythm on his traffic cone to accompany the chanting of the slogans.

There was: 'Corry, Corry, Corry! OUT! OUT! OUT!' And: *What do we hate?*

Coriander! (Not great scansion there, but still.)
When do we hate it?
NOW!

A couple of passers-by stopped and asked what the cause was all about, wondering if they were being filmed for some TV prank. Luke struggled to explain. He actually rather liked coriander. But it turned out there was an I Hate Coriander group on Facebook with almost 300,000 followers that had been going since 2013. Its mission statement was uncompromising: "We. Hate. Coriander.". The group shared anti-coriander content – Luke watched a video of some coriander being gratuitously flushed down a loo – and coriander war stories. Like the time a group member forgot to ask the waiter not to put coriander in their curry and then had to spend hours fishing nasty green bits out. Ugh, the horror! Luke could have got on board with I Loathe Apricots Day or I Hate The Smell of Lilies Week, but not this. And he certainly wasn't about to go to the campaign website and spend fifty quid on a black hoodie emblazoned with the slogan: "I HATE CORIANDER".

One upshot of all his outlandish initiatives was that Luke was starting to attract some media interest. Not exactly the national coverage that Dom had hinted at, but a local paper – the *Enfield Express* – had contacted Luke via his blog to ask if they could interview him. The reporter, a young lad fresh from a media studies degree who reminded Luke rather poignantly of a younger version of himself, popped round on Curling is Cool Day (February 23). Luke was in the garden with the kids, playing an improvised home-made version of the Scottish speciality featuring several uninflated lilos laid end to end, two mops, jets of water from Alan's power hose, and some empty Fray Bentos pie tins. Ziggy yelped along happily.

'It's such a fun thing you're doing,' said the reporter, who'd introduced himself as Tony, and had quickly proved himself as adept at this exciting new sport. 'But tell me, what made you want to raise funds for trigonometry?'

CHAPTER 21

Luke was back at Alan's a few days later to find out how much the kids got for a milk tooth these days. He'd promised to do Dom a show-and-tell for Tooth Fairy Day (February 28). According to a survey he'd read, the average tooth-fairy gift was £1, but some parents said they paid as much as £20 for the first one as it was 'an important milestone'. 'Milo seems to get £2 now,' said Alan with a smile. 'Although sometimes it does seem to depend on what coins the tooth fairy has to hand.'

Milo smiled back. 'I think kids these days are always happy to wait a day or two to make sure they don't get underpaid. And banknotes are always acceptable as well.'

According to the research, rates were going down: parents now aged thirty-five to forty-four received £3.64 on average per tooth when they were kids in 1982, which would equate to over £13 now. Clearly the kids needed to unionise, especially when you looked at the corruption they were up against. On social media, parents were confessing to some very sharp tooth-fairy practices: recycling the same pound coin again and again, taking the money from the child's piggy bank, or paying in Monopoly money. 'It was fifty pence in your day,' said Alan to Luke with another smile.

'Will you just give it a rest!' snapped Luke. 'For the last time, you are not my fecking dad!'

'Well,' said Milo, undaunted by this outburst. 'He kind of is.'

CHAPTER 22

Yazz028: Luke I want to see you!

It was the message he'd been waiting for. On February 26, which just happened to be Carpe Diem Day, Luke announced to the office that he would be going to Paris for a long weekend at the end of March. He had agreed to take up an invitation to meet 'a friend' at the top of the Eiffel Tower on March 31 – which, of course, just happened to be Eiffel Tower Day.

'Amazing!' said Holly with a smile. 'It's great you two are meeting up again! How long has it been?'

'Too long,' said Luke quietly.

Holly punched him playfully on the arm. 'Smug git.' But then this much-disappointed patron saint of crap dates smiled that lovely, generous smile of hers. 'I'm really pleased for you, Luke,' she said. 'It'll be amazing.'

MARCH

CHAPTER 23

Luke had managed to avoid answering Holly's 'how long' question because the truth was that it had been eighteen months and three days since he had last seen his true love. This also happened to be the exact length of time since he had first met Yasmine, another fact he did not like to dwell on/mention at all when discussing The One with the likes of Dom/Holly/Grace/anyone but Ziggy.

He would have liked to chat through all this with his dad – his actual dad, not Alan the cuckoo – but Dad was out in the States somewhere, negotiating cloud telecoms contracts (or something). It was great that he had such a successful career, and the cheques and pressies he sent from time to time were always very welcome (especially the cheques). But if he was honest, he could quite easily have done with a few less mini iPods and designer flip-flops over the years in exchange for a few more actual days with his dad. Come to think of it, he'd seen Yasmine more recently than he'd seen his actual dad.

Luke took advantage of Plan Your Solo Vacation Day (March 1) to thrash out the details of his stay in Paris. There were lots of things he'd always wanted to see, like the Catacombs, the Picasso museum, and the two ornate cemeteries where all the great artists were buried that looked so atmospheric in all the pictures. (French cemeteries in general were very cool, in his view.) He'd read about a tour of the sewers of Paris you could do, but he wasn't sure this was the most romantic option. He was also aware that Yasmine herself must live in Paris, or nearby at least. In the suburbs or a neighbouring town, perhaps. But he didn't want to come over all touristy, so he'd keep some of these things up his sleeve.

Come to think of it, that bridge where everyone put a padlock as a token of their eternal love – was that still a thing or was that a hopeless cliché now? He'd read somewhere that the bridge was in danger of collapsing under all that extra weight, which had to be a metaphor for something. Pledges and promises and gestures were powerful things: here he was planning to meet his one true love at the top of the Eiffel Tower, after all – which, if you didn't know any better, might seem a trifle clichéd too. But – and here his blank mind took to floundering helplessly – then what? After the gesture, what was the reality?

Luke studied a photo on his phone. It was the same photo that he'd scowled at in Alan's house. It showed a woman, his mum, with three children. Her face had the same expression – superficially fierce, but secretly amused and tender – that he saw hints of so often in Grace. Grace herself was in the pic too, perhaps five years old, her little legs dwarfed by a sheep she was clumsily petting. Coram Fields. Mum balanced a tiny baby on her shoulder: Milo. Luke stood behind them, a protective arm around the little ones and another on his mum's shoulder. He focused in on her eyes, as he'd done so many times before, as if some covert message could be intuited from her gaze. She must have been sick already. Was that a sadness in her eyes he could see? Or was that just a projection of what he knew after the event – that she would be gone within a year of this picture? Mum would have understood the Yasmine thing, she would have listened without judging. But she wasn't a pushover: she had a way of letting you be you, while still showing you what she thought was best and right. And coming from her (rather than, say, Alan, who was also in the pic, tucked away at the back) it never rankled, because you knew it always came from a place of unconditional love.

With an uneasy thumb, Luke swiped the photo away. It was hard to look at, even now. The old feelings of guilt and sadness always returned. He didn't remember much about Mum being ill, he'd always run away from the reality of it. Always hanging on at college longer than he needed to, always going away with friends, a couple of listless years teaching English in France and Spain. And then, eventually, the sheepish return to London. The back-sliding move into Alan's house. The years of sullen resentment that followed, until at last he'd got the bottom flat for himself. The crap content jobs. Dom. The dog. At least he'd always had 'the kids', as he called them. His half-brother and half-sister. Luke was only nine when his parents split, and he didn't remember any of it very well – more misery he'd learnt to block out, no doubt. But he remembered enough to know that things hadn't been rosy between them for a good while before that. But then Alan had steamed in, taken advantage of the situation, and his dad's frequent trips overseas for work had become the permanent fixture he'd known ever since. If ever there'd been a chance for his mum and dad to patch things up, Alan had blown that right out of the water.

CHAPTER 24

Luke and Holly had been mates for a couple of years now, ever since Luke joined Wordy Gigs. At that time, Holly, who was a couple of years younger than him, had been there for almost a year already.

'So come on then,' she had asked him on his first day. 'What was your test?'

'My test?'

'Oh, you know. The little creative task they always set in the interview. The one that tempts you into thinking that this place is some sort of arty ad agency where people sit around brainstorming ideas all day, rather than the industrial word mill we have come to know and love.'

Luke thought back. 'Er, let's see. It was something like: *Come up with a headline for a job ad aimed at recruiting new prison guards.*'

'And what did you put?'

Luke had written: *Screw. You?*

'Nice,' said Holly. 'You are a hack among hacks.'

'What was yours then?'

Holly quoted: '*Devise a way of engaging supermarket shoppers with a leading provider of poultry-based products seeking to position itself as a source of authoritative consumer information.'*

'Bloody hell! They just asked you that out of the blue?? What did you say?'

'I said they should compile a microsite of chicken and turkey recipes, complete with cooking, nutrition and storage tips, and drip-feed it all across social media.'

'Oh.'

'Yeah. And call the whole thing... Chickipedia.'

Luke guffawed. 'Okay. You win.'

Over the next few days, Holly had quickly schooled Luke in Greg and Phaedra's funny ways, and in the equally funny ways of content for search engines.

Your client wanted the bits of content you wrote on their behalf to be spread as far and wide across the internet as possible because it all helped them to rank higher in Google results. The only snag was that Google knew you were trying to create content just to game its search results, and it was especially down on 'duplicate content'. So much of Luke's work, he soon discovered, would involve the subtle art of 'repurposing' – writing ingenious variations on the same theme that were different enough not to be classed as copies, but similar enough that they didn't need to be signed off again by the client or have website owners complaining they were being served up sloppy seconds.

At first, Luke had assumed avoiding duplication meant being original, fresh or quirky in answering a client brief, but Phaedra soon put him straight.

'Luke – I asked you to rework those four articles about "vans in the movies" into a new blog post?' said Phaedra to him early on, in the course of a conversation he would later come to see as the beginning of the end of his honeymoon period, and his certain transition to the bus lane where he no doubt belonged.

Bus Lane

Noun. The stagnant rut that befalls certain unfortunate employees who always seem to get passed over for promotions, bonuses and job offers. Opposite of 'fast track'.

'Yes, Phaedra?'

'Well, you've added in loads of stuff that the client wasn't expecting.'

'Oh, sorry. I thought...'

'And half the original points aren't in here anywhere.'

'But surely you need something different?'

'Not *different*, Luke. Just... not exactly the same. Think *samey*.'

'Oh. Right.'

'Look, obviously it needs to be different enough so it's not identical. But it also needs to be similar enough so that the client can see it's essentially not new. I should have thought that was obvious.'

Luke held up the brand guidelines that had come with the brief. 'But it says in here that the client's tone of voice is...' and he quoted, '"irreverent, conspiratorial and surprising"?'

'Yes but not literally!' said Phaedra, with despair. 'They're a commercial vehicle insurer, for God's sake, not an avant-garde fashion label!'

'Okay, got it. But I'm guessing you don't want me to put that bit back in about vans that run on nuclear power?'

'Sure – why not? Sounds fun.'

'Well, I mean, that can't possibly be true.'

'Oh, don't worry about true, Luke. It's more *truthy* we're shooting for here. Okay?' And with that she swept off to the kitchen, where she was soon embroiled in a well-rehearsed fight with Greg about the return on investment of paying for cake on people's birthdays.

CHAPTER 25

As we were saying, Luke would have quite liked to share some of the sad and complicated stuff he was feeling, and Holly was often on hand for such moments. Unlike Dom, she didn't tell him he was being wet, or hold his insecurities against him. She could laugh at her own baggage, without ridiculing yours. She was a good listener, and usually available when the need for a last-minute whine-wine scenario arose.

Whine-wine scenario
Noun. A therapeutic drinking session for two co-workers, inspired by a sudden need to moan about rubbish relationships and/or how bad work is.

But she had been unusually unavailable of late, passing up on lunchtime walks and pub outings, and Luke soon discovered why. Miracle of miracles, Holly had stumbled on a chap who was actually half-decent, broadly normal and not obviously morally, socially or sanitarily problematic in any of the ways evidenced by her previous twenty-seven red-flag dates.

His name was Tom, and he was a gardener. (The spam email

writer hadn't worked out, incidentally, because about twenty minutes into the date it became clear that his main motivation for meeting Holly was to try and sign her up for a series of seminars on affiliate marketing. At a lovers' discount, of course. When she protested, he presented her with a complimentary mini car-hoovering kit so, you know, every cloud...) While Holly popped out for her third lunch of the week with Tom, Luke put his headphones back on and continued listening to a playlist he'd found of 215 of the world's national anthems. Well, it was National Anthem Day (March 3).

What could one say after such a mad completist effort? A few jumped out at Luke – Afghanistan's was surprisingly jaunty, American Samoa's reminded him of 'La Marseillaise', South Africa's was haunting – but most actually sounded incredibly similar. The tunes whizzed by in a nationalistic blur – Guatemala, Iceland, Lebanon, Zambia – and quickly started to sound interchangeable. This was because, it turned out, many of these hymns dated from the era of nineteenth-century nation-building, generally a bloody business requiring militant, self-aggrandising choons for its soundtrack.

Luke enjoyed the old and new tunes of Soviet states such as Kazakhstan, Turkmenistan, Tajikistan, Azerbaijan, and some of the old Soviet Socialist Republics. They had drama and depth, reminding him of the sweeping music at the start of an epic movie. Others that stood out included Japan, Kosovo and Mauritania. Iran's original pre-revolutionary anthem, 'Ey Iran', seemed to be much lamented, just as many considered the old East German national anthem better than the current pan-German one. (It seemed most countries had an unofficial anthem that everyone preferred to the official one.) And Montenegro's dark folk-based choral onslaught was indeed 'legitimately badass'.

Finally, Luke watched a YouTube video of a man standing outside the Palace of Westminster who was giving a rich baritone rendition of Ukraine's national anthem. Nine days into Putin's

brutal invasion, and the archaic words had been dragged into cruel
reality:

Ukraine is not yet dead, nor its glory and freedom.
Luck will still smile on us brother-Ukrainians.
Our enemies will die, as the dew dies in the sunshine,
and we, too, brothers, we'll live happily in our land.

CHAPTER 26

Holly breezed in the next day with a definite spring in her step. It was early days, but she had to admit that she did feel rather loved up already, she said, so much so that she wanted to introduce Tom to Luke.

'Why on earth do you want me to meet him?' said Luke.

'A wise person once said to me: "If you want to know whether someone is really suitable for you, see what they're like with your mates".'

'Who said that?'

'"And with children".'

'Was it Muriel?'

'"Also animals".'

'David Attenborough?'

'I don't know. No one. I made it up.'

'*You* said it, in fact.'

'Well, yes. But it's true, isn't it? You're most yourself with your mates. If your potential partner doesn't gel with them, that's surely not a good sign.'

'Fair enough. And, er, how many of your twenty-seven dud

dates have so far got to the meet-my-mates stage?' (He had a pretty good idea of the answer already.)

Holly put up some fingers then quickly put them down again. 'Er, this would be the first. I thought we could meet you for a walk on the weekend, maybe with Milo and Ziggy? Sunday?'

'Cool. What are you doing Saturday?'

'Ooh, probably just a lazy lie-in for the two of us. Saturday papers and sausage sandwich in bed, that sort of thing.'

'Sounds awful.'

'Why? What have you got planned?'

'I will mostly be hugging a shed and taking a selfie.'

'Because...?'

'Because tomorrow is Hug A Shed And Take A Selfie Day!'

'You lucky sod.'

CHAPTER 27

Luke disliked Tom from the moment he met him. He made him feel inadequate in pretty much every department. He decided to explore the reasons why in the form of a listicle:

10 reasons to dislike Tom

1. Tom has a real job. He has soil under his fingernails, and hard muscles from years of manful horticultural labour. While I go about researching pointless articles with titles like "How long does the average person spend on the loo in their lifetime?" (saniware wholesaler client), he is out there digging and sowing and building. My efforts might generate a couple of Facebook likes from a drunken Russian bot, but Tom's work yields toothsome fresh produce, fragrant flower beds, artfully architectural planting, verdant lawns and richly layered landscapes.

2. Animals love him. Ziggy greeted Tom like an old soul he'd run and frolicked with over many lifetimes. He had him dry-humping his leg with pleasure but also coming to heel and

performing tricks at the drop of a hat. Ziggy would have dropped me for Tom in a heartbeat. Indeed, he later seemed very aggrieved not to be going back home with him and Holly.

3. He's very good-looking. Sort of buff and rugged. Not disgustingly beautiful, but quietly pleasing on the eye, just as his manner is calm, strong and quietly confident, without being in any way showy or shallow.

4. He has great values. In our chats, Tom has shown himself to be politically engaged, well-informed on social issues, and with a strong sense of justice.

5. He's kind and sweet.

6. He's actually very funny.

7. Holly really likes him, and he obviously really likes her. He seems to genuinely care for her. When she speaks, his eyes light up. The way they hold hands or finish each other's thoughts – it's all so natural and spontaneous, dammit.

8. He seems to really like me. He takes an interest in what I say, and seems very pleased to meet someone who's 'an important friend of Holly's'.

9...

Luke decided to cap his listicle there, because the way it was turning out was becoming quite disturbing. Clearly he was in love with Tom himself, and the best thing he could do would be to go home and... And what? Retreat to his shed maybe.

Luke had got Milo to take a snap of him hugging the big old shed in Alan's garden. It had been there for as long as he could remember, and inside he found a box of his old stuff: goalie gloves, a battered skateboard, a few cheap trophies and medals from a very brief period of success as a cross-country runner. He had a sudden memory of sitting in here with his mum, dropping seeds into pots, pushing down the pungent, softly yielding soil, and applying a jet of water from the little spindly watering can that still sat on the work surface.

Alan would be pottering about in the background, he remembered now, always tinkering with the old electric mower or strimming the edges. There was a patch at the end of the lawn where they put up a goal for him one Christmas, he recalled now. He had a strange ancestral memory of his dad taking endless pot-shots and penalties to test his goalkeeping prowess. Only, his dad never really came here, did he?

Luke had a sense of past currents shifting. He would like to have gone back to the shed to re-examine these memories and see where this melancholy mood might take him. But of course the shed – with its earthy smells, compost bags and rows of secateurs – only made him ache for Tom now, and Sunday evenings were tough enough at the best of times.

CHAPTER 28

March was proving to be a busy, practical sort of month, and with Dom in and out again Luke focused on some quick wins and kiddie fun. On Lost Sock Memorial Day (March 9), he and Milo constructed an ornate lost sock station from an old piece of skirting board, some fluffy trolls and a range of old hooks and door-handles. They hung it on the inside of Milo's wardrobe door, where it soon acquired its first orphans.

On March 10, Name Tag Day, Dom played his Joker Challenge for the month: he stipulated that Luke had to get everyone in his Tube carriage to wear a name tag and introduce themselves to the person sitting next to them. Though he could be loud and silly with people he felt comfortable with, Luke was actually quite a shy person with strangers, and this sort of stunt would once have had him quaking with trepidation. But he'd done so many silly things by now, accosted so many random people with random requests, that he had started to feel quite blasé about such things. He had developed an out-of-body technique – first trialled in client presentations – where he pretended to himself that it wasn't really him who was doing this nonsense, just someone who looked and sounded like him. And when that failed, he always had those seven magic words to carry him through even the toughest assignment: *At least it's not National Gimp Day*. Words to live and die by.

Observing buskers and beggars soliciting cash on the Tube, Luke had noticed the importance of an early score. If you could get someone to donate some cash early on in your tour of the carriage, it made it much harder for the next person to refuse. But if the first few people in a carriage turned you down, the rest were pretty much duty-bound to follow suit; otherwise they'd be subverting the common will of the herd.

Herds meant safety in numbers, of course, and that's when Luke hit on the winning formula: Find a carriage with just one or two passengers in it; get them to sign up to the idea so that, as other people got on and the carriage started to fill up, a little caucus had formed all wearing name tags and pitching the idea to newcomers on your behalf. At this point, it was harder for the next incoming passenger to refuse than to join in. True, he'd had to go up and down the entire Piccadilly line for most of the morning until he'd perfected his technique. But sometimes the extra effort was worth it if you wanted the results.

'Oh this is rather fun,' said a posh lady at Bounds Green. Her name was Daphne, and she carried her laptop in an artfully miminalist wicker basket that Luke suspected was actually very expensive. She in turn recruited Kelis and AJ at Wood Green, and they in turn provided the reassuring smiles that got Patsy, Jersy and Damhait into the name-tag gang at Manor House. By the time Luke got off at Hounslow East, the whole carriage was chatting away like old friends, and he had some wonderful pics for the blog. Hounslow East was only about twenty stops beyond his own.

When he finally slunk into work, he was quickly ushered into Greg and Phaedra's inner sanctum, a long, wide, patchouli-scented office that was almost as big as the rest of the open office the other dozen or so staff shared, down a couple of steps, dominated by a wall-mounted large-scale Supermarine Spitfire model (his) and a full-length antique cast-iron dress mirror (hers). The pair sat together on the painfully vibrant fuchsia sofa from which they dispensed managerial diktats, nuggets of leaderly wisdom and – when, as now, the occasion demanded – double-headed bollockings.

'Luke,' began Phaedra.

'We're concerned,' Greg added.

'Shut up, Dad!' she said. 'This challenge of yours,' she continued. 'Wonderful cause, of course – my sister's best friend's daughter is on the spectrum herself – but is it, we wonder, becoming...'

'A distraction?' put in Greg.

'Dad!' Phaedra seethed. 'I can handle it.'

'What,' said Greg, quite unbothered by the evils his daughter was shooting his way, 'is the *value maximisation scenario* for Wordy Gigs here?' Not especially subtly, Phaedra now stuck two fingers in her throat and pretended to vomit violently.

'Don't worry, Luke,' said Greg in a voice that was meant to be chummy and light but actually came across as stilted and overbearing. 'I know my daughter is making faces at me behind my back just now. But she will soon come to see the wisdom of my words, as she well knows.'

The whole thing was excruciating. Luke had to put a stop to this, and there was only one way. He knew that Phaedra and Greg didn't really care what time he got in, so long as the work got done. And – call it a blessing, call it a curse – but he really did have a knack of crafting compelling content about plumbing supply merchants and office textile outfitters that tickled clients and search engines alike. All he had to do was convince dad and daughter that his Make Every Day Count challenge could benefit their business in some vaguely commercial way.

'So,' said Holly, after Luke emerged from the office, 'still got a job?'

'Of course. They've even made Wordy Gigs official sponsors of the Make Every Day Count blog! And we're going to offer a new service for clients – invent new Days for them. Backed up by lots of creative search-friendly copy of course.' Luke had explained to Greg and Phaedra that though a surprising number of fake holidays with a potential commercial angle were already taken – Aircon Appreciation Month, Human Resource Professional Day and Take Your Webmaster to Lunch Day, for example – there were hundreds more that could be invented to suit their needs/flog to clients: Kosher Taxidermist Day, Liposuction Practitioner Week and Anal Fissure Specialist Day, to name but three.

Holly pointed to Luke's name tag, which he'd forgotten he was still wearing.

'Luke Robinson,' she said. 'Who's that?' She looked at him oddly.

'It's a long story,' he said.

'But your name's Luke Milvaine.'

'Well, it was,' he said, 'until Change Your Name Day.'

'Oh right. But why choose that name?' She gave him another look. Or a second blast of the first look.

'It was just a random name picked from a hat,' he said. 'Dom and Milo did it.'

'Well, you can change it back now, can't you?'

'I could, I suppose. It's just it's taken me all this time to get my credit cards through in the new name.'

CHAPTER 29

And then, quite suddenly, and so much sooner than anyone could have imagined, it was the big one – National Wash Your Nose Day (March 11). This Day had been introduced by a manufacturer of sinus care products whose founder proudly declared himself 'an avid nose washer'. Luke, however, had decided to follow a more traditional route. For a small sum, he'd acquired a Jala Neti Pot, which was reportedly all anyone needed in order to partake of the ancient practice of yogic nasal cleansing.

Luke's special pot turned out to be little more than a cheap plastic jug with a longish spout and a nostril-sized hole at the end of it (Mum's little old watering can would have done fine, he realised now) but he had to say it was pretty effective. You filled the pot with warm water (ideally pre-boiled) and a teaspoon of salt (ideally Himalayan, but Luke only had table salt, which apparently was also okay). Then you simply tipped your head on one side over a sink, and directed the spout to pour water into one nostril until it flowed out the other. Once you got past the initial fear of drowning, it actually felt really very cleansing.

Luke noticed there was lots of positive feedback for the

product from people testifying to the pot's abilities to help with sinusitis, allergic rhinitis, congestion and all sorts of other conditions. One man commented, under the heading "Flushed with success": 'My wife seems to love this, although I refuse to know the details of what she does with it.'

CHAPTER 30

'So, how was the rest of your weekend?'

'Oh, you know. Dreamy.'

'Cool.'

Luke and Holly were giving out free packs of staples outside the Tube station. Michael the Cone, who had his own sandwich-board that'd he liberated years ago from an *Evening Standard* seller, had kindly allowed them to use it to pen today's message: "DON'T FORGET EVERYONE – IT'S FILL YOUR STAPLERS DAY!" (March 14). Surprisingly few commuters seemed keen to help themselves to the contents of Greg and Phaedra's stationery cupboard (liberation of which clearly came under the Universal Charter of Perkers' Rights) – probably, said Michael, because the staples weren't edible.

Universal Charter of Perker's rights
Noun. The unspoken but widely understood list of small items – pens, notebooks, soap, teabags, toilet rolls, USB sticks etc – which staff are morally entitled to pilfer from their office as compensation for the horror of having to work for a living.

'So... what did you make of Tom?'

'Oh, you know. Disgustingly perfect.'

'I knew you'd like him! He really liked you.'

'Did he? I'm glad. You two go great together.'

Holly smiled but said nothing. Luke knew she was trying not to look smug.

Next day, True Confessions Day (March 15), Tom had to go away to see his ailing mum, so Holly was at a loose end for once. She graciously deigned to join Luke in The Devonshire Maid, and along with the Guinness – and true to the spirit of the day – the confessions began to flow.

'Sometimes, when Phaedra's bollocking me for a typo, I feel oddly aroused,' said Holly.

'Pervert.'

'Your turn.'

'I think I'm in love with Tom,' said Luke.

'I'm glad you are,' she said.

'Why do you say that?'

'I suppose I just didn't really think it'd ever happen for me.'

'But it has happened!'

'I know! I guess. It's just, I can't shake this feeling that I'm doomed, I don't know why. Here I am with this lovely man – and I still believe it can possibly work out. Or that I deserve it.'

'Oh come on,' said Luke. 'You are an absolute catch! If I turned up for a blind date and it turned out to be you, I'd be well chuffed.'

Holly gave him a funny look. 'But you wouldn't though, would you?'

'What, be chuffed? Frankly, I'd be staggered that someone so attractive and normal needed to use a dating app.' It was a strange chat to be having, especially as they had both always been vocal supporters of the Office Nomance movement.

Office Nomance

Noun. A belief, usually borne of painful experience, that all relationships between co-workers are inevitably doomed to humiliating and very public failure. Motto: 'The couple that commutes together… always comes off the rails.'

'You are such an old man. Dating apps are for normals now too, you know. Anyway, I meant: You wouldn't go on a blind date.'

'Why not?'

'Well, you've got Yasmine, haven't you?'

'Oh yes! That's right. And you've got Tom.'

'Certainly have!'

The conversation moved to other topics. Holly confessed to an inability to open a pack of Twiglets without finishing the whole lot off, while Luke confessed that he didn't think he'd ever be good enough for his dad.

'Come on, Luke, take an emotional risk why don't you.'

'Did you not hear what I said about my dad?'

'Hello! *Twiglets* confession! I'm eating my heart out here!'

After exploring in some depth Holly's dysfunctional relationship with Marmite-inflected snacks that can still be obtained in a pseudo-tin format at Christmastime, they touched briefly on Luke's paternal psychodrama.

'He was always going abroad for work,' Luke recalled. 'Every time he came back, it was a special occasion.'

'Your mum and your dad… do you think they were happy?'

'Why do you say that?'

'Well, it's kind of strange he was away so much. He must have missed loads of milestones and special moments and stuff.'

'He was working hard. He just wanted the best for us.'

'And Alan?'

'He just steamed in and took advantage of Mum after the divorce.'

'Ah. So he didn't actually split them up?'

'I don't know. My mum said once there was fault on both sides.'

'Surely she meant on her side and your dad's side?' said Holly. Luke said nothing, so she persisted. 'When your mum died, how old was Milo?'

Luke swallowed a slow mouthful of Guinness. 'He was one.'

'Wow. So Alan was left with two teeny tiny kids to look after on his own. Plus you.'

'He didn't have to worry about me. I wasn't really around.'

'But what about before the kids were born? You lived with Alan and your mum till you were, what, sixteen?'

Another slow mouthful. 'Eighteen.'

'And what was he like?'

'Oh, you know, always pottering about in the background.'

'How do you mean?'

'I don't know. Mending stuff. Driving around.'

'He gave you lifts to places.'

'*Constantly!* He was always trying to be the dad. Used to be the only parent figure to turn up to my school football matches.'

'Sounds traumatic.'

'Always trying teach me stuff. Cricket, fishing, DIY. A real mansplainer.'

'You poor sod.' She paused. 'Tell me to sod off, but...'

'What?'

'Do you ever think you gave Alan a bit of a hard time?'

'Sod off,' he said, and they both wanted to believe he was joking. He swigged thoughtfully. 'It's hard to explain.'

'Night, mate,' she said, a little while later, giving him a hug.

'Night, mate.'

He watched her cross the bridge to the other platform. They stood facing each other for a while, exchanging familiar jokes and gestures over the rails, as each waited for their respective train.

CHAPTER 31

On Visit Your Relative Day (March 16), Luke popped down to the coast for a long-deferred visit to his aunt Maud. His mum's sister. She was a plain-talking, outdoorsy, very doggie type, and the day began with a brisk walk on the beach. Now that Luke had a dog of his own to play with her two bouncy, shaggy golden labs, Maud seemed much keener to see him. (Though, to be fair, he hadn't made much effort to keep in touch with her since Mum died.) Maud had sketched out a 'bracing but undemanding ramble' along the west coast of Hastings. It was all part of her plan to walk around the entire coastline of Britain, a project she had been pursuing already for nearly five years. Maud wasn't doing this as a continuous journey, because she could only fit in walks here and there, between work and other commitments. So far she had done bits of Cornwall, Wales, Yorkshire and various stretches of the south-east coast (she lived in Peacehaven). She had a big map on her kitchen wall where she tracked her progress, and in five years she had covered perhaps 1.15 per cent of the total target distance. So this epic walk, conducted over decades, would be a trip not just through space but through time; Maud hoped to turn it into a book, complete with her idiosyncratic watercolour sketches and acerbic notes made along the way. It was a wildly implausible plan, Luke reflected, and he loved it. It had shades of his own absurd project.

The pair set off in good spirits, with Luke only half-catching something Maud said about part of the walk not being fully accessible at low tide. Luke chose to ignore the signs warning of rockfalls from the cliffs, and the rather underwhelming good wishes of a local couple ('we think you'll make it'). As they walked on, the beach became rammed with giant, awkwardly angled squarish boulders, and the going became very slow indeed. Luke started to wonder if the tide times Maud had consulted were accurate ('they're actually for a town up the coast, but same difference') – and what the number for the coastguard was.

After nearly an hour they had barely covered a mile, and they reached the point where they had to decide whether to come off the beach or persevere beyond the point of no return. This part also turned out to be a nudist beach, and down by the shoreline they could see a rotund, pink chap happily stretching arms, legs and bits in the chilly March wind. They bumped into another nudist man climbing up a makeshift set of steps dug out of the muddy cliffside, with the aid of a makeshift rope bannister. Worryingly, he thought low tide was several hours later than Maud did. The light was fading, and in an hour or two it would be dark. 'Walk along past the bottom of the rocks,' he said, pointing at the shoreline. 'You can get along all the way there.'

From this distance the idea sort of seemed to make sense, so Luke and his aunt picked their way over more awkward giant rocks, waved to the naked pink man, who offered a tentative double-thumb gesture, and began stepping through the waves. From the cliffside it had seemed as if the sand was just beneath the waterline, and the pair were happily resigned to wet feet. A few yards on, however, and they were up to their hips, and clinging to each other for dear life. Suddenly everything seemed colder and darker, and the whole day was starting to look like the ominous opening scene of an episode of *Casualty*. 'Ah! So you thought better of it,' said the naked pink man as they squelched back to him. There followed a very British scene in which he explained in depth the best way back to Hastings town centre with reference to Maud's map, and everyone pretended not to notice his chilly pinkiness. As they picked their way off the beach, Luke was secretly so relieved to be alive that he was tempted to get his own kit off.

'It's nice to see I still recognise you, Luke,' said Maud drily, after they'd towelled off and retired to a dog-friendly pub in the Old Town. 'I don't know why it took you ten years to get down here, but still. You're here now, and that's a good thing.'

'I'm sorry, Maud,' said Luke. 'I guess everything got mixed up with Mum and...'

'It's okay,' she said, patting his hand briskly. 'No need to explain.' She sighed, looking deeply into her Guinness. 'Not a day goes by I don't think about her.'

They talked a little of his mum, and then Luke asked: 'What was my dad really like?'

Maud sighed again. 'I'm not one to bite my tongue,' she began, and then stopped again. 'How old are you now, Luke? Eighteen? Twenty?'

'I'm thirty-two.'

'Good Lord, are you really?' she said, gazing fondly down at Ziggy, who had wormed his way in between the labs by an open fire, and was now snoring on his back, brazenly flaunting his undercarriage to the world. 'In my head, you're still about seven.'

'Fraid not.'

'Well, look. Angie – your mum – never wanted me to say anything about this, and I've always tried to respect that. Alan wanted that too, though God knows why.' She sighed and swigged once more. 'But the fact is, Luke, that you're old enough and ugly enough to hear the truth. Especially as, who knows? It could be another decade before I see you again.'

'What truth?'

'Your dad,' said Aunt Maud. 'He was the most almighty arsehole.'

CHAPTER 32

·

After embarrassing her with a cringey card on Absolutely Incredible Kids Day (March 17; 'Ew, that is so wet,' was the not entirely unexpected response), Luke timidly asked Grace for her advice on National No Selfies Day (March 18). Luke never took selfies as a rule, but he thought he could mark the day by at least finding out how to do them. Grace reluctantly agreed to provide some advice so long as she could remain anonymous, on the grounds that the whole thing was definitely begging it.

'Look good,' was Grace's deceptively simple first hack. 'Delete almost everything,' was the second one; Luke's source told him that as a rule she deleted about ninety-nine of every hundred selfies she took. She finished with a cryptic reference to something called 'The Golden Hour', which turned out to be the bit of day just after sunrise or before sunset, when the sun isn't too overhead so the light is softer and shadows aren't too dark. Grace looked him over, and delivered her final thought: 'Look different. Try to be someone else.' It was just the sort of boost he needed ahead of his historic, do-or-die encounter with the woman of his dreams.

Dom discovered from Alan that the old lady over the road who always waved to them was actually Mrs Hart, Luke's old primary school teacher in reception class. He sensed there were some humiliating anecdotes to uncover here – at the very least a trouser-wetting episode or two – and so he challenged Luke to go and look up his old teacher.

'But where's the Day for this?' demanded Luke. 'I'm not doing it without calendric justification, and I can't see anything in here.' He held up their big bible of events. 'You can't just make me do stuff on a whim. Your challenges are becoming increasingly unreasonable and capricious as it is.'

Dom sucked complacently on his vapey thing. 'You seem to have missed the fact that it's actually Teachers' Day,' he drawled.

'What?'

'In the Czech Republic,' he added.

'Eh?'

'Commemorating, of course, the birth of John Amos Comenius.'

'Er, who?'

'The sixteenth-century Moravian educational reformer.'

'I see.' Luke thought of tabling a new motion concerning foreign Days, but really there were much tougher things that Dom had asked him to do. If he turned down this one, God knows what he might think of instead. (He'd noticed on another site that today was also National Something On A Stick Day; it was terrifying to imagine what challenge Dom might come up with for that.)

Mrs Hart lived in a friendly if wildly overheated residential home. Luke knew it was her, of course, and he remembered how his mum used to get him to take over satsumas and chocolates to her at Christmas. But it was a long time since he'd paid a visit. The wave of central heating as he passed through the home's two pairs of double doors at the entrance almost knocked him over. The carpets were blue everywhere, a strange muted sort of navy that matched the pastel-blue flock pattern that covered all the walls. There was something oppressive about how the same colour scheme went everywhere. Also on the walls, there were pretty scenes of cluttered harbours and groups of ponies in bucolic fields. There were vases of dried flowers at every turn too. And all was bathed in a complex smell that was distinctively institutional: some well-meaning blend of bleach, fabric conditioner, floor polish and mashed potato.

Luke climbed to Mrs Hart's room on the first floor. It was a generous, attractive room, the bed half hidden behind a folding screen. It must be at the wooden table and chairs by the window, with its bowl of fruit and tin biscuit barrel, that she passed so much of each day, observing the comings and goings in the road and smiling her blessing on it all. He stood at the window now, enjoying the unfamiliar vantage point over Alan's house, and all the gardens in between. From here, the houses looked strangely vulnerable, their lit-up windows forming facial expressions of varying degrees of sadness. It was the melancholy hour, when school and work were done, the day's productive core was fading, and nothing much could be salvaged now from time neglected or ill-spent.

'I'm sorry I haven't been over in so long,' said Luke.

'That's no matter,' said Mrs Hart with a smile. She had already offered him a boiled sweet and a fig roll, and now was opening an octagonal packet of Turkish Delight. Luke accepted, yet again. 'I see you all the time anyway,' she said. 'You haven't really changed.'

'I bet you say that to all the boys,' he said without thinking. Mrs Hart looked mildly scandalised. Luke had a sudden flashback to a pair of loud tartan trousers which she'd once made him wear all afternoon because he hadn't got to the loo in time.

'And the girls, I mean.' Mrs Hart looked confused. She had a wonderfully kindly face, soft pale skin framed by wisps of white hair with a delicate blue tinge. (So much blue in this place, thought Luke.)

'Sorry, I meant... It must be impossible to remember all the children you taught. So many faces, so many years. And they all want you to remember how special they were.'

She thought for a moment. 'True,' she said. 'But I have a few set phrases that stand me in good stead. "You always had a lot to say for yourself", that's a good one. Or, "I always knew you'd do something a bit different"; that one gets me out of a lot of holes. Then there's "I always said you'd go far" and "You were quite a character, even then!". People love that one. And then there's my favourite: "When they made you, they threw away the mould". They can't get enough of that one.'

Luke smiled. Mrs Hart fell silent, and took to miming a gentle chewing motion, which seemed to be her default non-speaking expression.

'But I knew you a bit better than most because we were neighbours,' she said. 'And I taught your brother and sister too. It was such a terrible shame about Angie. How's Alan doing?'

'He's okay.'

'That man. He's quite something, isn't he?'

'I don't know about that.'

Mrs Hart smiled. She pulled an iPad onto her lap. 'I do like your blog,' she said. 'It's just the sort of crazy plan you were always making. You always had some mad scheme on the go: dig to Australia, divert the New River into your garden, plant enough acorns single-handed to save the planet.' She smiled again. 'And Alan – he, well, he just went along with it all. Helped you try to build your castle in the air.'

'I don't really recall.'

'Never pooh-poohed your ideas. Never discouraged you. Just tried to make things happen.' A faraway look came into her eye. 'He'd have been a great primary school teacher, actually.'

Luke borrowed Mrs Hart's iPad to check in on his blog. His heart soared when he saw a new comment: *See u at the top Luke!!*

'I'm off to Paris tomorrow,' he said.

'That's nice, dear,' said Mrs Hart.

'Going to see The One.'

'The one what, dear?'

'The one for me.' He tried to explain about Yasmine, and how they met, and all the emails and how she was now cheering him on for his Make Every Day Count initiative. Mrs Hart looked sceptical.

'It all sounds very romantic,' she said doubtfully. 'But what about the skidmark in the toilet bowl?' Luke wondered if she was tiring and getting a little confused.

'Well, it was lovely to see you, Mrs Hart,' he said gently. 'Perhaps I should leave you now.'

She laughed. 'I'm not completely doolally yet, you know,' she said. 'What I mean is... true love needs to be tested by the boring, annoying, day-to-day stuff. It can't survive on grand gestures and crazy stunts alone.'

Luke edged his way out of her room a few minutes later.

'Good luck with your thing, dear!' she called out. 'I always knew you'd do something a bit different.'

CHAPTER 33

And so to Paris. Luke got a late-afternoon Eurostar, and made his way over to a hotel somewhere off Bastille. The rate had been suspiciously cheap, and he quickly realised why. The proprietor of the hotel actually lived and slept in the reception area, and was cooking his dinner when he arrived. The place stunk of stale body and lentils. Luke's room, as far he could tell, was basically a large toilet with a bed moved into it. For washing, there was a bidet rather than a shower, although there was a shower *curtain*, which hung on a clothes line to partition off the bed area from the loo area. On a small table by the bed, improvised from a cable reel that may well have been sourced from the very active and dusty building site next door, there sat a bare lamp in a wine bottle and a little ashtray fashioned from an old vinyl 33 melted into an approximate bowl shape.

Luke loved it all. Everything about his digs had the aura of hard-earned romance. The cruddier the billet, he reasoned, the sweeter the contrast with tomorrow's encounter. What a story this would all make one day, when they came to tell their little ones! (She would want little ones, he was pretty sure of that, though he

107

hadn't as yet asked her. Maybe ask tomorrow? Maybe too soon. Play it by ear.)

Next day he was up and out early. He could only get tickets for the Tower for 4pm, so he had time to take in a few sights. This pleased him: he wanted to be steeped in Paris when they met. So he whizzed over to the Catacombs, descended the many stone stairs, and wandered along the cool corridors of neatly stacked skulls and bones. Marat, Robespierre and Madame de Pompadour were all in here somewhere. The tunnels stretched for about two hundred miles, he read, although less than a mile's worth were open to the public. Luke wondered about joining the clandestine subculture of *cataphiles* – the urban explorers who were dedicated to penetrating these forbidden areas – but settled for buying some postcards instead. He had his own emotional labyrinth to negotiate.

After an indulgently touristy cruise on a *bateau mouche* over to the Musée d'Orsay, he walked to the Diana memorial (perhaps not the best omen, on reflection) then back to the bridge with all the padlocks on – definitely looking a bit clichéd now (unless of course Yasmine thought otherwise...?). Later he took tea in a cat café, which went by the gloriously French name of *Le Café des Chats*. Here a dozen rescue felines slinked supreme among a salon full of antique chairs and a very carefully regulated number of human clients. (He sent a pic to Milo: *DO NOT Show Ziggy this!*) Yasmine and he would come back here together, for sure. Unless she was allergic to cats? Unless she'd been here already? Was she a cat or a dog person? Or was she non-binary? Really, it was extraordinary the things he didn't know about her.

In the hardware section of Galeries Lafayette, a professorial-looking man passed him a leaflet and asked Luke if he'd like to join his online webinar that evening on Friedrich Nietzsche. He told Luke he was working on a new educational resource that explained the key themes of western philosophy through the medium of grime. If he weren't imminently meeting the love of his life atop the Eiffel Tower, Luke thought this must surely be his peak Paris moment, at least until he got swept up in one of the city's daily demos and found himself briefly agitating for pension reform for senior citizens. No trip to Paris would be complete without running into a *manif* of some sort, he mused. You could tell it was a French demo because all the flyers had footnotes.

All this activity, Luke knew, was an attempt to dissipate the nervous tension that was growing in him as the hour of the sacred reunion approached. It would also give him lots to talk about when they met; he just hoped he wouldn't come across like a demented Tripadvisor reviewer. (Especially as she probably knew it all inside out anyway.) (Or perhaps she looked down on all this stuff as hopelessly touristy, in the same way that Londoners never visited any of their own city's sights?) (Really, how did he not know any of this stuff about her? How come he hadn't asked her? What on earth had he been babbling on about in all those emails to her, a few of which he'd actually sent?)

Everything took so long. Luke had way too much time, time even to reflect on Dom's parting words of a couple of evenings back.

'So how are you feeling about the meet?'

'Oh, a bit nervous. But then, it's meant to be good to be nervous, isn't it? Gives you an edge.'

'I guess so,' vaped Dom. 'On the other hand, if you're so nervous you can't even speak coherently, let alone perform, you... could go to your grave haunted by regret. You know, because you fucked up your one and only stab at happiness.'

Luke pulled hard on the cork of another bottle. 'I do enjoy these chats, Dom.'

'Always happy to help, old boy. Look: see this challenge as a ring of fire. From the outside, it looks red hot and it's smoking and no one else will go near it. But one decent jump, one fearless leap, and you'll soar through into a vibrant new dimension of desires realised and happiness attained, shedding the skin of the old crappy Luke as you go. You know, the cruddy, timorous, alcoholic one.'

'I know him,' said Luke.

'And we'll see the new Luke emerge from the chrysalis of his courage. A man of charisma, audacity and creativity. A man to love.'

'I like him,' said Luke drunkenly. 'Thanks, Dom.'

'Unless of course, you catch your leg on the hoop as you try and jump through, and end up with your hair catching fire as you crash into the flames and emerge older and not much wiser. Also hideously maimed.'

The queue outside the Tower took an age. The queue for the lift took an age. But then, just as he was entering one of the Tower's Meccano feet, it was announced that the top of the tower was reopening. (It had been closed that morning because of *hauts vents*, high winds, as if even the Iron Lady herself was struggling to cope with the excitement.)

Up and up he wheeled in the lift, surely the very one that Superman had caught one-handed when Lois Lane was in freefall strapped to the underside of a plummeting car with a hydrogen bomb in it. Below and around him the whole of Paris swept suddenly out before him – the squares and churches, the spires and steeples, the gardens and bridges, the river, the Sacré-Coeur on the hill. So much beauty, and all backlit for the Golden Hour.

Luke was peering into Gustave Eiffel's little den on the top platform, and musing on what a fantastic chat-up line it must have made ('Fancy an *apéro* at the top of my tower?') when there was a tap on his shoulder.

Slowly, inevitably, as the world stopped spinning and time passed into eternity, he turned.

APRIL

CHAPTER 34

Luke woke early on April Fool's Day – jolted into brute consciousness by the anguished soul-jarring whines of some sort of industrial metal-grinding contraption on the building site next door – and reviewed, not for the first time, the cruel cosmic joke of which he was currently the exquisite butt.

There he had been, the whole of Paris swept out before him, peering into Gustave Eiffel's little den on the top platform, and musing about Gustave's chat-up line, when there'd been a sudden tap on his shoulder.

This, he thought. This is how it happens. This is how love is born and a planet is remade. Stuff like that. Slowly, with the world suddenly stilled on its Golden-Hour axis, he had turned to face...

...a funny little man with a fanny pack covered in maple leaves, a "J'aime Paris" baseball cap, and a T-shirt that said, "Actually, I'm Kind Of A Big Deal In Canada".

'Yes?' asked Luke, after a millisecond or thousand.

'You've got something on your trousers.'

Luke was wearing his deep-green trousers, the slightly velvety chino ones that Grace and Holly despised but that he thought made him look classy and not a little French. A strange mustardy semi-liquid was dribbled and smeared all down the front of one calf. (One would say it looked more like French Dijon mustard, rather than English or American-style, which was appropriate at least.) The semi-solid, boldly viscous and yet not unlumpy goo had run onto one of his tan Timberland rip-offs (another fashion choice his wardrobe advisers had not signed off on). It sort of looked as if an incontinent French rescue cat had shat all down his trouser leg and on to his brand-new shoe, and there was of course a good reason why it looked like that.

Could this be seen as a symbol or metaphor for something? Well, the whole long weekend had been marvellous fun. And it had been just about to become *incroyable*. Only: instead of turning all *ronron* and *chou chou* and *va va voom*, the weekend had now in an instant gone all *zut* and *ppppfffft* and *merde alors!*

It would have all been memorable and unique and special and everything, you see, were it not for the teensily inconvenient fact that Yasmine had never showed up.

CHAPTER 35

On his return on Saturday, Luke had expected interrogations from various quarters. But Dom had gone away again, and Holly – who could once have been relied on to be bugging him with nosey texts and calls as soon as he emerged from the cross-Channel Tunnel of Love (as he had prematurely dubbed it a few days ago) was clearly tied up with Tom somewhere. Ziggy at least was overjoyed to see him. Luke leant down for an extra-long session of ear nibbling, but the dog was for some reason more interested in sniffing the bottom of his trousers. The world continued to reek of metaphor, and not in a good way.

To take his mind off things, Luke climbed to Grace's bedroom. 'What?' she demanded, looking up for an eyeblink from her instant parallel processing of eleven different messaging platforms and social channels.

'It's April 2nd, Grace.'

'What?'

'International Pillow Fight Day,' he said simply. Grace sat up at once, threw down her phone and carefully placed her earbuds in their cradle thing. With an expert eye, she inspected the various pillows and cushions at hand, assessing each for give, strength and impact potential. She handed Luke a weedy little square thing, not much more than a farty cushion really, while she took firm hold of a massive plump deluxe bolster that looked like it could do a lot of damage in the wrong hands. In Grace's hands.

Luke put up some initial resistance, but his own paltry weapon soon split, and in the end he found it more expedient just to assume the foetal position and think of France as the powerful blows rained down on his head, back and legs. A dull, thudding, slightly vertiginous sensation would linger in his cranium for the next two or three days, but for now, this felt like just the place to be. Grace had strong wiry arms and a great deal of pent-up energy in need of an outlet, it seemed, while he found just then he had a deep, weepily masochistic desire to be repeatedly smashed over the head. In that moment, they were as one.

'Thanks,' he said afterwards, as he staggered towards the bedroom door and the floor slowly began to stop spinning. 'I imagine one normally has to pay good money for that kind of punishment.'

'Any time,' she said, casually replacing an earbud.

———

Next day, Luke took his mind off things further by celebrating Intergalactic Fish Fingers and Custard Day (April 3) in Alan's kitchen. As any serious Whovian could tell you, this date marks the emergence of the Doctor's eleventh manifestation, in the guise of Matt Smith. In his first episode, the new Doctor frantically searches through the fridge for a palatable meal, explaining that a Time Lord's food preferences change with each reincarnation. Things the old Doctor used to like – bacon, bread and butter, yoghurt – now all turn out to be disgusting. 'New mouth, new rules,' he explains. 'It's like eating after cleaning your teeth. Everything tastes wrong.' Finally, he hits on an unlikely recipe that just hits the spot.

Luke microwaved a dish of Tesco's finest vanilla custard, and encouraged the kids to dip in their Birds Eye fish fingers. 'Weird,' said Dom. 'I hate custard,' said Grace. 'Not as bad as I expected,' said Alan. 'I love this!' said Milo, who was now dipping pieces of raw carrot and red pepper in as well. As Luke wrote later on his blog, there was no earth-shattering taste revelation to report, but no great disgust either. Luke later discovered that Matt Smith didn't even eat fish fingers for that scene. He ate breaded coconut cakes instead. What an amateur!

Chapter 36

On his return to the office, Holly's expected questions were delayed as Phaedra and Greg had called an emergency meeting.

'Guys and gals, reality is tough,' said Greg. Phaedra sat next to him, hands over her ears.

Luke leaned in. This was a message he could get his head around. He wasn't sure how the bosses had got wind of his Paris news, but if they had ideas about next steps, he was all ears. He'd been expecting the usual Sales Borecast Meeting, but this was something very different.

Borecast meeting

Noun. The dreary hour-long Monday morning meeting at which the Head of Department regurgitates the latest set of mythical figures, and everyone else pretends to listen/care/believe them.

'As a business, we live for spikes and peaks and upticks,' said Greg. 'But right now, we are seeing troughs and dips and downturns.' Next to him, Phaedra began to drum her fingernails vigorously on the laminated table surface.

Greg fidgeted. 'Going forward,' he began again. 'In business, change as we know is the only constant.' Phaedra was now fidgeting almost violently beside him, crossing and uncrossing her legs and alternately sitting back and leaning forward like a teenager without a phone. 'Things are,' said Greg, 'very much what they are.'

'Oh do shut up, Dad!' she screamed at last. 'You are SO embarrassing!' Greg looked stunned, but he certainly shut up. There was a stunned silence all round. Turning to address the rest of the room, Phaedra stood up. 'Look, we're in the shit. If things don't pick up we'll have to let one of you go. Maybe two. By Christmas.' She sat down, suddenly calm. She turned to Greg and held out a hand by way of apology. But Greg was staring at her in awe.

'That's my baby girl,' he whispered.

'Aww, Papa,' she replied in a little girlie voice.

Everyone else quickly looked away; this new scene was so much worse than being bollocked or threatened with redundancy. The bosses filed out, presumably so Greg could drive his princess to her next gymkhana.

Muriel stood up. 'Well, that was quite the bombshell,' she announced. 'Now I know there's probably quite a lot to take in there, and I'm on hand if anyone needs a bit of shoulder or a cup of tea or, you know, a warming little hot lemon concoction, if you know what I mean.' She waved a box of tissues in the direction of the rest of the team, then leaned in for a conspiratorial whisper: 'Don't tell anyone, but sometimes I take a Lemsip even if I'm not sure I'm coming down with a cold! Just cheers me up on a melancholy day.'

'Thanks, Muriel,' said Holly. 'It sounds as though you've heard your job is safe at least.' Luke noticed that Holly said this in a way that didn't sound remotely bitter. Holly seemed genuinely pleased for Muriel. Mind you, he assumed that, like him, Holly was secretly elated at the thought of getting the boot from Wordy Gigs.

'Actually, I don't know that at all,' said Muriel. 'But this isn't my first rodeo. We just have to keep our chins up and not let things slip. Keep on respecting each other.' The others looked at each other in puzzlement. Who wasn't respecting whom?

'Take, for example, the incidents that have occurred in the kitchen area in recent days,' Muriel said. The team leaned in. This sounded serious.

'Unfortunately, and despite repeated requests, the surfaces continue to be littered with dirty crockery, squeezed-out teabags and random bits of packaging that people seem to assume will get cleared up by someone else.' The team leant away again. 'Sally – the office manager – and I do our best to keep the area clear – but the more we do, the more the rest of you take us for granted. Newsflash: We are not your mums!'

Muriel looked really rather animated, thought Luke. She was right, of course, but it was funny how this sort of thing got her more excited than her actual day job. Actually, no, scratch that. It wasn't surprising at all.

CHAPTER 37

'Wow,' said Luke, when he and Holly finally managed to escape. 'First the redundancy, and then the carnage in the kitchen area. What a time to be alive!'

Holly giggled. 'But never mind all that. *How was Paris???*'

Luke sat back in his chair and told her a tale of romantic river walks, crunchy croissants and toasty cuddles.

'We just picked up where we left off, really, completed all each other's sentences, all that. The time went so fast!'

'Sounds dreamy.'

'Oh it was.' Dreamy was the word. Unless it was delusional. The tale he told Holly was a lovely tale, the one he had desperately yearned to find himself living. Perhaps sometimes you could make something true by wanting it enough. Perhaps if he really concentrated hard, the story he was weaving could become a memory he was recalling. Perhaps, in a parallel universe, this was exactly what did happen.

'So, come on, then. Let's have a look at her. Show the dog the rabbit.'

'Eh?'

'Show me some pics. Let's take a look at Yazz. Don't worry, you can spare me the saucy ones.'

Luke made for his phone. 'Oh, it's dead at the moment. Show you later.'

'Fair enough,' said Holly, barely – but only barely – missing a beat. 'Now: where are we with the *Dictionary*, Luke? I believe you were preparing some toilet-based terms for the big book?'

'Certainly was, mate. Here's a few for you...'

Hang-bog expression
Noun. The look of disappointment on someone's face when they walk into the toilets, copy of the newspaper under their arm, only to find all the traps occupied.

Newspaper fairy
Noun. That mysterious being who gets up early every morning to place a fresh copy of the *Metro* in the right-hand cubicle of the blokes' loos on the fourth floor.

Cyclo-pathic rage
Noun. The intense annoyance non-bikers feel towards people who cycle to work then spend the first hour of the working day in the shower, getting changed, packing away their silly fluorescent and Lycra bits etc, etc.

Friday Tang
Noun. That slightly vinegary smell that accompanies you around the office after a lunchtime pint.

There followed a good-natured debate about whether some of these terms weren't a tad blokeish. But in the end both agreed that the *Dictionary* must encompass all elements of office culture, and no doubt other terms would speak to more women-friendly aspects of office life. Holly also announced that she was working on a cluster of terms related to office tea-making. It was to be, as might easily be imagined, an extensive piece of work, which could take a good few weeks to complete.

'Okay, but do please keep me updated on progress,' said Luke sternly.

'Yes, boss,' said Holly. At that moment, Luke pretended not to notice that his phone had just vibrated. Holly said nothing.

'The tea-making terms are a key area. I don't want to see them get kicked into Q5.'

Q5

Noun. The mythical three-month period that it would take:

(a) you to clear the backlog of tasks in your in-tray; or

(b) the company to hits its sales targets; or, more generally;

(c) any work task that it would be useful/valuable to complete but for which no one is nagging you.

CHAPTER 38

April was proving to be a rather existential month for Luke. There was the pain of the fact that Yasmine hadn't managed to appear, despite his waiting six hours at the top of the Tower, during which time he had made friends with an entire group of good-natured stags, all related, from Vancouver. Sensing his despair, the despair of a man abandoned by his lover at the very scene where millions before him had made their passionate pledges of undying *amour* (to loved ones who'd actually showed up), the Mckenzies of Vancouver had decided to take Luke under their wing. They were a big family, and to Luke in his blurry despair they were all alike in kindness and good humour. They all seemed to be impossibly tall and well-built too. But Luke was able to tell them apart because each had a different T-shirt slogan. "IT'S NOT A PARTY TILL THE CANADIAN SHOWS UP", said one. "MAKE CANADA GREAT AGAIN", said another. "I'M A CANADIAN DAD", said yet another, "LIKE A NORMAL DAD BUT SO MUCH COOLER". And Luke's favourite, a little more political perhaps: "EVERY TIME AN AMERICAN MAKES FUN OF ME FOR BEING CANADIAN, I GO TO THE NEAREST HOSPITAL AND GET MYSELF CHECKED FOR FREE".

The Mckenzies took lots of pics at the top of the Tower for the Make Every Day Count blog, then dusted Luke down and took him to a bistro for a *demi* or *douze*, by the end of which session Luke may well have poured out his whole heart and spilled the entire (non-)story of his grand (non-)love affair with Yasmine (The One).

'I know she loves me,' slurred Luke. 'She just has to break free of her handlers. She may be being brainwashed or love-bombed or something.'

'Okay,' said another Mckenzie with a slogan Luke hadn't spotted before: "YOU HAD ME AT POUTINE". 'That does seem like the most likely explanation.' (Luke had no idea what Poutine was at this point (he wondered initially if it was French-Canadian for 'Putin'), but he would find out a few days later in a Canadian bar near Covent Garden. This would be on April 11, National Poutine Day).

'Or...' slurred Luke. 'Orrrr.'

'Yes?'

'Or... It's a test.'

'A test?'

'Yes. She wants to be sure that I am fully committed to this before she breaks cover.'

'Jeez, Luke, I dunno,' said Canadian Dad. 'This is like something out of the Middle Ages.'

'Yes,' agreed Poutine Man. 'With elements of Cold War spy thriller and cult intervention.'

Luke was showing signs of unsteadiness by now, in ambulation as much as in mental reasoning, so the Mckenzies hustled him out of the bar, then treated him to a slap-up meal in a Parisian McDonald's. Ordinarily, Luke, who had studied French and fancied himself to be a bit of a Francophile, would have been scandalised to find himself swarfing a dirty burger in the heart of the world's gastronomic capital. But actually, the contrasts with a Brit Maccy D were fascinating. In a French *McDo*, the whole décor seemed more stylish; the tables were spaced further apart and even the chairs felt plusher. The menu was different too. For breakfast, there were jams and pastries, macarons and croissants. And for mains, there were things like Le McBaguette, 'le blue cheese and bacon' and 'le p'tit fondu', a burger with raclette and Emmental. You could even get beer! Focusing on such trivia got Luke through those first few desperate hours.

After the Mckenzies had checked that Luke was able to stand straight and had a reasonable chance of making his way back to his hotel, they queued up to deliver a volley of robust Canadian back-slaps and benevolent, spine-crushing embraces. There was the ritual exchanging of email addresses and reunion plans.

'Go, go, Yazz!' said Canadian Dad.

'Yeah – you got this, Lukey boy!' said Party Canadian.

'Bye, mate,' said Poutine Man. 'And give my regards to that Holly.'

'That Holly?' Luke didn't remember mentioning Holly.

'Yeah, she sounds really nice. I wouldn't mind looking her up when we get to yours.'

CHAPTER 39

April 6 was National Epitaph Day. Dom had tasked Luke about coming up with his own epitaph, and his mind kept running back to Paris, and – not irrelevantly – to the Catacombs. *'Arrête, c'est ici l'empire de la mort!'* Here, walking through the chambers of the dead, mottoes and inscriptions mocking the vanity of the living assailed you at every turn:

> *So all things pass upon the earth*
> *Spirit, beauty, grace, talent*
> *Ephemeral as a flower*
> *Tossed by the slightest breeze*

It was, he thought as he flicked through his phone pics to find a suitable image for the blog, the ideal inspiration to help you plan your own epitaph. But the harder Luke tried to come up with something, the more creeped out he felt about the whole thing. Should you even be doing your own epitaph – or should you leave it to anyone left behind who fancied the job? (If there were no volunteers, no matter; you wouldn't be around to know anyways.)

If you went for a humorous approach (along the lines of Spike Milligan's "I told you I was ill") the joke could quickly pall. Something of moment – perhaps a message about love or family – might be best, but then it wasn't easy to dodge the platitudinous. The best advice always came out as the most banal: Be kind. Make the most of your people. Want what you have. Do your best. Laugh at yourself. What should an epitaph be anyway – a well-chosen quotation, a summary of one's own life, or a thought for others still living theirs? "We're only the ones we love" or "He was quite good at catching peanuts in his mouth"? (Luke really was. And not just peanuts. Not everyone could say as much.)

Luke always remembered one of the first times he'd gone back to visit his mum's grave. Dad had insisted on taking charge of that stuff, and he'd gone for: "*Though you are so far away, we think of you 'most every day*". He remembered vaguely that Alan had wanted something different, quietly suggesting that 'there wasn't much of Angie in it'. But Dad had been insistent, and Luke had sort of been asked to cast the deciding vote. He'd been too dazed to really consider the words, and instead had just immediately sided with his dad. He'd wanted to curry favour with his dad, he saw now, and he'd wanted to hurt Alan. Both instincts had seemed entirely reasonable at the time. But a few years later, on walking round the graves, he'd noticed that several other tombstones bore exactly the same wording. It was obviously one of a number of tried-and-trusted formulas that cropped up again and again, like the swirly verses in old-fashioned greeting cards that no one ever read (*Daughters are a lot of fun/But you're a very special one...*).

The embryonic copywriter in Luke – along with the grieving son, perhaps – was offended. Naively, he'd assumed that the messages on tombstones always dignified the dead with their originality. And he'd assumed too, he saw now, that his dad would not have reached for something off the shelf either. But then, what did he really know of his dad? He decided to drop Dad a text that night, see how he was doing. And to pop in on Alan, to ask him a question it had never occurred to ask before.

In the evening Dom read through Luke's various attempts at an epigraph, with Ziggy and Milo in attendance. There was general consensus that the peanut one was very strong.

CHAPTER 40

And so to ASMR Day (April 9). Luke was vaguely aware of Autonomous Sensory Meridian Response, aka braingasms, aka those weirdly tingly sensations along the scalp and spine that can arise as a response to auditory, visual or tactile stimuli such as whispering, hair-brushing, towel-folding, page-turning, oyster-slurping, and the singing of Billie Eilish. But he hadn't been aware of the vast industry of YouTube videos – with views and followers in the millions – that had sprung up to service this, er, need.

Ahead of a show-and-tell on the topic commissioned by Dom, Luke decided to watch one of the most popular of these videos – forty-million-plus views and counting – which went by the catchy title, "Fastest ASMR: Dentist, Eye, Cranial Nerve, Sleep Clinic, Lice, Ear Exam, Ear Cleaning, Make-up, Spa!" He drew the curtains in the living room, cast his phone on to the big TV screen, and sat in murky silence as a young woman in a facemask appeared before him, claiming to be a dentist who needed to look at his teeth. One half of her hair, which seemed to cling to her scalp with unusual severity, was black, while the other half was silver. She began making faint whispery, clicky sounds, teetering on the edge of audibility, as she lunged at him out of the screen with a variety of implements. Luke felt odd, but there was no time to overthink because now he was at the optometrists, and the woman with the two-tone head, peering in too close again, was threatening to examine his eyes. And now the woman wanted to examine his cranial nerve! It was relentless. Luke began to feel slightly tingly, albeit in an anxious way. He skipped to the spa and make-up sections. But she would just keep looking at him, looming up out of the screen in her service-based fancy-dress costumes with her funny little clicky, whirry, whispery noises, and Luke found it all a bit oppressive. Almost as oppressive as the thousands of other videos by people who wanted to stare at him as they pretended to cut his hair or clean his ears or whisper a bedtime story.

Luke decided he needed something less confrontational and creepy, so he opted for a video called "One hundred sleep triggers in ten minutes". No face here, thank God, just a pair of hands. There was much tapping of fingers and scraping of nails across different surfaces. Notepad pages were thumbed. Metal suitcase fasteners and mascara tubes were flicked open and shut. Fizzy water was poured. Fingernails brushed a massage pad. Little plastic balls were gently shaken in a plastic case. Fingertips were drummed on a fancy handbag. (The nails really were the star of the show, thought Luke. He felt a sudden – unrelaxing – stab of anxiety for their owner: Did she have good nail insurance?) A make-up brush swished. Foam squelched as it was forced between knuckles. A pen was clicked, again and again. Sugar tongs squeezed. Drips of water in a bowl. All the sounds operated at the edge of one's sensory threshold, making them somehow both eerily abstract and yet oddly insistent. It wasn't unpleasant but Luke wasn't quite sure he was there yet. Maybe he could fake a braingasm? It was tough, this pressure to tingle to order.

Next day, he told Holly all about his experiences. She'd never heard of ASMR either (it was clearly a generational thing), so they sat in the darkened meeting room and Luke turned tingler-in-chief. He leant in close, trying to recreate for Holly the experience he'd not quite had, sub-audibly stirring spoons in liquid, whispering in her ear and oh-so-gently tapping crockery with his nails. He noticed how nice she smelt, a sort of subtle blend of vanilla and, was it, marshmallow? Her breathing was deep and regular, her eyes closed. He noticed how a little cluster of freckles daintily dusted her cheeks and the bridge of her pretty elfin nose. He couldn't help noticing how her sheer black top hugged her slim figure and how it rose and fell with her breathing. He was aware of a strange undercurrent in the room, a sort of tension he couldn't quite put his finger on. Holly was feeling something too.

'GET OFF ME, IT'S REALLY ANNOYING!' she shouted, sitting bolt upright and swiping him in the face with an angry arm.

Yes, thought Luke, putting down his sugar tongs and removing a fake nail. Definitely a generational thing.

Chapter 41

On Scrabble Day (April 13), Luke brought in his mum's old board and set up a lunchtime game. Holly was out to lunch with Tom, of course, but Muriel, Greg and Clive from Pay Per Click were happy to join in. Things got heated very quickly. Muriel was incensed when her word JIF was rejected – especially galling to her as she'd got the J on a triple letter.

'I'm sorry, Muriel, but JIF isn't a word,' said Greg.

'That is so ageist!' Muriel snapped.

'How do you mean?' asked Luke.

'It's the old name for CIF,' said Muriel.

'I hate to tell you this,' said Greg, 'but CIF isn't a word either.' When Muriel got all seven letters out with ZOFLORA, and met with the same response, she went into a deep sulk and looked ready to abandon the game.

Greg had once spent hundreds of hours playing travel Scrabble on train platforms while backpacking round India, he said, and his approach was fiercely strategic. He would sigh pityingly if another player gave away an S cheaply, and was quite capable of exchanging all his letters two or three times in a single game, a sure sign of an advanced player. His goes tended to create intricate nests of three

THANK YOU FOR THE DAYS

or four words simultaneously, whereas Luke was really only interested in trying to get all his seven letters out at once and hitting the fifty-point jackpot, something that happened once in a blue moon. In the attempt he was always trying out questionable words (eejit, OD'ed, runty) and forfeiting his go.

Muriel, meanwhile, had overcome her 'earlier disappointment and now pulled a 127-pointer out of nowhere – ACQUIRED on a double word, with the Q on a triple letter. Even Greg was impressed. Could this be the highest-ever Scrabble score? Er, not quite. In 1982, 'international Scrabble legend' Karl Khoshnaw notched up 392 points with CAZIQUES. (*Caziques* turned out to be the plural of a type of oriole, though no one was sure what an oriole was either.) The gang spent the rest of the lunch hour trying to work out how such a score would even be possible, but could only conclude that Karl must have made several other fancy words at the same time, Greg-style.

Surveying the board at the end, Luke wondered suddenly if Clive's efforts added up to some sort of cry for help. There was something odd about all the words he had put down: FREE, BEAT, SALE, QUICK, SAVE, CASH, CHEAP, SMASH, LOWEST, POTENT, HARDEST.

'Oh my God,' whispered Muriel, when he pointed it out to her. 'Poor Clive.'

'What is it?'

'His brain has been colonised by Google AdWords.'

'Oh that's what it is!' Luke replied. 'I asked him if he wanted a coffee just now, and he said, 'Yes please. ORDER NOW FOR INSTANT ALL-MAN ENERGY BOOST!''

CHAPTER 42

On Micro-Volunteering Day (April 15) Luke volunteered to help out at a local charity shop which raised funds for a local hospice. The shop was run by two people – Gaynor, who quickly emerged as the capable, hard-working one, and a bloke called Jim. While Gaynor ran about serving customers, unpacking donations, and pricing and arranging stock, Jim, a tall, stooped figure with a put-upon expression and the facial skin of a man who washed with scouring powder, sat in the back on a tall stool making endless cups of coffee and delivering sarcastic one-liners about the quality of items donated.

'Look at this old rag,' he said, holding up a bright-orange tank top. 'My *donkey* wouldn't be seen dead in that.'

'Do you have a donkey?' Luke couldn't help asking.

'Nah,' said Jim. 'Do you want a coffee? Pass the biscuits.'

Jim was good at looking busy. When Gaynor rushed in from the front, he would suddenly be seen wielding a broom or a mop or a steamer attachment, or offer to make a round of drinks. (Luke quickly noticed that Jim generally forgot to make more than one mug each time, and the biscuits rarely reached his co-workers.) Another of his dodges was to pick up some folded cardboard and say, 'I'm going out back', as if he was about to sort a load of recycling in the skip in the car park. But if you followed him out back, you'd just find him having a smoke by the door. There was no skip in the car park.

Luke came back to help the following week. A lady came in, looked at the books, and started weeping. It turned out she was upset to discover several Bibles had been given away and were now languishing in the shop. She couldn't bear this thought, so she bought them all. Luke later found another half dozen out back, so he put them out in case she returned.

Jim told him about the awful stuff that people gave away to charity shops. 'It's disgusting,' he said. 'You wouldn't believe what's in those bags.' He pointed with his coffee mug (his sixth of the morning, by Luke's estimate) to the ever-growing pile of bulging plastic bags, none of which Luke had ever seen him go near. 'Broken shite, food waste, soiled underwear,' he spat. Suddenly he pulled up a trouser leg to reveal a leg pitted with rashes and weals.

'Look at that!' he spat. 'The doctor told me I've got three different kinds of skin condition. Scabies, ringworm, fungus, you name it. He said: "Do you work in a charity shop by any chance?". I said: "Got it in one, doc!".'

'Shall we make a start on a few bags now?' ventured Luke.

'Nah. It's a bit late in the day,' said Jim. (It was 11.15am.) 'And anyway, I'm going out.' When he wasn't 'working' or out back smoking, Jim often popped out for high-level meetings with a bevy of cronies in the greasy spoon next door. 'Tell Gaynor I'm trusting her to hold the fort for a few minutes.'

Gaynor and Luke worked in silence for a while on the clothes out front. People often mixed up the sizes, or didn't put the clothes back on hangers, or just left them all piled up in the changing room. Luke wanted to ask Gaynor how she felt about Jim's contribution.

'Resentment is a poison and a prison,' she said, as if reading his mind. 'I am grateful to Jim for all the opportunities he gives me to practise!'

'That sounds very, sort of, Zen.'

'I should hope so.'

Gaynor expressed interest in Luke's Make Every Day Count project. 'In Buddhism, we say every day is a good day.'

'I'm just not really sure what the point of it all is really.'

'Ah, the point,' she said, smiling. 'What is the point?'

'You know?'

She smiled again. 'What is the point... of the point?'

Luke didn't know what to say. There was something infuriating about Buddhists and their smiles, as if they had discovered the meaning of everything but were too busy smiling about it to spit it out. But what Gaynor was saying now was really interesting.

'What if the point is just a pretext? The days repeat, and yet they are each unique. And this day, this Now, is actually all we have. So your challenge gives you a pretext – a destination for your journey.'

'But the destination doesn't matter?'

'Only as something for you to journey towards.' What was the point of doing anything, she said – from running a marathon to writing a book to raising a family – if you didn't enjoy the process? 'We always say things like, "It'll be great when this is over". But that is to relegate a huge amount of time and energy – all the process of getting there – to mere offcuts of experience. If we can enjoy the process, we're winning!' She leant across to the book section and passed him down a battered yellow paperback.

'Here, take this,' she said. 'When I see a copy languishing on the shelves, I could weep.' It was *The Tao of Pooh*.

CHAPTER 43

Much of April passed by in a blur of absurd challenges and minor humiliations. Desperate not to think too much about Yasmine (The One) and without his content sidekick Holly to hang out with, Luke took on whatever Dom threw at him with barely a murmur. On April 19 he combined National Garlic Day and National Amaretto Day in a dubious dish that gave him terrible breath, a rasping sore throat and burning insides for the best part of a week.

April 21 turned out to be Get To Know Your Customer Day *again* (how easy it was to forget that this Day was actually a quarterly fixture of the Silly Calendar), so Luke decided to check in on Reggie from Hornsey BoxLife once more. After a brief chat about search-engine performance and Google trends, Luke made the mistake of asking after Viv, Reggie's wife and mother, of course, to their two little ones. It transpired that Viv felt Reggie wasn't really pulling his weight. She'd gone away for a long weekend to 'reflect on shit' down at her mum's in Devon. Viv's mum had never liked Reggie; she didn't get the whole storage thing at all. He and Viv were both sleep-deprived, of course; but ironically, with the kids gone and missing them desperately, not to mention being haunted by echoes of his own childhood (did he mention his dad had raised him largely single-handed?) Reggie found he was now sleeping even less than ever. He also seemed to have no one else to talk to about any of this other than Luke.

'Thanks, pal,' he was saying now, between sobs. 'I don't know what I'd do without these calls.' Luke wondered if he was now committed to speaking regularly with Reggie from Hornsey BoxLife for the rest of his working life, and if so, whether he could charge some sort of retainer. But perhaps it wasn't so terrible, he thought, recalling Gaynor's words. Reggie needed someone to listen to him and there he was with ears to spare. It wasn't so terrible to be needed. He hung up after an hour and a half, a crick in the neck from where he'd been holding the handset, Reggie's wracking sobs – and tearful offers of six months' free storage – slowly diminishing to what sounded like gentle snores.

———

A couple of days later Luke was almost fired for trying to conduct an entire business meeting in Elizabethan English. *Marry, nuncle, methinks a regular cadence of four to six posts o' thy blog every four-week wouldst tickle Google's comical bone most preciously*, that sort of thing. The client, a supplier of industrial coatings, did not see the joke. The individual in question – a rather fogeyish chap dressed in tan brogues and bright-yellow cords – had in an earlier life tried to make it as a classical actor, and assumed that the whole thing was a set-up designed to mock his lack of success on the stage. So much for Talk Like Shakespeare Day.

For Holy Humour Sunday (April 24), Dom asked Luke to prepare a show-and-tell on the topic, "Are There Any Jokes In The Bible?". This seemed an unpromising area of investigation, but then as was well-known, there were no jokes in Shakespeare's so-called comedies, so who knew? In the event, it proved to be a rather fun assignment. A surprisingly large amount of thought had been expended on the question of humour in the Bible, and Luke found himself lost down a quite fascinating rabbit hole.

Luke thought he spotted some dark slapstick in the icon-bashing scenes in *1 Samuel*. When the Philistines capture the Ark of the Covenant, they display it in the temple of their idol Dagon. (Dagon sounded like a great car name, thought Luke. *Have you seen my new Dagon? It's the seven-seater hybrid. Quite a step up from the Malachi in my view.*) Anyway, God – the proper God, that is – kept knocking the idol over, inflicting more damage each time. First, the idol got thrown on its face, and was put back; but by the end, Dagon was found with his hands and head severed. '*Only the stump of Dagon was left,*' wrote Samuel, trying to keep a straight face.

There was definite sarcasm in Elijah's teasing of the priests of Baal (*1 Kings*), whose god – despite all their sacrificing and shouting and dancing – kept refusing to appear when called. '*At noon Elijah began to taunt them. "Shout louder!" he said. "Surely he is a god! Perhaps he is deep in thought, or busy, or travelling. Maybe he is sleeping and must be awakened.".*' Can't your god come to the phone right now? Elijah's Lord delivers on cue, of course.

And, now Luke thought about it, there was surely (Groucho) Marxist humour in the masochistic hyperbole of this line from the Sermon on the Mount: '*If someone forces you to walk with him for a mile, walk with him for two instead.*' But what if your oppressor only wanted to walk one mile? This was hilarious.

He was still giggling about going the extra mile when Dom challenged him to help a horse out on Help A Horse Day, a couple of days later. There weren't many horses to be found around Palmers Green, but Luke eventually found a stables in the countryside beyond Enfield that did riding lessons for kids. After overcoming the owners' initial suspicions – they had of course never heard of Help A Horse Day – Luke was put to work shovelling shit for an evening. That wiped the smile off his face. He thought of Gaynor, tried to love the shit he was shovelling and to focus only on the Now of the task at hand. Occasionally, it worked; but most of the time he just kept thinking, *I wish I was someone who didn't have to shovel horse shit.* Must be why they called it a practice.

On Global Pay It Forward Day (April 28), Luke stood at the barrier of Cockfosters Tube and swiped his card so the person behind him could travel free. The recipient of his random act of kindness was a young man with a heavy backpack who mumbled his thanks, but then stopped at the top of the escalator. 'Hang on though,' he said, turning back to Luke. 'I won't have your card to swipe out at the other end now. I'll probably have to pay all over again.'

'Where are you heading?'

'Heathrow Terminal 4.'

They were at one end of the long Piccadilly line, and the man was travelling to the very other end. 'Hang on.' Luke sighed. 'I'll just give work a call.'

CHAPTER 44

On Honesty Day (April 30), Luke cracked. He did in truth need to show some honesty to someone. He was – if he was honest – troubled by the thought that the only people who knew Yasmine hadn't turned up at the Eiffel Tower were a cockapoo and a random group of Vancouver men with a nice line in ironic T-shirts but little other connection to his life.

He might have chosen Holly, because she was Holly. But she was so caught up with Tom these days, that there wasn't really a moment to share such stuff anymore. And it would have felt like a betrayal too, in some weird way – there she was, so unlucky with blokes but finally happily coupled for once, and there he would be, coming along with his stupid sob story to take the shine off her moment. No, she deserved to be free of dispatches from the Annals Of Failed Love for a while.

It wasn't that Yasmine had forgotten him, of course she hadn't. It was just that she had *not* remembered him, and at a moment when he'd come quite a long way and when they'd made what he thought was a really rather specific and (again, as he thought) rather significant arrangement. They would get there in the end, he was sure of it. He would pass the test and persuade Yasmine and her handlers (whoever they may be) that he was worthy of her. But it looked like a long and bumpy ride, emotionally speaking, and Holly of all people was due a break from all that.

And so, one night, Luke printed out every last one of his plangent, painfully confessional, agonised, obsessive – and largely unsent – emails to The One. He knocked on Dom's door with his entire collection, his *Lettres à Yasmine*, his soul, his life, and read them out to Dom in a single self-mortifying burst of excruciated passion and thwarted grief. He read, for example, of the moment when he stood on the platform of the Gare du Nord as he returned from his Eiffel Tower weekend empty-hearted:

'*On the platform I found myself thinking of the moment when I'd waved goodbye to you that first/last time, Yasmine. We neither of us spoke while we were waiting; we both understood the illusion of that wait, understood that you had already left (Christ, how long before?). Those final moments were a wilful sadism, inflicted by a cruel god. I didn't understand it then, and I don't understand it now, Yasmine – now when in my darkest moments I fear that even your absence is no longer mine.*'

Luke paused as Dom embarked on a serious coughing fit. Clearly, the emotion was getting to him. This was serious stuff, and he did not want Dom to miss a word. Dom leant forward on his stick, clearly rapt. Now Luke dared share his fears for the future:

'*Must all things pass, Yasmine? Must this* possibility *be our only certainty? Or will I be left only with the dreams that haunt me – those anxious murkscapes in which I follow an exhausting trail of clues to your whereabouts across a city of complex grids and labyrinthine alleyways, only to discover that you are in a city of the exact same name and layout... but on another continent?*'

Luke, his heart and soul flayed bare at last, put down his printouts and sat back exhausted. He looked up expectantly at Dom. 'Phew,' he said. 'Well, what do you think?'

Dom vaped long and hard. For the longest time, he said

nothing. He vaped some more. Sometimes he nodded his head slowly, and sometimes he looked up as if to speak, but no words came.

'I know,' said Luke. 'It's a lot. Thanks for listening, Dom.'

Still Dom said nothing. He had picked up the printouts and was shuffling through them slowly, shaking his head here and gasping there, as if in the grips of a great emotion.

'No need to say anything, Dom,' said Luke, touching his flatmate's knee. Somehow what they had just shared went beyond words.

Dom vaped some more. 'Well, my dear, I'll tell you one thing,' he said at last. '*You absolutely can't write.*'

MAY

CHAPTER 45

On Read To Your Bump Day (May 1), Luke found himself sat on a crowded Tube, staring into the tummy of a woman with a very loose-fitting top to whom people kept offering a seat. She was dressed dramatically, with bold eyebrows and thick hooped earrings, and she refused every offer with firm stoicism.

Given the serendipity of his position vis-à-vis the unborn in her tummy, Luke got out Milo's old copy of *That's Not My Tractor* and started quietly reading aloud.

'What do you think you're doing?' the woman demanded.

'Oh, I'm sorry. It's just that it's Read To Your Bump Day, and I–'

'Do you mind?' another man butted in who had just got on, the sort who looked like he sold insurance by day but spent his weekends with the Territorial Army. 'Just give her your seat, for chrissakes.'

Now the woman turned angrily to this man. 'Why does everyone keep asking if I want to sit down?' she snarled. 'Do I look pregnant or something?'

Er, yes, the carriage didn't say. Luke hastily got on with reading *That's Not My Tractor* in silence. *Yes, yes, this is exactly the kind of book I like to read on my commute every morning*, Luke spat out to the rest of the carriage with a telepathic glare. The woman was still glaring at the last man to suggest she needed a seat; the back of his neck still burned a shameful red. Relieved to see the blame deflected elsewhere, Luke quietly turned to a rapt study of *Llama Llama Red Pajama.*

He yawned. He had risen early that day to mark International Dawn Chorus Day, stirring from sleep at 5.13am – only disturbing an angry Dom the twice – and liberating a sleepy Ziggy to walk out with him to a little pond in a genteel residential estate a few streets away from his.

Here, a pretty duck pond sat in the centre of a small park of quiet footpaths and ancient oak trees. It was fresh out but not exactly cold, and already light. Luke sat on a bench facing a little island in the middle of the pond. He was very much not a morning person, but having made the effort and dragged himself over here, he felt a tremendous sense of smugness at being up and about when so many other losers were still dribbling and groaning beneath their duvets.

It was, he was surprised to discover, insanely noisy at this hour. There were beeps and cries and screams, chimes and quacks and coos, many of them from creatures in trees and bushes he couldn't even see. A male mallard swept into land, and instantly took off again in formation with four others. A female mandarin was set upon by a posse of hostile tufted ducks. The Canada geese slapped heavily into the pond from their sleeping perch on the edge and began dipping their bills and strong necks underwater, funnelling sheets of water over their backs and shaking themselves clear again. Something dark and tiny flew low and very fast over the water surface. A bat?

This might have been rush hour for the waterfowl but it was clearly too early for the pigeons, two of which suddenly emerged from behind the screen of a skimpy alder, which swayed with their weight. Bleary-eyed and dishevelled, still in dressing gown and curlers, the pigeons angrily demanded to know what all the commotion was.

It had been a strain to get up so early and yet a strangely pleasant moment. Up at an unearthly hour, attention fixed only on birds and their noises, time for lots of staring into space and reveries about the past. A moment of mindfulness, you might call it. Gaynor would be proud of him. It all reminded him of how, when he was little, his mum would take him for walks in woods and countryside, encouraging him to identify plants and birds. (He missed his mum.)

CHAPTER 46

On May 3, National Two Different Shoes Day, Luke was sent to work by Dom wearing a brown brogue on one foot and a purple flip-flop on the other. He also had to wear a pair of skimpy shorts and a tuxedo jacket, to make sure that no one missed his unusual footwear combo. When Luke protested, Dom reminded him that such an outfit was entirely in keeping with the spirit of that day, which – as Luke must know – had been introduced in 2009 by one Dr Arlene Kaiser, an educator, coach and actor, to encourage people to experiment with the boundaries of social convention.

Luke hobbled off to the Tube. No one said anything to him on the busy journey into work, and by now he had been through too many such humiliations to really feel self-conscious anymore. He smiled to himself at the tolerance of London; people probably assumed that he had broken a bone in his foot and was nursing it back to health. As for the rest of his outfit, well, he was probably doing something for charity, or was on his way back from a party or something. At this hour, it would take a lot more than this to stir his fellow passengers from their morning trances or make-up sessions. He reflected that at this point he would probably have been more embarrassed if someone had actually asked him to explain what he was doing. No one had ever heard of half these Days he was marking, and he sounded more and more like a madman every time he tried to explain one. Once again he felt the shifty loneliness of the long-distance fake-holiday observer.

This day also happened to be Paranormal Day, and on the quiet Luke may have sent out a few psychic vibey spell rays in the direction of Paris. Sometimes at night he yearned so hard for Yasmine (The One) that he was amazed that she couldn't sense the waves of his longing lapping at her door. Or perhaps she did, and found it all rather alarming and needy. *Pas possible!* Because it seemed she did soon pick up on something in the lovers' ether: a day or two later, another comment appeared on the blog:

So sorry Luc. I wait for you but wrong day!

CHAPTER 47

Next day, May the Fourth (Be With You), Luke hung out with Milo. Alan was there too, as they sat down and worked their way through the first three *Star Wars* films. Luke had actually tried to get in touch with someone who practised the Jedi religion, but such people proved surprisingly elusive.

In the UK census of 2001, almost 400,000 people listed their religion as Jedi, as part of a protest about organised religion. There were still over 175,000 Jediists in the 2011 census, the same year that 6000 people listed their religion as 'heavy metal'. But Jedi followers were wiped out in the 2021 census, which did, however, reveal that there were eighteen Satanists on the Isle of Wight.

'Do you remember where you were when you watched your first *Star Wars* film?' asked Alan.

'With my dad,' said Luke. 'It was in town somewhere. *Attack of the Clones.* Maybe Leicester Square?'

Alan smiled. 'I remember you were obsessed with CP30. We had to get you every model going. Darth Vader figurines. X-wing fighters. The Millennium Falcon. The Death Star. That leggy Walkie thing.'

'The AT-AT Walker,' said Luke without hesitation. 'And I was never allowed the Death Star. You said we couldn't afford it.'

'It was very pricey, I remember that.'

'Dad sent me a special edition set from Dubai.'

'Yes, I remember that too.' Alan went out to check on the pizza they were to have that night. Grace eyed Luke oddly. She was scrolling through her phone.

'You weren't even born when the first *Star Wars* films came out,' she said. 'You'd only have been nine when *The Phantom Menace* came round.'

'Yeah,' said Luke. 'I watched them in the proper order. I saw all those early ones on video.'

'That would have been after your dad, er, moved away.'

'What's your point?'

'I bet you a hundred quid it wasn't your dad who took you to that film.'

'No?' Luke was aware of a strange screen of unknowing sliding away in a corner of his mind's eye.

'I'll bet you anything it was Alan.'

'What's your point?'

CHAPTER 48

One Sunday night, Dom called a meeting to plan upcoming days for Luke to celebrate. He had big plans for Naked Gardening Day, National Dance Like A Chicken Day, and Zombie Awareness Day, but – in clear violation of pre-agreed rules – most featured nudity or cosplay, and all involved very public exposure and humiliation. Luke was getting tired of Dom's increasingly formulaic sadism.

'I sort of thought this whole thing might be a bit of fun, Dom,' he said.

'I'm just trying to keep you honest.'

'But I've been doing it every single day! And keeping the blog up! When you're not here, I come up with my own ideas. I'm fully accountable – I don't need you to keep coming up with these stupid ideas. I'm getting on for halfway through the year, I'm fully committed – though God knows why – and you're not helping.'

'Ah, you'll miss me when I'm gone,' said Dom.

'Let's see, shall we?'

Dom said nothing.

'I mean, come on, Dom. Why do you even do this? What's in it for you?'

Dom said nothing again. But Luke, the lid off his frustration after months of gimp costumes and sleeping on roundabouts and accosting non-pregnant women about their non-existent bumps, was in full flow.

'Is it because you don't have anything else going on in your life? Do you not have any friends? Are you seeing anyone? Do you even have a job anymore? What actually is the point of you? Do you really not have anything else in your life?'

Dom looked absently at his own feet, vaping meditatively. Luke waited for him to mock him for repeating himself. But Dom only said: 'Not really.'

CHAPTER 49

As was his way, Luke almost instantly regretted his outburst at Dom. He was a softie at heart, and he hated confrontation. As a small child he remembered his parents rowing a lot, but also – as Holly had once suggested – he was perhaps unnerved by his own reserves of unexpressed anger. In any case, he worried now that he had gone too far with Dom, who had wrong-footed him by returning his angry questions, not with the usual banter, but with something much softer and sadder. Also, Dom had been behind a lot of the best challenges, and it was boring just setting them all yourself. Whisper it, but in some perverse way he wondered if he almost needed Dom.

Some silliness was in order. May 12 happened to be National Odometer Day, National Nutty Fudge Day, International Nurses Day and National Limerick Day all at once. With Milo's help, Luke managed to combine all these as follows:

There once was a High Court Judge
Whose insides were pure nutty fudge.
She drove 9.1 miles by car
To find her nearest ER
But the nurse said it just wouldn't budge.

Back at work, Luke was able to share some of this stuff with Holly at last. After weeks of being cocooned with lover boy, Tom, it appeared that she was free at last to hit The Devonshire Maid for a few drinks.

'So... how are things going with your man?' asked Luke, as the first swallow of the cold Guinness did its thing. They had already discussed a few new key terms for the great *Dictionary*, and now that Boast-it Note, Cereal Killer and Nervous Ticking had been accepted into the magnum opus, the pair were clear to move on to Any Other Business.

Boast-It Note
Noun. A totally unnecessary Post-it message left in a conspicuous place on your desk to remind others of your achievements e.g. 'Don't forget to cash biggest ever bonus cheque' or 'Collect salesperson of the year award – Thursday'.

Cereal Killer
Noun. The highly frustrating way the vending machine always sticks on the Nutri-Grain Breakfast Bar and never on the KitKat.

Nervous Ticking
Noun. The practice of adding jobs you've already done to your To-Do list and then crossing them off at once, in an attempt to ease your worry that you're not getting anything done.

'Oh you know – all great!' said Holly, a little too breezily. 'But tell me about Dom.'

Luke went into a lengthy tirade about his infuriating flatmate, and how his efforts to turn the Make Every Day Count challenge into a tiresomely sadistic exercise in one-way bantz had turned the atmosphere in the flat rather toxic. Holly listened carefully.

'It's a shame because, at the start, he really did help get the whole thing off the ground, didn't he?'

'He did, he did,' agreed Luke. 'But I'm up and running now. I've done all sorts. And if I'm honest, a lot of the most interesting experiences haven't been the silly stunt things. They've been the people I've met and the time to think about things.'

'I think this Challenge could be the making of you, young man. But do you really think you can stick it? Do you just wake up sometimes and think, sod it. I'm just gonna sack the whole thing off today.'

'Of course, I think that all the time. But then every so often something will happen as a result of doing this stupid Challenge that will make the whole thing seem worthwhile.'

'You like a grand gesture, don't you?'

'How do you mean?'

'Well, it's not exactly doing things by halves, is it? Like whizzing off to Paris on the spur of a moment.'

'Well, you know. You gotta do what you gotta do. When something's worth it, it's worth it.'

'Do you think you're more like your dad or Alan?'

'What sort of question is that?'

'Well, your dad likes a big gesture, doesn't he? He turns up out of the blue, after radio silence for months, with big pressies and some amazing outing planned.'

'He does like to make an entrance. I think you'd really like him.'

'Whereas Alan...'

'Alan?'

'Yeah, Alan. He just shows up every day, does the unglamorous stuff. Keeps the show on the road.'

Luke was aware of a strange sudden feeling in his guts, an unsettling mixture of anger, panic and defensiveness. 'Can I get you another?' he asked, desperate to send the moment away.

Holly looked at him levelly. 'I've still got half this one, thanks.'

'So... How come you're not seeing Tom tonight?' he asked on a sudden inspiration. 'I thought you two were joined at the hip.'

'Oh. Well, I... I don't know what it is. I've just got this feeling he wants a break from me. I dunno. I sometimes feel I just don't deserve–'

'Perhaps it's because you keep getting in his face with all these intrusive questions,' said Luke.

CHAPTER 50

At work next day, Holly and Luke sat conspicuously apart at the monthly sales and marketing meeting. It was a shame, because Muriel had come up with a classic presentation that would have afforded the pair of them many hours of enjoyment, both at the time and in play-by-play analysis. After a routine selection of slides in which Muriel ran through such standard topics as sales numbers month on month and year on year, sales growth by client and sector, new business targets and so on, she moved on to a brightly coloured slide on which each member of the team had been given a colour-coded strip on a bar chart. The standout performer, with a bright-green stripe that towered above all the others, was the one marked Greg and Phaedra.

'Well, thanks for pointing this out, Muriel,' said Greg. 'But really, there's no need. It's understandable that, as the founders of the company, we're going to contribute more sales than anyone else. But it really is a team effort. And you seem to have sold yourself very short here – you don't appear to have generated any business at all this month, which I know for a fact just isn't so. It's lovely that you give other people a boost, but don't forget to blow your own trumpet sometimes too!'

'Oh no, sorry, Greg,' said Muriel with a very serious expression. 'This isn't a sales chart.'

It did indeed have an odd heading: "TS Migration Index".

'What actually are we looking at here, Muriel?' asked Clive. 'What does TS stand for anyway?'

Muriel sighed. 'Were you not listening, Clive? That's no surprise, given you're the second highest bar on the chart.'

'Wait. Are you saying the bigger the bar the worse you are?'

'Yes,' said Muriel. 'TS stands for teaspoon. I have noticed a marked tendency in recent months for these innocent little items to go wandering from their kitchen home and wind up in all sorts of insalubrious nooks and crannies around the workplace. And I'm afraid when it comes to teaspoon migration – and really, that's a very polite way of putting it – you are the worst offender by a country mile, Greg!'

'Hang on, hang on,' said Greg. 'The chart says "Greg and Phaedra". It's not just me, is it?'

'I thought you might try and weasel your way out,' said Muriel. 'The chart has two names because you share an office. But let's do a deep dive...' Muriel clicked her clicker with gusto, and a new slide appeared that appeared to be a vertical plan of her bosses' shared office space. 'This heat map identifies very clearly the key sites of migration density vis-à-vis teaspoons,' she said. 'As you can see, the three most densely populated sites are all on your side of the room.'

Phaedra rolled her eyes. 'I don't even drink tea, Dad.'

'One of those sites is your top drawer,' said Muriel pitilessly, and Greg suddenly looked very shifty.

'You didn't–' he began.

Muriel shuddered. 'I saw things there that I can never unsee, alas.'

Luke dared to look across to Holly and seek out a small smile of satirical delight. But Holly just looked past him blankly.

CHAPTER 51

On May 21, World Meditation Day, Luke found himself in a Buddhist meditation class. Gaynor at the charity shop had recommended it. He had hesitated to enter the unassuming little building that doubled as a cub hut and church hall, but the people inside proved to be very friendly. There were tea and biscuits on offer, and no one made any attempt to take money or convert him to anything, let alone shove him roughly into the back of an unmarked van. He sat at the back of a small group of very relaxed-looking people. The sun was pouring through a large high window. At first there was a gentle hubbub of chatter as other attendees exchanged news and small talk. But gradually, as they awaited the arrival of the class leader, a gentle silence took over. Sat on the floor and trying to find a comfy posture, Luke was aware of all sorts of different background noises: the gurgling of water in pipes, the braking sneeze of a lorry, a distant pneumatic drill.

Ben appeared. He had a shaved head, and wore a thin yellow scarf around his neck. He was gentle and calm in his approach, taking his time to welcome newcomers and explain the steps of the class. They began by listening to their own breathing, feeling the breath enter and exit on the tip of the nose. Ben gave everyone a mantra to say on the outbreath. Each exercise or practice began or ended with the dinging of an ancient little gong, whose gentle tintinnabulations resonated long after they were sounded until they melded imperceptibly with the silence. 'If you get distracted or forget your mantra, that's absolutely fine,' said Ben. 'Simply acknowledge the interruption, and start again. That's the moment when the practice actually happens.'

After that they moved on to a meditation called the Metta Bhavana. Ben asked everyone to think of a person they cared about, and to wish them well. Over and over; think of the person, and wish them well. Luke thought of his Yasmine (the One). As he did so, he couldn't help wondering if she was thinking of him at the same time. Of course, she couldn't be expected to think of him as much as he thought of her... but did she think of him at least every day? Or every week? Did she think of him *at all*? True, she had gone to the Eiffel Tower, as he'd found out at last. But a bit of him wondered whether getting the day wrong wasn't a bit... Well, it wasn't a mistake he could imagine himself making, not when the emotional stakes were so high.

Fortunately, he was distracted from the unhelpful direction these thoughts were taking him by the next gong, and a new instruction: think of someone you feel neutral about, and wish them well. Luke chose Clive from Pay Per Click. 'May you be well, Clive,' he said a number of times, until the phrase started to sound ridiculous, and it was all he could do to stifle giggles. (Especially as he imagined Clive's own version: '*Free hot wishes for instant karma boost! Order before Monday, no fee, no strings*'.)

And then, finally, you had to choose someone you had a beef with, someone you actively disliked, and wish them well too. Luke chose Dom, but every time he tried to wish him well, the image of Alan kept popping into his head. And also Holly. He couldn't shake these images off, so in the end he visualised a sort of shaky split-screen in the back of his mind, with all three people projected on to it. He did his best to beam waves of good wishes at all of them, all at once. But then he began worrying that the waves might be too gentle or weak to do the job. So he visualised a sort of benevolent powerhose and began to jet his foes in the face with all his good karmic wishes. Not foes exactly. In his mind's eye, the faces seemed to flinch a bit under the onslaught, but somehow they held their ground.

'Hey,' a voice with a gentle Scottish lilt was saying now as its owner shook him very lightly on the shoulder. 'You can stop now.' Somehow Luke had missed the end of the class, had missed the final gongs and the salutation sign-off bit and the class breaking up. Wow, he must have gone very deep; he must have a real gift for this sort of thing. Ben would probably want to sign him up now, especially as there was no one left in the hall but the two of them.

'Sorry,' said Luke, shaking his head and returning his mind to the banality of everyday consciousness. 'I had no idea I was such a natural.' He couldn't resist a frisson of self-congratulation. 'Do you get many who get that deep on their first time?'

Ben smiled. 'Certainly none who snore so decorously,' he said at last.

CHAPTER 52

Is meditation good for the soul? Who knew, but next day, a Monday, Luke came into work with a sense of nettles to be grasped, elephants-in-rooms to be addressed, and rifts to be healed. He strode straight up to Holly, who was banging the vending machine in impotent rage, and handed her an envelope.

'What's this?' she asked suspiciously.

'Just open it.'

'"Happy International Being You Day",' Holly read.

'Sorry it's a day late,' he said.

'I did wonder,' she said. 'Oh well, better late than never.' She smiled.

'These are for you too.' He handed her a packet of Zebra Sarasa Grand Vintage Colour Gel Ink pens, which a little bird (Muriel) had told him was one of her current favourites. (Holly's love of stationery was legendary.)

Holly's expression turned serious. 'Luke. I'm sorry about... I didn't mean–'

'No, Holly!' said Luke with surprising force. 'Don't do that thing where you apologise for things that aren't your fault. *I'm* the one that's sorry. Really sorry,' he said. 'I was a twat in the pub the other night.'

Holly said nothing, but he saw that he had her attention.

'I was rude and insensitive. Everything you said was completely true. I didn't let you talk. I guess I'm a bit sensitive about my dad and all that. I just took it out on you.'

Holly sighed. 'I'm sorry too,' she said. 'I shouldn't have kept on about it. And I'm sorry I've been so preoccupied lately. I've not had much luck with men, and–'

At this extraordinary pronouncement, Luke pretended to faint with shock and executed a pantomime collision with the vending machine. There was a sudden metallic click followed by an unusually promising whirring sound.

'My God, I think you've done it!' exclaimed Holly, her eyes brightening in that nice way they had.

'Wait, is it...?' They put their heads together against the glass, to see what had emerged. Luke bent down to force the flap open.

'Oh,' he said flatly.

'Don't tell me,' said Holly. 'Another fecking Breakfast Bar.'

CHAPTER 53

Back at the flat, Luke wondered if the recent clash with Dom would lead to a prolonged stand-off between the pair. He disliked unresolved tension, and it hadn't been easy dealing with beef at home *and* at work. Ziggy seemed to have picked up on the atmosphere too. For several evenings running, he had displayed prolonged bouts of the zoomies, rushing in and out of all the rooms, chewing on all sorts of forbidden items (pens, pants, shoes, even Dom's walking stick), and refusing to settle even after a long walk out with Michelle and her Teddy.

But perhaps the meditative well-wishing had worked its magic. First up, Luke had made up with Holly, and now here was Dom, making out like nothing untoward had ever happened and even getting involved with all sorts of kid-friendly challenges himself. They went out tree-hugging on Love A Tree Day, and put on eyeliner and danced to Inkubus Sukkubus, Switchblade Symphony and Fields of the Nephilim on World Goth Day. Dom organised a fun scavenger hunt in the garden on National Scavenger Hunt Day, and tirelessly folded and flew disposable darts with Milo on Paper Airplane Day.

Truly, the days were flying by in a spirit of blithe bonhomie and innocent, collaborative play. The only slight hiccup in this happy period occurred when even Grace got into the spirit of things, offering to prepare a show-and-tell for Luke, Dom, Milo and Alan in honour of World Otter Day. Grace's presentation, forever seared on the memory of those who witnessed it, was entitled "Five Reasons Why Otters Are The Sick, Depraved Perverts Of The Animal World". Luke thought at first that Grace merely wanted to mess with their heads and send up the whole challenge, and why not? But it turned out that all her reasons were founded in scientific research, and she had brought the receipts.

Male otters engaged in hyper-aggressive sexual behaviour that sometimes caused the death of females, Grace lectured. They had been known to force themselves onto pups and to sexually assault/murder members of other species too, such as harbour seals. They hunted and killed in packs, and they could emit a fungus that was potentially fatal to humans. Perhaps most shocking of all, they were not averse to copulating with otter corpses. 'So don't be fooled by the slinky moves and impish good looks of these wildly misunderstood marine mammals,' Grace finished up. 'The cute otter is a PR myth. Otters are the depraved monsters of the deep who should never be allowed near our children or our cartoonists ever again.'

'Wow,' said Dom, after she had finished. 'I did not have that on my bingo card for this year.'

The eyes of Milo (who still secretly kept a small cuddly sea otter under his pillow) were wide indeed. 'What's necrophilia?' he asked at last.

'Ask Ziggy,' said Dom and Luke as one.

CHAPTER 54

At around 11.45pm on the last day of the month, Holly called Luke in tears.

'Tom's dumped me,' she said simply.

'That is a most unfortunate occurrence,' said Luke. 'Perhaps you could tell me more about the circumstances?'

'Luke,' said Holly suspiciously. 'Why are you talking like that? Are you being held at knifepoint by a Victorian grammar Nazi?'

'It's Speak In Complete Sentences Day, which is why I am speaking in this way.'

'Oh.' Holly sniffed. 'Could we not just drop all the bollox for once?'

'I am here to listen for as long as you need, today and every day.'

'Oh my God. What are you? Are you even my friend?'

'Yes, of course I am your friend. You know that I am your friend.'

'Okay, you frigging loon. You...' She sighed. 'Just don't talk at all anymore, okay? Just listen instead. Otherwise I am going to lose my mind.'

Luke wisely forbore from confirming that he was very happy

to accede to such a request. He was happy to not be required to speak too much, having found the whole day surprisingly taxing. 'I am very well, thank you.' 'No, I did not watch the latest episode of *Stranger Things* last night. Did you find it enjoyable?' 'No, I would prefer not to have salt on my toasted tuna bagel, please.' It was incredible how tedious it was having to talk in complete sentences, especially as Luke didn't seem to be able to do it without sounding like a reject from a bit of Jane Austen fanfic. But now, tasked only with a brief to listen, Luke and Holly stayed on the phone into the night, minute after minute, hour after hour, with Luke only uttering an occasional, 'His reaction does indeed sound really rather crap' and 'You are the sort of person who deserves so much better than this'.

Holly said she had always suspected she didn't in some way 'deserve' Tom, and that she kept suspecting the relationship was too good to be true. And, reading between the lines, Tom – who seemed like a thoroughly nice bloke – had struggled with her need for reassurance. Also, and no small matter this either, it emerged that he was planning to volunteer on a project in Papua New Guinea for a conservation charity for at least a year, starting in December; he seemed to have had no intention of including Holly in these plans or of deferring the trip in the interests of deepening their relationship. This gave everything they did together a transient, doomed feel, and, as Luke dared observe at one point, 'it does give one pause to wonder whether Tom has acted appropriately in embarking on a serious relationship without declaring his plans or creating an opportunity to consider with his partner how these might impact your chances going forward.'

Eventually Luke dared hope that his stupid sentences, coupled with the basic fact that he was still there, always there, were coming to have a soothing effect, and in time he lay back listening to the gently whispered sighs of a Holly who was slipping from hot, uncontrollable tears into gentle, subsiding sobs. A strangely intimate experience. 'In summary, I can only conclude that, despite so many favourable initial impressions, he was at bottom quite unsuitable and not remotely worthy of a person with your charms or abilities,' he said at last. At the other end of the line he thought he could hear someone quietly saying *pop-poppa* over and over again, but at last he realised that this was just Holly's own decorous way of snoring.

JUNE

CHAPTER 55

JUNE

Luke opened the email from his dad with hopes of news about a possible meet-up.

```
Hi mate.
   Great to hear from you. Sorry it's
been a while. Things crazy-busy here at
the mo. All hands on deck for a big
contract pitch. Could be the one that
puts me over the top into sitting-pretty
land!
   Hope to be in town before the year is
out. Look out for a pressie in your
inbox.
   Maybe we can get to The Emirates when
I'm there — watch your lot bottle it
again!!
   Dad x
```

The pressie came by email. It was a link to a voucher offering £50 off electronic goods at a range of selected stores. It appeared to have been sent by someone other than his dad, an assistant perhaps, though the official donor was marked only as "Corporate Giver".

Luke couldn't help feeling disappointed. By his reckoning, this was the first he'd heard from his dad in about twenty months. While it would be churlish to complain about being given free stuff, he'd been sent exactly the same sort of anonymous voucher the time before; it had actually proved very difficult to redeem, and he'd given up trying in the end. In any case, he'd really much rather have spent a bit of time with his dad. Not only that, but the words in the email were almost exactly the same as the ones he'd used in his last message. And the date at the top of the email – today's date – was his mum's birthday. His dad surely knew what that meant to Luke.

After work, Luke and Ziggy wandered down to the cemetery where his mum's ashes had been buried, safely berthed in the plot where her mum and dad had been buried before her. He found Alan there, knelt over the graveside, trimming the grass and stripping away weed and dead leaves.

'Hello,' he said. 'How you feeling?'

'Oh, you know,' said Luke. As he stood there watching Alan work – Alan the perennial gardener, always pruning or mowing or weeding – it occurred to him, perhaps for the first time, really, that this must be a difficult day for him too. How had this never crossed his mind before? He asked: 'And how are you?'

Alan looked up and away. A tear slid down his nose, which he surreptitiously wiped away. He nodded towards the tombstone, looked at the bare dates and the hopeless clichéd message. 'She'd have been fifty-three today.' Luke nodded. They shared a long silence, a silence that for once had no awkwardness about it.

'There's something I've been meaning to ask you,' said Luke.

Alan flinched. His voice, usually so infuriatingly businesslike and unflappable, was oddly wavering, even pleading. 'Please, Luke, let's not fight. Can we just not... today?'

'Oh no, it's nothing like that,' said Luke quickly. 'I just wanted to know: What words would you have put on Mum's stone if you'd had the choice?'

'Oh,' said Alan, clearly taken aback. 'Well, you guys chose the words, and of course I'm very happy with them.'

'Oh come on, they're dreadful,' said Luke. 'Like something out of a cracker.'

Alan gave a small laugh that seemed to Luke to encompass a universe of secret feelings. He wiped an imaginary stain from the metallic lettering. 'Wow,' he said. 'That's quite a question. Can I have a think?' Ziggy lay at the foot of the plot, and the two men stood in silence a while longer.

'By the way,' said Alan at last. 'Is today National Nail Polish Day by any chance?'

Luke held up his lurid orange talons. 'Got it in one.'

'You're bolder than me,' said Alan, holding out a pair of bright-turquoise pinkies.

CHAPTER 56

June 3 was National Repeat Day. As with so many of these days, it wasn't really quite clear what the point of the Day was, who started it, or how one should best observe it. And as so often, the special-day websites were reduced to making stuff up. *'National Repeat Day could be an opportunity for some and a bad omen for others,'* Luke read on one. *'Repeating a foot massage or a day with a dear friend would make this holiday special. Repeating a root canal or Hurricane Katrina are not suggested.'* Wow: words everyone can get behind, Luke thought. Although: even if for some perverse reason you actually wanted to, how would one go about *repeating Hurricane Katrina*? As a fellow content padder, a man who had once written 1200 lyrical words in praise of a special pumice-stone cleaner for toilet bowls (take *that*, Mrs Hart), Luke could empathise with this writer's plight. Sometimes, in the desperate need to fill a page, the stating of the bleeding obvious could suddenly turn quite surreal.

In such cases, Luke reasoned, you were surely free to find your own way to mark the day. Dom suggested that Luke should spend the day going round and repeating back to everyone the last thing they said. (The last thing they said.) He did so, all day, and three different people told him what a great listener he was.

June 10 was National Ballpoint Day. Luke knew how much stationery meant to Holly, and she was happy to be interviewed, albeit anonymously, for the Make Every Day Count blog about her obsession. Afterwards he wrote up the interview as a blog post. An extract:

'Hayley' (not her real name) is a self-confessed stationery addict. In honour of National Ballpoint Pen Day, she has agreed to speak in confidence about her issues for the first time…

So tell me about your addiction, Hayley. How did it start?

I think it started when I was at school, where my nickname was actually 'Kleppy' because I liked to steal from the stationery cupboard. It would be the highlight of my day if I could get a new exercise book. I would distract somebody and then jump into the cupboard. This was quite brave because it was right next door to the staff room and strictly out of bounds. It's just gone on from there.

And what does your stationery habit look like now?

Well, I own about 550 pens. I'm obsessed with notebooks, bulldog clips, Post-its and highlighters. I'm constantly buying more, and I have to keep up with the trends too – these Legami ones with the animal heads are intriguing me just now. I'm coming to terms with the realisation that I may have all the stationery I'll ever need for the rest of my life. But it won't stop me!

What do you look for in a pen?

Flow. Comfort. Weight. Balance. I favour blue over black ink. Makes-wise, I'm liking the InkJoy at the moment. By Paper Mate. You can get them in lots of different colours. They don't smudge. It's a gel pen that's really progressed over the years. They used to be pooey, but they're not anymore.

Er, pooey?

A pooey biro is the ultimate in horror stationery. That's a pen that emits too much ink when you're writing so you end up smudging your work. That's a trauma for me. If I accidentally wrote in a notebook with pooey ink, I would have to throw the notebook away.

Do you ever judge people who make poor stationery choices?

I think that when I see someone with a Bic, I do – on the inside – probably think a little bit less of them.

So are you super-organised and productive?

Not really. For instance, I can never find a pen. And I've got (counts) seven notebooks on my desk currently, all doing the same job. I can never remember which one of them I'm supposed to write in. But some of them are very pretty.

Why is it that so many of us are obsessed with stationery?

I think stationery can give you this momentary glimpse of a perfect life where we're doing everything right and we're completely in control. I guess it's a bit like people who build train sets: it's the promise of a world you can create and order just the way you want it. I read a lot of the productivity books too, like *Atomic Habits* and the *Bullet Journal* book. I am definitely in search of perfection. And if it's in shocking pink, so much the better.

·

CHAPTER 57

On World Blood Day (June 14), Luke signed up to donate blood, something he'd been meaning to get round to doing for about ten years. Next day was Magna Carta Day, and – with Dom away again – Luke decided there was nothing for it but to sit down and read the thing. Much of the text seemed to be about stopping King John doing whatever he liked – like ordering people to build a bridge for him on the spot, which apparently he liked to do just so he could try a different location for his hawk or inspect a kill. It was probably no surprise to learn that the document didn't offer much in the way of emancipation for women, or Jewish people; it was a bit short on narrative oomph too. First impressions were that it was quite repetitive and would need a lot of work to translate to Netflix. And no spoilers, but definitely worth keeping an eye on those cheeky barons.

A couple of days later, Luke found himself sprinting down the road in slippers and dressing gown to catch up with the bin lorry, which had swung by at its usual unearthly hour. When he finally caught up with the men, he handed over a box of Quality Street.

'Hi,' said Luke. 'I just wanted to say how much we appreciate you all. It's Global Garbage Man Day, you see. And, er, women.'

The man looked him up and down. 'We've heard about you,' he said. 'From Monika. Your postie.'

'All good, I trust?' said Luke nervously.

The man looked at the chocolates dismissively. 'There's four of us,' he said. 'How come Monika got a load of wine and we only get this?'

Behind and above the teddy-decked cart, Luke saw Mrs Hart shaking her head sadly.

'I'll have more for you next week!' called out Luke to the departing flourescent figures. 'Do you prefer wine or beer?'

The bin lorry started up again, but instead of making off down the road it nimbly reversed back to where Luke was standing. The bin man wound down the window.

'It's all a bit late now,' he said sadly, and Luke thought for one terrible moment that he was going to start crying. 'To think that you don't value what we do as much as Monika, that really gets me.'

'I'm so sorry,' said Luke again helplessly.

'Never mind!' said the man with sudden cheerfulness. 'A case of red and we'll say no more about it!'

'Right,' said Luke. 'And do you have any, er, preference for...?'

'Nah, whatever. Maybe... a Pomerol or a Barolo perhaps? Or perhaps something Argentinian, something with nice and chewy tannins, not overly flamboyant? You'll work it out. Be lucky!' And with that the bin lorry sped off down the road, in a flurry of discarded Quality Street wrappers.

CHAPTER 58

June 22 was Positive News Day. This looked like a toughie, thought Luke, scanning the day's top stories with their reports of health scandals, corruption, war and famine. He was enough of a media type to believe that only bad news really counted as news. Contrary to the proverbial expression, good news was no news at all, as any journalist could tell you. He read up about a Russian newspaper that had introduced a 'good news day' back in 2015. It saw its readership decrease by sixty-six per cent. He also remembered Sir Martyn Lewis being ridiculed for suggesting that news programmes should carry more positive stories.

We listen to the news to check that we're still alive, one of his old media studies lecturers used to say. Humans were apparently programmed to prioritise 'negative information' as an evolutionary survival mechanism: this was why "New snow and ice warnings issued as subzero temperatures close in" would always trump "Library waives forty-eight-year fine after Canada book return" or "Barry Manilow surprises punters at country pub". Good news was so hopelessly parochial and twee. Goody-goody news more like.

'Have you got any positive news for me today?' Luke asked Muriel once he got into the office.

'Actually, I have,' Muriel replied, waving a pile of stapled printouts.

'Let's hear it then.'

'I've just got hold of some breakthrough research from Germany looking at dish-washing best practice. The good news is that it confirms many of the tactics I've been advocating for some years. No doubt you're familiar with them.' She pointed to a row of close-typed, narrow-margined laminated sheets that were pinned up in a corner of the kitchen space.

'Give me the headlines if you will,' said Luke. 'I can use this on my blog.'

'Well, the Germans have boiled all the latest thinking down into six golden rules. Some of it is wildly counter-intuitive!'

'Really?' said Luke, pretending to start taking notes. 'Such as?'

'Do NOT pre-rinse dishes by hand. And always use the Eco programme if possible, even if takes longer.'

'Wow!' Luke hoped that this exclamation would have the effect of marking a sort of full stop on proceedings, but he had switched the Muriel program on now and it looked as though he would have to see it through.

'Yes! Also, it's a mistake to think that using more detergent will lead to better cleaning results. You know, like when you've got a very dirty load.' Muriel paused expectantly.

'*Really?* How come?'

'Because it can just lead to more foam, which can of course stick to items and impede rinsing.'

'Oh!'

'I know! But that doesn't mean you should rinse things by hand beforehand.'

'No?'

'No, siree. You're better off pre-rinsing them in the machine.'

'I'm going to have to stop you there,' said Luke, with the sudden inspiration of a man trapped beneath a falling ceiling. 'Because, as you may or may not know, today is also National Kissing Day, and I would like to ask your permission to kiss you. Clive, Phaedra and Michael the Cone have already permitted me, if that helps.'

'Very well,' said Muriel. 'It's the least I deserve.' She proferred her cheek, and Luke planted a big wet one. Just then, Muriel spotted Holly walking by.

'Hey, Holly! Come over here and kiss Luke!' she shouted.

'Excuse me?' said Holly.

'Oh, don't worry. It's only for charity. We've all had to do it. He's only raised about two hundred quid so far.'

Holly walked slowly over. 'Oh, go on then.' They each moved in for the–

'Oh no! I didn't mean–'

'Oh! I don't mind. I mean, what's a peck between friends?'

'That's what Michael the Cone said.'

As they'd leant in for the obligatory moment of osculation, Luke and Holly had accidentally found their lips touching. And then, just as accidentally perhaps, both stayed in position a beat longer than was perhaps strictly necessary, before each had quickly regained control of the situation and recoiled with comic force.

'Well, I've never done that with you before, Chandler,' said Holly. (They had long ago discovered that each had *Friends* in their Top 10 Guilty Pleasures list, along with *The Kardashians*, *Tangled* and eating cold pizza in bed. Neither had put down throwing a fake sickie as, in their line of work, with their bosses, both considered this a vital act of self-care and a civic duty rather than a guilty pleasure.) Holly looked a bit red, and Luke wondered if she was trying not to cringe.

'Sorry,' said Muriel. 'Could you just do that again, very quickly? Luke asked me to get a snap for the blog, and I think that one was all blurry.'

The pair complied. Having pressed lips to lips first time round, quite by innocent accident no doubt, it would have seemed churlish not to follow precedent next time round. They knew what to do, after all.

'Got it!' said Muriel, cackling furiously. 'Honestly, you two. Will you just get a room already?'

Holly's kiss would prove to be as stubborn as the most stubborn dirty-dish stain. Luke would feel its soft, warm imprint on his mouth for the rest of the day.

CHAPTER 59

Just in time for National Flip-Flop Day, there was a man on the telly who was sitting on a TV sofa with a dire warning. 'I am trying to alert the wider public to the dangers of flip-flops!' he stormed. 'People have died wearing flip-flops!' He said flip-flops were 'the most dangerous form of footwear in the world' and should be banned because 'they can kill'. Up close, he almost looked as though he were frothing at the beard.

Luke decided to explore the issue further. He could find no epidemic of flip-flop-related fatalities, though in 2018, there was a man in Wales who reportedly died after tripping over his flip-flops and sustaining head injuries when walking home from the pub. Then again, he had reportedly been drinking for several hours.

While not perhaps murderous, however, flip-flops had indeed been linked with lots of foot issues, he read, including fungal infections, tendonitis, stress fractures, hammer toes and poor posture leading to chronic pain in knees, back and neck. So perhaps the frothy-beardy man on the telly sort of had a point. But perhaps he'd be taken more seriously if he didn't have form for expressing some rather contrarian and eccentric views so forcefully. Someone on social media had set up an account with the sole purpose of documenting the best of these. They included a belief that Christmas cards sent with a second-class stamp should be chucked straight in the bin, and – Luke's favourite, and one he'd make sure Dom didn't get wind of – claiming that the best wasp repellent is to cover your body with Brussels pâté.

Luke and Milo donned their flip-flops a week later for Canoe Day. A neighbour had an old two-man canoe that had been languishing in the bottom of his garden for ever, and kindly let them borrow it. They decided to try it out on a stretch of the New River, a 17th-century man-made watercourse designed to bring fresh drinking water from Hertfordshire to North London. ('It isn't new and it isn't a river,' as the locals always liked to say.) Luke and Milo manhandled the vessel down to the water's edge, fought past a pile of building rubble dumped on the bank, and gingerly took to the waves. Luke had never noticed that the many bridges which criss-crossed the New River were so low as to be unpassable. While there were some pretty stretches that walkers ambitiously compared with the Canal du Midi, other parts – especially with all the fly-tipping – looked like the sort of place where you'd find the body at the start of a gritty police drama. They paddled rather awkwardly up and down a short stretch between two footbridges, but were soon assailed by a giant bird so angry they christened it The Anti-Swan. 'Can they really break a grown man's arm?' asked Milo, eyes wide in terror. 'I think we're about to find out,' said Luke. They were saved only by a passing jogger who inadvertently got even closer to the cygnets that the Anti-Swan was protecting (God knows why they needed protecting; the youngsters looked scary enough themselves, and like most teenagers they were already towering over their parents) and created enough of a distraction for them to make an awkward escape. Looking down through the shallow water to the canal bed, Luke spotted a giant dressed crab, a rusting unicycle, and what looked like a full set of carving knives.

'I'm sorry, Milo,' said Luke. 'That was a bit of a non-starter as adventures go. You were really brave though.' The lad had attempted to face the swan down with a broken umbrella, while Luke cowered behind him.

But Milo saw it differently. 'That was brilliant!' his half-brother raved. 'Please can we go again tomorrow? Bring Dad along? *Please?*'

Your *dad, you mean.* That was the sort of thing that Luke normally said when Milo said things like that. But today he didn't.

CHAPTER 60

As soon as you arrived at Wordy Gigs of a morning, you could usually tell what sort of day you were going to have by a glance at the expression on Greg and/or Phaedra's face(s). There were two basic settings, which Luke and Holly had categorised as Busy-Busy and Sulky.

On mornings when a new client had been won or a contract extended, Greg and Phaedra would be in high, self-congratulatory Busy-Busy mode, which was often when they were at their most infuriating. Phaedra liked to make loud phone calls that she thought demonstrated best practice in hardball client management. She'd drop loud, surreally macho statements like: 'I'm only dropping my pants to 2K because it's you, Jasper' or 'I'm going to guarantee you five per cent more leads than last year, Harpreet. We're going all in – my cock's on the block with this one'.

Greg, meanwhile, liked to stand over you – stage-whispering the fatal words: *'I'm not here! I'm the invisible man'* – while you tried to bash away at a blog post with a catchy title like *'So how much do you know about choosing a London gutter cleaner? Test your knowledge with our fun quiz.'* Or else he'd sit across from you while you ran through next month's content ideas with that new life coaching or tyre refit client. Greg would give little nods and grunts of encouragement, or occasional frowns or head shakes, while you struggled on under the double burden of (a) trying to pretend that you thought gutter cleaning or tyre refits was a deeply sexy and exciting topic, while also (b) having to ignore your boss, whose clunky, mansplainy presence was far more likely to make you lose your thread completely.

Afterwards he would always have a few notes. In Greg's mind, he was dispensing words of wisdom to his content protégés, rather like Titian helping one of his eager school of acolytes to fine-tune the way they did the tips of cherubs' wings. To Luke and Holly, he was more like the washed-up coach of a non-league footie side that gets relegated every other season, a man with about four or five nuggets of 'wisdom' to be dispensed with depressing regularity. Only instead of 'let the ball do the work' or 'we have to play how we know we can play', it was 'let's not boil the ocean' or 'Google is as Google does' or 'why not do a listicle?'.

But on June 27, the Sulky setting was in evidence. Shouting and door-slamming had been followed by an eerie silence as Phaedra swept out of the office in a cloud of mutual recrimination. Later, she and her dad would be stalking about the place, refusing to acknowledge each other's presence. Holly, an only child, said that such days reminded her of her childhood, which she recalled as a series of awkward silent mealtimes punctured only by the occasional stifled phrase such as 'ask your mother to pass the salt' or 'see if anyone [i.e. her dad, sitting two feet away] wants any more casserole'. On such days, she often reminded Luke to be grateful he had siblings.

'A brother or sister would have been an ally, an accomplice,' she told him. 'I wouldn't have had to bear the full brunt of all that tension.'

'I'm sorry your parents were so crap.'

'Oh, they were good people, really,' she said briskly. 'They were great individually. They just weren't meant to be together.'

'I guess my mum and dad were a bit like that.'

'But at least you got siblings later on.'

'I guess.'

'*Really?* You love hanging out with them. The best thing about this whole silly Day challenge has been you and Milo hanging out. And he looks up to you so much. They both do.' She sounded a bit choked. 'It's really cool.'

Luke wasn't quite sure what to do, so he put a limp hand on her sleeve. 'Well, it was just me when my mum was around,' he said.

'Oh, come on,' said Holly. If she was thinking that this wasn't strictly true as Grace had been around for at least some of Luke's childhood, she didn't mention it. Instead she said: 'I'd kill to have Grace and Milo in my life.' She looked at him shrewdly, and dared to add, 'And Alan.'

Just then Greg stalked out of his office and advanced on the two of them.

'Honestly you two – always at each other's throats,' he said. 'Can't live with each other, can't live without.' Luke and Holly looked bemused.

'So, Luke!' said Holly, trying to ignore this. 'What day is it today?'

'Monday.'

'No! What... *Day?*'

'Oh, right. Well, it's Sunglasses Day. Ice Cream Cake Day. International Pineapple Day, Industrial Workers of the World Day, Decide To Be Married Day... It's also National Bingo Day, funnily enough. Actually, Greg, we're popping down Mecca later if–' He gave Holly a quick enquiring look, and she nodded her head in instant understanding. 'If you fancy joining us?'

'Me and the wife started off like you two,' said Greg gloomily, ignoring the offer. 'We were in an emotional affair and didn't even realise it.'

'What's that now?'

'We both had other partners at the time, and they were always like, "How come you keep talking about this Anna or that Greg at work?".' (It was rare for Greg to mention Anna, who had no interest in the business and whom no one in the office had ever met. Not even Muriel, who'd been there since forever.)

Holly and Luke met each other's eyes for a moment, shook their heads helplessly. 'No, no,' Holly said, laughing. 'It's nothing like that. We're not, you know.'

'That's right,' put in Luke.

'He's with Yasmine, remember?' said Holly. 'In Paris?'

'Sure he is,' said Greg. There was a malicious look in his eye. 'Tell me, Luke, what's Yasmine's phone number?'

'Er, I'm not sure at the moment. She's between, er–'

'Okay, what's her email?'

'Ah, well. I believe that's changed too. You see–'

'All right, all right,' Greg cut in. 'That was a toughie. Just tell us the name of her street.'

Luke was suddenly very red in the face. 'It's not like that,' he began. But of course it was.

Holly was looking at him quizzically. She had the look of someone who was thinking, '*So just to be clear: The person you're obsessed with, the love of your life, the one (The One!) you've been boring us all silly about for the last eighteen months – you don't actually know where she lives, or have any of her basic contact details?!*' – only was too kind to say any of this out loud. He now saw an expression of terrible pity on her face, which was even worse.

'Why don't you two just decide to get married today?' Greg was saying now.

'Well, er, we,' Holly began. 'I've actually got a date tonight.'

Just then, Phaedra swept back into the office. She walked

straight past the three of them, looked straight through Greg, and slammed their office door behind her.

'This is me, I guess,' said Greg, and headed off after her. He paused at the door and looked around with an air of desperation.

'Has anyone seen Muriel?'

Holly and Luke shook their heads.

'Ask her to pop in if you do.'

Holly and Luke sat on in thoughtful silence.

'When are you going to change your name back?' said Holly at last. 'It feels weird, you going round with my surname.'

'It's not your surname as such,' began Luke. 'It was randomly selected from a list of the UK's most common surnames.'

'Yeah, yeah. Let's not go through all that again.'

'The ironic thing is that if we did decide to get married today, it would be quite convenient in a way,' said Luke. 'We'd both already have the same name.'

'Oh no you don't! I think I've provided enough material for your blog this year already without you tricking me into a fake wedding.' Holly produced a thick marker pen from her bag and bopped a big red blotch onto the tip of Luke's nose. 'If you don't get the name thing sorted out and soon,' she said, 'you'll be feeling the full force of my dobber.'

CHAPTER 61

Next day was Caps Lock Day. Luke worked hard to ensure that all his messages on this day had a momentous quality worthy of the persistent shift key. Like this one, which he sent to all staff:

```
DEAR ALL
    I MUST APOLOGISE IF I SEEM A LITTLE
GRUMPY AND OUT OF SORTS TODAY.
    I ORDERED MYSELF TWO CAPPUCCINOS FROM
MCDONALD'S THIS MORNING AND FOOLISHLY
THREW THE CUPS AWAY WITHOUT COLLECTING
THE STICKERS TO PUT TOWARDS MY FREE
SEVENTH CUP OF COFFEE.
    THIS IS ESPECIALLY GALLING AS I
ALREADY HAVE FOUR STICKERS SAVED UP.
    PLEASE DO BEAR WITH ME AT THIS
DIFFICULT TIME.
    LUKE MILVAINE ESQ
```

It occurred to Luke a day or so later that it was a good while – several days perhaps – since he'd last seen Dom. As the last day of

June was National Handshake Day – and with a palm that was still throbbing from the ninety-seven manual clasps he had so far secured – he thought it would be a nice gesture to grip the palm of the man who had done so much to spur him on. He had reached the not insignificant milestone of a half year's Days observed, so there was much progress to shake on. Luke knocked, but no answer. He tried again throughout the evening, but still no joy.

Ziggy whimpered and sniffed at Dom's door. He missed Dom in the uncomplicated way of unconditional love, a way surely inaccessible to any human who had ever had any dealings with him. He put his paws up and scratched. Amazingly, the door fell open. Luke peeked inside, feeling like a man on the threshold of breaching an unspeakable taboo. Dom wasn't there. Oblivious to the sacrilege, Ziggy pawed at the door of a little bedside closet. It clicked open, and about thirty jars of pills fell out, along with a familiar cuddly toy with a zip-up tummy. Ziggy got his teeth into this quickly, and the little scraps of paper with which Tipsy's tummy were filled started to spill out. Luke remembered the vote. He saw now that every single folded-up scrap of paper bore the same name: Robinson.

JULY

CHAPTER 62

July 3 was National Stay Out of the Sun Day, one of those all-too-easy-to-observe Days that don't require you to do anything and could easily be observed every day of the year (along with No Homework Day, No Make-up Day, No Housework Day, No Socks Day, No Pants Day and International No Diet Day). Dom still wasn't back, but Luke found that he felt compelled to stay accountable to his flatmate even more in his absence than in his presence, so he looked around for something else to observe and came up with Compliment Your Mirror Day.

It was a self-esteem thing, apparently – you had to look into the mirror and say things to the face that you saw there. The face Luke saw was his own, however, and he never found this sort of thing easy. So he went online to look up some sample 'mirror affirmations' and tried out a few:

I believe in my abilities and myself.

I can face this day and its challenges with strength.

Today I will let go of my fears, anxieties, and negative thoughts.

In this moment, I am filled with hope.

Every day, in every way, I have what it takes to be successful and confident.

That sort of thing. His face looked back most sceptically, so he tried to craft a few of his own:

Today I can be the partner my partner wants and needs.
Today I can be here for my family.
Every day, in every way, I am getting stronger and happier.
Whatever I work on today, I will give it my all.
Today I will focus on positive things and...

...And that was about as much as much as he could manage. Just saying these lines out loud made him hate himself. As he looked at his shaving-cream scribbles on the bathroom tiles that would make a photo for the blog, it struck him that these affirmations asked more questions than they gave answers. Who actually was his partner? How much did he do to support his family? How did he support his dad? How did he support Alan? Wasn't he family too, really? When had he last spent the day trying to 'do his best'? And why would you give your all just to keep the Google monster fed? Why on earth would anyone give their all to writing a piece of content entitled, "Ten reasons to ditch that exfoliating loofah back-scrubber"?

As always, this sort of 'spiritual' exercise left him feeling guilty and uncomfortable; never would he reach the giddy self-believing heights of a Salvador Dali, who wrote that every day he looked in his mirror and was astonished to discover yet again that he was himself the astonishing Salvador Dali, a man awestruck to imagine the extraordinary things that this extraordinary Salvador Dali would make and do with the new day.

CHAPTER 63

One morning early in July, Holly announced to Luke that she had discovered a new dating site that promised to deliver better matches. As a result, she had spent the weekend fine-tuning her profile, and already some promising leads were coming in.

'This guy seems nice,' she said.

'Why is he standing nearer the camera than everyone else in all his photos?'

Holly peered at the screen. 'I don't think that he is,' she said. 'It's just that he's, er, quite tall.'

The images looked like strange tricks of perspective. The man in question, a smiling, slightly stooped figure with bright-white teeth, a bold taste in patterned knitwear and an impossibly neat fringe, was indeed tall. Tall, really, was inadequate as a description of him. He was a giant, like a man from a fairy tale come to life. There was a woman in lots of the pics on his Facebook page, possibly his mum, who only came up to his knee.

'Well, well,' said Luke. A number of terrible childish gags and heightist remarks were sweeping through his cliché-ridden brain, including an irresistible urge to cackle like Sid James and say that he trusted everything was in proportion. Other co-workers were less restrained.

'No need to settle for the low-hanging fruit with that one.' Greg chortled over Holly's shoulder.

'Oh I say,' purred Muriel appreciatively. 'Ideal for reaching into those tricky ceiling corners, swishing away all the cobwebs.'

'Wow,' said Phaedra, peering over. 'When he dies, they're going to have to break his legs.'

It was quite a fun little conversational canter for a Friday morning, even with the strange dark turn Phaedra had introduced. Luke would normally have been quite happy to extend this topic for another good half hour or so till lunchtime, had not an airmail letter been dropped onto his desk, whose contents hit him with the force of a burning bush, a bolt from the blue and a strange voice in the wilderness, all rolled into one.

He ran into the end trap (no newspaper fairy needed today) of the men's loo one floor up and tore the letter open. It was from Her! The One!! She was sorry for her silence!!! She had thought of him because she was coming through London on her way back to Morocco!!! She felt bad because she hadn't been in touch!!!! Perhaps they could meet???!!!

Feigning his usual nonchalant office ennui, Luke sauntered casually out of the bog and back down to the Wordy Gigs kitchen, where he stood at the floor-to-ceiling window and gazed out over the streets of Farringdon, three floors below. He took in all the people down there walking about like ants, pretending they had a purpose in their lives – that bloke in the vest there, just smoking on his own; Michael the Cone playing 'Fly Me to the Moon' on his traffic one; those two men in hard hats chatting by a generator thing, hands on hips; a gaggle of Italian tourists, brandishing maps in the face of a baffled traffic warden; the cycle courier fixing his wheel; the taxi drivers in their rank, sharing a cab and laughing at something in the paper; the three civil-service types, all M&S suits and laptops and lanyards, on their way to some unspeakable meeting. And as he looked down he was filled with a vast all-seeing compassion for all those poor folk in the world who had not this morning received a hand-written, airmail letter from... The One.

CHAPTER 64

'Hello!' called Alan from the garden, as Luke walked back to his flat from the station. It was a sweltering day and he was batting away things in the air around him. 'Bloody Hell! Looks like it's Flying Ant Day!' On the telly, an unpopular Prime Minister was busy snarking his way through a rather ungracious resignation speech, but Luke's first thought was: Is Flying Ant Day really a thing? And if so, how does one find a way to observe it?

He sat out on Alan's pretty little verandah and pulled out his laptop. In his mind, the two events, the resigning and the swarming, were quickly confused. As a youngster, there had always been these swarms of ants round the house, which Alan and his mum seemed to regard almost fondly as the antics of a loyal opposition. He remembered watching his mum pour kettles of boiling water over the sprawling powdered battlements of the ants' nests. The departure of an unpopular leader felt like a purging of sorts too, but with a release of something diabolical in the process. He briefly wondered if the ants were toxic familiars the outgoing Leader had summoned to express his displeasure and further his evil will. It all made him think of those nasty flying monkeys that are set loose towards the end of the *The Wizard of Oz*.

Perhaps Dom – who'd been absent for a good fortnight now – would be home tonight, and no doubt he'd want an update on the Make Every Day Count challenge. Luke, who had even taken the unprecedented step of trying to call Dom a couple of times to see where he was, albeit without success, was suddenly anxious to behold his sardonic flatmate's sardonic features once more, and so he decided to prepare a show-and-tell on the subject of Flying Ant Day in case he should appear that evening.

It wasn't so much a day as a season, Luke discovered. The exact date of the annual swarming varied a little each year, and could last for days, even weeks. It usually coincided with a period of hot or humid weather, and often seemed to come after summer rain. As an established ant colony reached its limits of expansion, the sitting queen would start to develop eggs that turned, not into the usual flightless workers, but into winged ants – males and virgin queens. The goal of each new queen was to start her own colony, and to do that she needed to meet and mate with a male from a different colony. So the new fliers all came rushing out of their respective nests and took to the air, where they scattered to maximise their mating chances.

Larger flying females and smaller winged males could often be seen flying conjoined on their once-in-a-lifetime nuptial flight. Queens often mated with several males in-flight, after which the males all dropped dead within a day or so. On landing, the new queens bit their own wings off and started building their own new colony, with a big enough stock of sperm from that nuptial flight to lay fertilised eggs for the rest of their lives, which from now on would be spent entirely underground.

So the thick black swarms could be seen as a giant wedding bash. Unless they were a party throng celebrating the disgraced leader's passing? In any case, Holly was quite taken with ant life. 'This whole approach has much to recommend it,' she said when Luke told her about it. 'I quite like the idea of a big shagging spree, then bumping off all the males and retreating underground with my babies for the rest of my life.'

CHAPTER 65

Reading Yasmine's letter again, and toying with the idea of showing it to Holly, and even Greg (if only to shut him up), Luke wondered if it was actually the same letter he had devoured so ecstatically a few days before. It was as if opening the letter and exposing it to the banal office air had removed some of its charm and its joyous optimism. It was true that Yasmine was coming back through London, he saw now, but only as a stopover as her plane transferred back to Morocco. She had been thinking about him, she said, but mostly it now seemed because she was worried that he had '*developed expectations*' about their '*friendship*' that were '*not possible in this world*'. (The phrase '*this world*' would do quite a bit of heavy lifting for Luke over the next few days and weeks. He assumed she meant a world where mysterious, ruthless third parties conspired day and night to keep her from her shared destiny with him.) And what was this? The bit about meeting up seemed to have vanished, as if written in disappearing ink. Oh, ye dark gods! Cruel puppet-masters of destiny who toy with the heart's deepest desires! In its place, a new para seemed to have inserted itself into the letter, something (dictated at knifepoint, no doubt) about how Yasmine felt '*sad and bad*' about everything, but how sometimes in life it was necessary for people to '*turn a page*'. Wait. *Which people??? What page??!!*

'It sounds to me like she's trying to tell you something, dear,' said Mrs Hart. Luke didn't find it easy to talk to any of his friends about this, not even Holly, but Mrs Hart, well, this wasn't a very PC thing to say (or even think), but in his mind she was so old and detached from reality that telling her was no more incriminating than talking to Ziggy.

'Yes! But what is she trying to say?'

'I think she wants out, dear. She's trying to let you down gently.'

'I'm sure that's not it!' said Luke, worrying anew about Mrs Hart's diminishing cognitive powers. 'I think there are people round her who are trying to pressure her into ending our relationship.'

Mrs Hart was thoughtful for a moment. 'Well, they're doing a pretty good job, aren't they, dear?'

A light dawned behind Luke's eyes. A bright shining beacon of stubborn vainglory.

'This is the real test, isn't it?'

'Well, yes, dear. It's certainly testing my patience, I know that.'

Luke ignored the doddery, gibbering old fool. 'It's. A. Test!! She needs me to show her – and her... dodgy entourage – that I'm not the sort to give up!' he said. 'If she knows that I still believe in *us*, she'll find the strength to make it work.'

'Fig roll?' said Mrs Hart absently.

'Er, okay. Thanks, yeah.' They sat chewing in a companionable silence.

'I'll tell you one thing,' she said at last.

'What's that?'

'When they made you, they certainly threw away the mould.'

Luke smiled kindly. 'Thank you, Mrs Hart.'

'Call me a doddery, gibbering old fool if you like,' she continued, 'but wouldn't it be easier for you to court someone who actually wanted to be courted? Someone who maybe lived in the same country perhaps?'

'That's just the sort of thing Alan would say. Or Holly.'

'What's the occasion today anyway, dear?'

'It's July 11 – Cheer Up The Lonely Day,' said Luke, with a pointed nod towards his companion.

'Aw, my dear,' said Mrs Hart.

'Oh! Anytime, Mrs Hart,' said Luke.

'You poor love. How brave of you to reach out.' She patted his hand, and was now speaking louder and more slowly, as if concerned that he wasn't taking everything in. 'You come round and see me anytime.'

CHAPTER 66

On National Moon Day (July 20), Luke found himself mooning over a map of the moon. He found he rather liked lunar nomenclature, whose otherworldly, melancholy vibe seemed to speak directly to his own experiences on this planet: Sea of Crises, Lake of Forgetfulness, Lake of Fear, Sea of the Edge. How about the Lake of Absent Girlfriends, the Marsh of Heartbreak, or the Ocean of Unanswered Emails? With thoughts of a potential show-and-tell in mind for Dom, he found himself wondering: Where do these names come from – and who gets to decide them?

Luke discovered there was a sort of hierarchy of lunar features, starting with the *Maria* (seas) and *Oceanus* (oceans), and moving through the *Lacus* (lakes), *Sinus* (bays), *Paludes* (marshes) and *Terrae* (lands). These almost all had abstract or mythical names: Land of Cheerfulness, Bay of Trust, Bay of Rainbows, Marsh of Decay, Sea of Cleverness, Sea of Crises.

Then you moved into things like valleys and mountains, impact craters, dorsa (wrinkle ridges), rilles and escarpments. After that came the ordinary craters, of which there were so many that they had their own Wikipedia page. These were the ones that tended to be named after individuals. More were still being discovered, which meant more opportunities for someone to get named after one. Most of these lucky folk were scientists, engineers, astronomers and astronauts. There were craters near the Apollo basin named after the moon-walkers and the lost crews of Apollo 1, Challenger and Colombia, while craters near the Moon's poles were named after polar explorers like Shackleton and Amundsen.

Luke toyed with the idea of getting a lunar place named after Yasmine – Lake Of The One, perhaps, or Mare Jasminae. But the process wasn't easy, he discovered. You had to submit names for approval by the International Astronomical Union (IAU). The best chance of getting a name accepted was when the nominee was a high-achieving scientist or explorer and, ideally, dead. This looked like one challenge that might prove impossible even for Luke.

But then he read about the Shoemaker Crater – named after Gene Shoemaker, a specialist in craters, asteroids and comets, who but for ill health would have been the first geologist to walk on the moon. It contains a small portion of his actual ashes, brought aloft by the Lunar Prospector spacecraft in 1998. Though numerous space memorial flights have fired celebrity remains into space, Eugene Shoemaker is thought to be the only person who lies on any celestial body outside Earth.

'I could do that for Yasmine for next Valentine's!' Luke told Mrs Hart. He seemed to be popping in to see her most days now. 'No one's ever done that for their loved one before.'

'Sounds pricey though, dear,' said Mrs Hart, who was now humming 'Fly Me to the Moon'. 'How about a nice bunch of flowers?'

'But... imagine looking up at the sky and knowing that you're up there!'

'Wouldn't she have to be dead first though, dear?'

'Oh yeah. Well, maybe a lock of her hair?'

'Hmm. Or maybe get her something a bit more practical,' mused Mrs Hart, pointing at a shiny spread in a much-thumbed Lakeland catalogue. 'Why not get her one of these new air-fryers?'

CHAPTER 67

Next day, Luke got into work to find several all-too-familiar yellow squares of paper stuck to his phone. He prepared himself for a bout of PostNotal Depression:

PostNotal Depression
Noun. The terrible sense of existential weariness that overcomes a worker on returning to the office to discover a nagging flotilla of phone messages stuck all over their desk.

He calmed down a bit when he saw that all the messages were from one person. The depression quickly returned, however, when he saw who that one person was.

'Hi, mate,' said Reggie from Hornsey BoxLife. 'I know you were planning to call today but I just couldn't wait. Hope you don't mind.'

'Today?' Luke rolled the word around in his mouth and his head. His eyes flicked over to his Special Day wall planner. Oh dear Lord. Surely not. Could it be...? Already? Get To Know Your Customer Day *again*???

'No worries at all,' said Luke, recovering seamlessly and miming a dramatic thumbs up as Holly placed a tea in front of him with a sympathetic smile. Then she started taking pictures of him, and the rest of the gang gathered round. Watching Luke get to know Reggie from Hornsey BoxLife was one of life's little pleasures.

'So... how it's all going?'

'Oh, mate,' said Reggie sadly. 'Don't even ask.'

Okay then! Let's leave it there! were the words Luke would have liked to say next, but he knew that when Reggie said 'Don't ask', he actually meant, 'Please ask!'. Or perhaps: 'No need to ask me what the matter is... because I'm going to tell you anyway! Best to cancel all your appointments for the next three hours!'. Luke sat down and assumed the position of a good listener. To be fair, Reggie did actually have quite a bit of news to share, and it was hard not to feel sorry for him.

'She's kicked me out.'

'Who?'

'Viv.'

Weeding out all the sobs and hesitations, and all the repeated versions of the same story retold in various ways, doubtless for added rhetorical impact, and also trimming some of the *he said/so I said/then she said* parts of the narration – in which complete exchanges were reproduced, down to the smallest hesitation or conversational cul-de-sac – a transcript of the gist might read as follows:

'It's not her really. It's her mum. Viv's gone down there and her mum's poured all this poison in her ear about me. Says I'm not around enough. Says I don't understand Viv's needs. Says I'm a government sheeple for wanting to get the kids vaccinated.

'It's true I should have been around more. But I've been trying to build up the business. Viv always wanted financial security, she said she never had that growing up. But now she's come back and kicked me out. Changed the lock. Won't let me see the kid. Says

I'm a *toxic influence.* I asked her why. She said the fact I don't know is part of the problem. But 5G definitely comes into it, I think. She said her mum's nickname for me is Lizard Face.'

There was a strange tinny, echoey quality to Reggie's voice. 'Where are you calling from, Reggie?'

'Number 10A. It's on the left at the back as you go in. Ground floor. It's one of my favourites, actually. Lucky it was empty. Oooh! I could let you have it for twenty per cent off for the first year, once I'm done with it.'

'Wait: you're now living in one of your own storage units?'

'Just till we get things sorted. No point getting a flat or anything. I want to show Viv that I'm being financially responsible.'

And so the conversation went on. It was complicated. Viv was clearly a mad conspiracy theorist, or at least her mum was, but it turned out Reggie had struggled with a wee gambling addiction in the past. His current plan was to live in the storage unit during the week, and to camp outside the home from which he was currently banned on the weekends. He'd sleep in the Mondeo on the street outside her (their) place until it was time to drive back to Hornsey in time for work for Monday.

'Wow,' said Luke. 'That's quite a strategy.'

'Thanks!' said Reggie. 'The unit makes a nice break from the Mondeo, which I must say is a bit cramped. It's quite cosy in here – I've got fairy lights, a futon, one of those fancy air-dryers – the works. You don't normally get electric in these units but with my inside knowledge I found a way.' He gave a satisfied sigh, then added: 'All in all, I've got pretty much everything a man could wish for here.'

Except your wife and kids, and your home, Luke didn't say.

'Except my wife and my kids and my home!' said Reggie suddenly, bursting into tears again.

'You need to stop with these crazy gestures,' Luke heard himself saying. 'How is sleeping in a car on your own street going to help anyone? Believe me – I lived on a roundabout during a dark period in my life so I know what I'm talking about.' Luke did not dare to look at Holly at this moment, though he could feel her expression burning into the top of his head.

Reggie paused. Now that he'd got his torrent of woe out, he seemed to be hanging on Luke's every word.

'So... what should I do?'

Luke felt a sense of terrible responsibility. But – and this felt like a new sensation – he found that he didn't really mind. 'Just focus on the here and now, Reggie. Focus on today. What can you do today that will make things easier in some way?'

Reggie thought for a moment. 'You think I should move into the Mondeo full time?'

'No, Reggie, I don't. Viv will just think you're a loon. Your kids' friends will laugh at you. The neighbours will call the police.'

'What then?'

'Get on with your life. Show her that you are holding everything together until she's ready to get things back to normal. Write Viv a letter. Explain that you're here and ready whenever she wants to talk. Tell her you love her and you'll do whatever it takes to put things right. Apologise for whatever you've done wrong. Acknowledge that that might include things you don't realise or understand, and you're keen to put those right too. But don't grovel. Show some self-belief. Assert yourself! Say there are things in her behaviour that you can't accept and that you think a future together must mean working through differences and issues on both sides. While you are happy to try and understand her views, it's only right that she should make an effort to understand yours. In particular, your actions and beliefs regarding vaccines are perfectly aligned with mainstream medical science and it is perfectly reasonable to want to protect your child from harm or illness, especially in non-bonkers ways. Okay, scrub "non-bonkers" but you know what I mean. Also: look after yourself. Have some self-respect. Go and stay with a friend or get a room in a budget hotel. Stop stalking your wife. Get some sleep. Go for a run. Stay off the booze. Have a shave. And a shower. I bet you hum right now, don't you?'

He heard Reggie sniff. 'I guess I kind of do,' he said eventually.

'Wow,' said Holly after Luke had put the phone down at last. 'You really gave him both barrels.'

Muriel clapped her hands and cackled sarcastically. 'There is nothing quite so delicious as the spectacle of a man passionately dispensing to others that advice which he would do so well to follow himself.'

'Who said that: Oscar Wilde?'

'Should have been.'

'Oh God,' said Luke. 'I should have shut my mouth, shouldn't I?'

'On the contrary,' said Holly. 'That was pretty awesome actually. You know: I sometimes think there's a lot more to Luke Milvaine than he knows.'

'Than who knows?'

'Luke Milvaine. In fact, I actually think you deserve *this*.' She whizzed a shiny red packet over the carousel very fast in the direction of his face. Luke, no slouch in the field of AERO-dynamics, made a smart catch.

AERO-Dynamics

Noun. The art of catching chocolate bars thrown around a crowded workplace at high speed. First developed in relation to a fumbled Mint Aero, but now applied to items of confectionery more generally.

'Wow! How come? Did you...?'

'Don't ask. But it's yours. You earned it.'

'Let's share.' He ripped open the KitKat and broke off a finger for her.

'You don't have to, you know,' she said.

'Yeah, right.'

'I *knew* it!' she said, nibbling the edges of the chocolate finger in that way she had.

'Knew what?'

'Ziggy had his doubts, but I always knew you could be trained.'

Chapter 68

July 25 was Thread the Needle Day. Luke had the feeling the phrase could mean quite a few things, so he looked it up in Urban Dictionary. He was familiar with the gaming sense already: '*The act of killing someone in a shooter game by shooting the bullet through a narrow space at distance. Usually done with a sniper rifle and with only one shot.*' There was a similar sporting sense: '*If the quarterback completes a pass to a slot receiver running across the field while two or three defenders are converging.*' But there were also a handful of meanings related to going to the loo, and about half a dozen sexual ones, at least two of which sounded utterly impossible.

A few days later, on Uncommon Instrument Day, Luke popped down to see Michael the Cone, who was performing in his usual spot. In honour of this special Day (that he had, of course, never heard of until Luke told him about it), Michael did a rendition of 'Cavatina', the sublime fifth movement of Beethoven's String Quartet in B-flat major, followed by an atonal free-jazz piece of his own composition.

'Wow,' said Luke. 'I never knew you had so much... range.'

'Ah, you know how it is,' said Michael. 'You have to give the masses what they want. Your "Dam Busters" and your "Great Escapes" and your "Self-Preservation Societies". Most people rushing past – they just don't have time for the classy stuff.'

Luke asked Michael if he could have a go on his cone. It was much harder than it looked, and he was quite out of breath after a couple of minutes. He came away with a new respect for the cone-player's art, plus a mild case of gastroenteritis and £3.73 in very small change.

CHAPTER 69

July 26 was All or Nothing Day. A fitting day, then, for Luke to decide that he would find a way to meet Yasmine (The One) at the airport and confront her with the full force of his love. It was also Aunts and Uncles Day. Luke decided to give Aunt Maud another ring.

'Tell me more about my dad,' he said.

'Your dad was never really around much, don't you remember?'

'It's all a bit hazy.'

'Even when he and Angie were still together, he was always off out. He went off on so-called business trips at the drop of a hat. Never really lifted a finger round the house. Alan was far more of a dad to you than your actual dad ever was. That man is a saint. You do know that, don't you?'

'Why did they split up?'

'Hah! Why didn't she kick him out years before, is more the question. I suppose... You were very small. Angie probably thought that having him around was better than being on her own. Only she pretty much was, really.'

Luke said nothing. He found all this hard to hear. His own perceptions of his dad had been changing over the past few months, but it was all moving very fast. Maud sighed. 'Look. Your dad isn't a bad man, as such. He meant well, and he could be quite fun, as you know. He was just a bit hopeless, lazy and selfish. Oh – and he couldn't keep his dick in his trousers.'

'I feel you're rather stepping on your own point now.'

'Well, he couldn't. He had the best partner and a lovely kid at home, and he just kept looking elsewhere. Promised to stop loads of times. Angie gave him so many chances. But he just couldn't help himself.'

'Mum always said there was fault on both sides.'

'The only thing she did wrong, in my book, was putting up with it for so long. She just said that because she never wanted to tarnish your image of your dad. Especially once she knew she was ill.'

Luke was silent; Maud read his thoughts.

'Yes, yes, I know,' she said. 'And here I am trashing his good name,' she said. 'But really, Luke: wouldn't you rather know the truth?'

Luke thought about this for a good moment. He thought about Yasmine's last letter. The truth sounded kind of cool and candid, but he feared there could be something brutish and final about it too. In a similar way, he approved of colonoscopies and root canals and lumbar punctures, he just didn't really want to have anything to do with them personally if possible.

'Er, yes,' he said at last.

'Anyway, you don't have to take it from me,' said Maud. 'Why don't you just ask him yourself?'

'I do message him, but he's not exactly easy to get hold of,' said Luke. 'I don't think he's been in the country for at least eighteen months. I think he's in Dubai again at the moment.'

There was a sharp intake of breath on the other end of the line, followed by an impulsive rustling, rummaging sound.

'Here, Luke,' said Maud. 'Take this number down.' Maud dictated a landline number that began with the digits 01256.

'What's this then?' asked Luke. 'A new office contact?'

'That is your dad's home number. He's been living in Basingstoke since 2015.'

AUGUST

CHAPTER 70

The first day of the new month began with a rude awakening. Luke and Ziggy – who had taken to sleeping at the end of Luke's bed – were jolted into consciousness by an imperious rapping noise that sounded a bit like, indeed was, a co-habiting fiend banging on the wall with his walking stick.

'Luke! Ziggy! Kitchen in fifteen if you would, please. I need an update on the Make Every Day Count Challenge. Recent Days observed, plans for the next fortnight, review of ground rules. Milo's on his way. Quick smart: you know the drill!'

Luke was sort of pleased to see Dom back. He liked his mad gestures and extended long-term stunts to take place against a background of stable predictability. It was reassuring, after a Day spent shaking hands with strangers or speaking like an Elizabethan or walking houseplants round the neighbourhood, to return home and find all the old familiar things in place: Milo battering down the door to ask if Luke and Ziggy would come on the trampoline with him, Mrs Hart waving inanely down from her window, Alan out in the garden moving with slow, earnest purpose among his courgettes and his chard, and Dom taunting him for his lack of character, mediocre attainments, and poor life choices.

Dom was a hard taskmaster, a pitiless judge of human frailty (well, Luke's frailty), a so-called 'old friend' with the empathy levels of a drive-in morgue. He got away with all this because everyone assumed that no one could really be that big an arsehole. You felt obliged to assume the best about him – assume that he was secretly a huge softie with a soul so delicate he had to wrap it in the most thornily sadistic exterior. And Dom was happy to indulge you in this delusion.

Dom was scrolling now through the previous fortnight's blog entries. 'Looking in a mirror, phoning up an aunt, riffing on flying ants and lunar place names... It's all too easy, Luke! I mean: Where's the indignity? The pointless self-sacrifice? The exposure to easy ridicule?! We are *slipping* here, people!'

Luke pointed out that the summer months actually offered rather slim pickings for the Fake Holiday aficionado. Dom sighed and tutted, and said there would have to be consequences.

'Okay, boss,' said Luke with subtle sarcasm, and immediately regretted it. Dom gave every indication that he already considered himself to be Luke's boss as far as the Make Every Day Count challenge went. It didn't do to make him feel you didn't take his role seriously. It didn't do to poke the bear.

Luke had learned the hard way that when Dom suggested a Day challenge and you didn't look suitably dazed, demoralised or terrified by the idea, he would scratch his suggestion and come up with something even worse. So now, when Dom came up with something that Luke secretly thought was quite doable and only mildly embarrassing (and since National Gimp Day his perception of embarrassment had shifted quite considerably) he would pretend to shudder with apprehension.

This month, alas, Dom had awarded himself two Jokers – two Challenges that couldn't be refused so long as (according to the latest edition of the ground rules) they didn't break the law; and didn't involve nudity, cosplay, hallucinogens, unreasonable risk of injury or dismissal, or eating stoned fruit.

And this time, Luke had no need to feign terror.

Though he and Dom were bog-standard hopeless blokes straight from central casting, lacking in basic emotional intelligence, empathy or communication skills, it was nevertheless not possible for them to have shared a flat all these years without learning a few things about each other – well, for Dom not to have learnt a few things about Luke anyway. No one knew anything about Dom.

'Dom, I can't do that. Or *that*.' He had managed to pick perhaps the two things that Luke most hated and feared in the world. 'Anyway, they both fall on the same day, so I only have to do one.'

Dom's eyes narrowed. 'I did say Double Joker.'

'I just can't.'

Dom vaped thoughtfully. 'If you take on both these Challenges, I won't play another Joker till December.'

Luke shook his head. It didn't matter what Dom offered. This was naked fear, and it brooked no negotiation. He thought long and hard. How could he get out of this hole? He was duty-bound by stupid primeval rules of banterdom to see this stupid thing through. But fear was fear. And terror, panic, dread and horror... were terror, panic, dread and horror.

'Okay, Okay,' he said at last, with the quiet complacency of a poker player who knows he's holding the winning card and can now afford to have a bit of fun. (Luke had never actually played poker, or he might have realised this analogy wasn't a very good one.)

'I'll take on this Double Joker challenge... on one condition.'

Dom eyed him with sadistic suspicion. 'And what's that?'

'That you tell me where you've been the last couple of weeks.' Really, it was genius. Dom was super-secretive about his movements, and Luke knew from multiple attempts over the years that nothing would make him give up information about his sudden and frequent absences. Dom would have to back down, and Luke would escape his double doom without losing face. Look at Dom's face now! Already, he was sighing and shaking his head.

'Oh well,' he said.

'Oh well indeed!' trilled Luke in triumph.

'You'll find out eventually anyway.'

'Eh?'

'*Deal.*'

'Eh?'

'Roll on August 16th!'

CHAPTER 71

Luke tried to take his mind off August 16 by staging a water balloon fight for Water Balloon Day (August 5). It was a predictably one-sided and brutal affair, in which Milo and Grace leapt out from various hiding places around the garden and pelted Luke and Alan till they were sodden. Alan was surprisingly quick on his feet for such a tall man, and he began with some strong feints and dodges among the strawberry canes. But a poor choice of combat footwear – slip-on wellies – proved to be his downfall, and his resistance crumbled completely when he slipped on a growbag and collided with a plastic compost bin most comically. Ziggy got hit by quite a few balloons too, which he seemed to enjoy. Luke suggested they make special balloons for him filled with a canine body-shampoo solution, as the dog was beginning yet again to smell rather alarmingly of dog. ('It's funny how people always say *smells of dog*,' mused Dom later, 'When what we really mean is *smells of shit*.') After a while the kids dispensed with the balloons and simply tipped great buckets of cold water over the adults from the garage roof.

Milo lured Dom into the garden, claiming that Luke had fallen into the fish-pond. Dom came striding out, ready to take some pics of this delectable scene, and the kids poured an entire bucket of cold water on his head. The whole scene froze for a long moment. Dom had never really been got before. There was something about his pantomime evil aura (plus stick) that had always seemed to make him immune to such things. Why everyone should grant a cloak of impunity to the ongoing author of all their humiliations made no sense, but somehow that was the way their world had always operated. How would Dom respond?

He seemed a little shocked at first, gasping as the wave of cold and wet washed over him. He staggered a little on his legs, lost hold of his stick. 'Are you all right, Uncle Dom?' called Milo anxiously. Ziggy came over and jumped up at him with concern. (He also tried to run off with the walking stick, but it seemed well meant.)

Dom turned round, looked up and fixed his attacker with a steely glare. 'I'm quite all right, thank you, Milo. Did you manage to see who it was that assaulted me?'

'We didn't,' called down Grace, appearing next to her brother on the roof. 'It all happened so fast. They overpowered us!'

Dom paused, coughed a little, and wiped his still-dripping face with one of his lurid crimson handkerchiefs. 'Well, do you think you would recognise them if you saw them again?'

'It's possible. We could try.'

'Well if you see them out and about, let me know. I have quite the punishment in store.'

'What will you do, Uncle Dom?'

'I will round them up, tie them up against that wall over there, pin their ears open...'

Milo was agog. 'And what then, Uncle Dom?'

'...And force them to listen to the first ten chapters of Luke's novel.' Unseen by anyone, he had all the while been creeping over to the hose tap in the kitchen wall, which he now switched on and directed up onto the garage roof. Milo and Grace squealed in delight. Luke and Alan looked at each other and burst out laughing too. Who would have thought it? Dom was a good sport. Perhaps they should invent a new Day to mark the moment.

Chapter 72

In his show-and-tell for National Fresh Breath Day (August 6), Luke explained to a rapt audience of three (Grace, Alan and Dom) that bad breath has always been with us. He quoted Ovid from *The Art of Love*: '"She whose breath is tainted should never speak before eating, and she should always stand at a distance from her lover's face".' The ancient Egyptians invented a kind of breath mint three thousand years ago, made with spices like myrrh and cinnamon. For the Elizabethans, 'sweet breath' was a highly-regarded quality in a lover, and Shakespeare's Cleopatra fears the Romans' *'thick breaths, rank of gross diet'*. Luke was astonished to discover that, in a letter to her sister Cassandra, Jane Austen said of some neighbors: *'I was as civil to them as their bad breath would allow me.'* At this point, Grace stomped off. She had a date that night, and had hoped for some practical tips.

It was Listerine which created the market for a product that no one till then had really known they'd needed. Originally branded as an all-purpose antiseptic, Listerine was repositioned by the founder's son, Gerard Barnes Lambert, after he read about a condition called 'halitosis' in *The Lancet* in 1925. So began a long series of not-so-subtle campaigns tapping into a growing fear of germs and promoting Listerine as the scientific solution to a newly medicalised condition with awful side effects: social rejection, professional failure, spinsterhood. '*No matter how charming you may be or how fond of you your friends are, you cannot expect them to put up with halitosis (unpleasant breath) forever. They may be nice to you – but it is an effort.*'

A couple of days later, Luke and Milo were caught veg-handed as they tried to slip some gratuitous fresh produce onto various neighbours' doorsteps. 'What on earth are you doing?' 'What's all this crap?' and 'No fly-tipping' were typical of the responses they received.

'It's National Sneak Some Zucchini Onto Your Neighbor's Porch Day,' Luke began helplessly to another suspicious neighbour. 'Although Alan didn't have any zucchini, I'm afraid. He only had chard and these odd-looking conjoined squash.' He wondered if this would all sound more convincing if he knew what zucchini was.

'Okay,' said the neighbour. 'But why didn't you just knock?'

'Then it wouldn't be sneaking,' said Milo, with a disarming grin.

Sigh. It was hard work being a good neighbour. Perhaps if they lived in the country – ideally about a century ago – people would appreciate the gift of veggie edibles appearing miraculously on their doorstep overnight. It was a lovely idea, after all: in seasons where you had too much fresh homegrown produce, you secretly passed some on to a neighbour who might be in greater need. Sort of waste not, want not meets random act of kindness. But here in the city, there was so much suspicion and cynicism (not to mention lots of video doorbells) that such surreptitious gifting was almost impossible. With a mission like today's, you were instantly taken for a thief or a scammer or a weirdo. Admittedly chard was a terrible choice, the sort of thing appreciated only by crusty allotment-holders, and the oddly-conjoined squash seemed a pretty hostile offering too. The best people to give them to, Luke and Milo quickly discovered, were people who were out.

Luke wasn't sure what he could do with Middle Child Day (August 12), but Grace soon put him straight. Over the last fifty years, she explained, fertility rates had dropped significantly worldwide – in 1952, the average global family had five children, but by 2020 it was 2.4. This meant, of course, that the middle child – of which she was one, she said, sitting as she did between Luke and Milo – was quietly being squeezed out. 'And yet,' stormed Grace, 'no one even cares!'

'This is, like, the most middle-child outburst ever,' vaped Dom.

CHAPTER 73

On August 15, Best Friends Day, Luke asked Holly to lunch.

'But it's got to be with your Best Friend!' she protested with a smile.

'Well, I can't think of anyone else,' said Luke, 'so you'll have to do.'

They had a nice chat about various topics, including the redundancy threat (not really much of a threat since it would mean a chance to find a real job and not have to work for Greg and Phaedra anymore), and Muriel's new ringtone.

'It's driving me insane.'

'I know! And she has it so loud!'

'I wouldn't mind but she does that little dance too every time it goes off.'

'I suppose we shouldn't begrudge her – it makes her so happy. I reckon she gets people to keep calling her up just so she can hear it again.'

'That's as maybe. But I swear if I hear it one more time, I'm going to murder her.'

'You mean this one?' Luke stood up and did a little dance as he sang: '*You do the Shake n' Vac, and put the freshness back...*' Holly punched him hard in the stomach.

And so it was that a new term entered *The Dictionary of Office Life*: Dead Ringer.

Dead ringer

Noun. A colleague who has no idea that their new comedy mobile ringtone is provoking murderous thoughts throughout the office.

Holly had been oddly reticent about Tall Guy (as he was known in the office), and Luke was keen to prise out of her some details of what was really happening.

'He's really nice,' she said at last. 'We're taking it very slow.'

'How many times have you seen him?'

'We've had four dates, I think.'

'And what do you do?'

'Oh, go for walks, get coffee, feed the ducks in the park, that sort of thing.'

'Lots of outdoor stuff.'

'Well, yes.'

'And... does he have hidden heights? Sorry.' Luke regretted his flippant remark as he saw Holly's face fall.

'Here we go again. Come on, give it your best. Let's hear what you've got. *He stoops to bonk her* is my favourite so far.' Luke could tell she was putting a brave face on things.

'I'm sorry, Hol. Tell me how it's going. Really.'

'Oh, he's really nice. He's kind. He's just... I don't know. It's like he's...'

'What?'

'Really fecking tall! I know it shouldn't matter but it kind of really does. He can't fit into my Micra without turning it into a clown car. If we're standing at a bar I end up with neckache from shouting up at Mount Boyfriend all night. And it's a bit like hugging your dad.'

'But... if you like him?'

'I know, I know. None of this would really matter if there was a real spark between us. It's all so nice. But there's no... I mean, he'd never just sit and have a boozy lunch like this, making up silly words and doing the Shake n' Vac dance.'

'Well, we all have our unique talents.'

'It's just all so "pleasant" and "agreeable".' She put these two words in scathing scare quotes as she said them. 'I never come back from a date with him and think: God, that was so funny, I just couldn't stop laughing. Or, we just had so much fun I don't even know where the time went. You know, like we do.'

'We do?'

'Yes, we do.'

'Yes, but. You know, we're mates. There's no pressure on us. He's probably sitting there panicking about the best moment to go in for a kiss.'

'Trust me, I'll see it a mile off.'

'We don't have that pressure.'

'So what – you're saying you can't have chemistry *and* a good laugh with your partner?'

'Hey – I didn't make the rules.'

It was a nice long lunch, all the more relaxed and open-ended in the knowledge that Greg and Phaedra were away in Lanzarote for a week's 'business strategy brainstorming', so no one was waiting back at the office with a beady eye on the clock. A bottle of rosé had slipped down very easily, and Holly linked her arm in Luke's as they made their rather woozy way back to the ranch.

'Thanks for thinking of me today,' she said. 'Means a lot.'

'Think nothing of it, mate,' he said, and squeezed her arm.

'When I'm with you,' she said, 'I don't feel I have to try. Or worry about how you're going to react to something I say.'

'Thanks very much,' he said with mock indignation.

She punched him playfully. 'You know that's a good thing, right?'

'I know,' he said, after a moment. 'I feel the same.'

'I just don't get why you can't have that with a boyfriend. You and Yazz seem to manage it.' She looked at him searchingly a minute. Luke thought for a moment of Yasmine (The One). Conversation *and* chemistry? He wasn't sure they had either.

'You'll be telling me you have a divine right to happiness next,' he said.

'I know,' she said. 'It's a lottery. I just don't get how hard it is to meet someone who wants the same things you do.'

'You will! Your trouble is you keep selling yourself short. Trying to settle for all these deadbeats that don't deserve you.'

She smiled. 'You think I'm aiming too low?'

'I know you are.' She smiled at him again in an oddly pointed way.

'I know what you're thinking,' he said. 'You think I'm aiming too high.'

'I never said that,' she said. 'I just think that maybe, in our different ways, we both deserve better. Or we need to get better at aiming.'

'Oh God,' said Luke, with a glance at his watch.

'It's okay,' said Holly. 'The bosses are away, remember. We can't really be late.'

'No, it's not that. I've just realised it's the 16th tomorrow.'

'I'll be there.'

'Thanks, mate.'

CHAPTER 74

On the evening of August 16, Luke and Holly met Dom at Victoria and the three of them squeezed onto a fast-ish train to the coast. Dom was in good spirits, and had brought along a six-pack of Spanish lager.

'I honestly don't know if I can do this,' Luke said, yet again. 'Or the other.' The countryside flew past – fields flooded with the recent rain, home-made jumps for ponies, cluttered gardens and the open backs of terraced houses. Normally Luke loved to peer into all the windows, and imagine the lives of the people he whizzed past. He would look for evidence of passion among the saucepans, of teenage rows and newborn chaos. Today, however, the undulating rail seemed directly plugged into the line of panic that coursed through his bloodstream.

At the station they walked down to the beach. Luke felt so nauseous he couldn't speak. Dom had a hand on Luke's back, like a plain-clothes officer who has agreed not to embarrass a suspect with cuffs on condition that he comes quietly. 'You don't have to do this, you know,' said Holly, for perhaps the tenth time. 'No one is making you do any of this.'

'She's absolutely right of course, old boy,' said Dom vapingly.

'Fuck him,' snarled Luke with uncharacteristic venom. He didn't know why he was here. But he sensed dimly that the die was already cast. Even to have come this far was to have assented to the ordeal. The decision had been irrevocably taken days ago.

He didn't remember exactly when he had conceived such a horror of rollercoasters. He'd never been especially good with heights or with speed, so that of course came into it. He'd like to be able to say that he had a traumatic primal memory of being forced onto a ride when he was little, against his will, perhaps because he was desperate to curry favour with an elusive parent, okay, elusive dad. It sounded sort of right, but he had no memory of such a thing. What he did recall was that, every time he got a bit drunk, there'd be a moment in the evening when he felt his heart race and lurch and sway like he was being forced over impossible metal curves and arcs. He'd have to just brace himself and wait for the feeling to go away, while all round the oblivious evening chuckled and bantered its way on.

Now they were in the queue, just him and Holly. (Dom had tapped his bad hip and pleaded a medical exemption.) Luke actually heard a couple in front of him mention that it was National Rollercoaster Day. Ordinarily this would have pleased him mightily, as no one had heard of most of the Days he was observing, and Holly did try and engage them in conversation. 'Talk to me, talk to someone,' she kept saying. 'It'll take your mind off things.' She squeezed his arm. 'You don't have to do this, you know,' she said yet again. He pushed her hand away with an irritable shrug. Her attempts to reassure him only reminded him how shit-scared he was. He should have felt guilty for this, but all his feeling glands were full of fear; there was no space left for anything else. The queue took forever, time for his panic to reach near-frenzy levels. And then they were in, and a youth with pitiless metallic eyes was going down the line pushing down a pitiless metallic straitjacket around each victim's shoulders.

'Do something, do something!' he screamed. 'Take my mind off this bloody thing!'

On a sudden impulse, Holly leaned across and kissed him hard on the lips. It kind of worked, for a moment. The train shot off abruptly, then slowed down just as suddenly, then slowly started to build speed again. Their teeth banged with the first jolt, and their heads pulled apart.

This rollercoaster was called Ride The Rat. Part of it was outside, built on the top of a large amusement arcade, and Luke could see the twinkling lights of the seaside town and the glint of a million parked cars stretched out below him, and beyond that the sea itself, a patchwork of greys, dirty blues and wavy wrinkles. But then he couldn't see anything because he was just screaming and crying and praying and clutching Holly and swearing violently and shaking and bracing himself for imminent death. He did all these things, and all at once, as the little rodent train swept up and plunged down, and then appeared to be driving itself off the side of the building before executing a hard right-hander at impossible speed, and then plunged inside the building into a section in total darkness, where the ride corkscrewed one way and then the other, and you waited for it to shoot up but it plunged down into a black void, and your soul fell with it and then – just as you were resigned to terminal impact, and discovered there was no time for a life to flash before your eyes, not even one as banal and pointless a life as your own – you shot upwards once more and actually went right over. After this, the train slowed, and you began to shiver with relief, until the whole thing started up again, and you died a few more thousand deaths.

Afterwards, Holly, who had held him tight throughout, would show him the cluster-claw of bruises which he had imprinted on her forearm. Luke managed to still the worst of his weeping and whimpering before emerging from the survivors' tunnel in triumph.

'I'm alive!' he croaked.

'I don't mind rollercoasters as a rule,' said Holly, 'but I've got to say that was really quite mental.'

'Oh, indeed,' said Dom. 'It's considered one of Britain's top ten wildest rides.'

'Top ten *mildest* rides, you told me,' said Luke. 'That was the only reason I agreed to do it.'

'Did I?' said Dom. 'It's so easy to mix up one's M's and one's W's.'

'You can be a bit of an arsehole sometimes, can't you, Dom?'

'Oh come, come,' he vaped unperturbed, 'look at our young hero now. He is positively aglow! Tell me, young man,' he said, turning to Luke. 'Do you not feel you finally just came of age? In our society we lack the sacred initiation rites that other, doubtless more enlightened communities perform in order to launch their male-folk over the threshold from youth to manhood.'

'He's thirty-two, Dom.'

'And not before time, I quite agree.'

'And what about you, Dom?' pursued Holly. 'It feels like you could do with a spot of maturing too. What shall we do to initiate you?'

Dom looked at her with an expression Luke didn't think he had seen before. He couldn't put a name to it, but it lacked either malice or irony. Then he looked away.

'Oh,' he said at last. 'I'm sure the gods will come up with something.'

CHAPTER 75

After a pint in a nearby pub, the trio walked a few streets back from the seafront to another pub, this one called The Happy Hippo, outside which was a large banner featuring a laughing hippo and the words "OPEN MIC COMEDY TONIGHT! ALL COMERS WELCOME". Today was also Tell A Joke Day, which had given Dom the idea of challenging Luke to do a spot of stand-up. As Dom knew, the idea of performing stand-up was perhaps the only thing on the planet that Luke feared more than rollercoasters, and the triumphant glow from the first fear confronted was not enough to have him look at the second, so hard on its heels, with anything like equanimity.

The bar had a large, hangar-like back room with a small, raised platform at one end, facing about a hundred seats set out in narrow rows. Most of the seats were taken already by a crowd that looked youngish and quite hip: lots of piercings and tats everywhere, splashes of blue and pink hair, a fair bit of artfully sculpted beard.

Luke was on third. He didn't ask how; he just knew Dom would have set it all up. He would rather have gone first, get it over and done with. Jump through the ring of fire. If he caught fire, so be it, he might as well get on with the burning. There were fourteen acts in all, and third was far better than seventh or eleventh or last. This was not what he would have thought that he would have been thinking at this moment, he had to admit. The fact that he had not yet run out of the bar screaming down the road made him wonder if the rollercoaster experience hadn't perhaps changed him after all. He didn't want to do this, he dreaded it horribly; and yet, again, something in him had already assented to it. He'd died many times this year already. Did one more time matter?

Luke had had a horror of public speaking for as long as he could remember. He agreed with those surveys which always found that large numbers of people would rather die than speak in public. And stand-up was the ultimate public-speaking horror. Luke had recurring nightmares about this. Standing on a stage, pinned in the limelight, soul on the line, unable to stop himself spewing out toe-curling confessions and/or wetting his trousers while the horde stared on, crushing his paltry efforts at wit with wave after wave of malevolently mirthless laughter.

'I can't do this, I can't do this!' Luke wailed as his time approached. He kept standing up and sitting down again, as if he was about to bolt from the hall and run all the way back to London. When his name was called at last, he picked up his bag and turned to flee.

'Do it!' hissed Dom.

Holly looked at him in exasperation, then yanked Luke down by the neck, kissed him hard again, and shoved him towards the stage.

The expectant chatter died down as Luke swayed onto the stage. A few people tittered; he looked so terrified they imagined it must be part of the act. He felt lifeless, breathless, utterly unreal. He couldn't really see the people in front of him – Holly had advised him to remove his contacts, which did sort of help. He had decided not to say his name, or begin with one of those dreadful clichéd gambits that stand-ups always favoured ('How many of you came here by train tonight – put up your hands'). Instead he said, 'What do you do with a sick bee?' His delivery was deathless, muted. No one made a noise. 'Take it to the waspital.' A couple of people tittered. 'Why are Greek people always laughing?' he continued. And then, almost without waiting: 'Because they have a great sense of hummus.' There were a few guffaws, but also some groans. Luke could make out the fuzzy shape of Holly to the side of him right in the front. Even though he couldn't really see her, he sensed her as a warm, vague cloud of encouragement. Next to her, Dom's elegantly hunched frame emanated a quite different aura – quiet satisfaction at another expertly executed humiliation.

'Actually, he's the only reason I'm here,' Luke heard himself saying now. He pointed at Dom. 'He made me do this.' The crowd were silent again. 'What's a chiropodist's favourite flavour crisp? Cheese and bunion.' Still silence, though some coughing and stirring had started up. He looked over at Holly again. She was smiling at him, willing him on. He had a strange half-memory of her kissing him at high speed. Suddenly he forgot to care anymore.

'Yeah,' said Luke with venom. In between gags borrowed from his Asda Christmas cracker triumph, Luke started to talk about his life with Dom. 'Hands up: how many of you have a nightmare flatmate?' Quite a few, it seemed. Luke told everyone how he and Dom had had a bet to win the use of a chair, and as a result he'd had to sleep on a roundabout and dress up as a gimp on the Tube and talk to the bumps of women who weren't pregnant. A few chuckles. And Dom had a walking stick and no one knew why. And someone had given Luke a dog because he'd pretended to care about a schoolmate that had died by sniffing a cowpat. And he didn't actually know where his so-called girlfriend – the so-called love of his life – actually lived. He would like to find out, but he didn't seem to have a phone number or an email address that worked (the inbox to which he once sent his long, impassioned messages was now apparently full, perhaps with the weight of all his purple prose). Peals of laughter. And he hadn't seen his dad for years because he'd been working abroad. Only he hadn't really, he'd been in Basingstoke all this time, where he was basically hiding out from his son. Luke found his way into some sort of strange rhythm, where each of these humiliating confessions was punctured by another of his own made-up cracker gags. 'Why was the onion crying? Because it cut itself.' 'What's an airline pilot's favourite flavour of crisp? Plain.' 'Where do the English relay team train? Handover.' The whole thing started to seem like it had been artlessly crafted, and Luke spoke without an ounce of self-pity or emotion. Really, it was as if he was speaking about someone else.

By the end of his eight minutes – perhaps the longest eight minutes of his life, not counting the rollercoaster ride – the crowd were cheering and whistling. The MC – an abrasive man in sparkly glasses and bright-red jacket – invited the crowd to give Luke another round of applause. They cheered with gusto, until the MC said: 'Now why don't we get this Dom we've heard so much about up on the stage too?'

Dom stood at once. He was impervious to embarrassment; it was one of his superpowers. He hopped smartly up onto the stage, where, still holding his beer, he raised his glass to Luke.

'So,' said the compere when all the cheering and pantomime boos had died down. 'What have you go to say for yourself, our Dom?'

'Well, well, well,' said Dom to the compere. 'I must say I thought your opening routine was poor, but Luke really took it down several more notches. What an absolute shitshow.' It was all delivered with the deadpan callousness of Simon Cowell, and the crowd loved it. 'But tonight's been valuable – I think it's important for Luke to see that he really has no talent, in this or any other direction.'

'Meow!' said the MC. 'Why don't you tell us what you really think, Dom?'

Dom held up his hand until the crowd stopped jeering. 'All

right, all right,' he said. And again that mysterious expression. 'Today I challenged Luke to confront his deepest fears, not once but twice. And I am frankly in awe at his courage.' Luke, who was sitting back with Holly, waiting for the next put-down, felt a lump in his throat. Dom raised his glass. 'Let me just say now, while I can: Luke, you are a *fecking mensch*. You're not funny, obviously, but you are a *fecking mensch*.'

CHAPTER 76

Luke had promised to take Milo out on Geocaching Day (August 17), so he signed up for an app and they set off for what promised to be a fun day's quirky treasure-hunting. Their nearest site, according to the app, was a little enclosed garden next to a Victorian church that was locally famous for being home to an ancient oak tree. Previous finders on the app, Luke saw, had complimented the hider on the ingenuity of their hiding-place. There was even a pic of the spot, accompanied by a caption that said the cache was fully visible if you knew where or how to look.

Well, Luke and Milo looked and looked. The picture didn't quite match the scene they found; the section of fencing looked the same but the planting and flower beds seemed to have been moved around. They looked and looked some more but could still find nothing, even with the help of the extra hint. The only one who didn't show any signs of tiring was Ziggy, who loved rooting around in undergrowth and was delighted to discover his pals were, for once, up for an extended rooting and flushing session too. Part car aerial, part palm tree, his newly groomed tail wagged in furious delight. But after about a fruitless hour and a half, Milo was fed up, and they headed home defeated.

Looking through the app, Luke found it interesting to read other people's comments on their own searches, and what these said about them. '*I can't find it!*' wailed some, as he and Milo had done, assuming the fault lay with themselves, not the hider. Others, with arrogant certainty, stated baldly: '*It's not there.*' The implication: I can't find it, so it can't be there. Rather than log an embarrassed '*DNF*' (did not find) such people were more likely to mark a cache site as '*Needs Maintenance.*'

As with any self-respecting subculture, the policing of protocols was highly evolved – and Alehunter ('*interests: craft beer, angling, museums*', a man with 4714 finds to his name) was not happy. '*First of all thanks* 😊 *to the last person who irritatingly had the stupid idea of replacing the cache a few feet up in the hollow of a small evergreen* 🌲 *tree. Not Happy. It was after my fourth sweep* 🧹 *along the fence that I noticed it – this after 20-25 minutes pointlessly combing the area. I knew what I was looking for as the hint states it's at ground level which I am glad to say it is now! Sick of these silly buggers making life more difficult for us genuine geocachers.*' He did not sound like the sort of man who would take kindly to a bunch of free veg deposited on his doorstep.

Luke could sort of see how geocaching could become obsessive. You got to discover all sorts of interesting places, you could even travel the world, and there was a community of like-minded enthusiasts to connect with. Then again, life was short, and he was perhaps signed up for enough wild goose chases already.

CHAPTER 77

For his summer holiday, Luke went away for a week with Ziggy, Alan and the kids to a small resort in Dorset. It had the faded grandeur of a place that had once been popular with aristocrats and beautiful people of a bygone age, but now seemed rather on its uppers. In among the occasional artisanal cheese emporium and craft ale pop-up, there were big piles of rubbish along the esplanade, and rough sleepers on the beach. It was a fun week of not doing very much, reading books and hanging out on beaches, interspersed with day trips to a monkey sanctuary, two water parks and a rather dilapidated aquarium. Ziggy saw the sea for the first time and ran panicking away from the tide. Then he ventured back, and back again, and soon it was almost impossible to tear him away. He loved to wade in and retrieve a ball undulating on the shallow waves, though he would never go out of his depth.

There was no chance of a holiday for those (Luke) observing the Make Every Day Count challenge, of course, but at least there was no Dom to supervise, critique or censor Luke's lazy, holiday-style choices. He ate chocolate pecan pie on National Chocolate Pecan Pie Day, sponge cake on National Sponge Cake Day, and waffles on National Waffle Day. He went round with a big pink bow in his hair on International Bow Day ('bloody arty-farty Londoners', he heard a local snark). With Grace's help, he attempted a Brazilian blowout on Brazilian Blowout Day, and they all made an extra fuss of Ziggy on National Dog Day, an entirely unnecessary observance since the cockerpoo was spoilt rotten every day of the year. But this at least was one observance that Dom, who was secretly as soppy towards Ziggy as anyone, would have approved.

The only Day that week that was observed in less than perfunctory style was Be An Angel Day. Alan, who was getting more and more into the challenges, found a class in something called Horse-Riding With Angels, at a stables a few miles up the road. Okay, it wasn't actually *being* an angel, but they all agreed it was close enough. He dropped Luke at the place, which went by the name of Illumination Ranch, and retired with the kids to a nearby maize maze until such time as Luke messaged to say he was done, or just sent for help.

Luke found himself in a class with half a dozen well-spoken ladies in their thirties and forties, all regular angel-riders as it turned out. Their teacher, Maya, a jodhpur-clad lady of similar look and age, wore a bright-pink riding hat and spangly purple jumper, both colours Luke suspected were deeply significant at some intense vibrational level.

Maya began – and this apparently struck the rest of the group as an obvious, even banal thing to do at the start of a horse-riding lesson – by spraying a liquid in the air that she said contained the essence of a disembodied spirit guide whose messages she regularly channelled. Luke had little time to process this, though he did detect a pleasing vanilla-y scent that reminded him agreeably of Holly, because after that they all went straight into a little group meditation on horseback. Maya said a few words of aetheric welcome, something about energy and portals and veils. Then they all sat in their saddles in silence, with everyone urged to privately summon the angels 'in your own way'. ('*Come on, Angels – let's do this!*' said Luke in his head. It felt crass and clunky, but it was all he could think of.) Oddly, the horses seemed to join in with the prayer too, solemnly dropping their heads as one in silent invocation.

Next, it was the moment to choose an Angel Card from a basket. Each colourful little card carried an inspirational word like "*Joy*" or "*Forgiveness*" or "*Generosity*", a personally significant message to guide each rider through their lesson. Luke got "*Serendipity*". Then Maya said the riders should each choose a card for their horse. It wasn't entirely clear at precisely which particular gem of wisdom his mount's great flaring nostrils were pointed, but Luke did his best. 'Ooh look! Misty's got "*Patience*"! Well *done*, Luke!' squealed Maya delightedly.

So to the lesson itself. Luke had never had a riding lesson before, so he didn't have much to compare it with, but most of it struck him as probably pretty standard, except perhaps when he was advised to reflect on 'the serendipity of patience' and 'the patience of serendipity'. It sounded like dreadful nonsense at first, but there was something very agreeable about the crisp barn air, with its mingled smells of sawdust, fresh manure, and essence of disembodied spirit guide. As a nervous newbie, he'd been given a beautiful chestnut mare, Misty, who was gentle and responsive and not too tall. Luke had always been nervous around horses, but Misty was so calm and forgiving of his clunky technique – *patient*, one might say – that he soon started to enjoy the circuits they made together around the expansive paddock. And when Misty took to picking up her speed at his command – probably still only a light trot but in Luke's mind a dashing gallop – he started to feel really rather exhilarated.

Afterwards, over coffee in Maya's vast Aga-catalogue kitchen, the regulars all joyfully explained how they found they rode 'with a different energy' once the angels had been summoned. Everything was somehow lighter and less scattered. Similarly inspired and illuminated, the horses helped them work through issues, and the solutions they came up with were somehow always informed by that day's Angel Card. Luke was asked if he had anything he'd like to share. He talked a little about the serendipity of meeting Yasmine (The One), and how he was going to surprise her at the airport in a week's time.

'Sometimes, serendipity is not where you look for it,' said Maya.

'How do you mean?' asked Luke.

'Well, sometimes things look serendipitous because we want them to appear so,' she said. 'Whereas the truly serendipitous things... well, it is only when you stop looking for them that you can really *see* them.' Luke wondered if this was dreadful cosmic psychobabble, or if it was secretly very profound. Or perhaps it was both, or either, and which it was depended not on the speaker but on the listener's ability to understand and, well, *hear*. The coffee here was very nice, and he was still on a high from his horse. Then somehow he was talking about his mum, and his dad, and about Alan. He may have wept a little.

'Interesting: you say you work in content,' said Maya. 'But you do not say you are *content*.'

Luke quite liked the idea of angels, but as the conversation moved on, he was a little disconcerted to learn that Maya and her other students firmly believed that angels were only one of a whole pantheon of ethereal creatures, which also included nymphs, fairies and tree spirits. It had been an unexpectedly interesting, even eye-opening (heart-opening?) session, but he sensed that now was his time to return to the everyday levels of existence, before things got too controversial.

'I'm sorry,' he said to the group as he began texting Alan to say he was done, 'I can give you dybbuks, banshees and tulpas. I can entertain the possibility of indigo children and ascended masters. But,' – and here with regret he felt obliged to sound the only discordant note in an otherwise joyously harmonious morning – 'I find myself drawing a mental line this side of goblins.'

CHAPTER 78

At the end of the month, on International Matchmaker Day, Luke found himself at Heathrow airport at 7am. It was over a year and a half since he and Yasmine (The One) had last met. But there she was, over by the sunglasses stand, Terminal 2 airside. She looked wondrous, if a little surprised.

'It was just incredible,' said Luke to Holly in the pub that evening. 'We just picked up from where we left off.' As he eased into his story of the momentous day for his official Best Friend, he remembered suddenly that this day, August 31, was also Grief Awareness Day.

SEPTEMBER

CHAPTER 79

One of the tough things about the Make Every Day Count challenge was the fact that you had to do something every single fecking day for a fecking year, and that could get exhausting and boring, and a year was *so much longer* than people who hadn't attempted the challenge could ever possibly imagine, to the point where you had to wonder whether people who hadn't even attempted the challenge (pretty much everyone but him) even knew in any meaningful sense what a year actually *was*. Another was how you had to keep on chopping and changing every day. Luke often found himself fascinated by a topic or issue he'd never known anything about – like lunar place names or artists with scleroderma or the history of bad breath – only to realise next morning that it was time to hitch up his awareness-raising wagon and pitch camp somewhere else yet again. There were so many interesting things he found out about that he'd have liked to look into more deeply, but the calendar was relentless and with every passing day you were yanked on to the next thing.

To take one example, Luke's cursory research into Grief Awareness Day had led him to look into the famous five stages of grief outlined by Elizabeth Kübler-Ross. We all know them now –

Denial, Anger, Bargaining, Depression, Acceptance – and they are applied to everything, not just human death and dying but dealing with chronic pain, being made redundant, losing a pet, and even more trivial things like an author dealing with a negative book review or a gamer disappointed with a long-awaited upgrade of their favourite shoot-'em-up.

Luke guiltily remembered that he had (with some misplaced ingenuity, though he said it himself) contributed to this process of trivialisation on more than one occasion, most recently in a blog post entitled '*The 5 stages of processing the disappointment of a rejected van cover claim*'. In this piece, Luke argued that the sure sign that you had reached the final stage of Acceptance was when you drew a line under the disappointment and decided to take your van cover needs elsewhere, ideally to the provider on whose website this ingenious article was published.

Now, however, listening to an audiobook of Kübler-Ross's *On Death and Dying*, Luke discovered that the stages she outlined weren't meant to be taken as some sort of universal template at all. They didn't even relate to bereaved people, but were based on Kübler-Ross's own anecdotal observations among a specific group of terminally ill people who were confronting their own imminent demise. As various studies have since concurred and as she herself said, grief is not a linear process; the stages aren't clearly defined hoops that you could jump through in any simplistic trajectory of "progress". Luke himself knew enough about grief to know that it looped here, there, and everywhere, two steps forward and five steps back, round and about and all over the place.

He was thinking all this because September 1 was Letter-Writing Day. Aside from his unsent missives to The One, it had been years, perhaps decades, since he last wrote an actual letter to anyone, although back in the day, when he'd lived abroad, he recalled he used to send them all the time just so he'd get some back. It had been a way of staving off loneliness and homesickness, two sentiments he had never publicly admitted to.

Who then to write to? He could write to his mum, but something about the artificiality of the exercise repelled him. He could write to his dad, but what really would be the point? He could write to Yasmine yet again, and here the Kübler-Ross stuff might come in handy. He could also, should also – as his conscience kept nagging him – write something to Alan.

Complicated. Writing a letter felt portentous. It wasn't like just banging out an email or fat-thumbing a few random words in a text (*Beer @Crown? Thu nite lemme no)*. It raised difficult questions, like what you might say that could be worthy of the form, and who you might want to say it to. Tricky. The obvious thing to do was to park all these difficult questions and focus on the logistics instead. If he was going to write a proper letter, Luke decided, he should have the proper kit. He recalled that his mum had always used one of those old-school zip-up leather letter-writing cases, with a pad of proper blue Basildon Bond letter paper tucked inside, together with various pockets and flaps that contained stamps and envelopes, an ink pen and cartridges. On a sudden impulse, he went over to Alan's and asked him if he knew where the case was. Incredibly, Alan still had it, tucked at the back of a compartment stuffed with boxes and folders on a high shelf in the big pine wardrobe in his bedroom.

'Your mum was a great letter-writer,' he said, fingering the case fondly.

Luke took the case back to his, and inspected the object with reverence. It still had a few cards and letters tucked in one pocket, including a message from her sister, Luke's aunt Maud, and another from her own mum. Looking at the dates, these must have been messages she was planning to reply to, but ran out of time.

Luke found his mum's fountain pen still in its place. The ink had dried up but there was a blue cartridge in another little pocket and after a bit of fiddling and scribbling, he managed to get the pen writing again. He turned to the pad, wrote a name with the very pen his mum had once held, and then paused, deep in thought. Ziggy had miraculously appeared by his side. That dog would turn his nose up at all the fancy special-recipe dogfoods they bought him, but he could sniff out a bit of cold toast from ten miles away. Luke was about to put pen to paper again, when he noticed a loose sheet of the blue paper, folded once at an approximate angle, just jutting out from the back of the pad. He flicked to the back, and found a half-finished note:

My love, I'm sorry I wasn't very with it when you came in today. You do so much, you are our rock. Thanks to you I don't fear for the kids. Don't worry about Luke and don't let him provoke you — it's a hard age for him but in time he will come to appreciate what

Well, that was enough to bring on a touch of the Kübler-Rosses.

CHAPTER 80

On Saturday, September 3, Grace, Milo, Dom and Alan joined Luke for what would prove one of the toughest days of all in the whole year: Digital Detox Day. Dom had set them all a test to see who could last the longest without their digital fix, with the promise of a special prize for the winner. But really, Luke mused: how hard could it be? He began the day with a lie-in, lazing around in bed with an old copy of *Private Eye*. In the bath he'd planned on reading his Kindle – Muriel and Holly had both recommended *The Salt Path* and he was keen to get stuck into the e-book. But Dom ruled that e-readers were technically digital, so Luke had to find a 'real' book to read.

Still only 9.47am; it was amazing how slowly time went when you had no screen to look at.

He flicked through *Chase's Calendar of Events* with a view to planning some more challenges for later in the month, and then decided to update the blog on his recent Day experiences. But he wasn't allowed to type anything because laptops were digital, said Dom, and so – in case anyone was wondering – were smart TVs, bank cards, traffic lights and microwaves. This meant no use of the car, no easy cooking, no ordering pizzas over the phone (even a landline one). And no telly. Luke made a stab at writing up some blog posts by hand, but the thought of having to type them all up again afterwards exhausted him, and he soon gave up.

There now followed a lengthy debate between Alan and Dom about the actual difference between analogue and digital, which quickly became far too technical for Luke to follow. It was clear that Alan – as an engineer – actually understood this stuff, while Dom was mostly reliant on poshly confident bluster, Rees-Mogg style. Alan argued that most microwaves were technically analogue, but Dom countered that the display was digital. In which case, asked Alan, why was it all right to use the washing machine still, which also had a digital display. Dom replied that Milo was washing his shirts for him, for pocket money, and if he didn't get that pink one he liked done today, Grace wouldn't be able to earn her ironing money. Despite this blatant infringement, Dom's wider point actually won out, which was that today's challenge should be all about people unshackling themselves for one day from their over-reliance on the internet and passive electronic stimulation. Alan said he heartily agreed and handed out gardening gloves. 'Nothing more analogue than weeding the fruit trees or rotating the compost!' He smiled. 'Come on, there's lots to do!'

Luke went to do his bit. Whisper it, but he actually quite enjoyed a bit of gardening when he ever got down to it, and was especially keen on mowing and strimming: it was satisfying to see all that rampant greenery brought to order and cut down to size. Mowing the lawn delivered a pleasing before-and-after effect that was surprisingly therapeutic, and there was an aesthetic pleasure in teasing out an elaborate geometric shape in the well-kept green surface. But Dom now called out their kitchen window to say that mowers and strimmers were digital, and only hand implements were to be used. Alan made as if to respond, but then he just smiled, shook his head, and got back to weeding a flower bed. He handed Luke a pair of shears and a scythe to hack out all the weeds that had grown rampant around the veg patch. This turned out to be very hard work, but the blades of both implements, which Alan had done a good job of keeping keen over the years, could at least be applied to their targets with cathartic savagery.

'Are we sure he's not mixing this up with National Amish Day?' called out Luke.

'I think even the Amish are allowed to use farm machinery,' said Alan. 'But it's fun to get back to basics once in a while.'

Grace was the first to crack. She ducked out of Digital Detox Day at 10.44am when she discovered that Dom considered Snapchat and Instagram to be 'digital'.

'Oh, you are chatting the most!' she wailed. 'If I don't reply to my friend in the next minute, there's going to be a disaster!'

'Why, is there an emergency?'

'There will be if Matt thinks I'm airing him!' Matt was the new boyf, or so Milo said. Grace would volunteer no information on the topic herself.

'To air is human,' mused Dom. 'To forgive divine.'

'Stop waffling,' said Grace. 'Also, my Snap streak is over 450. Do you expect me to sacrifice all that work for a stupid medieval bet?' In discussing the flatmates' maturity, Luke often said that his half-sister was apt to confuse the words 'middle-aged' and 'Middle Ages'. Grace replied that she wasn't confused in the slightest.

Milo was next to crack. He did a bit of half-hearted weeding, threw himself around the trampoline for a bit and then retired inside. Then things went suspiciously quiet, and when Alan and Luke went in to suggest a session of board games, they found Milo playing Tank Battle on an old iPad.

'I can't believe you gave in so soon, Milo!' said Alan.

'I didn't give up, I just made a mistake,' he wailed.

'If that's so, why are you sitting under a table?' asked Dom. 'Hidden under a duvet.'

Luke took Ziggy for a long walk. He liked to listen to music or audiobooks as he went round the park and in and out the woods

THANK YOU FOR THE DAYS

that Ziggy loved, but today he was forced to go cold turkey. He was especially disconcerted to realise that he wouldn't be able to check the football scores on his phone, a religious ritual he never neglected.

Instead, he had a nice time chatting to a handful of fellow dog walkers he hadn't seen for a while. He bumped into Michelle.

'How's it been?'

'It's not been great.' Michelle was pleased to see Ziggy, and pleased to see that the blog had raised a bit more money to support people with trigeminal neuralgia. But work had been stressing her out, she said. 'Public speaking and telly always do.'

It occurred to Luke that he had no idea what Michelle's job was. 'I'm a Deputy Detective Chief Inspector with the CID,' she said. 'Murders, mostly. You might have seen me on *Crimewatch*.' It rarely occurred to Luke that all these park characters had full lives beyond the ball thrower and the poo bag, so on his way round he took to asking the jobs of all those he chatted to. He discovered a food stylist (Shih Tzu), a French polisher (labradoodle), a motorway control-room coordinator (two whippets), a Royal Mail lorry driver (Airedale), a British Gas engineer (a husky and a Pomeranian) and a kids' TV producer (two dachshunds). The only awkward moment was when they asked him what he did.

'I'm an SEO copywriter and strategist,' he went with first of all, but even he didn't believe this. 'I... Oh, you know, marketing,' he took to saying. And finally: 'I just type shite for a living.'

Milo, Dom, Alan and Luke spent a few hours after dinner playing board games. Only Alan and Luke were still live contestants in the Digital Detox challenge, of course, but the others were happy to join in as they played Labyrinth, Scrabble, Connect 4, Cover Your Assets and a strangely addictive railway-themed world domination game called Ticket to Ride. Learning the rules took a good half an hour. Then they tried Mind, in which the group had to use telepathy to put numbered cards down in the right order. You start off with a hand of one card each, with the aim of going all the way up to twelve cards per hand. It took a good while to get the hang of this deceptively very simple game, but when they eventually managed to get all the cards out in order with a hand of seven cards each, it felt like a spooky hive-mind triumph. After that, Dom slipped off to the living room to watch *Match of the Day*. It looked as though Alan and Luke would get to share the spoils, but on his way to the loo Luke was caught peeking through a crack in the door at the football.

'Congratulations, Alan! And here is your prize,' said Dom handing over a small squat box.

'Thank you, Dom.'

Alan opened up the box to discover a very basic Casio digital watch, perhaps the cheapest digital object in existence. Its strap was a lurid pink colour.

'Why thank you, Dom!' said Alan wholeheartedly. He immediately strapped it to his wrist and began showing it off to the rest of the group.

'And Luke – you made a valiant effort. You don't go away empty-handed either.' He produced another little box. 'Yours isn't quite such a nice bright colour, though.'

'Thank you, Dom.'

'No need to open it now, I've still got to get a battery for it.'

'Okay, thanks,' said Luke. He put the box to one side. 'So: the challenge is done, the prizes have been dispensed, and I now know that Arsenal lost. It's been a tough day but actually a really interesting one. Thanks, Dom. How about a last game of Scrabble, everyone?'

'Dear God, no,' said Alan, diving for his phone.

CHAPTER 81

Be Late For Something Day (September 5) was devised by the Procrastinators' Club of America in 1956. (They'd meant to do it sooner but...) Luke was still writing his letter, which he had put off finishing since the start of the month, so he decided that counted. He made extra sure by failing to complete his letter on this date too.

At lunchtime, he and Holly nipped out for a sandwich. Holly had a chicken and avocado panini, while Luke went for tuna on a toasted bagel with a squeeze of lemon. They were both very fond of the old-school sandwich bars, not a few of which could still be found dotted around this area, places run by generations of Italian families whose members didn't give you a look of utter bafflement if you asked for Marmite on your toast. (Though they must never have eaten it themselves, as they always spread it far too thick.) The pair began on a musical, provisionally entitled *Holborn Viaduct*. This bold new updating of *Romeo and Juliet* would centre on the doomed love affair of a young man from a traditional sandwich bar who falls in love with the woman from the head office of an all-conquering barista chain who has been sent to buy up the quirky old place and turn it into yet another generic franchise. Sort of

West Side Story meets *You've Got Mail*, with extra avocado and no dill pickle, please. The production promised some unforgettable songs, including the heart-breaking 'Don't Treat My Feelings Like No Sandwich Fillin'' and the show-stopper, 'D'you Want Butter With That? (Or Are You Still on That Diet)?'

All this, as Luke pointed out, was great fun but could not be allowed to blur the reality that Holly was late in delivering her key section on tea-making for *The Dictionary of Office Life*. Holly apologised again to the New Words Committee (members: Holly and Luke), but reminded its co-president (Luke) that being late for things was very much the point of this Day. Holly then presented a couple of new terms for the technology section: Frown Time and Techno-burble.

Frown Time. *Noun.* The unrecoverable time spent frustrated and unable to work, with a deadline looming, while you wait for someone to come and fix your computer.

Techno-burble. *Noun.* The contrived and painfully unfunny banter that takes place between colleagues as they wait for an IT issue to be sorted out ahead of a presentation – 'Just talk among yourselves for a moment!' – with everyone pretending to enjoy the chat but things getting noticeably more tense and impatient by the second.

'Luke,' said Holly.

'Yeee-eees,' said Luke.

'I guess we should talk about, you know.'

'What? Is it Tall Guy? Do you need me to make one of my calls?'

'No, no. Well, yes actually. Maybe. No, I was thinking of what happened on August 16.'

'My rollercoaster stand-up triumph day? What about it?'

'Well, what I did. Before the ride started.'

'Oh.'

'And before you went on stage.'

'Oh that. I hadn't really thought about it.' He had, actually. Holly looked embarrassed.

'It's okay,' he said. 'And thank you.'

'Thank you?'

'I know you just did it to take my mind off things. All that fear and terror. Dom put you up to it. I'm very sorry to have put you through that. You are a True Best Friend.'

Holly said nothing. She seemed to be weighing things up in her mind. Then she nodded, as if to herself, and said nothing some more. There was a silence which neither of them seemed able to break. The rasps and gurgles of an ancient espresso machine filled the moment.

'Luke,' she said at last.

'Yes?'

'Do you mind if I have your pickle?'

Chapter 82

On their return to the office, there was a definite note of gloom in the air that could not be fully accounted for by Muriel's earlier announcement, shocking as it was, that Wordy Gig's commercial washroom supplier was discontinuing its line of tubeless toilet tissue. Five or six of their co-workers were gathered around Muriel's machine, staring at an email.

'It looks like one of us is definitely for the chop,' said Muriel.

'Really! Who?' said Holly and Luke together, with inappropriate glee. The two couldn't refrain from breaking into a little jig.

'That's not really in the spirit,' said Clive. 'It could be one of you two, you know,' said Clive.

'Oh God, I wish!' said Luke, clasping his hands together in prayer.

'Ooh yes please!' said Holly to the heavens.

CHAPTER 83

September 10 – Hug Your Hound Day – was one of the easiest yet, but Bald is Beautiful Day (September 13) presented rather more of a challenge. Luke decided not to wait till Dom issued the inevitable challenge, and went round to his local barber. He was a friendly Algerian man who kept things very simple; everyone – regardless of what they asked for – came out with exactly the same classic short back-and-sides haircut. Unless, of course, you asked him to shave off all your hair completely.

Luke felt very odd afterwards. Sort of refreshed and liberated, but also sort of itchy and ridiculous. He'd been warned that men who shave their head can often be seen as rather threatening. But his scalp was pale white and vulnerable, like the tip of a large nocturnal worm unwittingly exposed to daylight. Some people gave him a sad, sideways head tilt, and he wondered if they thought he had cancer.

'Good Lord,' said Dom. 'That's rather drastic. Well, fair play to you, though I must say you look absolutely awful.'

'Well, you'd have insisted on it, so I just thought I'd get a jump on the challenge.'

'Yes, yes,' said Dom, taking snaps for the blog and apparently not really listening. 'Really quite grotesque. Like a sort of alien penis. I wouldn't have suggested that for a moment – I was just going to get you to wear one of those bald caps for a day that actors use in films.'

'Oh.'

At work on the following Monday, people couldn't stop petting him. Holly in particular seemed to enjoy running her nails through his fuzzy stubble. 'It's like having a living fidget spinner on tap,' she said. 'You could just sit in the middle of meeting rooms as something for people to play with when the presentation's getting too boring.'

'You'll never get laid off round here then,' said Clive.

CHAPTER 84

There was no obvious Day that could be made the pretext for the key personal challenge that Luke had set himself this month, but September 17 – Locate An Old Friend Day – seemed about as good as any. With the help of the IT guy at work, Luke had managed to trace the Basingstoke phone number Maud had given him to a physical address. He had really no idea what to expect. Holly had offered to come with him, but this was something he knew he had to do alone.

The address did not correspond to a PO Box, as he'd half suspected, or even to any kind of office, as far as he could see. Luke nosed Dom's Audi down quiet suburban streets and between blocks of residential flats until he came to a large green clearing surrounded by narrow roads on three sides. In the middle of the clearing, nestled among a little copse of deciduous trees, there stood a squat building that looked as if it might once have been a café or a play school. A little area in front of the building was lined with Astroturf and enclosed by a low picket fence. A little wooden sign attached to the fence announced: Donny's Dog House.

Luke checked the satnav again. There seemed to be no mistake. His dad's full name, he remembered, was Peter Donald Milvaine.

He was processing all this when a short squat man emerged from a path he hadn't noticed before, one that looked as though it led into some woods proper and would make a good spot for dog-walking. This was a good thing, because the man had five different dogs on leads, all of them complying with varying degrees of enthusiasm as he called to them and led them back to the building.

'Morning,' called the man, whose middle name was indeed Donald and who walked straight past him.

'Morning, Dad,' called Luke uncertainly.

The man stopped. 'Bloody hell,' he said. He peered back, almost furtively, and five dogs turned as one to look at the source of this interruption. Two of them sat down, one started nibbling on some long grass, and one started whining in the direction of the doghouse. The fifth, a cockapoo, came up to Luke and started sniffing his hand.

'I've got one of those,' said Luke.

'Lovable little shit,' said his dad.

'Back at you,' said Luke. He had been so nervous about this moment up until a few minutes ago, but he found now that the bathos of it all put him quite at ease.

'Oh sorry, not you,' said his dad. 'Or rather, not the shit part.' It was his dad who was doing all the flustering now. He peered at his son. 'There's something different about you. What is it?'

Before the conversation could proceed, one of the dogs jumped up and grabbed a chicken chew from a bum-bag that was loosely slung around Pete's waist. The others all followed suit, and soon he was shouting sweatily at his charges to behave.

'Sorry,' he said at last, after he had finally imposed some semblance of canine order. 'Here – help me get the beasts inside.' He led the animals through the gate into the picket enclosure, unlocked the front door of the Doghouse, and let them all off their leads. Inside, there were water bowls and doggy toys and little doggy obstacles and doggy baskets to sleep in. 'Fancy a cuppa?' said Dad, tugging at a sliding door with some difficulty to reveal a poky little kitchenette. Luke nodded, and Pete began filling a kettle covered in black Dalmation spots whose handle was shaped like a dog's tail, and whose spout was a dog's head.

Pete stared at his son again. 'There *is* something different about you. I can't put my finger on it.'

'And you, Dad.'

'How do you mean?'

'Well, last time I looked you were "a Senior Business Development Director advising high-growth emerging-tech scale-ups looking to expand into new territories, specifically in the Middle-East region",' he recited. As of this morning, this was still the wording of his dad's LinkedIn profile.

'I must get round to updating that,' said Pete. They sat sipping their teas. 'Do you know what a Business Development person does?'

Luke thought of Muriel. 'Do they by any chance... spend hours building the business case for purchasing a fridge deodoriser for the office that costs £4.99, when they're supposed to be drumming up some sales and keeping everyone in a job?'

'Yep. Sales,' said his dad, who appeared not to have heard the fridge bit. 'In sales, you live and die on your performance, and I, er... under-performed once too often.' It made a lot of sense. As a dad, Pete had been something of an under-performer too.

'So you moved back here and started... this?' Luke took in Pete's doggy empire with a sweep of his arm that tried hard not to be ironic. 'Quite a surprise move.'

'Oh, not really,' said his dad. 'I've always quite liked Basingstoke. I needed somewhere to get back on my feet. Especially after the divorce came through.'

'Wow.'

'I know! I didn't really see it coming.'

'I meant, wow, I didn't know you'd been married again.' Peter looked shiftily at his feet. Luke noticed a cluster of angry boils on the back of his neck. He was sweating heavily, and little patches of flaking skin peeked through his thinning salt-and-pepper hair. 'You'll be telling me you've got another kid next.'

Pete Milvaine looked shiftily at the floor again. He uttered a short sound that sounded a lot like: *two*.

'Jesus, Dad,' said Luke. '*Two kids*!'

'I've got pictures somewhere.' He fished in his bum-bag for his phone but couldn't find it.

'Were you ever going to get in touch again?'

'I was! I am!' said his dad. He stood up and tried to pace around the kitchenette, but there just wasn't space. The dogs saw him coming and rushed over for some attention, poking their wet noses through the little stair gate that he had pulled shut behind them. 'I just didn't want you to see me like this. I wanted to get the business properly off the ground.'

'Oh, Dad. You don't need. I really don't...'

'You'll see!' said his dad. 'One day there'll be a Donny's Doghouse in every town from Farnborough to Fordingbridge! We'll be the leading doggie daycare solution provider for the whole of northern Hampshire!'

'We?'

'And possibly even southern Berkshire and western Surrey too!'

'We?'

Pete was peering at him again. '*What is it*? Have you got new glasses?'

Luke scratched and stroked his bald scalp most blatantly. 'Got it in one, Dad.'

'I *knew* it!'

His dad made as if to walk towards Luke, then sat down again. His eyes watered, Luke saw; he walked with a slight limp, and even the mild exertion of tea-making seemed to have left him out of breath. 'It's good to see you, son,' he said at last.

As Luke drove away, he was filled with a strange mix of conflicting emotions. He had expected to be angry, and quite righteously so, at this man who had fathered two more kids and been back in the country for years without bothering to tell his firstborn son. A man who never remembered his first wife's – Luke's mum's – birthday, or the anniversary of her passing. But, as Maud had suggested, there was nothing malicious or even deceitful really about Peter Milvaine. His key flaw was a sort of generalised crapness which, without Luke's mum's saving influence (or that of a second partner, who had not unsurprisingly ended up throwing in the towel) was now allowed to flourish quite unchecked. You might pity him, but it was hard to summon up the energy to hate him.

He drove on, keen to get home before it got dark. He wondered if he had inherited the crapness gene, and if there was an antidote. But above all, he felt strangely lighter, the way Ziggy shook himself in happy liberation when you took his harness off. He was looking forward to seeing his dog. And he had a letter to finish.

CHAPTER 85

The next few days passed easily enough. Holly, who still could not leave Luke's fuzzy scalp alone, took him shopping on Build A Better Image Day (September 18). She helped him pick out a new pair of jeans and a shirt in a style and pattern he'd have never considered for himself, but which attracted a fair few compliments when he wore the outfit to work the next day. (On that trip they also made a few detours into Primark, Zara, Mango, Boots, New Look, Monsoon, FatFace and Kookai for 'a couple of bits' that Holly, the office shop steward, said she needed, which he couldn't really begrudge her.)

Shop steward. *Noun.* The shopaholic who cajoles others into accompanying them to the same half-dozen crappy shops every single lunch break – only to return with nothing but an overpriced sandwich. Says the shop steward: 'That was fun; must do it again!'

As they shopped he told her about his dad. 'It's stupid, really. All these years, I've been worried about what he thought of me. I felt I was never good enough for him. And now I see...'

'That he was never good enough for you,' put in Holly. 'Oh God, sorry,' she said, biting her lip. 'Too much.'

'No, you're right. And it turns out *he* was ashamed of what I'd think of *him*!'

'Well, I'm sure Ziggy will approve if they ever meet.'

'Oh yes. All those interesting doggie smells.'

'So do you think you'll see him again? And what about these two new half-siblings?'

'We'll see. To be honest,' he said, smiling at her, 'I need to focus on my real family, if you know what I mean.' Holly gave his arm a squeeze. She thought she did.

Talk Like A Pirate Day (September 19) came and went in a puff of throat-rasping anticlimax. At the start of the year Luke had been looking forward to this one, which had struck him as the definitively silly day, a milestone of popular jollity and glorious pointlessness. (This was before he'd heard of National Hug A Plumber Day, Talk Like Yoda Day or International Dog Biscuit Appreciation Day, of course.) In practice, however, it just meant standing around saying things like 'Ahoy, me hearties' and 'Avast, ye scurvy bilge-rats!' – until after a few minutes you realised you didn't actually know that many pirate expressions, and also, that talking like this didn't half make your throat sore. In 2012, President Obama had tweeted: '*Arr you in?*' But perhaps Peak Pirate had since sailed off over the horizon. Today also happened to be Meow Like A Pirate Day, which made about as much sense.

On September 24, Punctuation Day, the pair – flush from their success with *Holborn Viaduct* – got the whole office involved in their composition of a libretto for a new musical comedy, provisionally entitled *Well, (Dash) My. [Colon]!?*? If it ever got to the stage, this was a show that was sure to break new ground, because every character in it was a punctuation mark. Highlights included the lively full-cast opener 'Let's Eat Grandma! (Commas Save Lives)'; the breathtaking romantic duet, 'Left Bracket, Right

Bracket (We're in this together)'; the heart-wrenching solo, 'Even I Don't Know What I'm For' (sung by the semi-colon); and the big dance-number finale, 'Ain't No Full Stop To This Love!'

CHAPTER 86

A couple of days later, Luke finished his letter at last. He had enjoyed wielding the fountain pen, feeling the flow of ink on paper, and watching the visible signs of progress as the lines snaked down to the bottom of the page. (He'd even remembered to place under his page the thick-lined guide sheet that came with every letter-writing pad, the way Mum had shown him once.) The rhythms of letter-writing came back to him: the opening scene-setting (*'it was National Letter-Writing Day recently so I thought I'd drop you a note!'*), the recipient-focused section where you have to answer both sides of the conversation (*'How are you? I was so glad to hear that nightmare boss finally left – it must be a load off your shoulders not having to face them every day'*), the clumsy attempts at seamless segues – *'and speaking of dogs (not that we were really)...'*. The task became absorbing, the pages of wonky spider-doctor scrawl mounted up, and soon enough the finishing line approached. Luke got on a roll, writing such chatty letters to Aunt Maud, a lecturer from college he'd kept in touch with on and off, an old pal from a previous job, and Mrs Hart.

Then he wrote one very last short one, without any pleasantries:

Alan, I found the enclosed in Mum's letter-writing set. I thought you might like to see it. It confirms something I'm ashamed not to have understood until very recently: You were (are) the very best dad I (n)ever had. I'm sorry it has taken me so long to see it, or say it.

He toyed with the idea of adding an *x*. Too soon, he decided; maybe in a couple more years. He put the note, along with the unfinished one from his mum, into a blue Basildon Bond envelope, which he slotted into the shoebox under his bed.

CHAPTER 87

The last day of the month also happened to be pay day *and* a Friday, a happy coincidence which made a night in The Devonshire Maid pretty much mandatory. Once the first round was ordered, the table fell to speculating as to who might be for the chop. Clive said he'd overheard Phaedra and Greg saying that a writer would have to go; they could use freelancers instead and reduce costs.

'I bet it will be me,' muttered Clive into his pint of snakebite, an odd choice of beverage that Luke had never seen consumed outside of a student bar before. 'LAST DAY SALE: EVERY CLIVE MUST GO!' he extemporised. 'TIME'S RUNNING OUT! TAKE ADVANTAGE WHILE STOCKS LAST.'

'I don't think it will be you,' said Muriel. 'Not with skills like that.'

Squashed up next to Luke, Holly was keen to hear more detail of Luke's glorious airport encounter, which for some reason he had not said much about in the weeks since the momentous event occurred.

At first, Luke simply repeated how, on International

277

Matchmaker Day, he had got up early and made it to Heathrow airport for 7am. He didn't mention that it had been over a year and a half since he and Yasmine (The One) had last met. But there she was, over by the sunglasses stand, Terminal 2 airside. Looking wondrous, if a little surprised. She might have been even more surprised by the version of events that Luke was now presenting to Holly, in which Yasmine not only agreed to share all her contact details with Luke, but also tentatively agreed to come and stay with him for several weeks in London, after which they hoped to return to Paris to live together in the New Year.

There is another version of what happened, one less romantic, perhaps, but rather more historically accurate. Luke would share it with Holly eventually; it just needed five pints of Guinness Extra Cold, a weird vodka jelly thing that Clive was passing round, and an ill-judged pint of snakebite.

Yasmine, it turned out, had been surprised to see Luke because they had in fact made no arrangement to meet. She was just touching down in Heathrow to get a transfer to Morocco, as she'd said in her note, going back for a family wedding. Funny route, not exactly direct but cheaper for some reason. She was kind enough not to ask Luke what he was doing there. This excused him from having to explain all the internet research he'd had to go through to try and work out what flight she might be on.

'I just thought it might be fun to surprise you,' he'd said. He'd found it weird to have to go through security, and have his rucksack searched and everything, when he wasn't even intending to fly anywhere. He explained to Yasmine that he had a mate who worked at the airport and could get him into the departure lounge. Anyway, now they were together, they had by his calculations an hour and forty-two minutes till her flight would be called. In her message, she'd talked about '*turning the page*'. All he had to do was to get her to completely reverse her decision, and to agree to come and live with him. (Or he could live with her, he wasn't fussy.) And he had, shit, ninety-seven minutes to do it. Then again, it was only *one* page.

Ordering coffees took seven-and-a-half minutes, but trying to chat in the busy queue was awkward, and they soon fell silent. After sitting down at last, the talk remained, to Luke's distress, small. Yasmine shared vague news of a family he had never met; he did likewise. She said she was well, and that her croissant was not too flaky; her coffee, however, was a little disappointing. They sat by a big window overlooking the very runway where he could already see her plane being readied for departure. At no point did she mention the blog.

As she got up to go to the loo, she smiled towards him, and he felt the earth slide again. Behind him, a coffee machine hissed and grated, and a barista banged and whistled. He felt he would never get over the poignant beauty of her face, that gaze at once shrewd and kind and unknowable, or the very shape and colour and aroma of her.

She had left a lipstick on the table. He fingered it with reverence, as a server fussed about him, scooping up saucers and wiping surfaces. He picked up a paper napkin and began to scrawl a message with this crayon of rouge that had kissed her actual mouth:

I will always love you

Seeing her making her way back from the loo – God, another four minutes lost! – he folded the napkin and tucked it away on his lap, well out of sight. They tried to talk some more. But the coffee machine was too noisy and the second hand of the clock raced round too fast; somehow, the conversation never took off.

The very moment her plane was called, she got up to leave. Her hastiness pained him. As she stood, they hugged awkwardly, and he went to drop his secret message into her bag. In his mind the gesture would be romantic, powerful, inevitable. But instinctively she put up a fierce arm, and there was a moment's awkward tussle.

After they had parted at the transit gate, he slipped behind a pillar and watched her walk away. He looked on as she opened her bag, pulled out the napkin, glanced quickly at the words, slowly scrunched the serviette and very gently, almost apologetically, dropped it into a passing bin.

Back in the café, as he sat staring at her half-drunk coffee with the miraculous imprint of her lips on its rim, he was disturbed to hear his name being urgently announced over the loudspeaker. It was the final call for the last remaining passenger on his flight to Astana, Kazakhstan.

After talking his way out of the terminal – and resisting the surprisingly strong urge to make use of his one-way ticket to Kazakhstan (there was of course no mate who worked at the airport) – Luke wandered among the taxi ranks and horizontal escalators of Heathrow. He tried hard not to look up, fearing (quite without foundation) that he had the power to make planes explode just by looking at them.

Out here, in the post-Her world, the very air stung. Callously, people went about their business, scraping clunky suitcases along gum-spattered pavements, chasing clunkily after errant toddlers and fecking vaping. They looked unhinged and pointless, every last one of them.

A sign attracted his attention: **Chapel**.

It took a while to find. The signs seemed always on the verge of turning up a dead end and, as he trawled under flyovers, across bus concourses and through narrow concrete passageways, it was as if the chapel did not want to be found, or not by someone who was not prepared to seek a little. But here at last it was. A circular concrete tomb-like thing, submerged in a traffic-lashed roundabout and overlooked by a bland multi-storey car park. Down the steps he went, down past the plaques to dead people, and into the central chamber. Here, under glass, a prayer book stood open at the anniversary of a fatal air crash from 1972.

A service was just winding up, and soon the sky pilot was telling his tiny congregation of passengers and airport workers to 'go in peace, to love and serve the Lord'. Out they all filed, leaving Luke alone in this strange, overlooked citadel to the Lord of the Heavens.

You only love an idea of me, she had once written.

Candles. At least there were always candles. He lit one for her now, saying a prayer for her safe return. It seemed the most he could do.

Back on the Tube, and heading into work through the morning rush hour, he beheld a poignant scene. Another couple separated by cruel circumstance – she with a seat, he forced to stand in the vestibule, the pair edged ever further apart by the rabble, unable even to say a proper goodbye when it came time for the man to get off at Leicester Square. Mutely they exchanged farewells across the uncaring carriage, eyes fixed unblinkingly on the day ahead as each swallowed the great grief of separation with mute dignity.

Luke had a lump in his throat. He fancied the couple would not see each other till perhaps 7.30pm tonight now – later still, if the woman didn't finish that presentation on 'Key sales drivers in the cloud-based e-payment space'. As he got off, Luke saw the man's eyes seek out his beloved's one last time, but she was already busy touching up her plum pout with a lip pencil.

He remembered suddenly that today, August 31, was also Grief Awareness Day.

Holly listened to this account, much of which only emerged on the slow walk to the Tube station, with impressive attention for one who was more than half-cut and rather desperate to pee. She gave him a hug. He gave her a hug. She asked him if she was a bad kisser. He said she wasn't.

'Why do you keep hugging me?' he asked.

'Because it's Hug A Vegan Day,' she said.

'Oh yeah. I told you that.' She hugged him again.

'But I'm not a vegan.'

'Never mind,' she said. 'I'm sure you try.'

OCTOBER

April may be the cruellest month, but October is the off-whitest. For Luke anyway. Which shade of off-white he wasn't quite sure; he consulted various websites and discovered that paint people have identified 150 different shades of off-white, and he despaired of ever pinning down the one he saw in his mind's eye, especially as he wasn't a very visual person, and the things he saw dimly in his mind tended to recede and shrink if he tried to look at them directly, the way dreams do. After a cursory browse he hit on a colour called Cloud White, which seemed about right.

Luke had always seen months, like numbers and days of the week, as colours. Grace did too, and they sometimes compared notes.

'I see January as a sort of mauvey pink,' he said.

'Ew, bro!' She snorted. 'It's bright yellow.'

'March is a sort of brown colour,' he said. 'Like a long muddy river.'

'Stop waffling – it's silver!'

'February is a sort of mottled green and white,' he said. 'Like the tiles in the bathroom when I was a kid.'

'Hah! Orange.'

And so they went on, pleasantly agreeing to disagree. December was a deep black spotted with tiny silvery stars for Luke, while for Grace it was a velvety scarlet. October, in fact, was the only one they agreed on.

'I believe we're mildly synaesthetic,' said Luke, after a quick browse on Reddit. 'It could mean we have slightly better IQ and memory than other people.' On the online forum he looked at, it turned out everyone saw different colours. One person railed at a fellow poster who said they saw April as '*pastel blue*'. '*How can you say that? April is a crystalline, almost translucent whitish ochre. Duh!*'

'Although – it doesn't sound very intelligent that everyone has their own personal palette,' he added.

'I'm going to ask broski about this,' said Grace, in what Luke took to be an unguarded reference to her boyfriend. 'I can't get with someone whose colours don't gel with mine.'

'Fair point,' said Luke. 'Let me know how you get on. Maybe we could have another chat about this on Glossy Gold Day?'

'Sure,' said Grace. 'Why wait till Friday though?'

'I mean Monday night!' said Luke. 'Oh dear Lord. Everyone knows Friday is Dark Greyish Blue Day.'

'I can't do Monday,' said Grace.

CHAPTER 89

October 1 was the first day of Emotional Intelligence Awareness Month. Luke didn't do Months as a rule – this far, he'd stuck strictly to Days – but he found himself drawn to a quiz called '*How Emotionally Intelligent Are You?*' Secretly he'd imagined he'd score quite well in most of the key areas – self-awareness, self-regulation, motivation, empathy and social skills – but Dom and the kids caught wind of what he was doing, and quickly took over. The assessment that emerged, based on their answers, was damning.

Luke learnt that his default mode was anger, he was easily frustrated, and he struggled to regulate his own feelings or understand other people's. There was much work for him to do: he needed to work on mindfulness, keep an emotion journal, and ask others for feedback. He needed to note his triggers of anger and practise deep breathing, learn to celebrate small wins and get better at setting longer-term goals.

On empathy – 'the fundamental people skill' – he scored only fifty-one per cent. The solution: 'Start by just thinking about other people's perspectives. Imagine how they may be feeling, and use active listening skills to understand them fully when they express their emotions to you. Try not to interrupt or talk about your own feelings.'

'It's funny,' as Luke told Mrs Hart later that afternoon. 'I'd imagined that the Make Every Day Count Challenge would sort of make me a better person. I sort of imagined that at the end of the project I'd feel that I'd grown in some way. But in fact, I just seem to be becoming more stressed and enraged by the day.'

'Perhaps you *are* getting better, dear,' she said. 'Only you're starting from a very low base. Imagine how bad the results would have been if you'd done the quiz at the start of the year.'

'In my defence, I have had quite a time of it recently,' he said, a touch defensively. Mrs Hart knew all about Yasmine and his trip to see Dad of course.

'Oh well, the only way is up, isn't it?' she said absently. 'Fig roll, dear?'

'I guess.'

'I did tell you your dad was a bit hopeless. And as for that foreign affair, well, come on, it was never going to last, was it?'

'Thanks a bunch, Mrs H.' He had been planning to write a blog post about her for Guardian Angel Day (October 2), explaining how she was always looking out for him and literally keeping an eye on him from on high, but he was starting to think better of the idea. But then it struck him that this was probably not a very emotionally intelligent reaction, and that he was supposed to be trying to see things from other people's point of view. 'I wonder if I can guess what you're thinking,' he said.

'Go on then.'

'You're thinking: When they made him, they threw away the mould.'

'Got it in one,' she said. 'I always knew you'd have a lot to say for yourself.'

CHAPTER 90

On October 5, Luke popped round to see Alan. They chatted awkwardly for a while in the kitchen, and then Luke handed over his letter at last. And then, because he was just a bloke with an EQ rating of fifty-one per cent, he turned and fled.

A couple of hours later, Alan knocked on Luke's door. Ziggy leapt up at him, because Alan always brought the best treats. But for once, Alan had forgotten. He looked like he'd been crying.

'Oh God, I'm sorry, Alan,' he said. 'I didn't mean to upset you.'

Alan said nothing.

'I was just trying to put things right,' he persisted uncertainly. 'Not that I mean I can fix it all, not just like that. I just... Oh God. It was National Forgiveness and Happiness Day, and...'

'Luke!' shouted Alan. He looked rather overwrought, as if he was wrestling with something he didn't want to, didn't know how to say.

'Me forgive you!' Luke said, almost pleading. 'Not you forgive me! Oh God...'

Alan spoke at last. 'Do you have a beer?'

'Of course! Only... Please try and understand where I was coming from.'

Alan put a hand on Luke's arm. 'If you don't give me a beer right now and stop talking, I'm going to come right over there and hug you.'

Luke gulped, one hand on the fridge door. 'Coming right up!'

They chatted for a long time, of this and of that: football, work, the garden, 'the kids'. They did not really speak of Luke's mum – Alan's partner – or of the letter, or of the years they had shared in the shadow of that death. But these realities underpinned everything else they spoke about. Luke's resentfulness seemed to have evaporated, and in turn Alan's reserve – a natural defence developed against the former, no doubt – was starting to melt away too.

Luke found himself telling Alan about Yasmine, and about his trip to Basingstoke. Alan nodded and listened, and Luke found that he was a very good listener. (Blimey: at this rate, Mrs Hart could be out of a job.) He didn't tell Luke what he should do next or where he had gone wrong, which had until recently been Luke's abiding impression of his – come on, say the word – *stepdad's* attitude towards him. Only, now – and surely this was worth a few EQ points in itself – now it struck him that Alan had never perhaps been quite like that, except in so far as his role of fill-in parent had demanded it. Luke had only chosen to see him that way because of his unresolved anger about his mum and dad separating, and his mum dying, and – as he had perhaps dimly sensed, even at the time – his dad not really being much good at the dadness. Alan had showed up, day in and day out; he had given Luke a home and family life as best he could. He had always taken responsibility for him, always kept him safe, always been there. He had tried to make life fun, in so far as Luke had let him. He had done all the grunt work of parenthood, and received none of the rewards or the gratitude. But it was gratifying that – despite being an obvious mensch – Alan himself was not so well-endowed in the EQ department that he could bring himself to talk about any of this stuff any more easily than Luke could.

'I like the sound of that Muriel,' said Alan. 'She reminds me of your mum.'

'Muriel?'

'Yeah. She sounds like a right laugh.'

Luke felt a sudden need to change the subject. 'I suppose you knew my dad was in the country?'

'I had my suspicions. Should I have told you? I'm sorry. I didn't know how to–'

'No,' said Luke firmly. 'That's on him.'

CHAPTER 91

Luke came into the office on October 10 to find an argument in progress that he realised he could pretty much record and transcribe straight into his blog. Greg was singing the praises of Columbus Day.

'He was a genius! The architect of the modern world!'

'Why don't you just call it Happy Continental Genocide Day?' said Muriel. She was so het up that she had even taken a break from descaling the kettle. She explained that President Biden had now endorsed Indigenous People's Day on the same date.

'Oh, come on,' said Greg. 'That's just virtue-signalling. Italians have a right to celebrate their heritage.'

'So start an Italian-American Heritage Day,' said Muriel.

'You could combine it with National Spaghetti Day – January 4,' put in Luke. 'It's thought that Day was begun by Italian immigrants to the States at the start of the twentieth century.' No one paid him any mind. Good Lord, he was boring.

'Columbus helped to found the Atlantic slave trade,' Muriel was saying now. 'He captured hundreds of Taíno people and shipped them to Spain to sell for gold. The conditions were appalling, and most died on the way. He fed live babies to dogs in

291

front of their parents, sold children into sex slavery, and turned the corpses of indigenous people into dog food. This is all just culled from his own writings, by the way.'

'Well, the pre-Colombians did bad things too,' protested Greg. 'They had slaves and carried out torture and executed babies.'

'Oh, and by the way, you do know that America had already been discovered, don't you?' Muriel continued, ignoring him. 'Oh, to have the entitled arrogance of a stale pale male, who can stumble onto a country that had already been inhabited for millennia – and still expect people to be giving him the credit for discovering it centuries later.'

'Oh lighten up,' said Greg. 'He made the States what they are today.'

'He never actually set foot in the States! He landed in the Bahamas.'

'It's lucky your job is safe,' Greg muttered, retreating to his lair.

CHAPTER 92

After one emotionally courageous conversation with Alan – and in the desperate hope that all this was racking up the EQ points – Luke decided he was ready for another. He knocked on Dom's door, to ask him why he went away all the time. He had a few other follow-up questions in mind too, such as What do you do for a living? and Who are you? Dom had promised to answer such questions after Luke's stand-up/rollercoaster triumph, and it was only the euphoria of surviving that double-brush with death (coupled, perhaps, with the incongruous experience of being kissed twice by Holly rather forcefully, a memory he found himself returning to more and more these days) that had distracted him from pursuing Dom for an answer.

But first he handed over a nice cup of tea and a plate of biscuits. Dom took up the offerings with a suspicious air.

'What's all this in aid of?' he demanded.

'Oh, its October 15 – Grouch Day, of course,' replied Luke.

'Haven't we had this one already?'

'I think you're confusing today with Do A Grouch A Favour Day.'

'Well, what's the difference?'

'Oh, none at all, as far as I can see,' said Luke. 'You know how the calendar goes – there are duplicate and overlap days all over the place. Did you know there are at least three different days just for doughnuts? By my reckoning there are thirty-one different days that are chocolate-themed in some way. In fact, the whole area of foodie Days is really quite an interesting topic in its own–'

'I know why you're here,' Dom interrupted. 'You want answers.' He sighed. He looked a little older suddenly, Luke thought. 'I'll answer your questions, so long as you promise not to spout any more guff about chocolate-themed Days.'

'Well, I... Okay.'

'It's only fair. I did promise. And you certainly held up your end of the bargain.'

'I did.'

Dom ushered Luke into his room. It was bigger than he realised, and smelt pleasantly of something aromatic. Incense, was it? A piece of intricate piano and double bass was playing quietly, which Dom said was the work of 'a Polish jazz trio I'm rather partial to'. There was a long shelf of black Penguin classics, with an emphasis on the Russians and the Romans. Luke had never pegged Dom as a spiritual man, but he also spotted a Bible, and a series of books with titles like *The Imitation of Christ*, *The Cloud of Unknowing*, *The Way of Perfection* and *The Dark Night of the Soul*. On the wall by the bed, tucked out of sight behind a nightstand, Luke spotted a discreet Orthodox cross. On the wall behind the door, there was an artful arrangement of postcard prints of Biblical scenes (Caravaggio? Titian? Rembrandt?). Tacked to the back of the en-suite door, meanwhile, there was a rather larger picture of a young Keanu Reeves, buff and poignant, from his *Speed* days.

Really, Luke did not know Dom at all. There was so much to take in, he almost didn't catch some of what Dom was now telling him.

'I have a thing,' he was saying. 'It's in the family. Every so often I have to go and get some treatment or have a check-up.'

'Are you okay?'

'Absolutely. I just need to make sure I manage it. As I do.'

'And... your family?'

'Oh, they're not really around much, I'm afraid. We had a falling out. And then some of them died.' He gave a hollow, mirthless chuckle. 'It's easier that way, really.'

'But... are you okay? I mean... What is it?'

Dom swatted the question away with a dismissive sweep of his stick. 'Oh, no you don't. We're not going there. I will not have you googling.'

'Is there anything I can do?'

'Oh, dear Lord, no. Please do not start flapping. I couldn't bear it if you turned into a *flapper*.' He pronounced the word with great distaste.

'So... what then? Just pretend we never had this conversation?'

Dom sighed. Clearly he felt he'd conceded far too much already in the way of personal history, and Luke's flapping was testing his patience.

'Luke,' he said, in a firm and yet uncharacteristically gentle voice. 'What I'd really like you to do... is complete the Make Every Day Count challenge. Morally, I suppose one might concede that The Chair is yours already.'

'I take it you're referring to National Gimp Day.'

'Indeed. But observing and, dare I say, helping to shape your daily challenges has actually rather cheered me up this year. It has – how shall I say – enhanced my quality of life.'

Luke gulped. 'Wow. Dom. I don't know what to say.'

'Oh, think nothing of it. I've rather overdone the compliment because I was hoping to shut you up.'

There was a quiet beep and Dom looked at his watch. 'Come on, they'll be kicking off soon.'

Luke stood for a moment in Dom's sanctum as if trying to

soak in as much detail as possible. He had a suspicion he might never be admitted again, and he knew Holly would expect a detailed description. The medicine bottles were nowhere to be seen now, he noted.

'Come on,' said Dom. 'There's no extra time in this one, remember.'

CHAPTER 93

Luke came into the office the following Monday to find Holly hard at work on an intricately colour-coded Excel document. October 17 was Spreadsheet Day, Boyfriend Day and Forgive An Ex Day, and this unique combination of events had given her an idea.

'I'm putting together a database of all my failed dates and relationships. Huh! If you can call them that.'

'And the colours?'

'I'm looking for patterns. Trying to see where I'm going wrong, so I can avoid the dodgy ones next time round.'

The spreadsheet was a work of intricate analysis. The men were arranged by chronology, left to right. Each of them was assigned a vertical stripe, the length of which – Clive's dodgy jokes aside – related to the duration of their association with Holly. One column detailed where they met – pub, wedding, dating site, client meeting, crochet class, giving blood, and so on. The colours in the chart related to the key issue which Holly determined had been the cause of the relationship breaking down. She admitted this part was a work in progress, but so far she had allocated about twenty different shades, to denote things like: Emotional Immaturity;

Mother Issues; Rampant Mansplaining; Sexism; Politics; Artistic Differences; Physical Challenges; Communication; and Hygiene. Some of the men had been given multicoloured bars on the chart, implying that they had fallen down in more than one of these areas.

But the column which most drew Luke's attention was the one furthest to the right, headed 'Additional comments'. There were some corkers here:

– Arrived carrying a heavy tool bag, then insisted three times in the first five minutes that he wasn't a serial killer.

– Failed to make eye contact once in four and a half hours. Either looked at the floor or at a spot two feet above my head.

– Referred to me as 'the little lady'. As in: 'And what would the little lady like to drink?'

– Blamed most of the world's ills on (using big scare quotes) "global bankers".

– Just after we met, said: 'Can you walk ahead of me because I've farted?'

– Insisted on picking up the tab for the meal, then said: 'It's no bother. I pay for sex all the time!'

Luke was alternately absorbed, entertained and appalled by these little vignettes. He was also impressed by the effort Holly had gone to. There was comedy here, of course, and perhaps a touch of self-therapy. But there was also, he thought, a genuine effort to understand where she was going wrong. 'If you'd applied half as much effort and thought to your actual job as you've done to this,' he said in his comedy snarky Greg voice, 'we probably wouldn't be thinking about laying you off.'

'Where *am* I going wrong?'

'The only thing these blokes have in common,' said Luke, 'is that none of them are good enough for you.'

'Oh, pshaw,' said Holly dismissively. 'Stop waffling.'

'He's right,' said Muriel. 'Come on. Why do you keep throwing yourself at these unsuitable blokes?'

'You tell me.'

'So you won't run the risk of getting hurt by someone who might actually mean something to you. By really falling for someone who's your equal. Putting your heart on the line.'

'I liked Tom,' said Holly quietly.

'Well, yes,' agreed Muriel. 'But Tom liked men, didn't he?'

'No! Fruit bats and tree-kangaroos were more his thing. But you're right – I do need to add another colour for "secretly gay". You'd be surprised.'

Luke asked: 'What about you, Muriel? When did you know that your Martin was the one?' Little was known in the office about Martin, except that he and Muriel spent most their non-work time trying to stop their boys destroying the house or bickering about whose turn it was to put out the recycling (Martin's. Always Martin's).

'Oh, I'm not sure he is,' she said. 'But we've been together twenty-three years now, and it is important to have someone to moan about. And he knows his way round a hoover, I'll give him that.'

Holly looked genuinely confused. 'Are you serious, Muriel?'

'How do you mean?'

'Well, if you're not sure, what hope is there for the rest of us?'

Muriel stopped and turned to face her. 'Martin is my rock,' she said. 'He's my best friend. My lover, very occasionally. My life.'

'But I thought you spent half your time arguing?'

'Only about little things, like who's the most sleep-deprived, or which wildlife doc we should watch next. But bickering is a good thing, done right.'

'How so?'

'It's like a constant renegotiation of the terms of the relationship,' she said. 'Otherwise you get stuck in roles. Pigeonholes. And if one day you decide that role doesn't suit you anymore, or you realise your partner is abusing their role at the expense of yours, it can be very hard to fix.'

'That's really interesting,' said Holly.

CHAPTER 94

Luke and Holly went on a date together that weekend. Only not with each other. Tom was back and keen to see her; Holly had asked if Luke would come along too. She wasn't sure how she felt about Tom's reappearance, and thought that having someone else there would offer a bit of emotional cover.

Luke needed to find a date too, of course, so he asked Gaynor from the charity shop. He'd done a few more shifts over the course of the year, and always enjoyed his chats with her.

'I'll come tonight on one condition,' she said.

'What's that?'

'That if we have sex, you make a conscious effort to try and withhold your sperm.'

'What's that now?'

'Your sperm is your life force. By retaining it, you can direct that energetic essence up your spine and into your brain, where it can nourish the soul and enhance overall well-being.'

Luke thought for a moment. 'Why don't we just agree not to have sex?' he said at last.

'That'll do it,' she said.

In the event, he needn't have worried, because the moment

Gaynor saw Tom, she had eyes for no other. Tom likewise was quickly fixated on Gaynor.

After a while, Holly pointedly asked: 'Shall we just move the chairs round so you two can sit nearer each other?'

'Oh – would you mind?' said Tom, quite oblivious to her sarcasm. Holly and Luke ended up chatting at one end of the table, though their conversation was hampered by the gales of laughter coming from the other end.

At the end of the meal, Gaynor said she needed to get back for her cats. One of them had been poorly recently, and this was the first time she (the cat) had been left on her own since being released by the vet. No one was in the least surprised when Tom offered to walk her to the Tube. They all stood to say their goodbyes, and everyone pretended it had been a lovely evening and *we really must do it again.*

Holly and Luke sat on in the pizzeria, almost the only people left.

'What's the betting that cat will be jumping on two people's heads tomorrow morning?' said Holly, with a trace of bitterness.

'I'm sorry, Holly,' said Luke. 'I know you really like Tom.'

'*Liked* him.'

'Well, if it's any consolation, he won't be allowed to orgasm.'

'Not really.'

She said nothing more for a while, just stared into her Baileys. 'It'll be okay,' she said stoutly at last. 'I've been here before. After a while, it's hard to get too upset about someone who's just not that into you. I mean, one of the basic requirements of a partner is that they're really into you, right? That's a very attractive thing, assuming you're into them of course.'

'Well, we did a good thing tonight,' said Luke. 'We brought together two people who really are into each other.'

'I know! Who could have predicted that?' She paused. 'And what about you, Luke? Did you like Gaynor? Or was she just…? How are you feeling about…?'

'It's okay,' he said. 'You can say her name.'

'Nadine Dorries.'

'Funny. Yasmine. I'm getting there. A lot of it was in my head, I can see that. But we really did have a connection. I wasn't a complete loony. Or a stalker, honest.'

'Of course not. No one thought that.'

'They did.'

'Well, not *that* much.'

'But if I'm honest, I didn't really know her. I thought I could win her with big gestures and all that. The only thing I don't get is why she wrote me all those encouraging messages on the blog.'

Holly was silent for a moment. She said, 'How do you... How do we really know that was her?'

'If it wasn't her,' said Luke slowly, 'then who?'

It was all getting very *Scooby Doo*. Holly frowned at Luke, Velma to his Fred. (Or was he Shaggy? In any case, for the record Luke had always thought Velma much sexier than Daphne.) 'Who do you think?'

CHAPTER 95

Incredibly, it was Get To Know Your Customer Day yet again. Luke had made a point of highlighting it in his calendar so that he would be mentally prepared for the latest instalment of Reggie from Hornsey BoxLife's rollercoaster life, or as much as one could be. Reggie's monologues made Luke think of what women always said about childbirth: 'If you truly remembered what it was like, you'd never let it happen again.'

In the event, Luke was pleasantly surprised by Reggie's news. He had taken some of Luke's advice, and was slowly putting his life back together. Viv had fallen out with her own mum over the royal family – Mum was firmly Team Kate and Wills, and was disgusted to learn that her daughter was in Harry and Meghan's camp. Reggie had rented a little flat near his storage place, and had 'quit the cheese-string habit' (Luke did not know if that was a euphemism, prison slang perhaps, or a literal statement, but he knew better than to ask). He was now allowed to take his daughter to pre-school and pick her up afterwards on most weekdays. He was also allowed to make her packed lunches, take her to ballet, dental and GP appointments, and to babysit her when Viv went out, which was only two or three times a week. Viv even occasionally allowed him to stay over (on the sofa-bed, of course) if she was out clubbing late.

'It sounds like Viv has got herself a full-time nanny,' said Holly afterwards.

'Oh, you know, baby steps.'

Luke had also decided to observe Count Your Buttons Day (October 21), but wasn't sure if this meant the buttons on his clothes or on all his electrical appliances and gadgets. Either way, it was a most boring exercise, but – and this was perhaps the original point of the Day, though no one seemed to know – he did come across three buttons that were missing on various shirts, and two more that were about to go.

He recalled that Alan had once shown him how to sew on buttons to help him get a badge in Cubs, so he popped round for a refresher. The beers came out and soon the two of them were sitting contentedly on the sofa, a footie match on in the background. Luke found himself telling Alan about his recent chat with Dom, and the disastrous double-date with Holly.

'That reminds me a bit of how I really got to know your mum,' he said quietly. 'I mean, I'd known her for ages at work, like to say hello to. But we'd never really spoken, you know?'

'So what happened?' He tried to sound casual, but he was suddenly desperate to hear more.

'Well, she'd gone out to meet some guy on a date. A second date, I think it was; she wasn't sure about him but she wanted to give it one more try. Anyway, she was really early for some reason; which was very unlike her of course. I happened to be in there...'

'Doing what? Sitting on your own?'

'Well, I'd been with some other people from the office but they'd left. I was about to leave myself but I got on a bit of a run on the trivia machine...' Alan's love of pub quizzes was legendary.

'Say no more. And Mum – what did she do?'

'She came over and started watching. Before long, of course, being her, she started shouting out answers. Hopeless on sport and science, of course, but she knew all the arts and gardening and politics questions, so between us we cleared up.'

'You hit the jackpot?'

'Oh, two or three times, I think.'

'So what happened when her date turned up?'

'I don't quite remember. I know he joined us for a bit. But we were getting on like a house on fire, and I think he must have just drifted off somewhere.'

'That poor bloke.'

'I know. We weren't proud of ourselves. But...'

'But what?'

'Oh no, it's nothing.'

'Come on, you can say it.'

'Well, we were just so *happy* to be there, with each other. Something just clicked.'

'When did she break the bad news to you?'

'About what?'

'About her kid. Me.'

'Oh! Straight away. She was so proud of you. She couldn't have been with anyone who didn't get that, didn't want to share it.'

'But still,' said Luke. 'A sulky eleven-year-old kid, with all his spots and baggage. It's a bit of a passion-killer.'

'When I fell for your mum, I fell for the whole package,' he said. 'I wouldn't have had it any other way.' He didn't dare look up; this was fragile, uncharted territory between the two of them. But he needn't have worried, because Luke had suddenly discovered that his half-sewn button required his full, intensive attention.

'You made her very happy,' he said, almost under his breath.

'It's funny,' said Alan. 'You can search high and low for The One. And then sometimes it can turn out they were right there in front of you all the time, only you just never saw it.'

CHAPTER 96

Luke now entered another rather literal phase of the Make Every Day Count challenge. He wore Crocs on Crocs Day, ate a crisp sandwich with fries while he and Dom watched a video of *Chucky* on October 23 (National Chucky Day, Greasy Food Day and Crisp Sandwich Day), and went out into the garden with Ziggy and howled at the moon on Howl At The Moon Day. The following day, American Beer Day, did not go unobserved either.

He didn't know if his co-workers had got the memo about October 27 (Cranky Co-worker Day) but they certainly did not disappoint.

'Oh, for the love of God!' wailed Muriel, pointing with disgust at a magazine spread about DIY household hints. 'Can we please let go of the idea that you can clean windows effectively with just newspaper!!'

'Aaagh!' shouted Holly, holding her phone with her fingertips, as if it had just been picked out of an unflushed loo. 'If I see one more picture of a bloke on this dating app holding a big fish, I swear I'm going to run amok with a large wet haddock.'

There followed an entertaining office debate about the best fish to slap someone with. Luke suggested a mackerel, which is relatively easy to grip and long enough for optimal slappiness. Muriel argued in favour of a flatfish such as a brill or turbot – 'great surface area for maximal impact, light to carry, and a nice neat little tail to grab hold of'.

Clive opined that it really depended on whether you wanted to humiliate someone or inflict proper physical harm. 'If it's the latter, you could go for a frozen pike – packs a real bony punch. Or maybe an electric eel. You get maximum flexibility and reach, plus deliver a decent shock. Just make sure you're wearing your Marigolds.'

A cycle courier who happened to be waiting at reception now weighed in. 'For me it would have to be the rainbow trout. Good size, not too slimy so you can get a decent purchase. Decent slappiness-to-concussion ratio. And the colours will give a lovely bright arc through the air as you strike. Efficiency, violence and flair – the rainbow trout's been my go-to for years!'

'Fancy going on a date tonight?' called Holly.

'Sorry, love, no can do,' said the biker. 'I'm running to the top of a skyscraper.'

CHAPTER 97

Greg and Phaedra were both in extremely cranky moods. They had been in and out of their office all morning, slamming doors and shouting cryptic barbs at each other. Greg had not even joined in the fish-slapping discourse, which was not like him.

In the afternoon, Luke and Holly were called in to the inner sanctum. They stood at the end of the double-desk, with Phaedra and Greg looking down the long room at them.

'Do sit,' said Greg.

'Actually,' said Phaedra. 'Do we want them to sit?'

'Well, I think it's only...'

'It's okay,' said Holly. 'We'd rather stand.' They both knew what the chat was about, and standing did indeed feel the more appropriate position.

'Luke,' Greg began.

'Yes?' said Luke.

'Holly,' he added.

'Yes, Greg?'

'As you know, Wordy Gigs has experienced some headwinds of late, and the company – as a company – has struggled to hit some

309

of its more ambitious growth targets. Some time ago, we signalled to you both that – were market conditions not to reassert themselves in a more favourable light in a timely fashion – it might become incumbent upon us, as leaders and shareholders, and indeed to secure the viability of the company overall…'

'Oh, for the love of God!' Phaedra burst out. 'Holly and Greg, we told you a while back that things weren't great, and if they didn't pick up, we'd have to let one of you go.'

'That's right,' said Greg. 'And when we came to assess your relative capabilities, both of which are of course considerable, it became incumbent upon the senior management team, which in this instance may be understood to be these two people seated at this end of the table…'

'*Jesus*, Dad! We have to let one of you go, and we've decided that's you, Holly. It's nothing personal. We're very sorry. You'll get a good payout and a great reference. Shall we say end of November?'

'I see,' said Holly.

'You can't! That's not! Why…?' Luke tried to exclaim various things but none of them really made sense. He looked at Holly, who appeared close to tears, but whether with upset or relief and joy it was hard to say. A not un-small part of himself was gutted that he wasn't getting out. Really: What did a guy have to do to get the boot round here?

Greg was looking intently at his daughter. 'That's my girl,' he said. 'I'm so proud of you right now.' Luke made his excuses, and slipped out before the nausea kicked in. But Holly stayed behind.

'Thank you for letting me know,' she said quietly. 'Can I ask the reason for your choice?'

'Ah yes, well,' said Greg, looking at Phaedra with an I'll-handle-this-one-darling expression, while she just rolled her eyes. 'We had to factor in a number of, ah, factors into the decision-making process, in order to arrive at a multi-factorial decision that–'

'Oh, for a large halibut!' screamed Phaedra. 'Look, Holly.

Luke's cheaper than you, and he's less likely to go off and have babies. I'm sorry but there it is.'

'Would you care to repeat that?' said Holly, reaching for her iPhone's record button.

'Repeat what?'

CHAPTER 98

That night, a three-line whip for the pub, Luke was in triumphant mood.

'God, you are so lucky, Holly!' he kept saying. 'I'd kill to be getting out of here!'

'Yes, so you keep saying,' said Holly.

'I mean, how long have we been dreaming about this? I feel like you're doing it for the both of us. *You are living the dream!*'

Holly looked rather glummer. Luke was oblivious, but Muriel noticed. 'Ignore him, he's just trying to put a brave face on it,' she said. 'He won't know what to do with himself once you're gone.'

'Oh, I think he'll manage,' said Holly.

'How are you doing?'

Holly sighed. 'Oh, you know, Muriel. It's one thing to daydream about leaving. It's quite another when it happens to you. Wordy Gigs has been like a sort of family to me. Weird and dysfunctional, but sort of home.'

'Sounds like a family to me,' said Muriel. 'We're all going to miss you so much. But why don't you fight it? That thing Phaedra said – it's outrageous. You could get a payout from a tribunal for that!'

'Oh, I couldn't face it. And besides, she was paying me a compliment in a way. At least she was straight with me.'

Several drinks later, Luke found himself propping up the bar next to Holly. 'You lucky sod,' he said drunkenly. He waved over at Patsy, the new receptionist, who he'd been huddled in the corner with for much of the evening. Holly felt a sudden stab of irritation.

'It didn't take you long to move on,' she said, nodding in the direction of Patsy.

'Eh?'

'You're desperate to get shot of me, aren't you?' she spat.

Luke did a good impression of a half-cut bloke who didn't know what to say. It wasn't really an impression.

'No more Holly cramping your style. Well, I'm with you on that.'

'Holly,' said Luke. He had at last noticed that she was upset, apparently, but still didn't know why, and certainly not why he was the chief culprit.

'It's time we went our separate ways, Luke,' she said. 'We've been getting in each other's way for too long. Has it never occurred to you that *you* are the reason I never meet anyone nice and normal? Every time I meet someone, they always say: *Who's this Luke bloke? Why do you keep going on about him?* And I always go home wondering why I have more fun with you than any of them.'

'We're mates,' said Luke hopelessly.

'We're not mates, though, are we?' she persisted. 'We're... emotional crash pads.' This was probably not quite the right expression, but it would have to do. 'We're together all the time. We enable each other's emotional crap. We're like... mutual reverse romantic co-dependents.' Again, this phrase would have to do. 'We each need the other one to fail so that we can feel better about our own failures. We each encourage the other to fuck up because, really, how on earth would the other one cope if one of us actually managed to meet someone?'

'I don't know what you're talking about,' said Luke. 'I was with Yazz for...'

'Yazz? Oh, give me a break. That was all in your head. Even Mrs Hart could see that. Ziggy too, probably. You made it up to make yourself feel superior to me.'

'Holly, I really don't know what you mean. I'm really sorry you're leaving. I was happy for you because I thought it was what you wanted. We talked about it loads of times, remember?'

'Actually I will be happy to leave,' she snapped back. 'Because now I'll be free of all this crap at last.'

She knocked back the last of her spritzer. But there was rather more left in the glass than she realised, and she had to put a hand to her face to stop the bubbles coming out of her nose. Then she picked up her bag, and stalked out of the pub.

Luke watched her depart. 'And I had such a nice day in the country planned for us for Saturday,' he said to Muriel.

She raised a quizzical eyebrow.

'Hug A Sheep Day,' he said.

NOVEMBER

CHAPTER 99

Holly's last full month of employment at Wordy Gigs began with her and her official Best Friend still not speaking. Luke had to go sheep-hugging with his young stepbrother Milo (in the end, they had to settle for petting some lambs at a kids' zoo near Tooting). And Haunted Fridge Night, which Luke had planned as a classic curtain-raiser for Halloween, had been a complete write-off.

Luke's way of pretending none of this was happening was to double-down on his flirting with Patsy, the new receptionist.

'Can we please stop calling Patsy the "new girl"?' requested Muriel in a memo. She's a *woman*.' She refrained from adding that she was a single mum of two, who happened to be seven or eight years older than Luke.

Luke, whose relationship record was generally patchy, had never dated someone older than himself before, and the whole idea was most intriguing to him. Not that they were exactly dating; it was more him hanging around inanely by the photocopier and making her endless cups of tea.

'Oh, for God's sake, please save him from himself,' said Muriel to Holly, after a few days of this. 'It's too painful to watch.'

'Nothing to do with me,' said Holly.

'Can't you reach out to him via the medium of his special Days?' persisted Muriel. 'Today is Cliché Day, which feels horribly apt.'

'I wash my hands,' said Holly. 'And besides, I've got a hot date tonight.'

'Really? Who with?'

'Steve.'

'Ooh, do we know him?'

'Yeah, you know, Steve.'

'Steve the cycle courier guy?'

'The very same.'

'Interesting. What's he like?'

'Really nice, actually. Very considerate. Always brings a helmet for me.'

'I should hope so.'

One night Steve and Holly went out for a drink in Muscadello's, the wine bar round the corner where Greg and Phaedra always took clients or reserved an area for (dread phrase) formal 'client drinks'. To Luke's mind, nothing was more inimical to spontaneous fun than the prospect of being corralled into the roped-off area of a bland wine bar, segregated from the people at large, and forced to make small talk with the people they had to slave for all day. For that reason, Wordy Gigs' foot soldiers never went to Muscadello's on their own time, so it was the ideal spot to avoid scrutiny. Hiding in plain sight.

Holly and Steve were by now on their third date (as she would later tell Luke). They had progressed to the slow-goodbye-kiss stage but, despite the absence of any obvious red flags on either side, neither seemed in any rush to progress their intimacy. Steve was funny, even eccentric, and they had a good laugh. They talked about telly and about work, about celebs and about holidays; but somehow their conversation never got past the second base of warm chit-chat.

'Hey,' said Steve. 'Isn't that Luke over there?'

317

Steve called Luke over, oblivious to Holly's frosty glares and to Luke's obvious embarrassment at (a) having been caught drinking in this odd place; and even more (b) the fact that someone had obviously just thrown a glass of red wine in his face.

'Here – look who the cat dragged in!' he said with a chuckle. 'Come on, mate, why don't you join us? Tell us all about it.' Holly did not look best pleased, and Luke in his turn thought it was odd that Steve would invite a third person to crash his intimate little tête-à-tête.

'Let me guess – you came here for a drink with Patsy,' she said. She looked like she had meant to ignore him. But he was here now, and in spite of herself, she was obviously curious.

'I did.'

'And you thought no one else would come here.'

'Sort of. As did you, no doubt.'

'But then: you put your foot in it in some way,' said Holly, ignoring him. 'She misunderstood you, and you ended up with a face full of Malbec.'

'Yep.'

'My God, you've got a gift,' said Steve admiringly. 'How could you possibly have known it was Malbec?'

CHAPTER 100

Luke and Holly stayed on chatting in Muscadello's long after Steve left. He said he had to be up early in the morning for a training run. He was preparing for an ultrathon – running one hundred miles through the dark up a mountain in Wales or somewhere – and he had to be up at dawn to get the miles in.

'So training is a big deal for him then?'

'The man is obsessed. I mean, there's not an ounce of flab on him, he's like Bruce Lee.'

'I feel quite inadequate already.'

'Tell me about it. Every time I reach for a Haribo I sense this aura of judgement wafting my way. He certainly wouldn't approve of all this.' She gestured at the third bowl of salsa and melted-cheese-drenched nachos which had mysteriously appeared on the table, a special offer for National Nachos Day.

'I suppose it takes up a lot of his time?'

'He showed me his training schedule. He's got about two evenings free in the next six months. Anyway – enough about all that. What I want to know is how you managed to get wine thrown over you by your older woman.'

'Oh, it was a religious thing.'

'How do you mean?'

'Well, she believes in reincarnation and karma and all that. We had quite an interesting chat – as you know I'm a big fan of *The Tao of Pooh*.'

'Right.'

'But then I asked her if she believed that people who are disabled or chronically ill are paying for the sins of past lives.'

'Blimey. Me and Steve are still working through our jokey *Love Island* analysis stage.'

'Well that would have been the safer bet. Somehow everything kicked off. She said karma was widely misunderstood and it was much more complex than non-practitioners could possibly understand. I found a quote from the Dalai Lama about the disabled thing, and we went back and forth a bit more, and then she just snapped and... Here we are.' He gestured to his red-soaked shirt.

'Did you like her?' asked Holly.

'I thought I did,' said Luke. 'But I can't stand it when people are so certain about things that no one can possibly know for sure about. It sort of provokes me.'

'I can see that,' said Holly. 'But are you sure about anything?'

'I'm sure about family, friends, the things in front of me. But beyond that... I thought I was sure about Yasmine, but of course, that was mostly in my head.'

Holly wiped a drip of red wine from his chin. 'Well, I'm sure of one thing: you must have done something pretty nasty in your last life to deserve this.'

CHAPTER 101

Next day, Luke got a bit of a lift from one of the fake holiday websites whose email newsletters he'd signed up for. It was headed '*Congratulations for November 15!*' Intrigued, Luke opened the message. '*To us, every day is a special day,*' it said. '*But November 15 is going to be extra special. Why? Because it's your birthday, of course! You didn't think we'd forget, did you?*'

The Calendar people had a very special gift in store: '*As our present to you, for the whole of November 15 you have our permission to refer to the day as 'National Luke Milvaine Day, and to celebrate it in whatever way you deem appropriate. Just make sure to take some pics, share on the socials, and let us know how it goes!*'

Luke sat back in his chair, breathing deep sighs of satisfaction. It was everything he had ever wanted, and the fact that his birthday was actually in June was neither here nor there.

In the event, the Day was rather hijacked by Muriel, who had discovered that November 15 was also Clean Out Your Fridge Day. At least that was what it was supposed to be. She had convened the team for a show-and-tell on the topic, and the troops had duly sauntered into the big meeting room, with its beanbags, hanging aloe vera plants, and stencilled wall-quotes from Maya Angelou,

Mark Twain and Stephen King on the power of storytelling. In retrospect, it was a surprisingly big turnout for one of Muriel's domestic pep talks.

The overview slide that whizzed in gave no indication of what was to come:

- What's the difference between regular cleaning and 'deep' fridge cleaning?
- Tools for the job
- Preparing the fridge
- To bleach or not to bleach?
- The deep-clean workout
- Final thought: Can you go too deep?

Muriel embarked on a couple of slides. She said some very sensible things about how the folds on the fridge door can harbour 'malevolent crumbs and debris', and why it was important to hoover the coils at the back of the appliance, but then she rather abruptly stopped.

She clicked her clicker, and the next slide whizzed into place. Contrary to Luke's expectations, it was not an image of a fridge interior, or an ode to the benefits of baking soda. It was an image of Holly next to an image of Luke. There was only one line of text on the slide and it read:

What are we going to do about these two?

'Thanks, Muriel,' said Greg, stepping in. 'Some very valuable thoughts there. But as most of you know, we have gathered here for another reason. Today we ask: Holly and Luke – what is it with these guys? And what can we do about it?'

Greg clicked the clicker again and a comedy emergency hooter started hooting. At the same time, a graphic flew in from one corner of the slide, zigzagged around the screen and ended up superimposed on the images of Holly and Luke, who now appeared to have been stamped with the official-looking words: "THIS IS AN INTERVENTION!". Luke noted that the pics of him and Holly were now flashing and sliding towards each other, then away again, in a naive animation loop that soon started to make him feel quite queasy.

'*What is this?!*' said Holly. He had never seen her look so agitated.

'What the feck?' said Luke.

'Okay,' Phaedra continued. 'Clive,' she said, throwing a pack of coloured markers in the direction of the Pay Per Click man. 'Scribe for me if you will.'

'Got it, boss. Content KISS & TELL. Hot Lovers Reveal All!' Clive took up his station by the big whiteboard and starting jotting down key phrases as the discussion took off.

Muriel was looking equally disgusted. 'Whatever this is,' she said at last. 'It's not right. And I don't just mean the hijacking of an important fridge-cleaning talk.'

'Oh come on!' said Greg. 'These two can't see the wood for the trees.'

'Someone's got to help them help themselves,' put in Phaedra.

'Yes, that's right,' said Greg pompously. 'All the speculation, it's very disruptive for the rest of the office. It's starting to impact productivity.'

'Oh well,' said Muriel sarcastically. 'We can't possibly have that, can we? Not when the obvious alternative is to publicly humiliate two of our friends and colleagues.'

'This is sick,' said Holly, and got up to walk out. But she paused at the door. She looked as if she was still struggling to process the surreal events that were unfolding before her. It was all wrong on so many levels. And yet: it was hard to look away.

'Okay,' said Greg, oblivious. 'Let's do this thing! Let's spit-ball, let's mind-map, let's brainstorm! Let's throw some shit at a wall! Who wants to go first?'

No one said anything.

'Okay, me first!' said Greg. 'Holly's unsuitable dates: What's all that about?'

'Well at least she was trying to meet an actual person!' said Muriel.

'Muriel!' Luke and Holly hissed as one.

'Sorry,' said Muriel sheepishly. 'It's like I can't help myself.' Holly half nodded. She half knew what Muriel meant.

'Never mind Holly!' Phaedra was saying now. 'What about Luke and his Yasmine fantasy? I mean, hands up all those who think she actually exists?' Luke put his hand up, and Holly did too, rather more slowly. No one else did, however.

'You do know we are actually here? In this room with you, *right now*?' spluttered Holly.

'*Yeah*,' said Luke, unconvincingly. He too sort of felt a need to see where all this was going.

'Let's hear the evidence first, please, Holly,' said Phaedra. 'There is a protocol to these things, I think we will do well to observe best practice.'

'Could I just say...' Luke began again.

'Not now, Luke,' said Greg. 'You've caused far too much trouble already.'

Holly and Luke sat in silence as the team discussed their love lives, their hopes and aspirations, their obvious suitability for each other – and their perverse insistence on sabotaging their own happiness.

'Call the first witness!' ordered Greg.

A Zoom call was now initiated, and up on the big screen popped a slightly fuzzy image of Dom. He was vaping at the kitchen table in his and Luke's flat. Milo and Ziggy were sitting next to him.

'Dom, thanks for joining us this morning,' said Phaedra. 'Give us your take if you will.'

Dom vaped slowly. 'Well, I've known for over a year that they were meant for each other in a crass, doomed sort of way,' he drawled. 'Luke has a sort of naive hopelessness which she clearly found quite endearing, while Holly has the sort of inhuman levels of compassion and understanding required to put up with him.'

'Quite so, quite so. And I believe you even tried to steer them together in some ways?'

'Oh yes,' he drawled. 'Just little things, you know. Getting them to kiss each other or tricking them into sharing the same surname. I thought that'd be a pretty big hint.'

'So it *was* you with the surnames!' said Luke.

'And me!' said Milo proudly.

'Well done, Milo,' said Phaedra. 'And what do you think about all this?'

'We love Holly!' he said simply. 'Luke stops being grumpy when she's around.'

'I'm not grumpy!' Luke protested. 'And shouldn't you be at school?' Just then it seemed that the Zoom call was dropping out, but it turned out to be Milo, Dom and Grace guffawing uncontrollably. Ziggy started barking too.

'Oh, dear me,' said Dom, wiping tears of mirth from his eyes. 'Not grumpy! Now I really have heard everything.'

'If you were so set on bringing us together, Dom,' said Holly suddenly, 'why did you fake all those messages from Yasmine?'

Dom vaped thoughtfully. 'It's a fair question,' he said at last.

'Well?'

'It's a thing Luke does. He sets himself impossible quests so that he doesn't have to deal with reality. All I tried to do was show him that the whole Yasmine thing was one such fantasy.'

'Thank you, Dom. That's very interesting. And why do we think he wants to stop himself from having a normal relationship?'

'I think, if I may, some of this goes back to Luke's mum.' Luke was astonished to hear Alan's voice. 'I think losing her at a young age, plus dealing with his parents breaking up before that, left him with some very deep wounds.'

'Alan!' said Luke and Holly as one.

'Oh God, I'm sorry, Luke,' said Alan. 'This whole thing is wrong on so many levels. I've been lured here under false pretences. Greg asked me to dial in for a chat about your job. A sort of virtual Bring Your Parent To Work Day, or something.'

'That was on November 4,' said Luke.

'Not that I am your parent, exactly.'

'Why is Luke even here? – that's another good question,' said Holly, of all people. Really, it was so hard not to join in. 'I mean – it's obvious he hates the place.'

'Or is it himself that he hates?' said Clive, whose chin was dotted with little red blotches from his board marker. He turned and added the words *toxic masculinity* to the whiteboard. And then, as if moved by some urgent impulse he could neither control nor understand, he added: *podcast??*

'And what about Holly?' asked Phaedra.

'Oh, she's absolutely lovely,' said Alan. 'I'm always telling Luke she reminds me of his mum. Oh! God! Sorry, sorry. There I go again.'

'You said Muriel did!' protested Luke.

'Did I?' said Alan, peering at the screen. 'I'm so sorry, I get all the names mixed up.'

'Oh, Holly – that's easy,' said Muriel. 'Holly chooses unsuitable dates to sabotage her own chances of love.'

'And why do I do that?' Holly had spent the first few minutes of this session staring wild-eyed around the room as if trying to find a single person who shared her level of outrage at this surreal violation of, of, well, everything. But slowly and inevitably, the conversation – concerning as it did her own self – had started to draw her in.

'You suffer from low self-esteem,' Muriel said with great certainty. 'Low self-esteem is our great gift to the world. It's what keeps women's magazines in business.'

Luke glanced over at the whiteboard, which Clive had rapidly been filling up with scribbled notes:

Luke
Stupid quest junkie
Hopeless romantic??
Can't see wood for trees
Dodgy dress sense (quick win)
Primal wound + dog
Why so grumpy?

Holly
Low self-esteem
Able to put up with Luke
Much too nice
Like Luke's mum (in a good way)
Stop reading ladies' mags
Running away from happiness??

'You can run away from Wordy Gigs,' said Greg with the air of a man delivering a piece of wisdom for the ages. 'But you can't run away from yourselves.'

'Er... I'm not running away,' said Holly with admirable restraint. 'You laid me off, remember?'

'In a technical sense, true,' said Greg. 'But I think my wider point stands.'

'We're all waiting for our lives to turn into stories,' a voice was saying now. 'You know – "I was struggling until I met X or started doing Y, and then everything took off from there". We all like to think of our lives as satisfying narratives following a meaningful pattern. But there is no narrative: there is only dread, guilt and fear. Money and material gain, if they come, only hollow us out; the having never quite delivers on the wanting. Trapped and restless, we bounce around through life like crabs at the bottom of a kid's bucket. Illness, infirmity and insanity snap at us from the shadows. All will be over soon.' The voice was oddly tinny and echoey, as if speaking from an enclosed metallic space.

'Oh, dear Lord,' said Luke. 'Who invited Reggie from Hornsey BoxLife to this?'

CHAPTER 102

Next day was International Check Your Wipers Day. Dom – who like Luke had made no mention of the intervention – got his flatmate to go up and down the road, inspect all the wipers and put little notes on the windscreens of those that looked like they needed replacing. Mrs Hart waved her encouragement, and only two car owners threatened to assault him.

The previous day's events were not easy to process, so Luke basically didn't try. He got on with walking the dog, updating the blog, and helping Alan in the garden. He told the office he would be working from home for a few days, and in reply to one of his emails Muriel mentioned that Holly was working from home too. Neither of them had made any effort to speak to the other.

November 22 was Start Your Own Country Day. This one was started at the 1939 New York World's Fair – in retrospect, a most inauspicious year – to honour 'those free-spirited souls who dared to hope and believe in a better world where they too could declare any land their own'. After browsing a list of micro-nations on Wikipedia, and deciding that starting his own country was rather too much bother, Luke wandered on to a geopolitical role play site where you could pretend to invent a nation, and see how it panned out on the world stage.

He filled out a detailed questionnaire that got him thinking surprisingly hard about his politics and his values, and soon the result emerged. Characterised by the site (a tad sarcastically perhaps) as a "Left-wing Utopia", the Republic of Milvania turned out to be *'a fledgling, environmentally stunning nation, remarkable for its punitive income tax rates. The democratic population of 5 million Milvanians are free to do what they want with their own bodies, and vote for whomever they like in elections; if they go into business, however, they are regulated to within an inch of their lives.*

'The enormous, socially-minded government juggles the competing demands of Welfare, Education and Healthcare. The average income tax rate is 55.7 per cent, and even higher for the wealthy. The developing Milvanian economy, worth 123 billion kronor a year, is led by the Information Technology industry, with major contributions from Furniture Restoration, Basket Weaving, and Pizza Delivery. State-owned companies are common. Average income is 24,689 kronor, and is distributed extremely evenly, with little difference between the richest and poorest citizens.

'Crime is totally unknown, thanks to a capable police force and progressive social policies in education and welfare.' Luke noted that the national animal chosen for Milvania was *'the squirrel, which frolics freely in the nation's many lush forests'*. More sarcasm perhaps?

Within seconds of his country coming into being, Luke was bombarded with messages from other 'countries'. They all seemed to want Milvania to join their community, trading bloc, region or military coalition, promising to give him a better chance of succeeding at the game. This could all be fun to carry on with and get more involved with, he thought. But then so could a lot of things. Like geocaching perhaps. Life was short, and he had a nagging suspicion there was something else he was supposed to be focusing on.

Though he had barely noticed it before, Alan had always been quite political. When Luke told him about the game, he said, 'Instead of looking at ways to start your own country – how about looking at ways to make this country better?' Luke said he didn't know how; Alan immediately handed him a sheaf of leaflets and a list of streets to deliver to. Luke did as he was asked. It was an uneventful couple of hours, with the exception of a tongue-lashing from a stressed-looking mum with two small kids hanging off her who said that money earmarked for 'low-traffic zones in posh neighbourhoods' could be better spent on hospitals, and a weepy tirade from an elegant elderly gent who complained that the mayor was spying on him.

'How?' asked Luke.

'Through my air fryer,' said the man.

CHAPTER 103

'Fancy a coffee?' Holly asked Luke a couple of days later. It was the first day they were both back in the office after the, you know, the thing.

'Good God, no,' he said. 'I've had about ten already. It's National Espresso Day.' Jittery and restless, Luke had typed and retyped the same sentence very fast, about fifteen times over. This was unfortunate, as the sentence in question was '*Aiming to please: How to minimise washroom splashback.*'

'Tea then?'

'Sure.'

As they made their way down to street level, Luke breathlessly exclaimed to Holly that 'espresso' was number nineteen in the UK's top twenty most commonly mispronounced food words, according to a recent survey. It was one of the most commonly misspelled too, he said: people often wrote it with an *x*. He quizzed her on a few other commonly mistaken food words, such as *acai* (pronounced ah-sigh-ee) and *maraschino* (which should be pronounced ma-ra-skeeno with a hard K sound).

'What's the number one word?' asked Holly. He seemed oddly obsessed, so she decided to run with it.

'That's *tzatziki* – pronounced tsat-si-key. I think I would have got that one, but then I do live in London's kebab capital.'

'Luke,' said Holly. 'Are you just going on about all this to avoid talking about that fecking intervention?'

'Of course not!' said Luke. 'Now *bruschetta* is another one I always get wrong.'

CHAPTER 104

Luke was amazed to discover that there was such a thing as National Alan Day (November 28), and he got together with the kids and Dom to make a big fuss of his stepdad. They had a fun evening, playing lots of board games and watching *Meet the Fockers* on the telly. Alan kept apologising for his role in the intervention, but Luke told him not to feel bad. He'd been duped himself.

'So... have you managed to get it together with Holly yet?' said Grace, ignoring Alan. 'Come on, everyone can see it.'

'Well, it's not up to everyone else though, is it?'

'Oh, come on. Why are you always trying to get in the way of your own happiness?'

'I'm not, Milo. And who told you to say that, by the way?'

'Ziggy.'

Luke and Holly finally went for a drink the next night. They began by discussing a few new terms for *The Dictionary of Office Life*. Possibly thinking of Clive, Luke had come up with:

Thirst aid officer
Noun. The bloke in the office who is always up for a snifter, any lunchtime or evening of the week. Usually a figure of pity, he becomes invaluable on the night you've just been dumped by your boyfriend/girlfriend and can't find anyone else to drown your sorrows with.

While Holly contributed:

Tibbles
Noun pl. The small pools of tea that randomly appear up to three days after spilling a full cup over your keyboard and desk.

'So you've made a start on the tea-making section at last,' he said.

'I have indeed. Plenty more where that came from,' she said. 'Though I'm going to have to hurry – my leaving do's in two weeks.'

Luke was silent for a beat. 'We can still carry on with the Great Work though, can't we?'

Holly said nothing. After that, the conversation wandered awkwardly and circuitously to the very fringes of the topic which had doubtless been preoccupying both of them for days. Outrage seemed a good way in.

'Honestly, the cheek of them all. Ambushing us like that.'

'I know! And especially when Greg and Phaedra had literally just made me redundant.'

'I've never seen a group of people so up for a chat about fridge-cleaning.'

'Of course, it's all very silly. The protocols of Office Nomance are very clear.'

'Absolutely. I mean, if it was ever going to happen, it would have happened already anyway.'

'Right.'

'I mean, it's a ridiculous idea,' said Luke, after a round or two. 'What if everyone just went round getting together with their best mate?'

'Well, quite.'

Three or four drinks later, Holly asked: 'What if we just kissed?'

'Eh?'

'You know, just so we could tell them we'd tried it and it wasn't right.'

They kissed. Luke would always remember the moment as an intoxicating vanilla swoon.

'Wow,' he said at last. 'I've not done that with you before.'

'Well, not except during moments of mortal fear and under strict orders from Dom,' she replied.

'Yes. I mean, they were great too. Do you think Steve will mind?'

'He's so busy training I don't think he'll notice. And Patsy?'

'Oh, she said we could try again...'

'In another lifetime,' they both added, as one. They kissed again. Though the first voluntary kissing experience of a few moments before had set the bar very high, this follow-up could not be described as anything but an improvement.

'By the way, Luke, what day is it today?'

'Oh, November 30th. Let's see – I believe it's Personal Space Day.'

'I'm not sure you're doing a very good job of observing that one.'

'No?' said Luke. 'Okay, let's see. It's also National Mississippi Day.'

'Kississippi Day, more like.'

'That is the sort of dreadful play on words I've come to rely on you for.'

'It could be our Day.' She smiled, and they kississipi-ed again.

DECEMBER

CHAPTER 105

It had been a hell of a year, Luke reflected, as he stepped out with Ziggy for a frosty morning walk. Luke had taken on a ridiculous challenge that no one thought he'd stick to for a week. And though he ached for the day when he could wake up and not have to worry about accountably appreciating a mail carrier or helping a horse or speaking in Shakespearean English – a day when he could just ignore whatever Day it was and do absolutely nothing, all day – he was certain now of seeing this thing through to the bitter end. If this was a marathon, he was in mile twenty-six. Admittedly the point of it all was still not really clear, but then epiphanies never arrived promptly for Luke. 'No experience is ever wasted,' as Alan liked to say, and Luke – at last in a place where he could be receptive to Alan's thoughts – dearly wanted to believe this was true.

What else? Well, he had come to understand the true nature of his dad. He had been bitterly disappointed at first by what he'd discovered, and cross with himself for not having seen through his dad's bluster before. But his dad was such a pathetic figure now he was more to be pitied than condemned; and really, the evidence had always been there, it was only his wishful thinking that had shielded him from the rather sad reality.

Then, too, he had healed his relationship with Alan. Alan had been his parent in the day to day, which is the only place that really matters, the only thing we really have. And this made sense, because Mum had chosen him and knew that when she had to leave, her son would be in good hands. (Mum had also chosen Dad, of course, but then every rule...)

Finally, Yasmine. And Holly. The year had sealed the end of his 'affair' with the one (who had never been, as it turned out, The One) and brought him together with the other, a real person in the here and now, who (incredibly) might just be into him too, and who was already his best friend. It was a heady mix of the familiar and the strange, to be heading out on romantic dates (Italian films, Afghan food, muddy puppy walks) with the same person in whose gossipy company you'd spent years bitching about your co-workers, commiserating on crap dates and keeping hair out of their pukey face when Clive spiked the sangria at the office Christmas do. Holly and he had both always been looking for someone and they'd done lots of their looking together. Only they'd not thought to look at each other, to see that the person that might be for them was the one right in front of them. Not that he'd said much of this stuff to her yet; they were taking it slow for now, as felt right for something with the potential to be rather awesome. But things were definitely very tingly.

With the days running down to a triumphant conclusion, Luke 'National Gimp Day' Milvaine felt pretty gung-ho about the remaining challenges now. Quite gratuitously, he wore a fetching green frock to work – and attracted quite a few compliments on the overground – on Wear A Dress Day, for example. But December was the slowest month of all for silly fake holidays, and he was often reduced to quite literal, mundane activities. He played basketball with Alan, Grace and Milo on Play Basketball Day; he wore brown shoes on Wear Brown Shoes Day, and an ugly sweater on Ugly Sweater Day. He took to Duolingo on Learn Arabic Day; dragged himself with Holly round a club till the early hours on World Techno Day; and concocted some home-made slime with Milo on National Slime Day.

There was a panicky half hour when Ziggy appeared with a green tongue and everyone feared he had ingested a big dollop of borax susbtitute; some feverish googling did not provide much reassurance. (There were so many things dogs couldn't or shouldn't eat, Luke had discovered over the course of the year, including everyday things he'd never have guessed like chocolate, raisins, garlic and onions. If he put the word 'can' into his Google search bar, it auto-completed: 'Can a dog eat...') Fortunately, it turned out Ziggy had merely chewed on one of Milo's felt-tip pens. He was rewarded for his bad behaviour with half a cold sausage, which must have seemed to Ziggy like a good morning's work.

CHAPTER 106

Sunday, December 11 was International Mountain Day, which gave Luke the idea of taking Holly away for a weekend in Snowdonia. They began with a blissful night in a cosy BnB. Another high point was the long scramble up Mount Snowdon itself, at the top of which each of them said some rather cryptic and beautiful things to the other. Back down at the bottom of the climb, after a descent which seemed to take even longer going down than up, Holly announced that her phone's signal, which had been patchy on high, had returned.

They climbed into the Audi which Dom had most generously lent them for the weekend, and began the long drive home. Holly was strangely quiet, but Luke put it down to a mixture of message backlog and the dreamy quality of the whole weekend, which he felt had taken things to a whole new level between them.

Luke drove them back to his, and – with Holly smiling but still rather quiet – they popped in to give Mrs Hart the plant they'd bought her for National Poinsettia Day.

'That's very kind of you, dears,' said Mrs Hart as they handed the gift over. 'And do you know the legend of the poinsettia?' She asked this as if addressing a class of seven-year-olds. The couple both felt slightly patronised, but also compelled to sit at the elderly lady's feet for Story Time.

'Many years ago, a poor little girl called Pepita was very sad on Christmas Eve. And do you know why?'

'No, Miss.' The pair were trying to be ironic, but secretly they were both loving every infantilised moment.

'Because she was so poor she had no gift to present to baby Jesus at midnight Mass. But her cousin Pedro said to her, "Pepita, even the most humble gift will be acceptable in Jesus's eyes if given in love". Well, Pepita listened to those words... and do you know what she did?'

'No, Miss.'

'She gathered a handful of weeds by the roadside and made them into a little bouquet. She was very embarrassed, but she had nothing else so she decided to lay them at the foot of the nativity scene. And do you know what happened?'

They both shook their heads.

'Suddenly, the bouquet of weeds burst into blooms of brilliant red, and all who saw them were certain that they had witnessed a Christmas miracle right before their eyes!'

'Aw, Mrs Hart,' said Holly. 'That's beautiful.'

'And so are you, my dears.' She beamed. 'Now: Who would like a fig roll?'

'Oh! Thanks, Mrs Hart,' said Holly. She lapsed back into silence, munching ruminatively.

'Now I do believe there's something on your mind, Holly dear,' said Mrs Hart. 'Would you like to share it with the rest of the class?'

CHAPTER 107

There was, of course there was. The course of true thingy never does quite run thingily, now does it? And here it came.

'Luke,' said Holly at last, as they cuddled up on the sofa with Ziggy, who was flaunting his puppy junk again, in a shameless bid to woo Holly for himself.

'What is it?' He hadn't known Holly very long as his – what, girlfriend? Dare he call her that? – but he had been her close friend a long time and he knew when something was up. A strange dread crept over him.

'Sorry I've been a bit quiet,' she said.

'That's okay,' he said. Those two words were doing quite a bit of heavy lifting, because of course what he actually meant was: *'Is Everything Okay? What Have I Done Wrong??? Please Don't Leave Me!! Was I Terrible In Bed? Do I Smell!? Just Tell Me! I Can Fix It Whatever It Is! Please Don't Tell Me It's Over!!! Oh God, Don't Say You Want To Go Back To Being Friends!!!'* Something like that.

'I... got an email today,' she began.

An email. This sounded less drastic than the things he'd been dreading. 'Don't tell me – it's from Ancestry.com,' he said with a laugh. 'It turns out we're half-siblings.'

'No, nothing like that,' she said with a laugh that quickly petered out. 'It's about a job I applied for.'

'Oh! Brilliant! What is it?'

'It's Features and Lifestyle Editor for a new magazine aimed at travellers and expats. It's got amazing benefits. A big commissioning budget. And I'd be in charge of the whole thing.'

'Wow – and they've offered it to you?'

'Don't sound so surprised.'

'I'm not! You know I'm not! I'm just trying to work out whether I'm officially allowed to jump up and down yet.'

'Yes, they've offered it to me. It's like, *double* my salary at Wordy Gigs.'

'Yay! Go you!' He hugged her with pleasure. He'd been glad for her when she'd found a way out of the old place, but he'd always felt funny about still having a job when she didn't.

'I know!' she said. 'And all tax-free.' She sat on the end of his bed and waited for the words to sink in.

'That's amazing!' he said. 'Go you!' Then he sat down on the bed next to her, as the words sank in.

'Wait, where is it?'

'Abu Dhabi.'

CHAPTER 108

After that, things suddenly felt a bit weird between them. They chatted of this and that, but never of *the other*. Holly said she didn't mind a romcom, and Luke – who was a serious student of the genre – put on one of his favourites. But without thinking he had chosen *Sleepless in Seattle*, which – being all about thwarted love at a great distance – quickly created a bit of an atmosphere. Long before it was over, Holly announced that she needed to get back to her place, as it was her last week at Wordy Gigs coming up and she had stuff to sort out. (He said he should also get an early night, as it was National Cocoa Day tomorrow.) No doubt, though she didn't mention it, she had stuff to pack and things to sort for Abu Dhabi too.

On the walk to the Tube, the pair fell into yet another thoughtful silence. Luke wondered idly to himself whether Holly would have a lot of stuff she needed to store, and if so whether Reggie from Hornsey BoxLife might offer her a discount. There were so many more relevant things he wanted to say, but none that seemed altogether reasonable or non-desperate. Eventually he managed, 'And when do you go?'

'It would be December 31st.'

He had neglected to observe Lost and Found Day on December 9, but it seemed now that he had inadvertently invented its dark sister – Found and Lost Day. As the clouds hid the moon and the cold rain began to fall, he remembered now that tomorrow – as Dom would no doubt take great pleasure in pointing out – was also National Violin Day.

They kissed goodbye at the barrier, and it seemed as if they were kissing goodbye for the last time.

Chapter 109

A couple of days later, Luke came across a note from Dom on the kitchen table. It bulged with the key of his Audi, which Luke understood from the message he was now to consider his own.

You've kept me going this year, the note began. *I've lived it through you. I'm sorry if I made it too hard. I just wanted you to keep going. I wanted you to see it through – for both our sakes.*

There was more in this vein, but none of it made any sense. Where was Dom? And why, after years of sarcasm and low-level humiliation, would he turn round and gift him his Audi? Luke would have liked to ask him, but there was no answer when he knocked on Dom's door. A couple of days later he was emboldened to turn the handle. To his surprise, the door opened. To his even greater surprise, all Dom's things had gone. The posters and postcards were folded neatly on his bed, but of his clothes, books, toiletries (and pills), there was nothing to be seen.

Luke slipped the note into the shoebox under his bed. He found there the little watch box that Dom had given him before. Assuming it was the same satirical Casio non-gift that Dom had presented to Alan, he had never bothered to open it. But he did so now, and discovered a rather different timepiece: a beautiful

Baume et Mercier Classima 10415, with silver dial in sun-satin finish, elegant gilt hands and Roman numerals for hour markers. Red-brown leather strap, impeccable Swiss quartz movement. All of this he got later from the internet, of course, which adjudged the Classima – and Luke had never before felt so *seen* – as '*a fitting wristwatch for the modern gentleman who appreciates tradition*'. But what set Luke off wasn't the beauty of the gift, or its surprising value (which he couldn't help also googling) or even the fact that it had come from Dom, so much as the inscription on the reverse:

> *For Luke, Master of Days.*
> *Who really can write (a bit).*
> *'No present like time'*

CHAPTER 110

Holly's leaving do began like so many other leaving dos and birthday drinks at Wordy Gigs. The event was an excuse to down tools early, and Luke was happy to comply with Phaedra's request to leave off his latest opus, '*Nipple guards and anti-chafing creams: A runner's guide*' (new sports-shop client) and head to the kitchen in search of glasses. Soon the Prosecco was flowing, and everyone came out to listen as Greg made another of his terrible speeches. It proved to be an absolute corker of the genre, even by his own exemplary standards.

'Holly!' he began promisingly. 'To help me put together this little speech, I naturally emailed round among your colleagues to ask for a few thoughts and memories.' He shuffled his bits of paper. 'Here's one: "She always makes sure the ladies' loo is fully stocked with posh handwash".' Someone cheered. 'Not something I've been able to verify at first hand, I hasten to reassure you all.' A couple of listless titters.

'Several people mentioned all the items around your desk, Holly! Like your ever-growing collection of ceramic poodles, or the piles of printouts you keep by your feet, which you claim are vital background reading and in no way represent a conflict of interest with your role as our company's Fire Prevention and Awareness Officer.'

'*Oh, dear Lord,*' muttered Phaedra loudly.

Holly was shaking her head. People were turning to one another in confusion. But Greg was oblivious.

'But seriously, folks, the word that comes up most when anyone talks about you is "support",' said Greg.

'"She's always there when you need a shoulder to cry on. To my certain knowledge, she has helped people in this office through two divorces, three bereavements and a serious case of bullying" – said someone who wishes to remain anonymous.'

'Office bullying?' Phaedra hissed. '*Which twat wrote that*?'

Greg's eyes appeared to be welling with tears. Luke remembered he was only just back from an extremely lengthy client lunch. 'And that's the thing about you,' he was saying now. 'You are always there for other people. You are the heart of this office, someone who encourages everyone to see their workplace not just as somewhere to live out their nine to five-thirty but as a *community*. A place where people look out for each other. Just so long as you remember to put your bits in the dishwasher!

'And so everyone, raise your glasses... to Muriel!'

'Oh, Jesus Christ,' hissed Phaedra. 'We decided to keep her, remember?'

'Thanks for those kind words,' said Muriel, deadpan. 'This is actually Holly's leaving do, though.'

'Technically, yes,' said Greg. 'But I think my wider point stands.'

Muriel had arranged a collection, and the gang presented Holly with a chic Lulu Guinness cabin-spinner carry-on case.

'Let me add something,' said Luke suddenly. He was as surprised as anyone to hear himself speak. 'Holly, you are the best colleague any of us could have wished for. We are so proud of you for getting out and wish you every success as you embark on your exciting new adventure.

'To Holly! And all who sail in her!' Luke raised his glass, almost savagely, and the fizz sloshed everywhere. At the end there it seemed his voice got a bit wobbly, and he had to run out of the room in search of 'more ice'.

Muriel quickly produced a mop and began vigorously applying herself to the spillage.

CHAPTER 111

Luke sat in the cubicle and inspected his phone. He was amazed to notice a new message had popped up on the Make Every Day Count blog – from Yazz028, of all people.

Your presence is requested at the chapel at Heathrow Airport. Noon, December 31st. In the meantime, try not to mess things up. Search for the biro inside yourself!

He set this aside, because the day's festivities were now gradually spilling over into the dreaded roped-off area in Muscadello's. The staff knew the drill: use up the money the bosses had put behind the bar here as quickly as possible, then sneak away from the enforced merriment and seek sanctuary in The Devonshire Maid. Here, there was more toasting of Holly and joshing of Luke for his teary speech, which he didn't mind really because it meant that his conduct had not been considered so odd or embarrassing that everyone had to dance round it. Luke updated Holly, whom he had not really spoken to for a few days, on the note from Dom, and the new comment on the blog, presumably also from him.

'So... how are you feeling about the big day?'

She looked at him oddly. 'Oh, you know. Weird.'

'It's always nerve-wracking to start with. You know, that first-day-at-school feeling.'

'And how do you feel about it?' She had always been braver than him.

'I, well, weird too, obviously. I kept my cards very close to my chest in my speech.'

Holly put a hand on his arm. 'It doesn't... It doesn't have to be the end of everything, does it?'

Luke stiffened. He looked away from her as he said, 'I'm sorry. The distance thing. My dad, Yasmine, you know. I just... can't be commuting to the Middle East every five minutes.'

When he turned back, there were tears in Holly's eyes, but her next words were spoken more in anger than sorrow.

'I told you I'd been offered the job,' she said. 'You never asked me what I was going to do about it.'

'You booked a flight!' said Luke.

'I'm surprised you didn't book it for me,' she spat back.

CHAPTER 112

Did it count to observe a Day by doing something you would've done anyway? Luke had long agonised over this point, but there was no Dom around to hold him to account, and besides, there was very little going on calendar-wise. At the fag-end of the year the fake holidays were themselves taking a holiday. So, on Christmas Eve, Luke was happy to observe Last-Minute Shopping Day, heading off with Alan and Milo to Asda for a motley selection of last-minute purchases – bread sauce mix (essential), presents for unexpected visitors, foil, extra bread, milk and coffee, spare chocolates, stuffing mix. The shop was full of everyone else doing the same thing, and an odd parking regime had taken over. A squad of phone-staring lads in hi-vis jackets were directing everyone to drive into the underground section of the car park, quickly leading to total gridlock, while the fenced-off upper bits remained virtually car-free.

But it wasn't all bad news, as the disruption gave locals a good opportunity for a moan on the local neighbourhood app. A post on this topic attracted thirty-eight replies, and quickly degenerated into another version of every other thread on the app. A few highlights:

>> Chaos at Asda... virtually empty upstairs car parks with space for 100s...and cars backing up along the main road !!! I was told by a marshall to go to asda enfield !!! How ridiculous – I'm off to sainsburys to spend my £200.

>> It's done to stop ignorant drivers parking in mother and baby or disabled spaces when they are not entitled to. We should applaud the action rather than be quick to shoot them down.

>> I was buying a couple of last-minute things. I saw a woman with a trolley full of stuff and 5 kids... Seriously, who leaves all Xmas shopping to Xmas eve!?

>> Maybe a busy woman with five kids???

>> All from different fathers?

No one had compared things to the Nazis yet, but it was clearly only a matter of time.

CHAPTER 113

Hi Holly, typed Luke late that night.

I'm sorry about how things went at your leaving do. I just wanted to make sure you got the attached before you go. I know you've been busy so I thought I could cover this one for you. Hope it's okay – do let me know if you have any comments or queries.

Luke Milvaine Esq (Co-chair, New Words Committee.) xx

The attachment in question was the fabled and much-delayed section on tea-making for *The Dictionary of Office Life*. Luke was about to hit *send* but at the last minute switched to *schedule send*. He set it to go on December 31 at 7pm.

The scheduled send thing was a great strategy he wished he'd worked out years ago. When working at home, he could bang out a piece of copy in an hour, schedule it to send a couple of hours later, and earn himself a couple of hours' free time. If, like Luke, you had a gift for spouting plausible bollox at high speed you could effectively earn a full-time wage for part-time hours. It was also good, he saw now, for highly charged moments of existential crisis in your life, when your future happiness hung in the balance and you didn't know what to do about it. You could schedule your email, and defer thinking about it for a little while longer.

Around this time, he also received an email from the nation-making role play site. It turned out that, in the country of his own making, the combination of a compulsory new organ-harvesting scheme and some Big Brother-style surveillance measures put in place by his heavy-handed police force were creating the conditions for widespread civil unrest. The subject line read: 'APOCALYPSE LOOMS IN MILVANIA!' 'Tell me about it,' muttered Luke to himself, as he entered into a brief reverie in which he and Holly invented a country of their own and all difficulties were resolved. A place where she didn't have to choose between her job and her relationship, and where he didn't have to choose between the woman he loved – and…

And what exactly? He fingered Dom's inscription. *No present like time.* Infuriatingly, the words became more profound and multi-layered with every rub. Dom – *profound*? It was hard to take.

'*Ah, feck it!*' he shouted at a quizzical Ziggy. Ziggy had been dozing on The Chair, but sleepy as he was he couldn't stop his tail starting up its joyous throb. Luke hit *send*.

CHAPTER 114

On Christmas Day, Luke wrote a blog post reflecting on the year but taking care not to use the twelfth letter of the alphabet. This was because December 25 was also 'No L' Day (geddit?) – an observance allegedly coined by Alfred Hitchcock, who was fond of a pun. He used to send out Christmas cards displaying the whole alphabet, only with one letter missing. Clearly he was quite the hoot.

> I woke up at 6ish [Luke wrote, L-lessly] and knowing we had peeps (Auntie Maud, Mrs Hart, etc) arriving for the festivities in a few hours, I decided to get Ziggy's morning canter out of the way. We set out in the frost and were at the park by 7.30am. It's not supposed to open before 8am, so a sign said, but the gate was ajar, and with thanks we stepped inside. Ziggy roamed and quartered the woods he so enjoys, chasing scents and tree rodents, with a joy that moved me. I sat on a big piece of chopped wood and watched my dog, for some reason shedding a tear from time to time. From nowhere it had become one of those unexpected moments where you sense yourself a part of

something more, and for a moment your being streams, in a happy-sad way, out of time.

Later on that day, Luke took Milo and Grace with Alan to unveil the present he had sorted for his stepdad. Present wasn't perhaps quite the right word, but he knew at once from his stifled sobs that Alan got it. They stood around his mum's grave, with its new words – the words Alan, who loved her most and best, then as now, would have chosen:

ANGIE – MUM, PARTNER, SISTER, FRIEND
SO LOVING AND SO LOVED
THANK YOU FOR THE DAYS

Luke wrote thank you notes on Thank You Note Day (December 26) and made a fruitcake on Fruitcake Day (December 27). He enjoyed the blog post that Muriel had written for their office-cleaning client for December 30: '*37 Uses For The Wonder Powder That Cleans Everything It Touches!*' Lots of other enterprising outfits had found ways to tie in a marketing message with Bicarbonate Of Soda Day, from purveyors of kitchen science books and life hacks, to drain and plumbing experts, to wine merchants: '*Did you know that you can use baking soda to remove red wine stains?*' A soap maker in Jacksonville, Florida, reminded everyone that '*without baking soda there would be no bath bombs!*' Luke's favourite tie-in was the advert for a new thriller about a serial murderer who always made an extra-good job of clearing up their carnage. It was called *Obsessive Compulsive Killer.*

He kept the Make Every Day Count blog updated too, and looked out for more messages from Dom. There were none, unless you counted the one in spam that said, '*See you in the Chapel on the 31st*'. This still made no sense, and besides, he could not be making plans for December 31st.

Luke and Holly had exchanged a couple of tersely inconclusive calls in the interim. He knew she had been away a lot too, visiting friends and relatives to say goodbye, so it hadn't been easy to meet or chat. But perhaps both had had the same thought: better to leave things as they were rather than drag out the agony unnecessarily. Some things are just not meant to be, and no doubt that would all make sense one day too.

Chapter 115

And yet: here he was, catching the first Tube on New Year's Eve. There was no mate at the airport to get him airside, as had been painfully well established, but he could, what, at least go and say goodbye properly? It was what friends did, wasn't it? He wondered if there would be a gang of people there to send her off, and how he would deal with that (the last time he had publicly addressed the reality of Holly's departure would be unlikely to make his All-time Top Ten Moments of Grace and Poise list). Ah well. Something else not to think about too much.

As a man with form in springing not-always-welcome surprises on women at airports, he was confident that he knew the flight Holly would be on, and would be there early enough to catch her at the check-in area. Even if she had checked in online, she would still have a suitcase to hand in, so it should be hard to miss her. It was silly that he had bought flowers really, even if he knew (from Tom the gardener) that the pink roses, peonies and gypsophila he'd arranged with care into an informal bouquet were her favourites, as she couldn't of course take them onto 'the aircraft'. (Or plane, as he liked to call it.)

Luke's usual headphones were broken, so he was using his

tinny little phone ones. Just after Covent Garden, an angry-looking man in expensive Lycra gear – a clear candidate for some righteous *cyclist rage* – began tapping him on the shoulder and gesturing at his ears.

'Can I help?' said Luke as calmly as he could manage.

'Excuse me, mate, can you turn your music down?'

'I'm sorry?' said Luke, to buy himself some processing time.

'Your music. It's blaring out. No one can hear themselves think.'

'Oh, sorry.' Luke paused, but couldn't resist adding, 'Actually this is *Father and Son*, by Sir Edmund Gosse.'

'You what, mate?'

'It's an audiobook.'

'Sorry, mate,' said the cyclist unapologetically. 'I don't do trip hop.'

CHAPTER 116

At the airport, Luke raced round to the check-in area. There were five hours till the flight took off; it seemed implausible that he could have missed her. And yet, as the minutes turned into hours, he came slowly to accept that miss her he had. Holly must have gone through early. He traipsed back out of the terminal, forlorn bouquet in hand, until a sign caught his eye: CHAPEL.

He knew the way at least. There was a painful echo of his last failed airport trip, in oddly parallel circumstances.

At first my taking over your silly Day challenge was just a way to lash out at you, Dom had written in his note. *Not for anything you'd done but for what was happening to me. But you ended up giving me something to go on for. I lived a little more this last (last) year, thanks to you.*

Luke followed the signs, tracking unerringly along passageways, under flyovers and across bus concourses until he found again the entrance to this odd concrete cylinder on its traffic-lashed roundabout, and began his spiralling descent. He paused uncertainly in the doorway; a service of some kind was in progress. Suddenly Luke gave a start of something like joy, for there in the front row was Dom. He raced up to him but stopped just in time.

It wasn't Dom. But it was someone who had to be related to Dom. He had the same patrician stoop, the same long tweedy coat, the same way of sceptically steepling his fingers. An older brother perhaps? The priest said something about 'your servant Dominic' and a lady standing next to the Dom-a-like began to quietly sob. The Dom-a-like put his arm round her. Other stifled sobs and coughs could be heard from around the chapel. Luke had the sudden sense that everyone was here for the same reason.

Luke froze in mid-aisle, suddenly self-conscious. He turned. At the back of the space, tucked behind a couple of larger hunched figures, Luke saw a movement. It reminded him of the time he, Mum and Alan had once sat in a hide when he was a kid, waiting hours with a group of earnest birders for a kingfisher to emerge from its nest. When the moment finally arrived, and even though he hadn't really understood the significance, Luke had shared in the euphoria and relief, and even got a chance to look at the marvel through a long-distance lens.

A leaflet caught his eye. *A Mass For The Repose Of The Soul Of Dominic 'Dom' Crispin.*

The movement again, somewhere at the back. A pale-pink hand waving, albeit very discreetly, as one might wave at a service for the dead. Luke quietly crept round to the back pew, and squeezed in next to Holly.

He understood suddenly that Dom was dead, and that he had lured Holly here, just as he had lured Luke. It was his last play, his Double joker for Make Up Your Mind Day (December 31).

Holly squeezed his arm, and looked up at him in a way he would never forget. There were so many things to shed tears for just now. Sticking out of her little handbag (no Lulu Guinness carry-on case, as far as he could see) he noticed a printout of the tea-making section he'd written for *The Dictionary of Office Life*:

Tea-leaf

Noun. The co-worker who never offers to make the tea, but always grabs the chance of a cuppa when someone else offers. Aka **Tea-baddy**.

Brew Dog

Noun. An apparently very eager tea-maker whose drinks are so rank that people are beginning to suspect it's a tactic to get out of further drink-making.

Lone Wolf

Noun. A furtive, unsociable figure who refuses all offers of a drink from other people, and only ever makes a cup for themselves.

Herbert

Noun. The smug healthie who, when you offer to make a round of teas, pulls out their own liquorice, cinnamon and hibiscus sachet, then proceeds to recite laborious instructions for its optimal infusion.

Nag-bag

Noun. The infuriating co-worker who always makes a very small but ostentatious round of drinks very early in the morning (before most of the office have even sat down to work), then spends the rest of the day moaning about how it's time for more tea but it's definitely not their turn.

Tea-totaller

Noun. A person who will never turn down an offer of a drink, even when they clearly have a steaming half-full mug on their desk already.

Sip-tease

Noun. The infuriating colleague who regularly hints at making a round of teas, but never actually follows through.

Mutual infusion pact

Noun. A strict agreement between two or three co-workers to only and always make drinks for each other *and no one else*.

Kettle prod

Noun. The person at the next desk you used to spend all day chatting and laughing with. The one who made work bearable, even if they never put enough milk in and always forgot to take the bag out.

The one that left for that job in Abu Dhabi. The one you keep meaning to email to say, *Hey, you stole my David Bowie mug!*

The one you never got round to telling was just your cup of tea.

Epilogue

TOMORROW AND TOMORROW AND TOMORROW

JANUARY 1, 2025

Weddings are funny things, aren't they? Well, this one was. For starters Holly said she wasn't sure about marriage so she'd rather call theirs a 'commitment party'. Not that it changed anything; everyone just assumed it was a wedding anyway, and then they heard the word 'party' and were even happier. The day after New Year's Eve might have seemed an odd choice for a wedding, but Luke pointed out it was very 'on-brand' for Holly and him, a couple determined to make every day together count. And no one else seemed to mind either; they all just carried on the party from the night before, happy to defer the hangover for another 24 hours.

Luke and Gav's old school mates were all out in force in their Make Every Day Count T-shirts. Luke had scheduled the stag do for a good week before the main event, to give himself time to recover, and this proved to be a wise move. After the big night no one could remember much of what had actually happened, although Gav's Marvel-mad brother had got into a row with the bossy one and the boozy one about the merits of rival cinematic universes. The bow-tied one had thrown the Helmet of Truth at someone else's head, and an attempt had been made to place the

Golf Flag of Destiny in a bodily cavity where it didn't rightly belong. Gav would have been proud.

The ceremony was co-officiated by Janine the Chief Psychic Demonstrator and Gaynor the Taoist. Holly and Luke walked down the aisle to a haunting rendition of The Kinks' '(Thank You For The) Days', played beautifully on a specially decorated traffic cone by Michael the Cone. Janine had kindly allowed the service to take place in her temple, with the reception in its pretty, dog-friendly backyard. It was a clear, crisp, starlit night, and the flaming torches, firepits, lanterns and quilted blankets that Janine had laid on made for a wonderfully warm and atmospheric occasion.

Gaynor gave an arresting sermon in which she asked everyone to turn to the person next to them, give them a big hug and shout: 'I forgive you!' People looked a little quizzical and self-conscious at first, but it certainly broke the ice. In her address, Janine made it clear that she had predicted the love match all along, when she first met Luke. It had been an instant intuition, gifted by Spirit.

('When was that then?' Luke had asked her during their marriage preparation sessions. 'You remember – when I suddenly heard the word *Ivy*.' 'Eh?' 'The holly and the ivy, silly! And all at Christmas.' 'I'll give you that,' said Luke, who had been in the habit of making up far more contrived stuff for his day job.)

All the old gang from Wordy Gigs were there, of course. Muriel, who had to be forcibly restrained from cleaning the venue's oven, cut a fine rug on the dance floor with Martin. Their four boys all came along too, and ran round the dance floor firing NERF guns at each other. Greg arrived with his wife, Anna, and the pair were soon Lindy-Hopping it up a storm to any tune that came on, whether country, Latin pop or R&B. Phaedra arrived with a mystery man in tow, with whom she sat canoodling in a corner for most of the night.

Dom's brother and mum, whom Luke had met at the airport chapel, were in attendance, and Dom was much mentioned and celebrated. He had arranged that service himself, it transpired, a week after his own one-way flight to Switzerland. His family laughed along with everyone else at Luke's stories of the demanding challenges his flatmate had put him through, though he was careful to focus on the gentler, funnier ones than the more heartless, sadistic ones.

Grace, who had taken to the role of Best Man with relish, was not so delicate. Somehow, with the help of the IT department at Wordy Gigs, she had managed to uncover some candidly uncensored images of National Gimp Day – images Luke had been assured were deleted and erased beyond any hope of retrieval. These were not for the faint-hearted, and the Prosecco went down extra-fast after that.

Alan, whom Holly had asked to walk her down the aisle, gave a quietly impassioned speech about the year Luke had been through, the journey it had meant for everyone, how proud he was of his stepson, and how happy in his choice of bride. His words were simple and true and kind, and no one could fail to be moved by them. Alan had shown up every day and he had always wanted the best for Luke, both to honour his beloved partner and because that's how he was. Luke tried to say some of all this in the joint speech he gave with Holly. He was wildly incoherent at times, faltering and nervous, with a little bit of sobbing here and there, but there was so much good feeling in his words that everyone knew exactly what they meant and who they were meant for.

Luke's dad didn't speak, which seemed like the best option all round. But he was very much present, relishing his role as Keeper of the Beasts. For, as one sensed Ziggy had stipulated, it was a very dog-friendly wedding, and the venue was one where the animals could wander around freely all night. Michelle, who accepted a cheque from Luke on behalf of the Trigeminal Neuralgia Association, brought Teddy, Aunt Maud bought her two labs, and there were quite a few others. Pete ran his dog creche into the evening. He came along with twelve-year-old twins from his second marriage. Nothing could have rained on Luke's parade that day, and this concrete evidence that he had another couple of step-siblings his dad had forgotten to mention was so superbly on-brand for his old man – and so in the spirit of the more-the-merrier vibe of the day – that he and Holly raced to embrace them. The girls were soon spotted in the backyard, blowing bubbles at the dogs with Milo.

Mrs Hart came too, of course, in her best frock and hat. She quietly munched on fig rolls throughout the whole ceremony and told numerous people that Luke had always had a lot to say for himself. But Luke knew Mrs Hart better than that. As he fondly explained in his speech, she had been a friend and mentor to him throughout the year, wise and candid, and Holly still dined out on the poinsettia story.

There were a few messages from fondly absent friends too. The boys from Vancouver sent the happy couple a lovely message in the way they knew best – his and her matching T-shirts emblazoned with the words, "THAT HOLLY IS SO COOL I KEEP THINKING SHE'S CANADIAN". Reggie from Hornsey BoxLife couldn't make it either, but he had the best possible excuse – after a brief dip, he was now back in the family home for keeps, and enjoying a three-week make-up cruise with the missus. As a wedding gift he offered the couple twelve months' free storage, with the option to upgrade to twenty-four months at a very reasonable rate. No rush, think it over.

Holly did get to Abu Dhabi, albeit only for about a year. Luke came out a lot, and managed to work from abroad for several weeks at a time. After his initial panic, Luke decided that he was uniquely placed for the challenge of time apart: he had kept a meaningless challenge going for a year, and an imaginary relationship for even longer; holding on to something real for twelve months would be a doddle. Holly then returned to the UK when another job came up, this time as website manager for a prison reform charity. Luke, meanwhile, decided to leave the copywriting game altogether, and retrain as a primary school teacher. Thanks to his Special Days challenge, he said, he had ideas for at least 365 lessons and assemblies. Holly said it was good that he'd be off when the kids were out of school, and they shared a secret smile.

'So,' Luke whispered in Holly's ear as they swayed with clumsy joy to the first dance, Jonny Cash's 'A Thing Called Love'. 'This is the first day of the rest of our lives.'

'I wouldn't have it any other way,' she whispered back.

'Me too,' he said. 'But – how are we going to play it?'

'How do you mean?'

'Well, usually I like to set myself some sort of challenge. Sort of gives me focus.'

Holly thought for a moment, then leaned in for a soft kiss. He stood back, taking in her smiling perfection. She kissed him again, lightly dobbing him on the nose.

Then she said: 'Let's just take it one day at a time, Mr Robinson.'

Also by Dan Brotzel

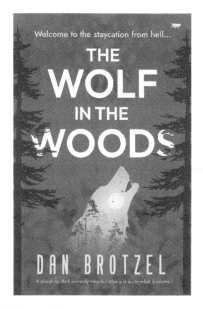

The Wolf in the Woods: A gripping and dark comedy where nothing is quite what it seems

"One of my top reads this year... a full-blown page-turner... perfect... laugh out loud in that Dark humour way." — **Reader review**

BUY NOW

APPENDIX 1

From the dawn of time to I Hate Coriander Day:
A brief history of fake holidays

National Bubble Bath Day, National Hermit Day, National Barbershop Quartet Day, British Pie Week, Adopt-A-Rescued Guinea Pig Month... I have always been tickled by these funny pseudo-holidays, and I'm sure I'm not alone. A staple of the PR and awareness-raising arsenal, they offer easy catnip for the lazy journo looking to spice up a slow news day, the DJ with a chat slot to fill, the inspiration-starved assembly-giver or sermoniser.

When I began as a magazine journalist back in the 1990s, I remember we had a little card desk calendar of UK special Days, mostly health-related. It always fascinated me, though by today's standards the calendar was painfully thin, not even one per day. When I looked into them on a whim a while back, I discovered that there are now *several thousand* Days, Weeks and Months, many originating in the US but often cropping up in the UK now too. So began the research that would eventually turn into *Thank You For The Days*.

Most of us only come across the odd special Day when we hear one mentioned in the media, but when you see a full year's worth altogether the effect is bewildering. Some are profound and important (World Cancer Day, International Day of Forests, Zero Waste Week). Some are popular fixtures (Red Nose Day, Blue Monday, Take Your Dog to Work Day). Some are nakedly commercial (National Stationery Week, International Dog Biscuit Appreciation Day, Anti-Frizz Month courtesy of Alberto V05). Some celebrate ideas or concepts (Pi Approximation Day, DNA Day, World Logic Week). And some are just silly (CAPS LOCK DAY, Lost Sock Memorial Day, International I Hate Coriander Day).

Suddenly I found myself wondering: *What would happen to a person if they tried to observe a different Day every single day for a calendar year?* Also, why do we have all these weird Days, who gets to choose them, and what's the correct etiquette for observing them? Here's a little of what I found out...

The idea of 'a special day for something' is probably almost as old as the idea of a calendar. The seasons and the skies imposed a cyclical shape on our sense of time, and gradually we added our own anniversaries so that we could mark the miraculous coming-around-again of things. Empires celebrated famous victories and religions remembered their martyrs on their execution dates.

Undoubtedly we have always made and unmade holidays in the image of our prevailing culture too. Accession Day, for example, marked the coming to the throne of Elizabeth I on November 17, 1588. But it was celebrated long after her reign, far into the 18th century, as it became a focus for English anti-Catholicism. Elizabeth was seen as a figurehead of the Protestant Revolution, and effigies of the Pope and Devil were traditionally burnt on the Day.

In our time, the resurgence of St Dwynwen's Day – the Welsh feast day of lovers, on January 25 – can be seen as a reassertion of Welsh language and culture. In the US, Columbus Day is currently engaged in existential combat with Indigenous People's Day for calendric supremacy on October 10. And the suggestion of a Margaret Thatcher Day – an idea first mooted in an unsuccessful Parliamentary Bill of 2013 – continues to provoke and divide.

Chase's Calendar of Events – Luke's companion and the most venerable resource in this area – distinguishes between *holidays*, which it regards as 'religious, civic (governmental), or folkloric' – and *special days*. This book is about the latter group, which *Chase's* divides into awareness days, advocacy days, commercial days and "for-fun" days.

These for-fun days have many other many names too – National Days, fake holidays, holidates, Facebook holidays, micro-events, unofficial observances... Whatever you want to call them, they've been around since at least the 1900s. National Raisin Day was introduced by California raisin-growers in 1909, who boosted it with flyers, newspaper ads and radio spots. On the day itself, menus with dishes featuring raisins appeared in eateries, dining cars, hotels and steamships all around the country, all backed up with material praising the quality and health-giving benefits of Californian raisins issued by schools and local and state governments. The slickness of the promotion suggests that this was already a familiar mechanism to the marketers of the day. Other early observances included Friendship Day, launched by Hallmark in 1919 in a subtle bid to sell more cards; Be Kind to Animals Week (1915); June Dairy Month (1937); and National Salad Week, which in the UK goes back to at least the 1950s.

In the US, 'when people really wanted to be sure an observance gained formality, they went to Congress to get proclamations and actual legislation to make it so,' Holly McGuire, editor-in-chief of *Chase's Calendar of Events* told me. To stay official, Days have to be re-proclaimed every year, as still happens with staples like

Mother's Day and Memorial Day. But some Days lingered on as popular observances anyway, boosted by interested commercial parties. National Ice Cream Day, for example, was proclaimed for a few years in the 1980s by Ronald Reagan. In lauding this 'nutritious and wholesome food', his real goal was to support a US dairy industry that was already burdened with a surplus 500 million pounds of cheese. Unofficial #IceCreamDay is still going strong, though now it's all promos and shout-outs.

From the 1990s, Congress began to wind down its proclamation activity, and other authorities stepped up. Getting into *Chase's* has long been a benchmark of respectability for Day-makers. The first edition, published in 1957, contained 364 entries over thirty-two pages, and sold for $1; the 2023 edition runs to 750+ pages, contains 12,500+ entries and costs around £75. Another key player today is a North Dakota business called National Day Calendar. It certainly sounds official, and if they accept your Day, they will even issue an official-sounding proclamation. But these are Days with names like National Chocolate-Covered Raisin Day, National Dimples Day, and National Something On A Stick Day. Not national, or indeed holidays, in any formal sense – and the recognition has to be paid for. (Incidentally, Joe Biden has shown a renewed appetite for federal Proclamations, including firsts like National Indigenous People's Day and Juneteenth, which commemorates the emancipation of enslaved African Americans.)

The explosion of unofficial special Days coincided with the rise of the internet and especially social media. Tellingly, the respective founders of National Day Calendar, *Foodimentary* ('*celebrating 365 food holidays with classic recipes*'), and Days of the Year, a leading UK-based site with a large US audience, were all digital early adopters. Though many of the Days they curate and create might seem silly and gimmicky, they are worth a fortune to their beneficiaries. '*Whimsical as these days seem, the creation and maintenance of national days are a phenomenon with massive financial implications,'* writes James Hamblin in *The Atlantic.* *'Many such days are used – or were even specifically invented – to coax people to talk about products and services. This happens on a scale that traditional advertising almost never achieves. Even spending millions on a Super Bowl commercial cannot command so much favourable attention to a product – given freely and enthusiastically by unassuming consumers who blast it into the timelines of everyone they know.'*

Just how many Days there are now is impossible to count exactly, though it's certainly in the thousands. National Day Calendar estimates it has 2200–2500 on its site. No one could ever really keep track of them all now because they continue to proliferate, there is no standard way of quantifying them, and, as Holly McGuire says, 'people just start them left and right and let them languish'. The calendars are littered with Days that no one can quite remember who started or what they are for, as I discovered many times.

Beyond federal or regional mandate, usually at the prompting of a special interest group, the other big Day-making authority is the United Nations. The UN currently has over 200 live Days, Weeks and Months (it also does Years and Decades), most of them formally agreed by the General Assembly or by one of its agencies. Each has its own website, backed by extensive information and in-depth resources, and they are some of the most-visited pages of the UN's entire digital output. Charities and brands launch Days too. But so, frankly, could you or I.

'Our feeling – passed down from co-founder Dom Chase – is that anyone can create a special day,' says Holly McGuire. Or as Tom Torriglia, a musician credited with creating National Accordion Awareness Month (June) in 1989, put it: 'It was established as simply as me deciding it would exist.'

But for your Day to be really real, you do need some sort of audience. As Holly McGuire says, 'It's like, if a tree falls in the forest, does it make a sound?' You can give your Day a sort of quasi-official status by getting it mentioned on one or more of the big calendar sites like National Day Calendar, Checkiday (which both charge) and Days Of The Year (which doesn't). Celebrity endorsement and social-media buzz can do the same job, as when Brendon Urie from Panic! at the Disco got 15,000 likes simply for posting a pic of himself in his favourite boxers tagged #nationalunderwearday (a Day sponsored by online retailer Freshpair). Or when President Obama tweeted '*Arr you in?*' on Talk Like A Pirate Day in 2012.

Some people are called to be serial Day-makers. Adrienne Sioux Koopersmith of Chicago, self-styled 'America's Premier Eventologist', has coined around two thousand 'holidates', as she calls them, including Poetry At Work Day (January 10), As Young As You Feel Day (March 22), and Ant Appreciation Month (August). Food blogger John-Bryan Hopkins, 'the godfather of food holidays', has revamped the whole area of edible Days with his *Foodimentary* website, book and calendar, downgrading observances for the likes of lard and frozen food and introducing things like National Comfort Food Day (December 5) and National Pizza with the Works Except Anchovies Day (November 12). Thomas and Ruth Roy of Pennsylvania have slid over eighty of their creations into *Chase's*, including Quirky Country Music Song Titles Day (March 27), Hug An Australian Day (April 26) and Particularly Preposterous Packaging Day (August 7). *Chase's* has a page on its website where people can send in suggestions. National Day Calendar says it receives thousands of submissions every year too, of which it approves about thirty.

It's niches all the way down on the internet, and if you can find yours, the next step is to mobilise your community and start monetising. At the time of writing, the I Hate Coriander Day people (February 24; mission statement: "We. Hate. Coriander.") have grown their Facebook group to over 185,000 followers. An

'Official I Hate Coriander OG Hoodie' will set you back A$74.95 (about £40).

Mind you, if anyone can start a holiday, the opportunities for axe-grinding and self-promotion are obvious. One of the Roys' Days, not currently in *Chase's*, is Snow Plow Mailbox Hockey Day (January 23). The explanation feels deeply anecdotal: *'It's wintertime, and time for snow plow drivers everywhere to see how many rural mailboxes they can knock over. Twenty extra points for boosting one into the next township.'* In Turkmenistan in 2002, self-appointed President-for-life Saparmurat Niyazov set about renaming all the months of the year after the country's key heroes and national symbols. January he would name after himself, he told a People's Council, while he planned to call the month of April 'Mother'. As the BBC reported: 'In response, a speaker at the Council suggested calling the month by the full name of the president's deceased mother, Gurbansoltan, which the president said he would consider.' (The suggestion was indeed adopted, but all the names were switched back after the dictator's death in 2008.)

Even without autocratic diktat, the evolution of a day from whim to canonical internet fact can move very fast. As Hopkins said in a 2014 interview of his foodie day choices: 'The first year, it's just me telling people to take my word. By year two, the news people believe it because it was around the previous year. When year three comes, it's like it was written in the Bible.' Google quickly confers an official aura on fake holidays, as National Day Calendar founder Marlo Anderson similarly noticed. 'By the time a day becomes woven into calendars and memories,' as he told James Hamblin, 'no one seems to care or remember whether it is "official" or not.'

Then again, 'all holidays are made up in a way, when you think about it,' says Sam Alderson of Days Of The Year. 'But I'm not sure it matters how formal or whimsical the origins are – whether it's a Presidential proclamation or a social media meme that's taken off. If it's something that engages people and they enjoy celebrating in some way, it's all good!'

How, then, should you actually *observe* a Day? Fun, literal and respectful seem to be the watchwords, according to the (self-appointed) experts. 'On International Talk Like a Pirate Day, people say "Arrrr!" and "Matey!". On National Chilli Day, 'they eat chilli,' Holly McGuire advised me. 'On Haiku Day they read or write haikus.' National Day Calendar's motto is simply: "Celebrate every day". With health-related days, there's always money to raise and lots of information to absorb. Says Sam Alderson of Days Of The Year: 'I think as long as it's coming from a sincere part of you and you're not taking the mick, particularly of the more serious days, then any celebration – even in the smallest way – is fine.' Happy Days!

APPENDIX 2

Hidden Pain:
An interview with Aneeta Prem, CEO, Trigeminal
Neuralgia Association UK

Imagine having a form of facial nerve pain so bad that you are unable to work and rarely leave home. A dentist removes all your teeth, even though the pain isn't dental. It might take you up to twenty years to get a diagnosis, if you ever get one. Yet there is no drug treatment for what you have, only a highly invasive operation with a patchy track record of success. Your condition isn't registered as a disability so you may end up fighting to keep your house. You spend days in the corner of a room, rocking with pain and the side effects of painkillers and antidepressants. Loved ones abandon you because they can't cope with all your complaining, and you may even be driven to contemplate suicide.

And yet no one has even heard of what you have.

All of the above is a real scenario, as I learnt in an eye-opening conversation with Aneeta Prem, black belt judo instructor, magistrate, campaigner against forced marriage and female genital mutilation – and sufferer with trigeminal neuralgia. When she was first affected, she hadn't heard of it either – 'I couldn't even spell it.'

Anita first felt the pain about twelve years ago. 'I remember I was driving, and I began to feel this excruciating pain on the right-hand side of my face. I kept feeling I wanted to chew on something.'

Anita went to the dentist and asked to have a wisdom tooth removed. She had an X-ray and was told there was nothing wrong with the tooth. But she had it removed in the end anyway, because the pain was so bad. Still it wouldn't go away. Eventually she was referred for an MRI scan, which took two years, but that also turned up nothing. Anita decided she must be making the pain up.

'I was under a lot of stress – dealing with debt, moving house, setting up a new charity (she also runs Freedom, which deals with forced marriage and FGM). I was doing a lot of TV, meeting the prime minister, giving talks. I just thought my mind's in overdrive and I'm making up this pain because I've got too much to deal with. I thought it was all psychological.

'So I never spoke about it, never told anyone. But I'd be constantly rubbing both sides of my face. I remember in court someone saying to me, "You never smile. You look really grumpy all the time". I thought, that's a really sad thing to say about somebody, I must try and smile a bit more. But I had very little to smile about it. Life was really difficult.'

It took Anita nine years to get diagnosed. 'A locum at my GP sent me to a neurological centre, where at last they told me. I just burst into tears. The specialist said: "I'm so sorry, it's a really tragic condition to have". And I said, "No, you've given me a label. I'm just so happy I haven't made this up".'

Anita was offered an operation 'where they drill into the back of your skull and release your trigeminal nerve.' But the surgery is scary – one person has died following it, and strokes are not unknown. 'My mother was terrified I would die, and I was very anxious too. I started planning for my death, trying to get our finances in order, thinking who'd look after my mum. I became obsessed by folding my clothes in a particular way, Marie Kondo-style. If I was going to die, my drawers had to be immaculate.'

After surgery, Anita had double vision and took several weeks to learn to walk again. She'd been making videos of her recovery, and BBC and Channel 5 were interested in covering her experiences. She made contact with the Trigeminal Neuralgia Association around this time, and ended up as its CEO. But the surgery didn't work.

So what does it feel like, this invisible pain? 'The most common phrase you hear from sufferers is it's like someone's zapping you with electric shocks or shards of glass being pushed into your face. The surgery can be a lifeline for people but I still have about a hundred attacks a day, maybe more. I know of many people who've had the surgery and are managing to live with medication, but that means sitting in the corner being addicted to their life-changing medication: high doses of painkillers, antidepressants, anti-epilepsy drugs.'

Anita often doesn't know when the attacks are coming. 'They're definitely brought on by stress and being tired. If I'm doing a TV interview or some public speaking, I can guarantee I'll have no pain. But the second I come off after that hit of adrenaline, the attack will be extreme. I'm worse in the evenings, and it often keeps me awake at night. But most people with this don't work. They can't. And many of them are on their own because their families or partners have just had enough of someone that's in constant pain.'

Trigeminal neuralgia is sometimes known as 'the suicide disease', says Anita: 'Many shy away from that label, but I don't because it gets people's attention, and it can be true. The pain is so bad, there is no real recognised cure. Even after surgery, some people feel that the only option is to take their own life to end this life of misery and pain.

'On our helpline we've added the Samaritans as an option when you dial. Because a huge number of people just believe there is no hope left. Last year a lady contacted me to say that she was spending Christmas on her own because her family had completely had enough of her moaning about her pain. But she wasn't moaning about it. She was expressing that she couldn't cope with pain that's like root canal times a hundred. And people will say, Yeah, I get face pain. But this is not like any normal face pain. All the dentists I've spoken to say it's the worst pain they've seen. It is off the one to ten scale.'

There is so little awareness of this condition that no one even knows how many people it affects – one in 50,000 is the best estimate for the UK – or what causes it, or how to account for its development. 'Everyone's pain is slightly different. It's very unusual to have it on both sides, which I do. For some people it goes into their eye. For some, it goes into their nose and teeth so they can't brush their teeth, they can't open their mouth, they can hardly eat and have to go on a liquid diet. For some people it can go away for months, and then come back. Others are in long-term remission; there's no rhyme or reason to it.

'There hasn't been the research there should have been because there's no money in it. Most people are really lucky if they get diagnosed. For some it can take twenty years. A lot of people I speak to have had every tooth in their head removed, because they think the pain must be dental.' Anita is appalled at those dentists who are going on removing teeth in this way without proper investigation.

To try to bring the pain to life for others, Anita had the idea of literally visualising the pain. 'I thought, how do you show a hidden disability? How can you describe the pain when none of us have got the words? How can you relate if you've never been dug at with a razor, or stabbed with a pen?' For the TMA's first awareness day, 'I got a professional make-up artist to come to my house, paint the trigeminal nerve on my face, but also put glass in my face so people could better see what it feels like for me. We've all got this nerve, just not all of us have got blood vessels resting on it that cause this constant agony.' When Anita's mum saw her daughter made up, 'she just burst into tears.'

Anita is fighting to get trigeminal neuralgia recognised as a disability. 'People are losing their houses or fighting to get their PIP (Personal Independence Payment, which replaced Disability Living Allowance and is supposed to help with extra living costs 'if you have a long-term physical or mental health condition or disability'). They're losing everything because no one's heard of this. No one's talking about it.'

The cost of living crisis has added a new dimension of pain. 'The cold is a trigger for many of us. I wear hundreds of layers, a hood and a big red hat because the cold air touching my face can trigger an attack. I'm being attacked by air, for goodness' sake! I did a little video about this the other day, and one of our members in her eighties said, "But I can't afford to put my heating on." It's really hard if you are having to make a choice between heating food and paying your bills, and you can't get free prescriptions for anything unless you're signed off sick. But people feel ashamed to say they get extreme pain from the wind or a cold draft, or putting on a polo neck, or water hitting their face when they shower, or they can't wash their hair or brush their teeth. They think they won't be believed.'

A disability that's both hidden and little understood has to punch above its weight in the awareness marketplace. 'If you're talking about cancer, we can all relate to somebody we have lost or know of. But when you're talking about something that no one's heard of or can't even pronounce, people just go, *Oh dear*. It's very difficult. Sadly many of our sufferers don't make media-friendly case studies because they're struggling to even function.'

Anita is using her own profile to get media coverage and raise awareness on social media. But she says if she could find a magic tree right now, she'd start somewhere more fundamental. 'If someone gave me £2 million tomorrow, I would set up a retreat to give people respite. Help them to learn some pain management techniques, give them good quality food, get them some time away, teach them and their families about mindfulness.' Every two months, she organises a talk for members with a leading expert. A recent one was on medical cannabis – an approach that is delivering positive results for sufferers in the US and Canada but where the UK has been very slow. 'There are trials of medical cannabis in the UK, but patients have to pay hundreds of pounds a month, which risks excluding many of the people who could most benefit. It's the only UK trial you have to pay for.'

Another benefit of these talks, which are open to family and friends, is that it helps others see the reality of the pain, she says. 'Not just hearing from a person that they are in pain, but hearing experts say how bad that pain is, has been incredibly validating for our members. To be truly believed takes away some of the shame.'

[All information correct as of September 2022.]

- *Trigeminal Neuralgia Association UK: www.tna.org. uk/raising-awareness*
- *Trigeminal Neuralgia Awareness Day is October 7.*

Acknowledgements

This book began life as a journal of my own attempt to observe a different special Day for each of the 365 days of 2022. So I must begin by thanking Moira and Bob at Sandstone Press who first encouraged me in my silly idea.

Very sadly, Sandstone went into liquidation just before that book – *Awareness Daze* – was to be published. So my next thanks must go to Betsy Reavley at Bloodhound Books, who saw the potential for a fictional version of my memoir, which in time became *Thank You For The Days*.

Thank you to everyone who read early sections of this (and the earlier) book and provided feedback and encouragement: Michael Grant Smith, Sarah Riley, Rob Pointer, Eve Brotzel, and all the members of the Conway Writers' Group. Thanks especially to Alex Woolf and Jenny Fielder, aka my mum, who made extensive comments on early drafts. (As Mum noted, Bring Your Parent To Work Day is the first Thursday of November.)

Thank you to Aneeta Prem, Sam Alderson and Holly McGuire for sharing their knowledge, and to Carina, Cath and Jem for their contributions to various office scenes and definitions. To Isla and Poppy for language advice. To Faber Books, for permission to quote from the poetry of Philip Larkin. To Tara at Bloodhound for her production magic, and to Ian Skewis for his insightful editing. And to my agent Ger Nicholson, for all her encouragement and support.

Final thanks to Teddy, the real-life Ziggy, who'd like to point out a glaring omission in the book for May 1 – National Cockapoo Day.

As for *Awareness Daze*, at the time of writing I don't have a new print publisher, but the title is available as an audiobook from WF Howes.

A NOTE FROM THE PUBLISHER

Thank you for reading this book. If you enjoyed it please do consider leaving a review on Amazon to help others find it too.

We hate typos. All of our books have been rigorously edited and proofread, but sometimes mistakes do slip through. If you have spotted a typo, please do let us know and we can get it amended within hours.

info@bloodhoundbooks.com

Made in the USA
Columbia, SC
23 December 2024

50516235R00238